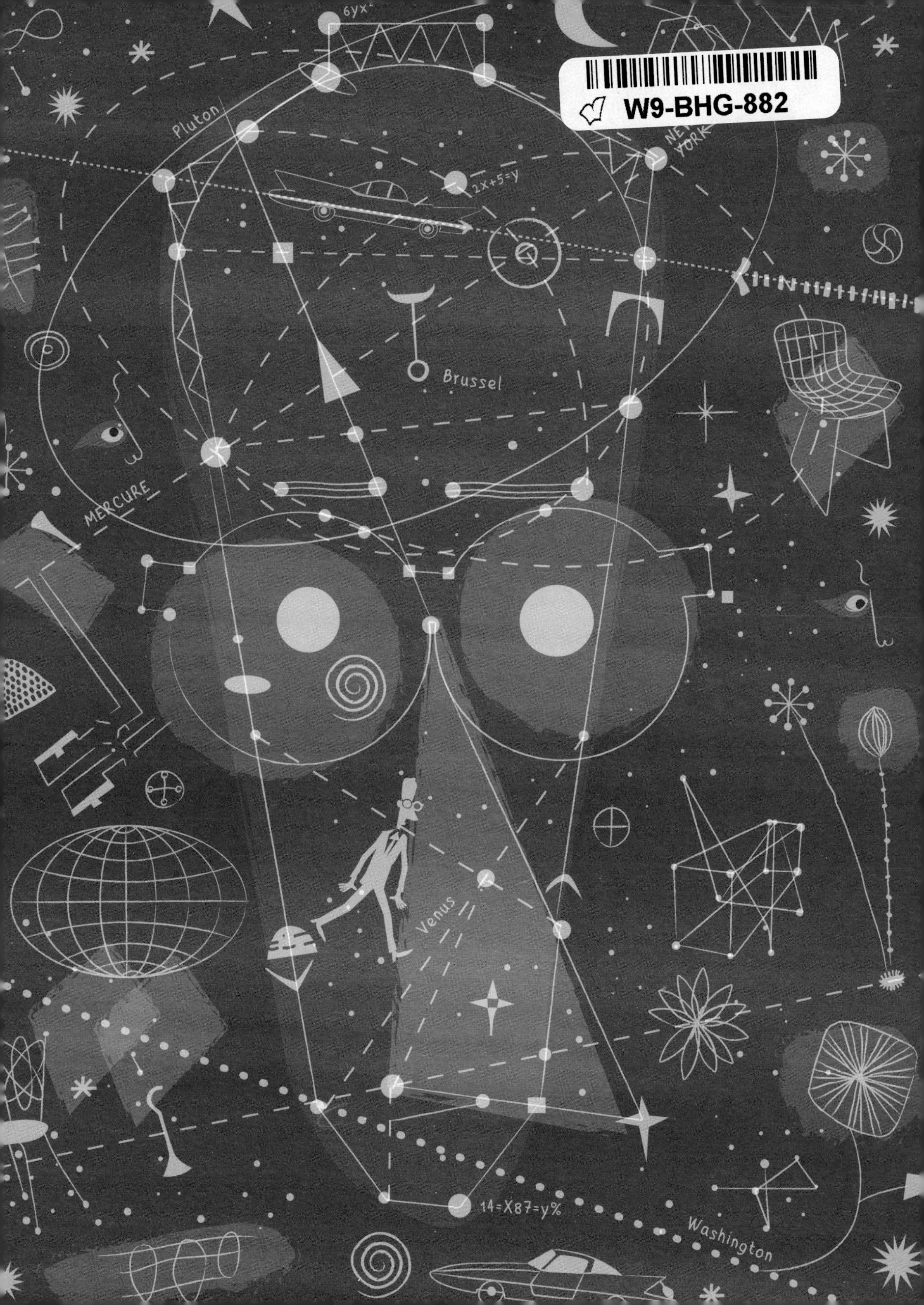
Pluton
NEW YORK
2x+5=y
Brussel
MERCURE
Venus
14=X87=y%
Washington

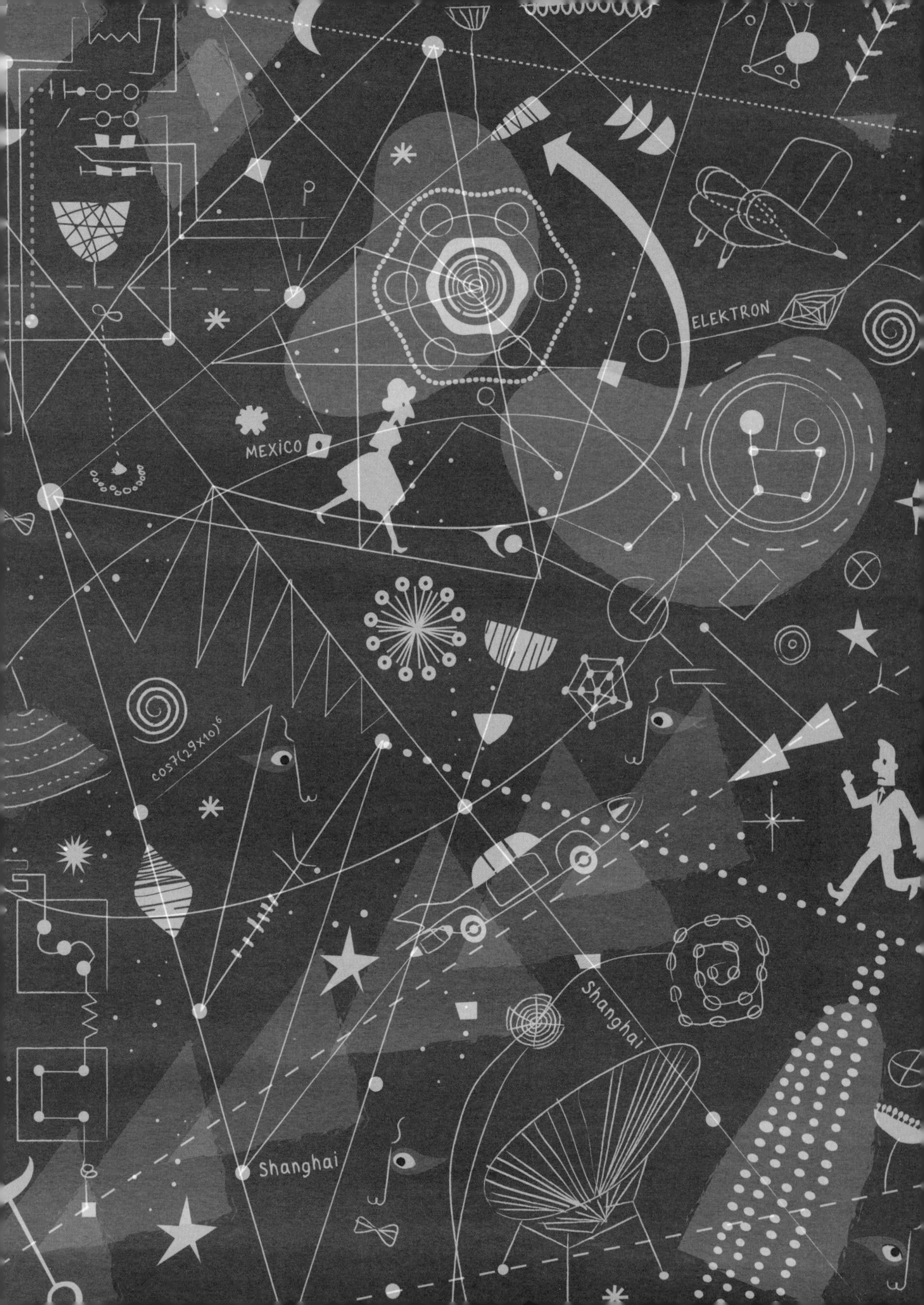
ELEKTRON
MEXICO
$cos7(29x10)^6$
Shanghai
Shanghai

Thierry Smolderen

Alexandre Clérisse

ATOMIC EMPIRE

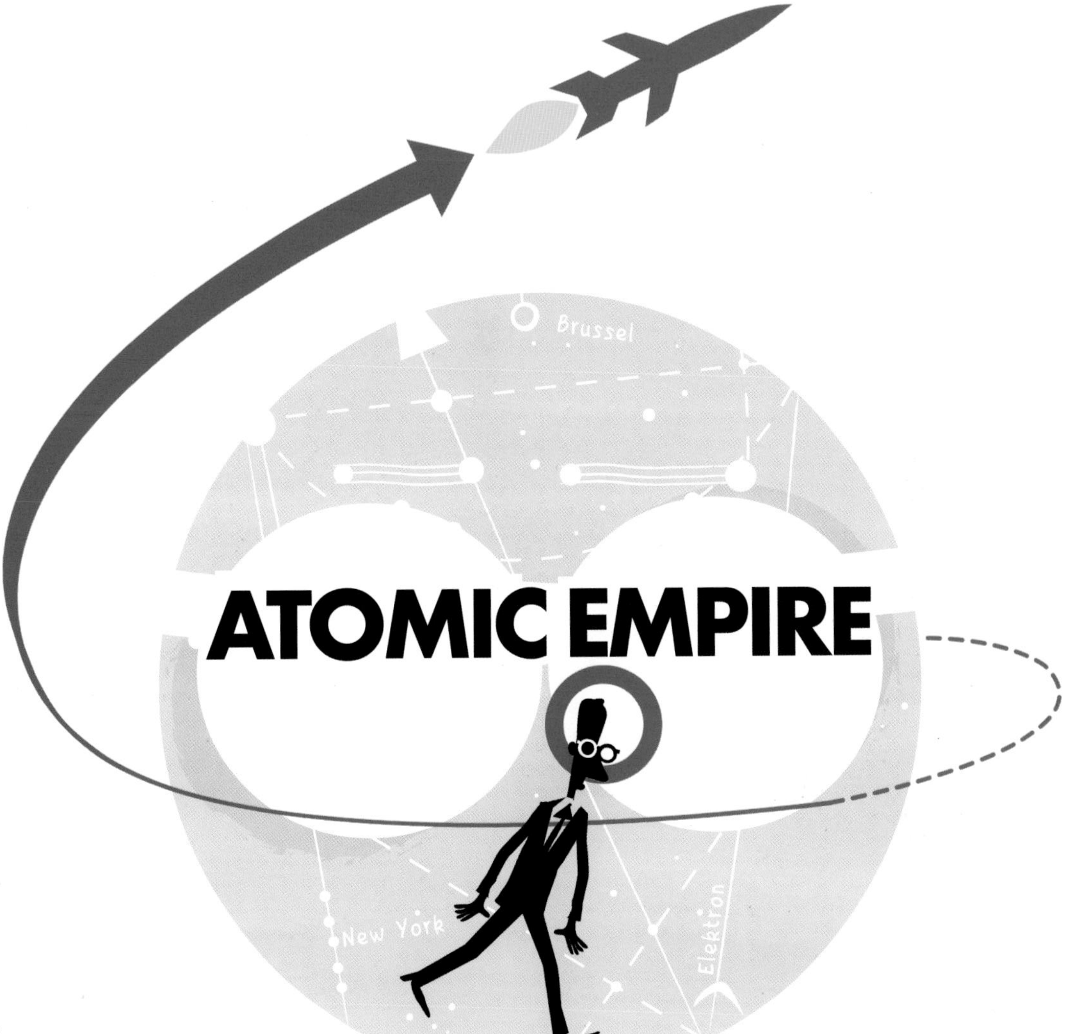
Brussel
New York
Elektron

IDW

Facebook: **facebook.com/idwpublishing**
Twitter: **@idwpublishing**
YouTube: **youtube.com/idwpublishing**
Tumblr: **tumblr.idwpublishing.com**
Instagram: **instagram.com/idwpublishing**

ISBN: 978-1-68405-311-7   21 20 19 18   1 2 3 4

EDITS BY
JUSTIN EISINGER AND
ALONZO SIMON

DESIGN BY
RON ESTEVEZ

PUBLISHER:
GREG GOLDSTEIN

Originally published by Dargaud as *Souvenirs de l'empire de l'atome*.

Greg Goldstein, President and Publisher
John Barber, Editor-In-Chief
Robbie Robbins, EVP/Sr. Art Director
Cara Morrison, Chief Financial Officer
Matt Ruzicka, Chief Accounting Officer
Anita Frazier, SVP of Sales and Marketing
David Hedgecock, Associate Publisher
Jerry Bennington, VP of New Product Development
Lorelei Bunjes, VP of Digital Services
Justin Eisinger, Editorial Director, Graphic Novels & Collections
Eric Moss, Senior Director, Licensing and Business Development

Ted Adams, IDW Founder

WRITTEN BY
THIERRY SMOLDEREN

ART BY
ALEXANDRE CLÉRISSE

LETTERING BY
FRANK CVETKOVIC

TRANSLATION BY
EDWARD GAUVIN

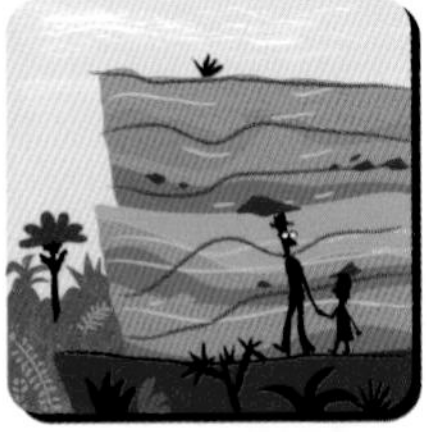

Mexico. 1964

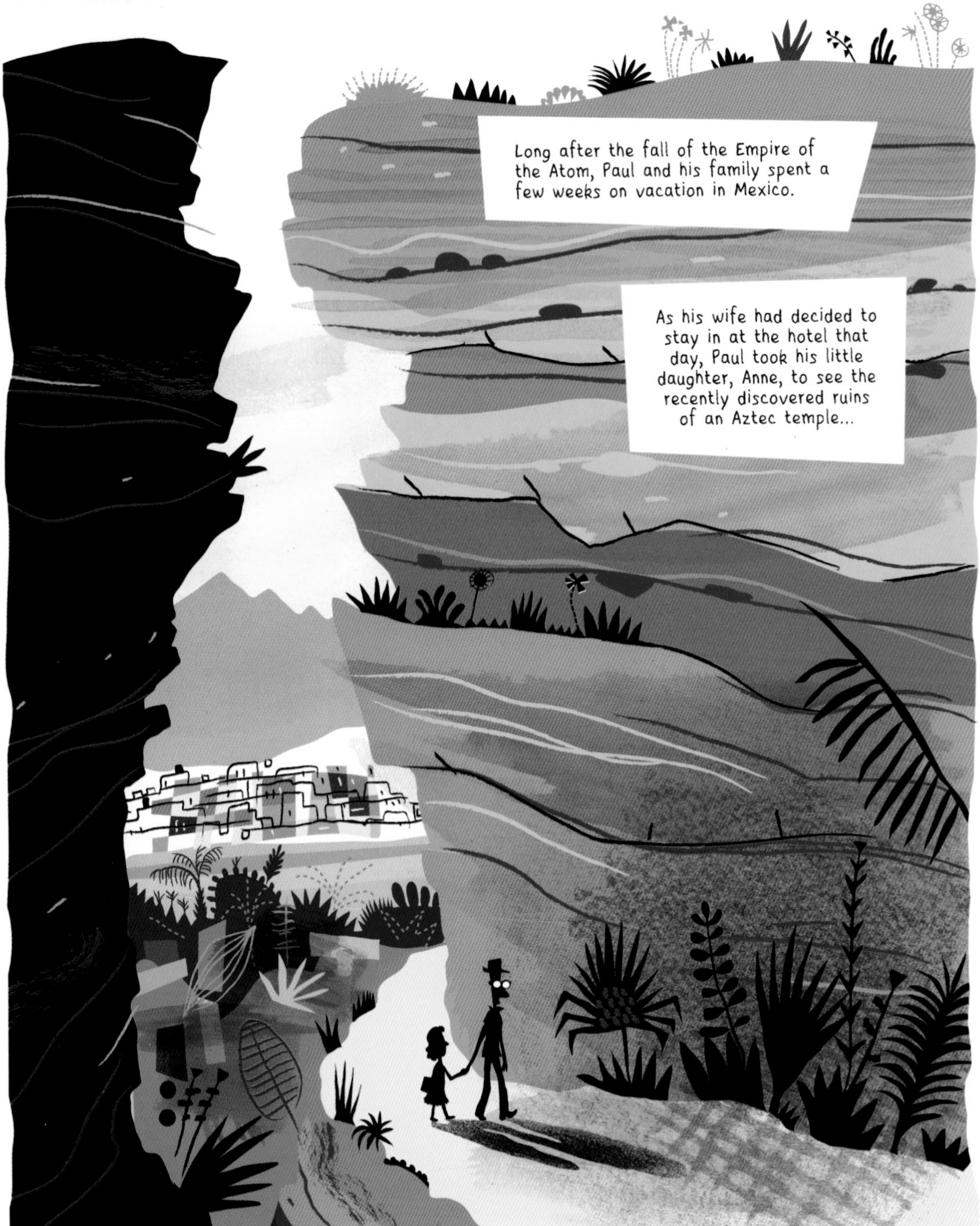
Long after the fall of the Empire of the Atom, Paul and his family spent a few weeks on vacation in Mexico.
As his wife had decided to stay in at the hotel that day, Paul took his little daughter, Anne, to see the recently discovered ruins of an Aztec temple...

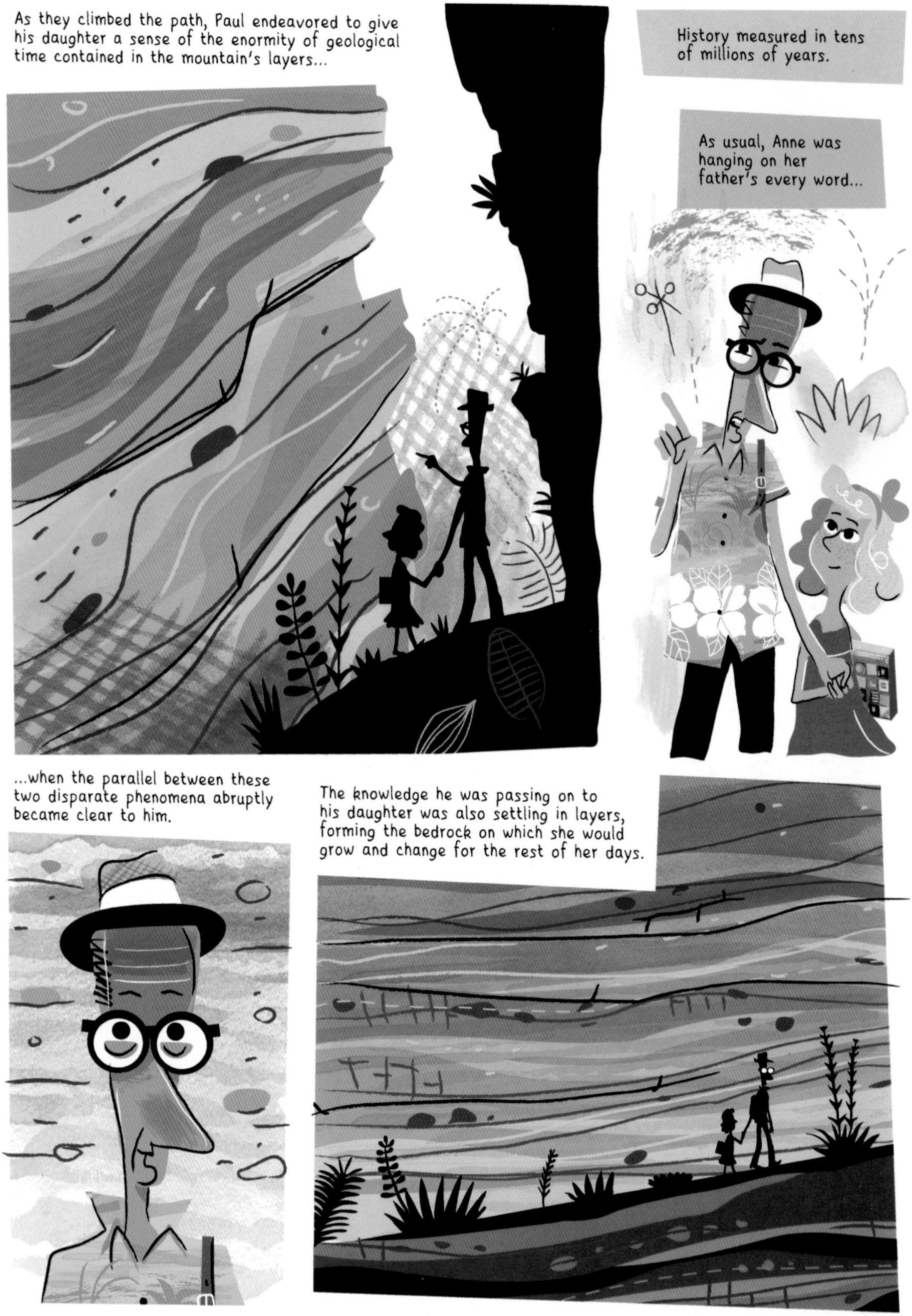
As they climbed the path, Paul endeavored to give his daughter a sense of the enormity of geological time contained in the mountain's layers...
History measured in tens of millions of years.
As usual, Anne was hanging on her father's every word...
...when the parallel between these two disparate phenomena abruptly became clear to him.
The knowledge he was passing on to his daughter was also settling in layers, forming the bedrock on which she would grow and change for the rest of her days.

When they reached the top of the mountain, there was no temple in sight.

They sat down to picnic on a big slab of rock. Afterwards, Anne got out her game of Memory.

And, taking turns, they began to flip over the cards.

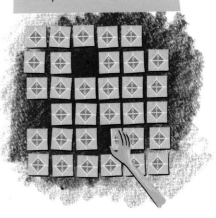

Aw, phooey! The little girl. Fine, then—*i'll* flip over the Christmas bulb!

For your second card... why do you always go for ones we've already seen?

Does it annoy you?

No. But why?

'Cause you go after me. if *i* found the mate to a card we've both seen, i'd be giving you the point!

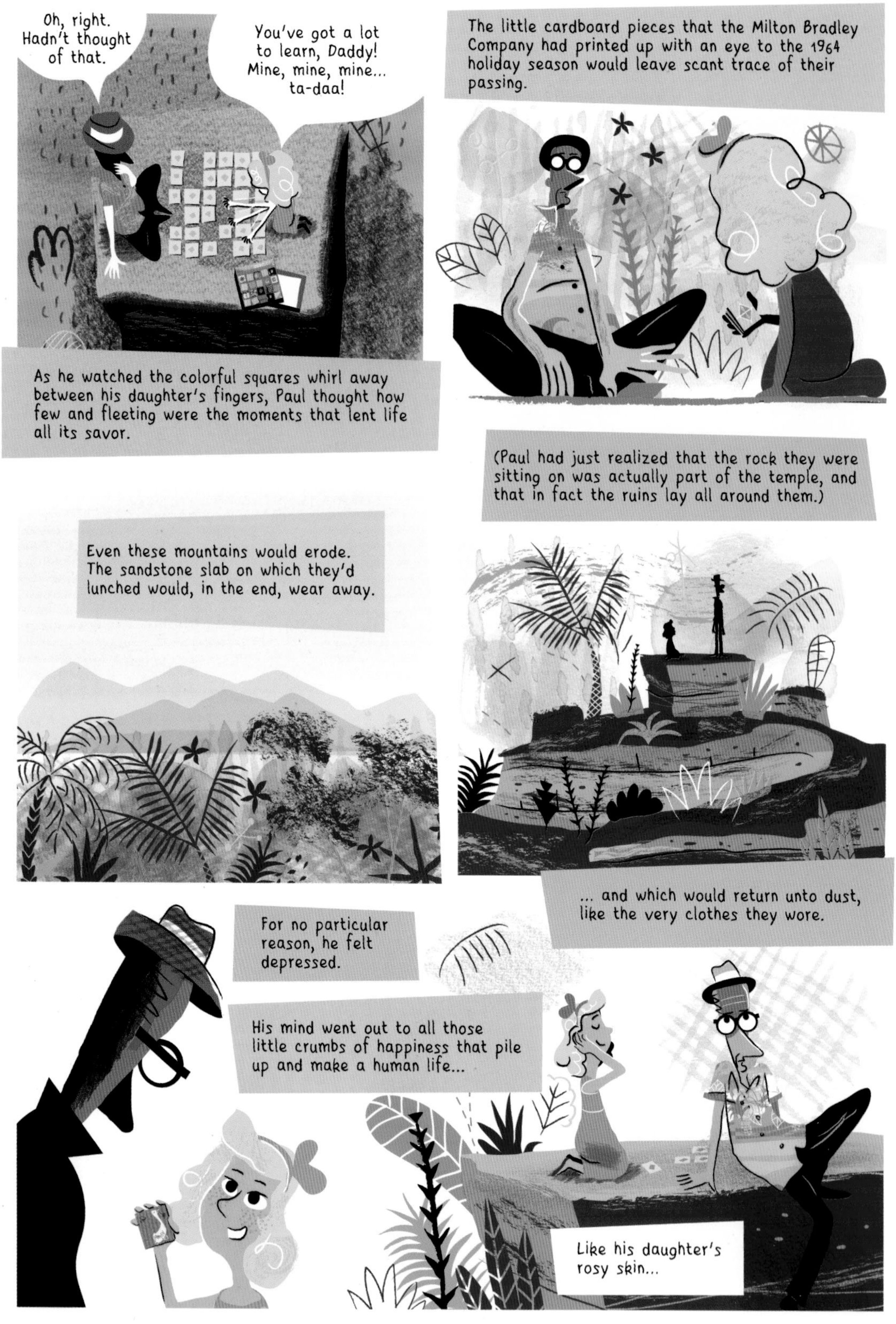
Oh, right. Hadn't thought of that.
You've got a lot to learn, Daddy! Mine, mine, mine... ta-daa!
As he watched the colorful squares whirl away between his daughter's fingers, Paul thought how few and fleeting were the moments that lent life all its savor.
The little cardboard pieces that the Milton Bradley Company had printed up with an eye to the 1964 holiday season would leave scant trace of their passing.
Even these mountains would erode. The sandstone slab on which they'd lunched would, in the end, wear away.
(Paul had just realized that the rock they were sitting on was actually part of the temple, and that in fact the ruins lay all around them.)
... and which would return unto dust, like the very clothes they wore.
For no particular reason, he felt depressed.
His mind went out to all those little crumbs of happiness that pile up and make a human life...
Like his daughter's rosy skin...

Or the cheap pulp on which his latest science fiction story had just been printed.

OCTOBER 1964
50¢

galaxy

THE TACTFUL SABOTEUR by FRANK HERBERT
THE CHILDREN OF NIGHT by FREDERIK POHL
THE 1980 PRESIDENT by MIRIAM ALLEN DEFORD

SOLDIER, ASK NOT
A great new novel of the
Friendlies and the Dorsai!
by GORDON R. DICKSON

Should I finish playing on my own? I'm warning you, I'm keeping all my cards!

Do you know what we're sitting on?

Moss.

Nope. This stone slab is where temple priests laid out their human sacrifices. Hundreds of Aztecs were flayed alive on this very spot.

Flayed alive?

Peeled just like tomatoes, while they still lived and breathed.

Can you even imagine the scream you'd let out if someone tortured you like that?

Eh... they've been dead for forever!

i can hear them still.

Screams like that make the very stars shiver till the end of time.

Well, well... what have we here? We had a car like this when I was little.

It's been a while since I've seen it!

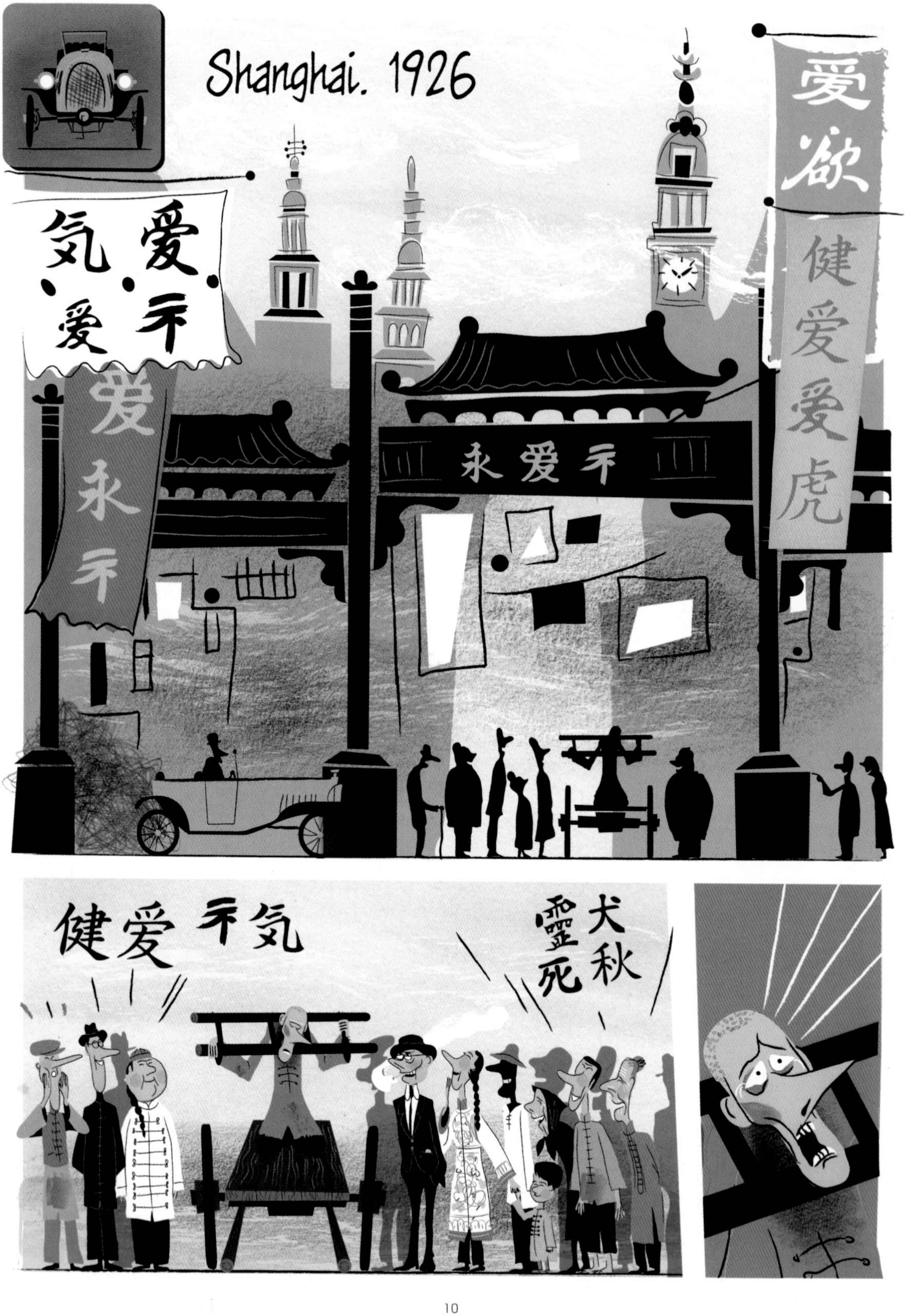
Shanghai. 1926
氖爱
爱亍
爱
永
亍
永爱亍
爱欲
健爱爱虎
健爱
亍氖
犬秋
靈死

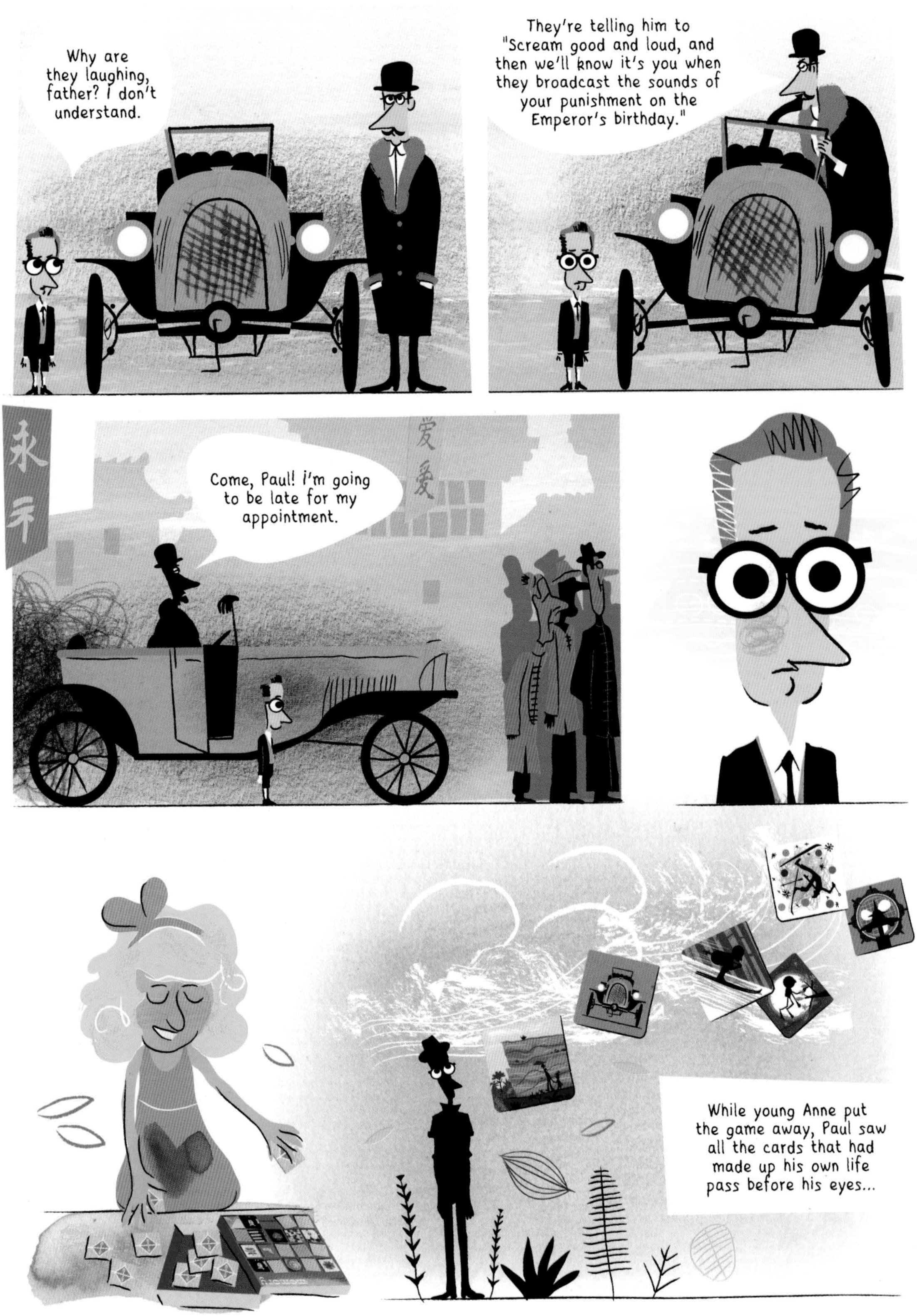
Why are they laughing, father? I don't understand.
They're telling him to "Scream good and loud, and then we'll know it's you when they broadcast the sounds of your punishment on the Emperor's birthday."
Come, Paul! I'm going to be late for my appointment.
While young Anne put the game away, Paul saw all the cards that had made up his own life pass before his eyes...

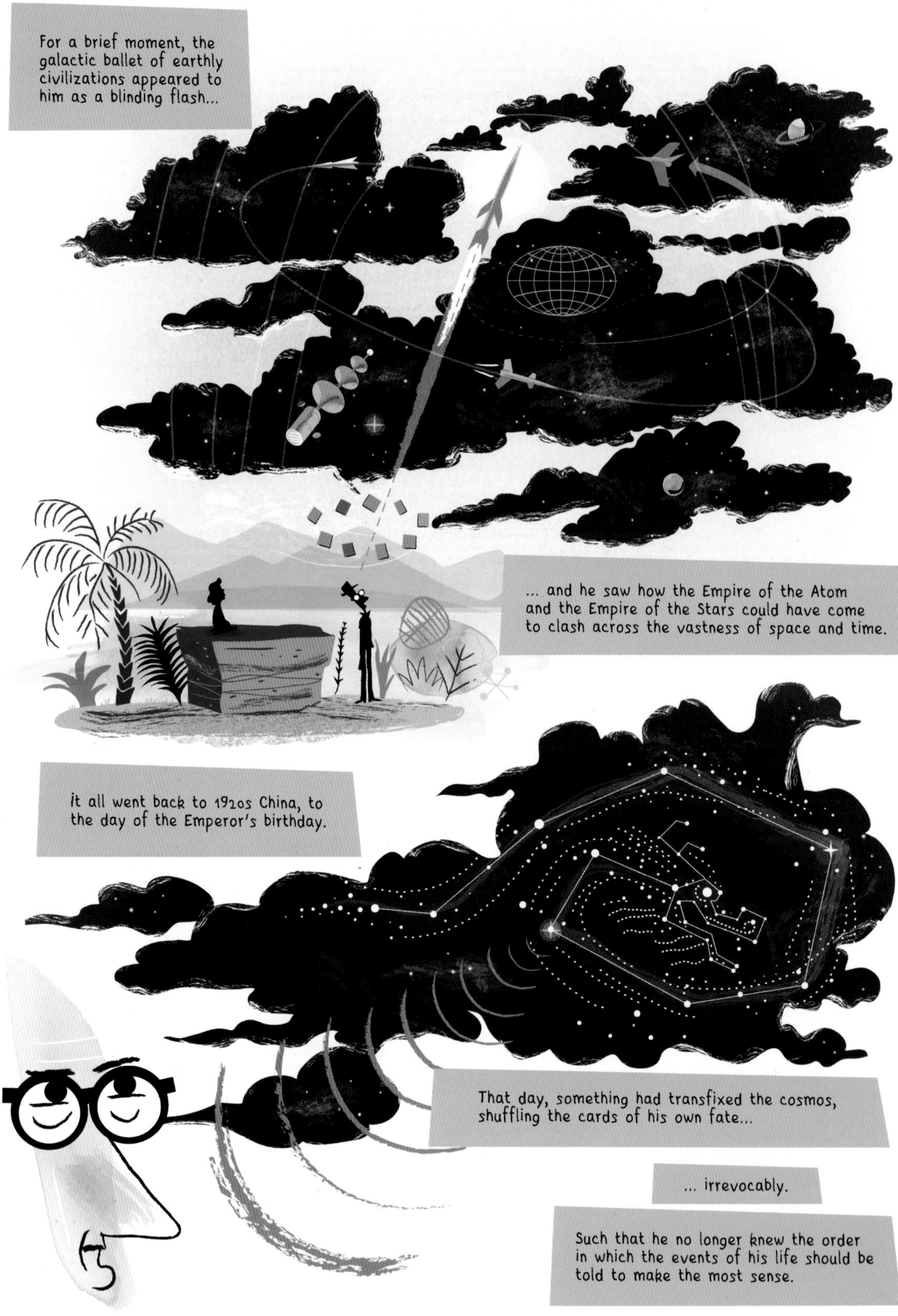
For a brief moment, the galactic ballet of earthly civilizations appeared to him as a blinding flash...
... and he saw how the Empire of the Atom and the Empire of the Stars could have come to clash across the vastness of space and time.
It all went back to 1920s China, to the day of the Emperor's birthday.
That day, something had transfixed the cosmos, shuffling the cards of his own fate...
... irrevocably.
Such that he no longer knew the order in which the events of his life should be told to make the most sense.

chapter 1

Swimmers of the Ether

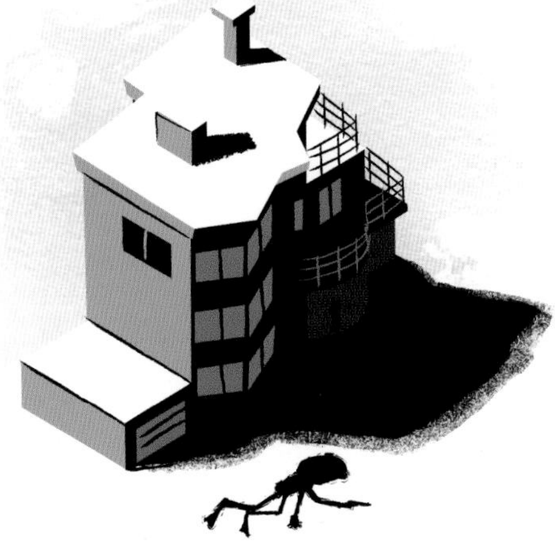

Brussels. April 1, 1958 (six years earlier)...

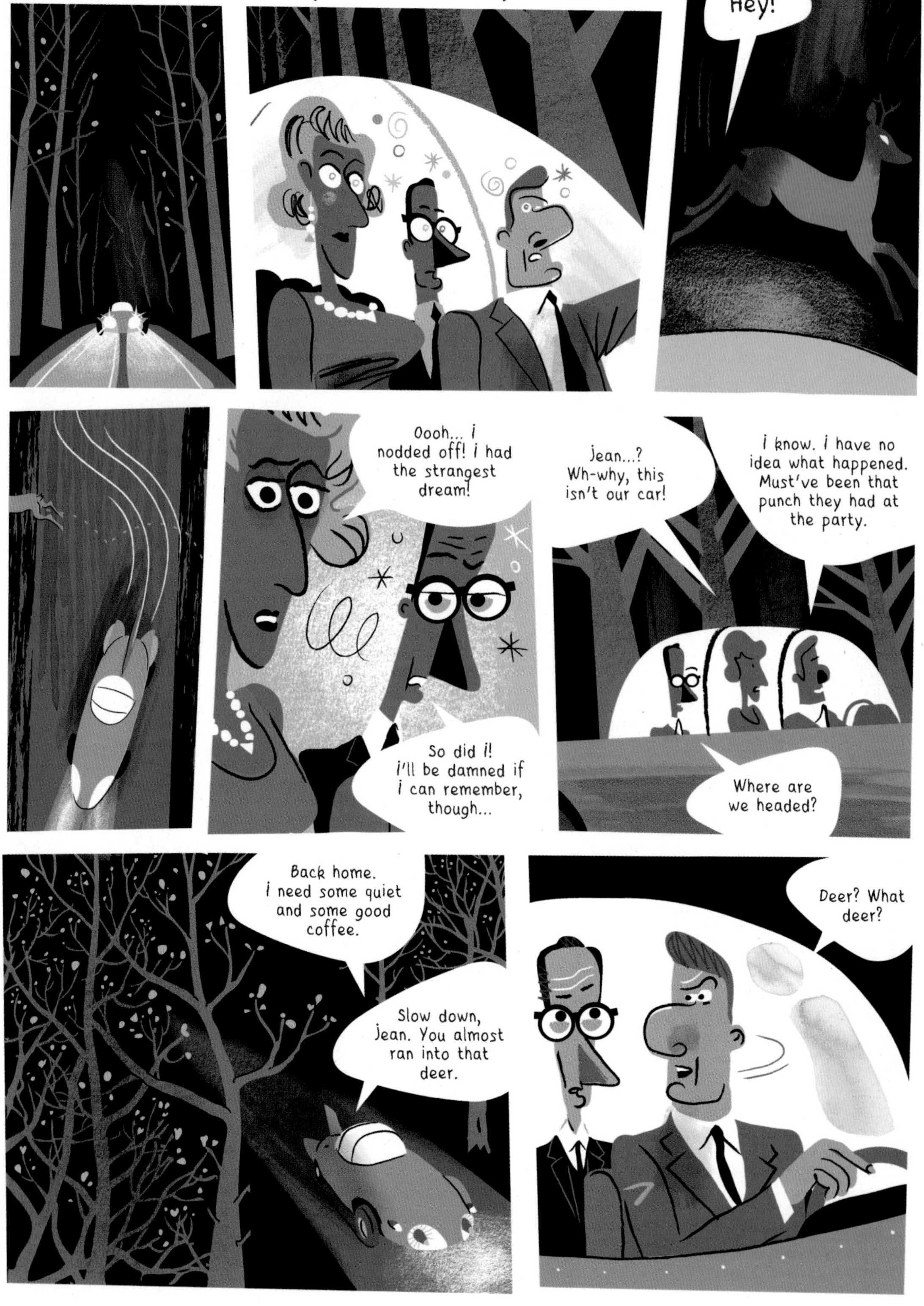
Hey!
Oooh... I nodded off! I had the strangest dream!
So did I! I'll be damned if I can remember, though...
Jean...? Wh-why, this isn't our car!
I know. I have no idea what happened. Must've been that punch they had at the party.
Where are we headed?
Back home. I need some quiet and some good coffee.
Slow down, Jean. You almost ran into that deer.
Deer? What deer?

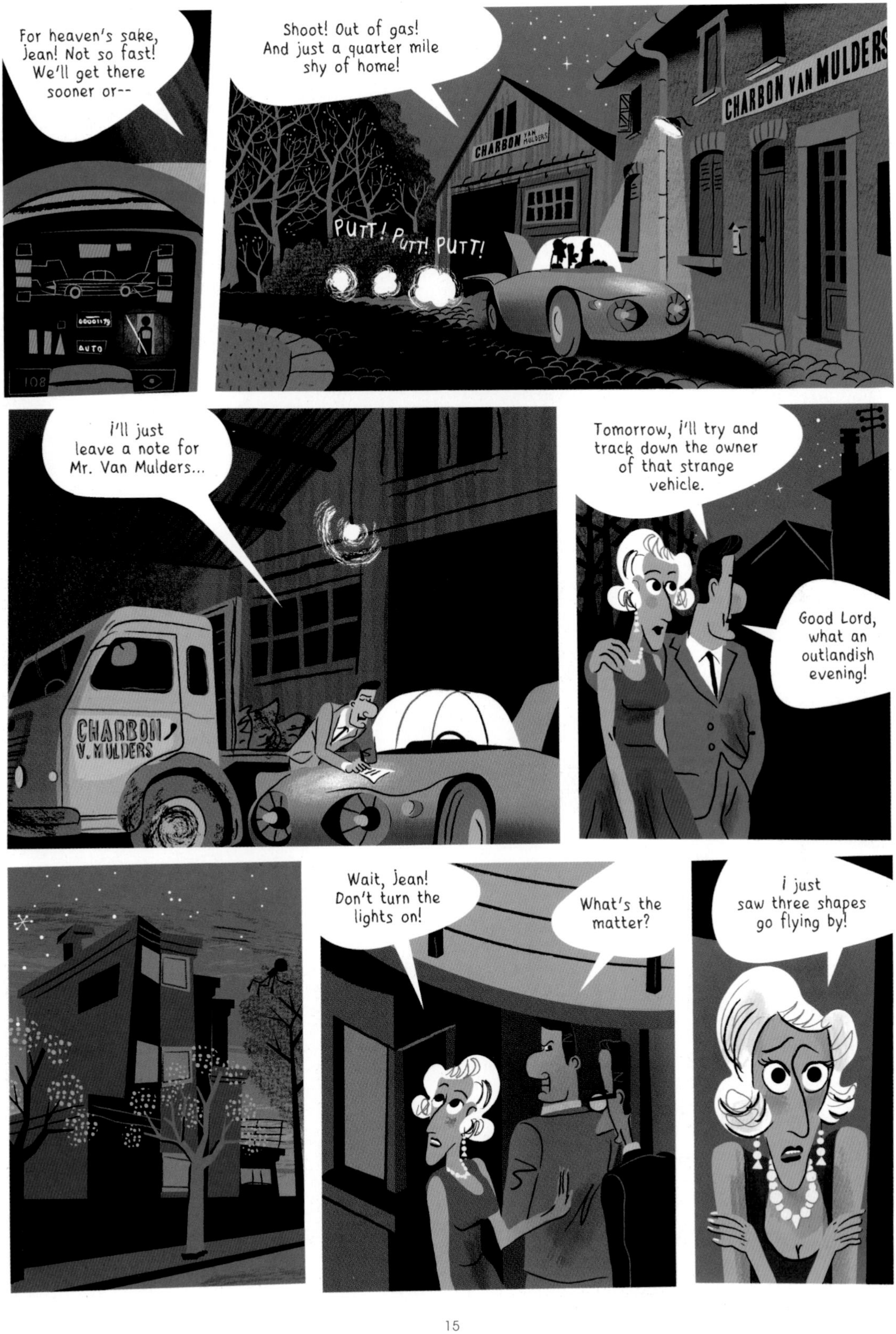

For heaven's sake, Jean! Not so fast! We'll get there sooner or--
Shoot! Out of gas! And just a quarter mile shy of home!
CHARBON VAN MULDERS
CHARBON VAN MULDERS
PUTT! PUTT! PUTT!
AUTO
I'll just leave a note for Mr. Van Mulders...
CHARBON V. MULDERS
Tomorrow, I'll try and track down the owner of that strange vehicle.
Good Lord, what an outlandish evening!
Wait, Jean! Don't turn the lights on!
What's the matter?
I just saw three shapes go flying by!

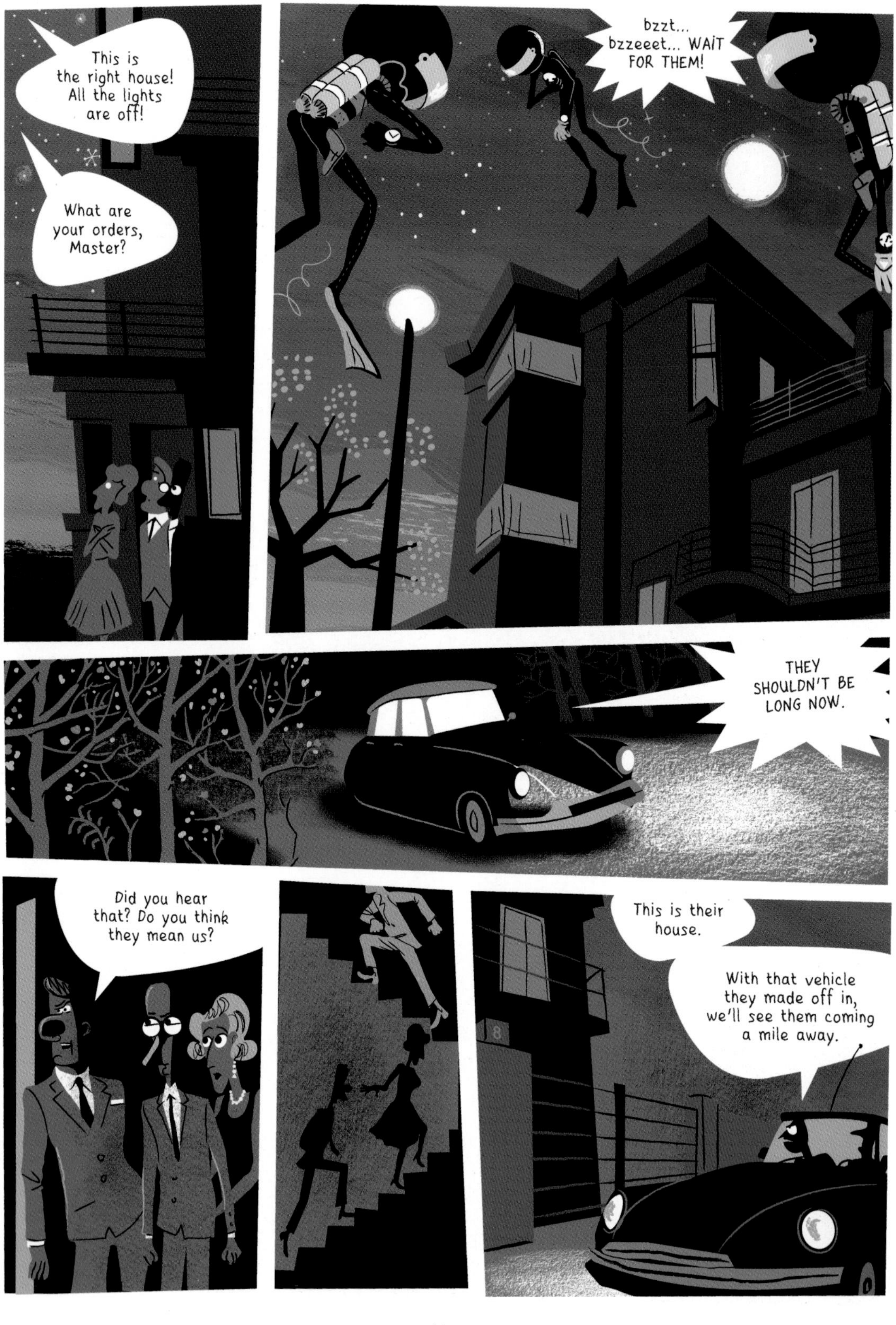
This is the right house! All the lights are off!
What are your orders, Master?
bzzt... bzzeeet... WAIT FOR THEM!
THEY SHOULDN'T BE LONG NOW.
Did you hear that? Do you think they mean us?
This is their house.
With that vehicle they made off in, we'll see them coming a mile away.

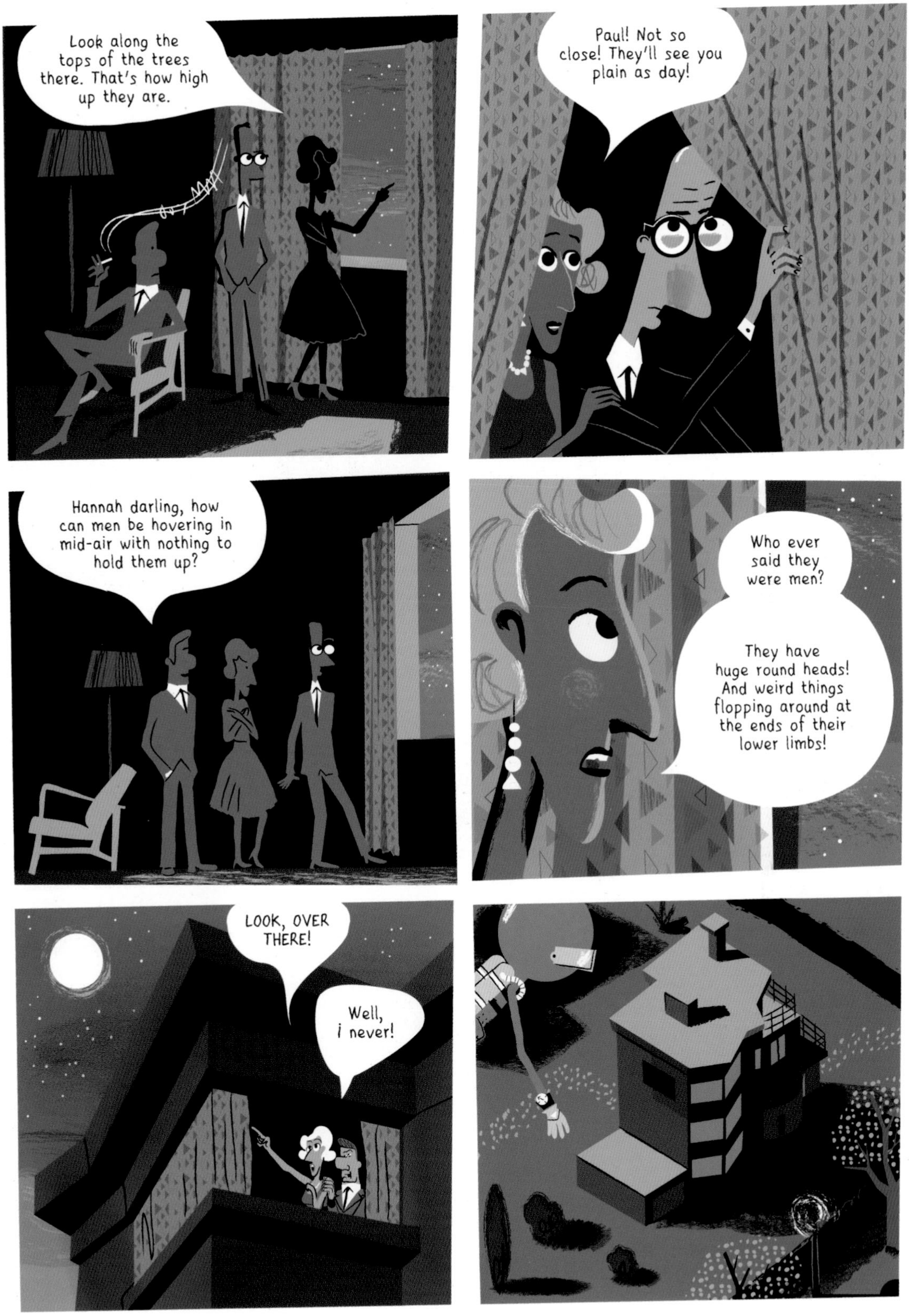

Look along the tops of the trees there. That's how high up they are.
Paul! Not so close! They'll see you plain as day!
Hannah darling, how can men be hovering in mid-air with nothing to hold them up?
Who ever said they were men?
They have huge round heads! And weird things flopping around at the ends of their lower limbs!
LOOK, OVER THERE!
Well, i never!

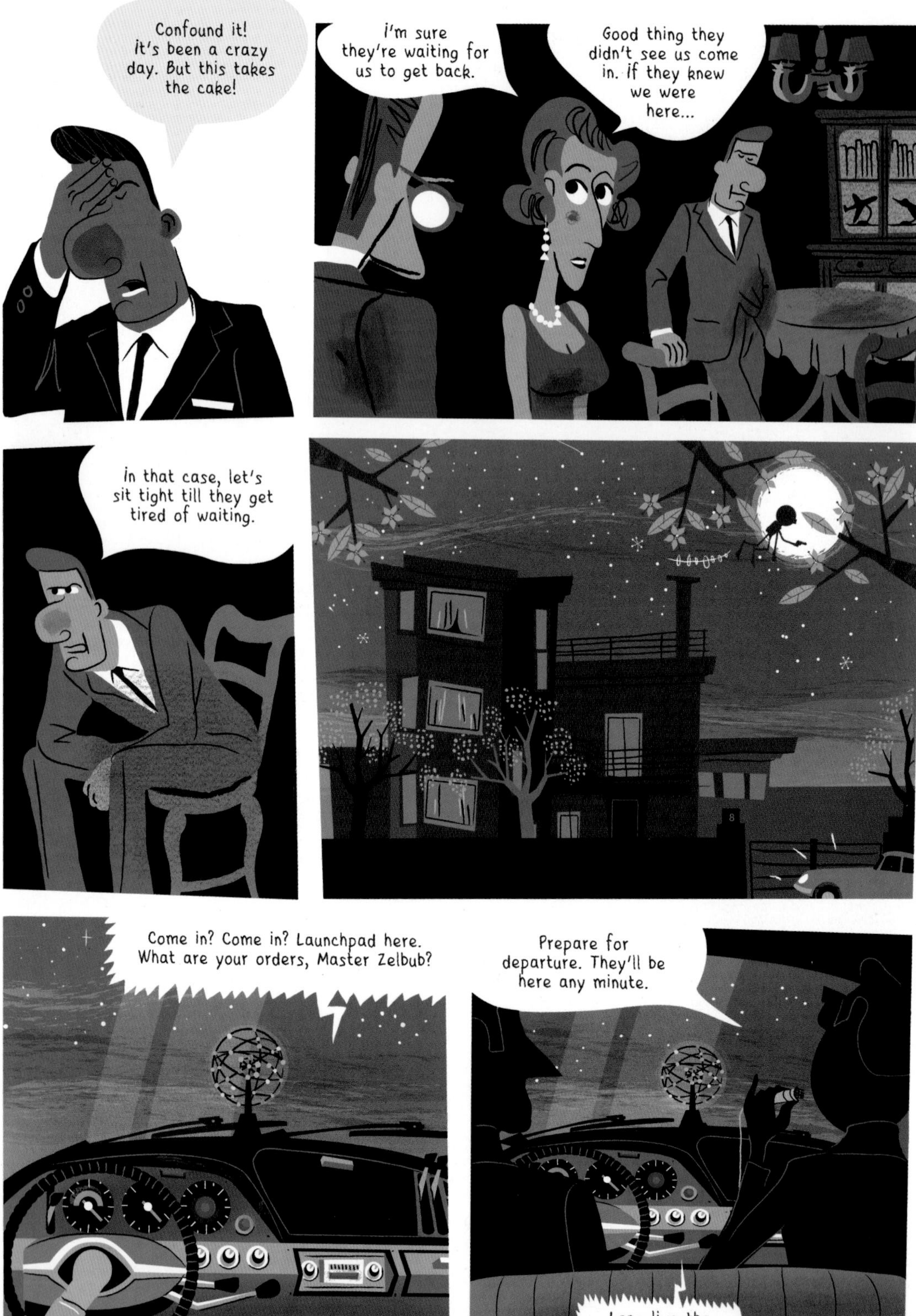

Confound it! It's been a crazy day. But this takes the cake!
I'm sure they're waiting for us to get back.
Good thing they didn't see us come in. If they knew we were here...
In that case, let's sit tight till they get tired of waiting.
Come in? Come in? Launchpad here. What are your orders, Master Zelbub?
Prepare for departure. They'll be here any minute.
Long live the Empire of the Atom!

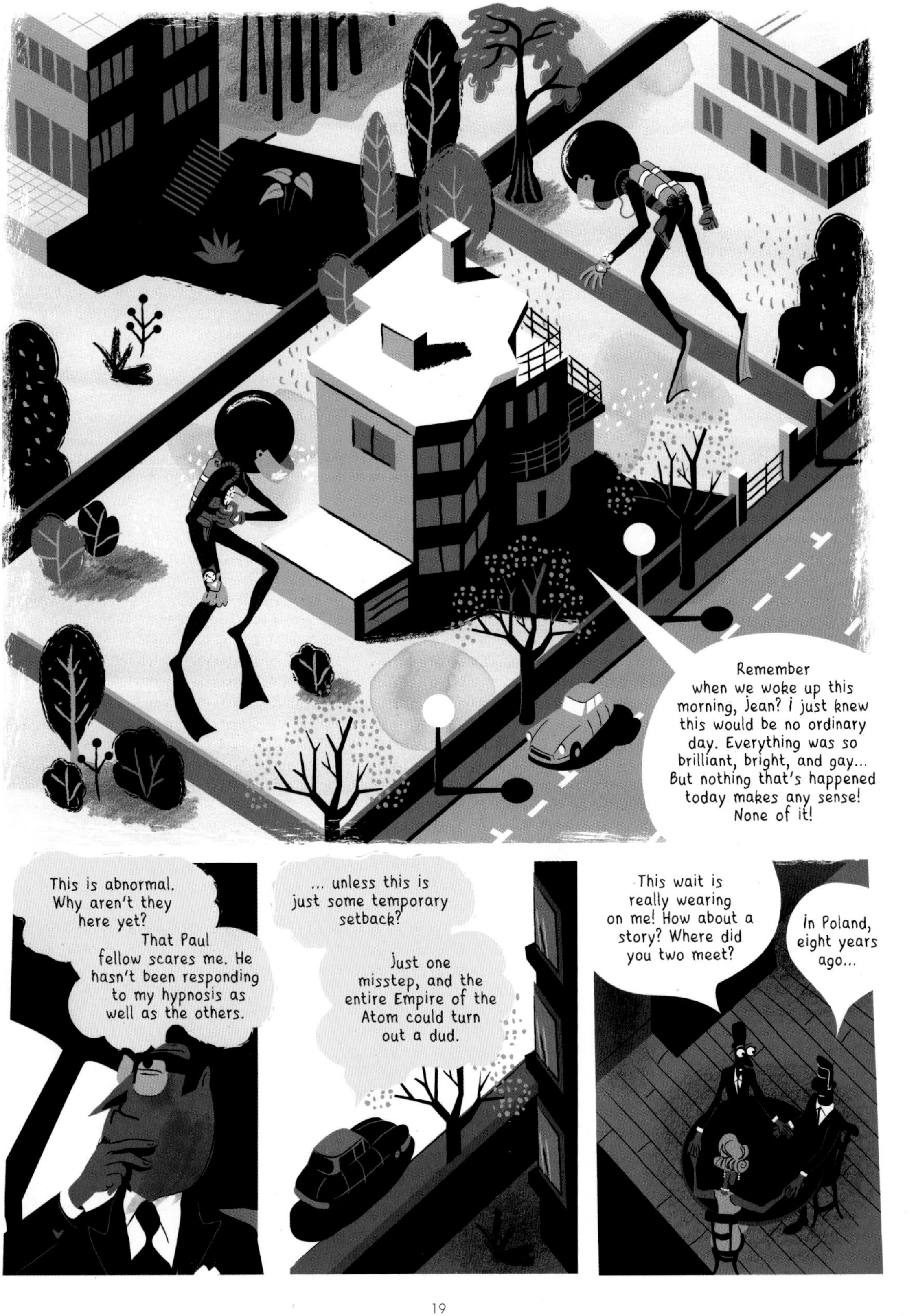
Remember when we woke up this morning, Jean? I just knew this would be no ordinary day. Everything was so brilliant, bright, and gay... But nothing that's happened today makes any sense! None of it!
This is abnormal. Why aren't they here yet?
That Paul fellow scares me. He hasn't been responding to my hypnosis as well as the others.
... unless this is just some temporary setback?
Just one misstep, and the entire Empire of the Atom could turn out a dud.
This wait is really wearing on me! How about a story? Where did you two meet?
In Poland, eight years ago...

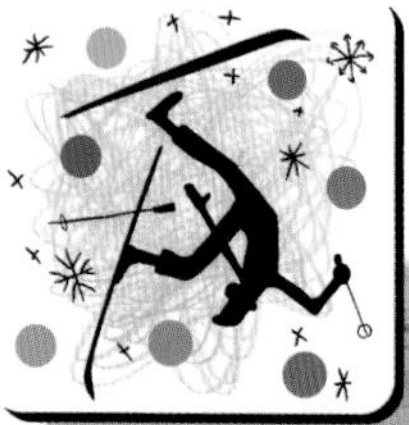

Zakopane, Poland. 1950

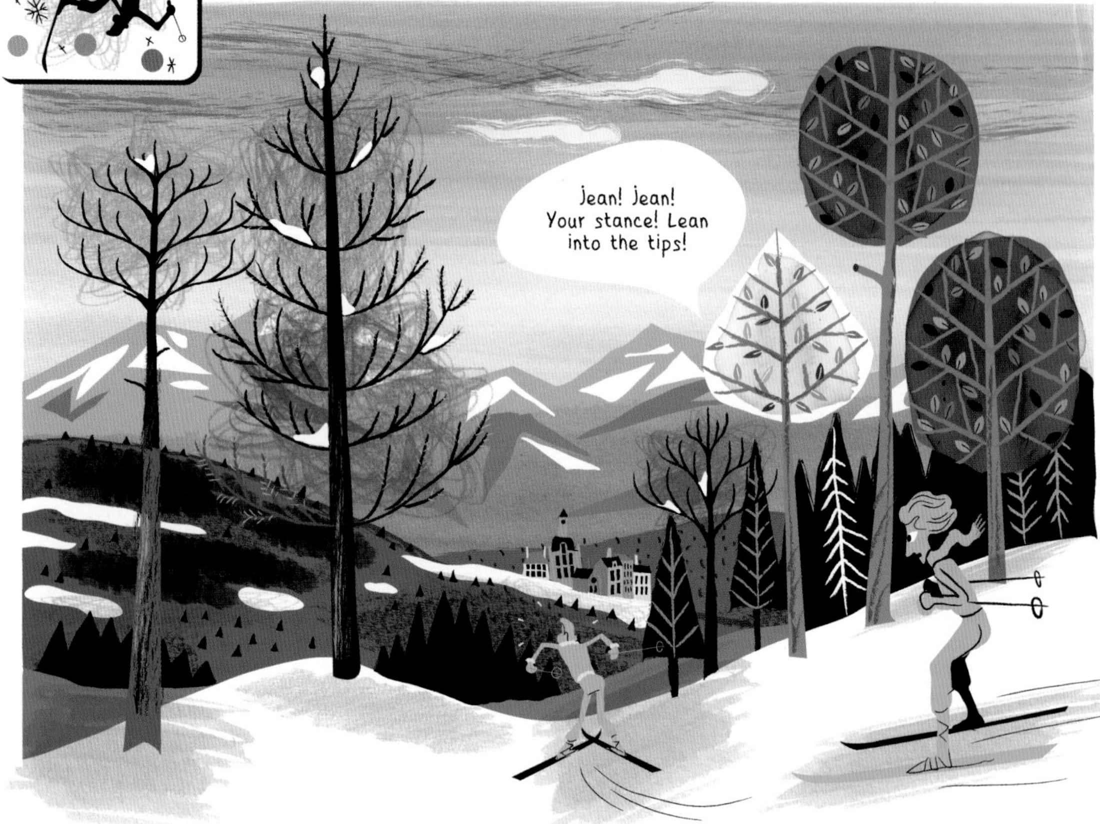
Jean! Jean! Your stance! Lean into the tips!

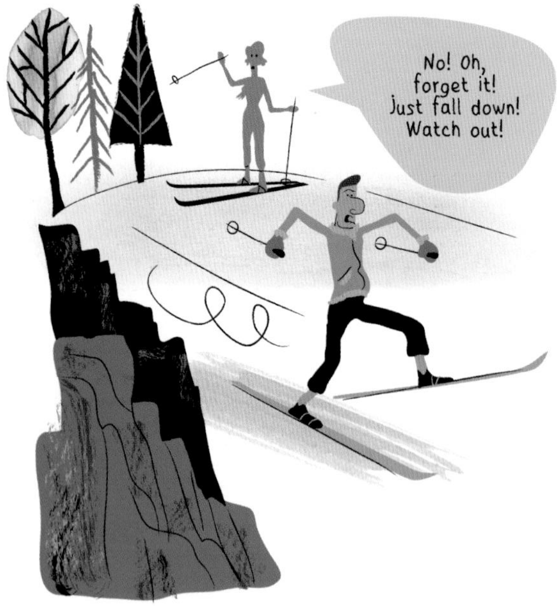
No! Oh, forget it! Just fall down! Watch out!

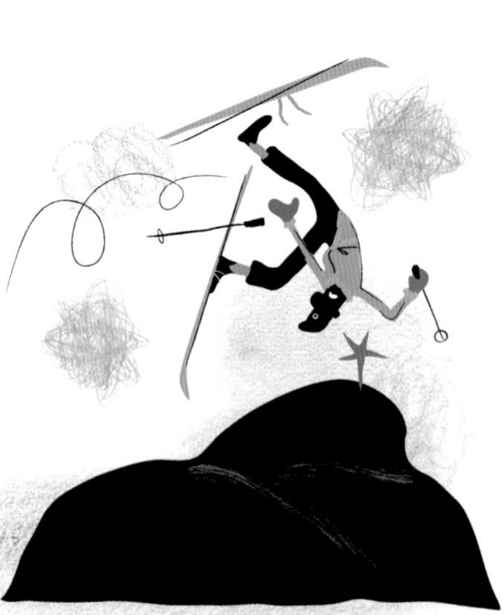

i'm fine, Hannah! All in one piece.
Don't blame yourself. it's this Communist snow of yours rejecting me as a petty bourgeois!
if you're ever in Belgium, you know where to find me. i'll be waiting.
Are you sure? it could take months.
i know. Never fear. i'll wait for you.

But we were not to meet again for six years.

I was in Hungary in 1956. When the Russians came marching in, I decided to try my luck.

There was nothing I could do for my parents now... and I'd kept the number Jean had given me.

I'll never forget that phone call as long as I live.

Sint-Genesius-Rode. November, 1956

Jeannot! Telephone! It's urgent!

I think it's your Polish crush!

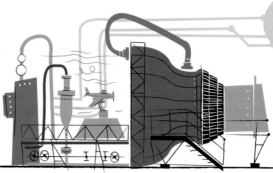

She's got the right accent, anyway. She's waiting for you at the Gare du Nord! Flat broke.

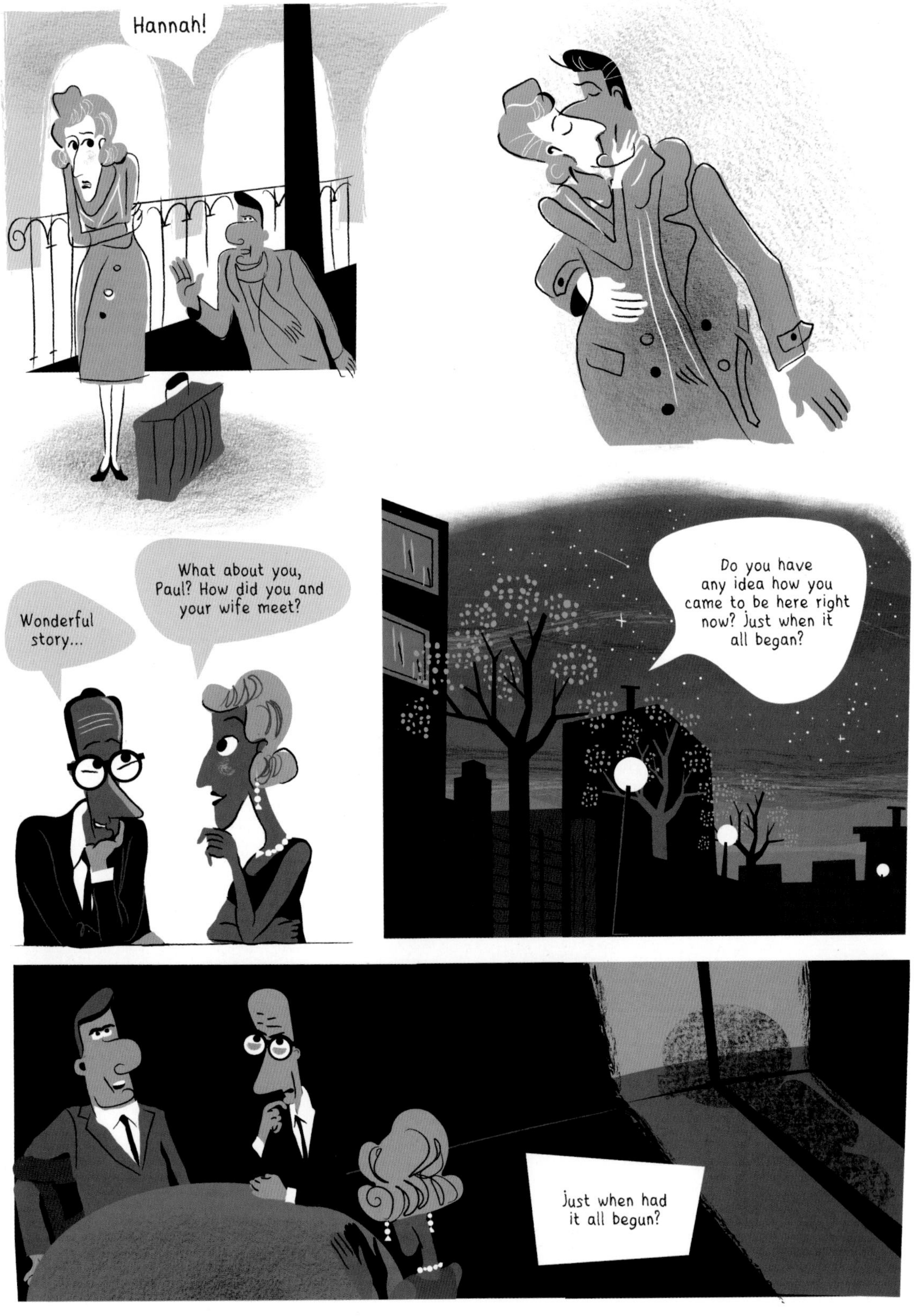
Hannah!
Wonderful story...
What about you, Paul? How did you and your wife meet?
Do you have any idea how you came to be here right now? Just when it all began?
Just when had it all begun?

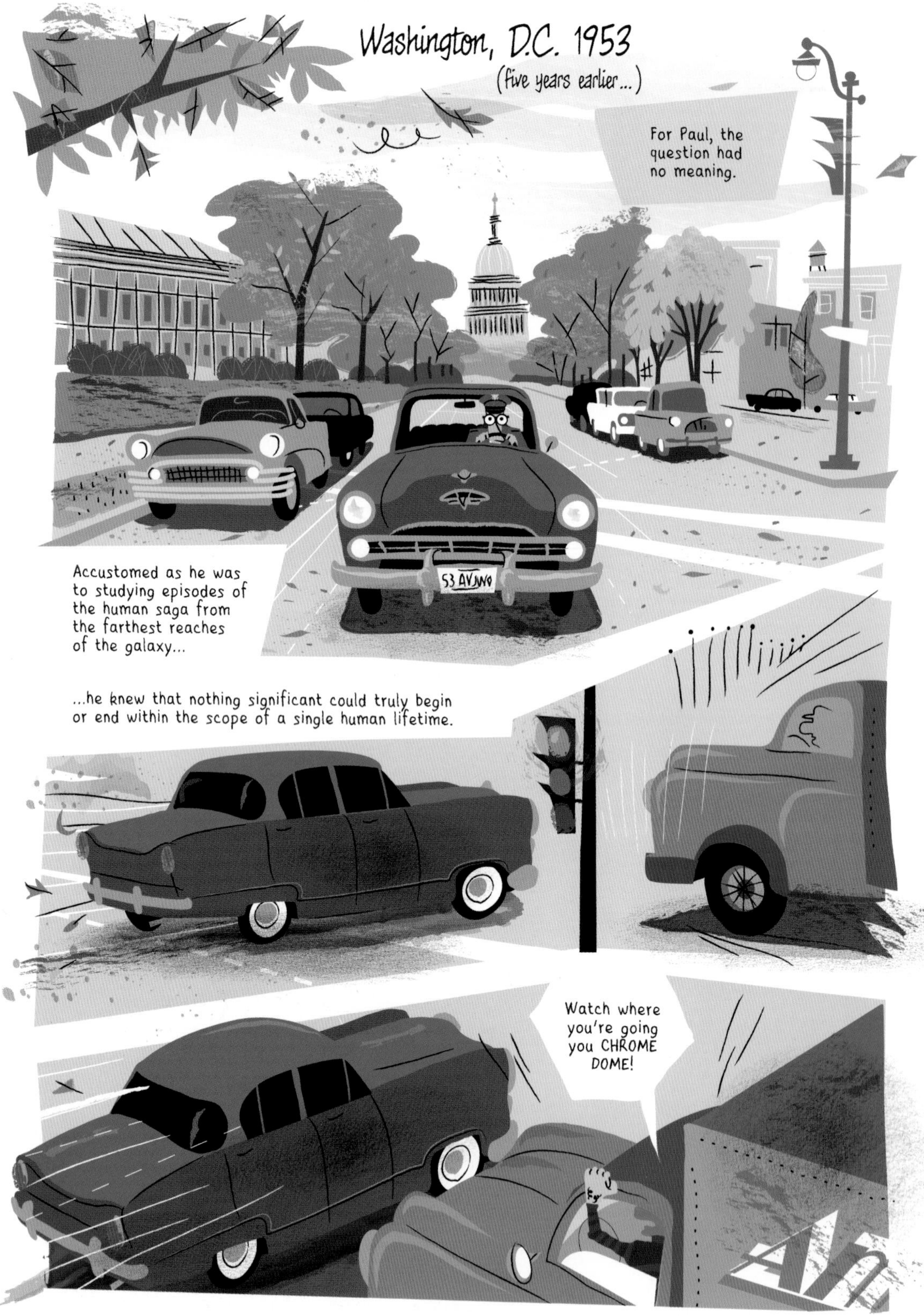
Washington, D.C. 1953
(five years earlier...)
For Paul, the question had no meaning.
Accustomed as he was to studying episodes of the human saga from the farthest reaches of the galaxy...
...he knew that nothing significant could truly begin or end within the scope of a single human lifetime.
Watch where you're going you CHROME DOME!

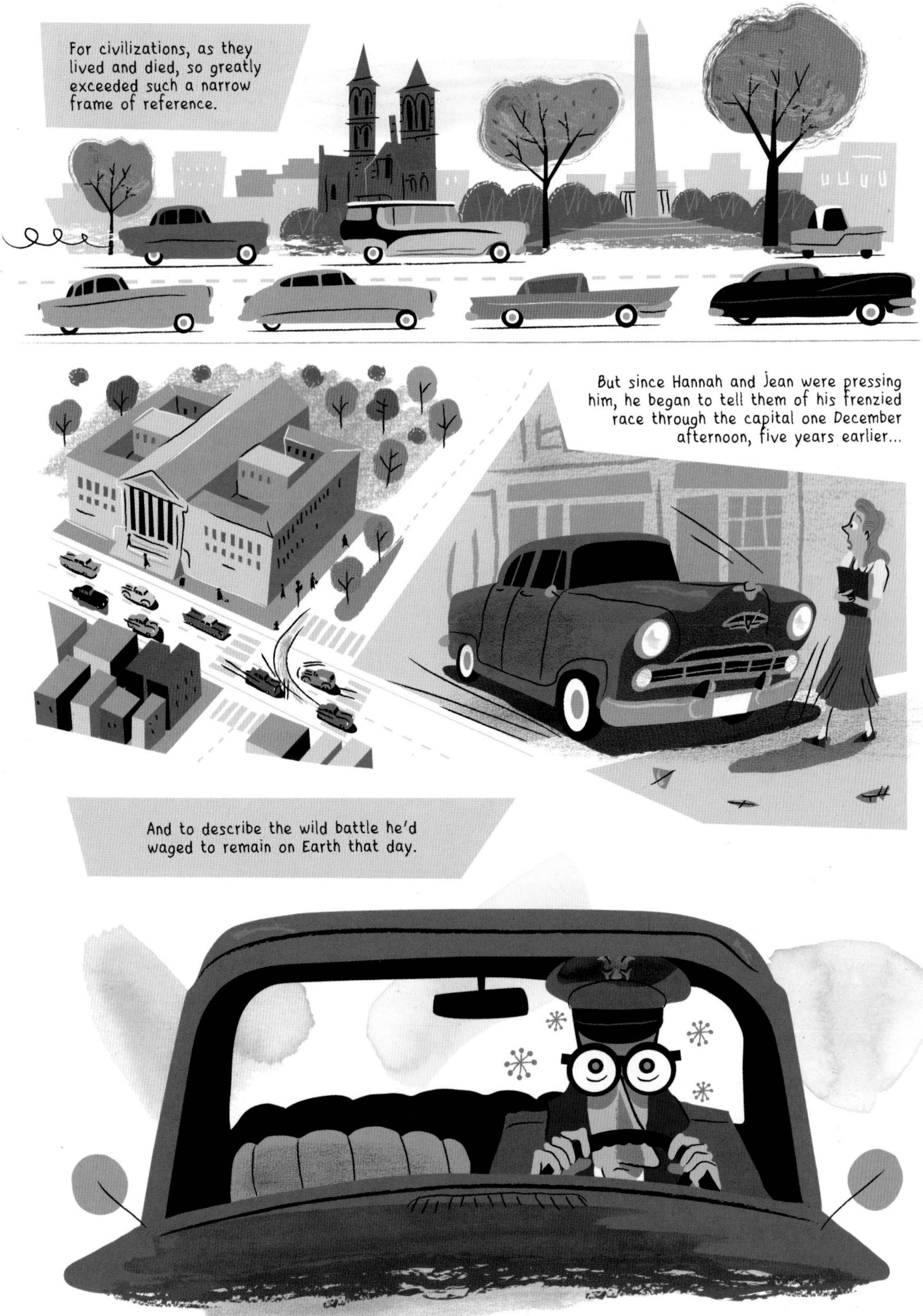
For civilizations, as they lived and died, so greatly exceeded such a narrow frame of reference.
But since Hannah and Jean were pressing him, he began to tell them of his frenzied race through the capital one December afternoon, five years earlier...
And to describe the wild battle he'd waged to remain on Earth that day.

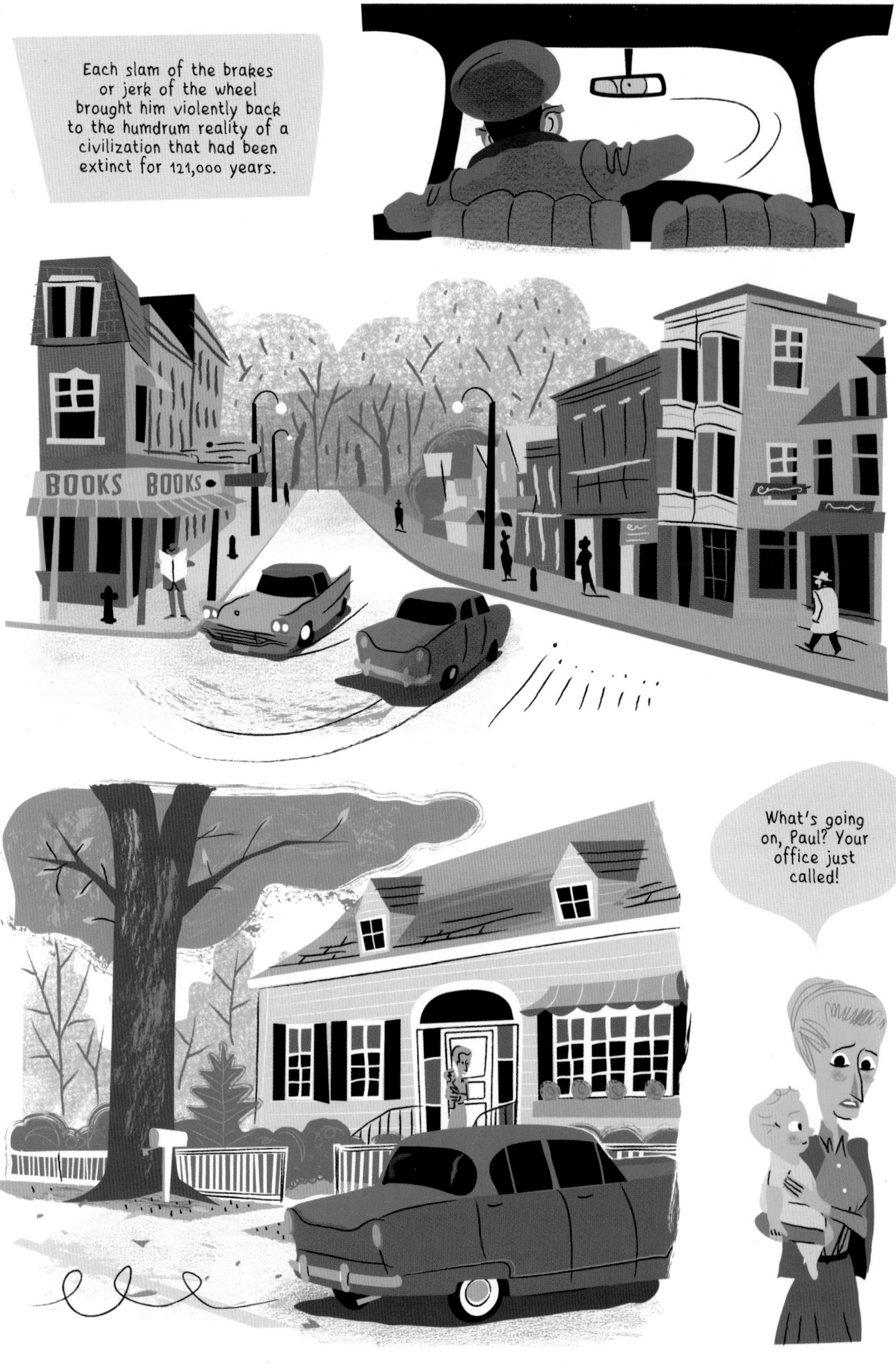
Each slam of the brakes or jerk of the wheel brought him violently back to the humdrum reality of a civilization that had been extinct for 121,000 years.
BOOKS BOOKS
What's going on, Paul? Your office just called!

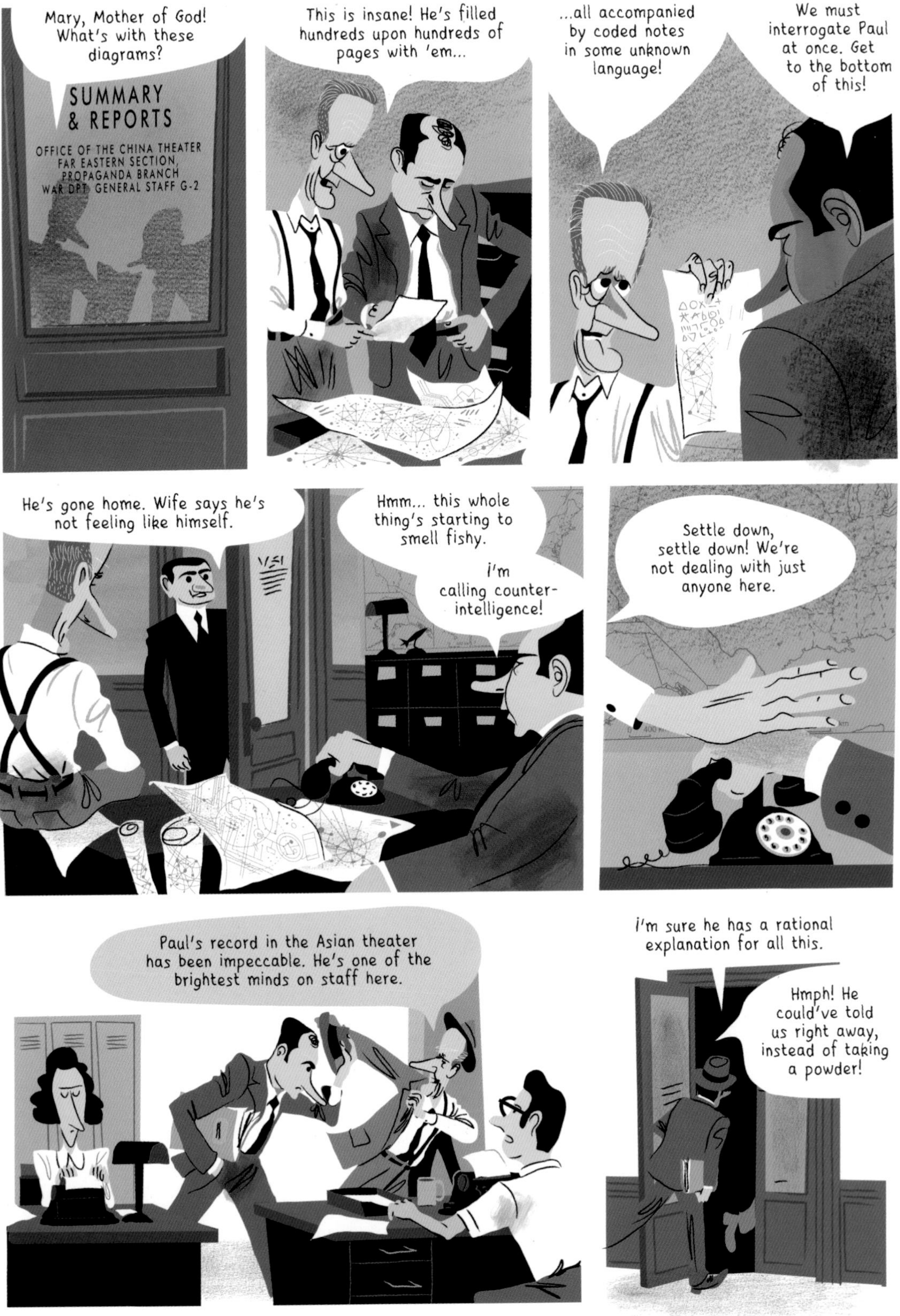
Mary, Mother of God! What's with these diagrams?
SUMMARY & REPORTS
OFFICE OF THE CHINA THEATER
FAR EASTERN SECTION,
PROPAGANDA BRANCH
WAR DPT. GENERAL STAFF G-2
This is insane! He's filled hundreds upon hundreds of pages with 'em...
...all accompanied by coded notes in some unknown language!
We must interrogate Paul at once. Get to the bottom of this!
He's gone home. Wife says he's not feeling like himself.
Hmm... this whole thing's starting to smell fishy.
I'm calling counter-intelligence!
Settle down, settle down! We're not dealing with just anyone here.
Paul's record in the Asian theater has been impeccable. He's one of the brightest minds on staff here.
I'm sure he has a rational explanation for all this.
Hmph! He could've told us right away, instead of taking a powder!

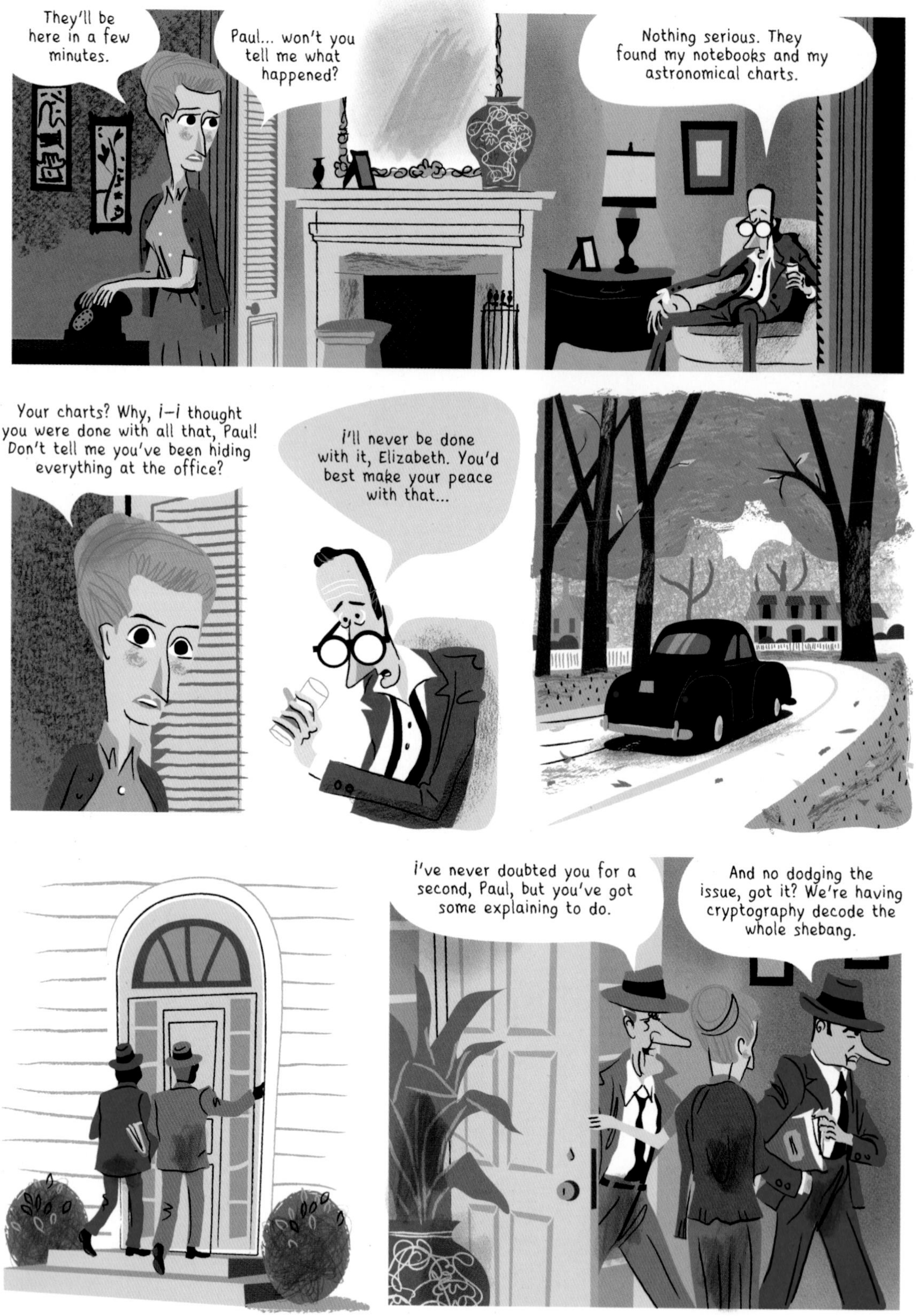
They'll be here in a few minutes.
Paul... won't you tell me what happened?
Nothing serious. They found my notebooks and my astronomical charts.
Your charts? Why, i—i thought you were done with all that, Paul! Don't tell me you've been hiding everything at the office?
i'll never be done with it, Elizabeth. You'd best make your peace with that...
i've never doubted you for a second, Paul, but you've got some explaining to do.
And no dodging the issue, got it? We're having cryptography decode the whole shebang.

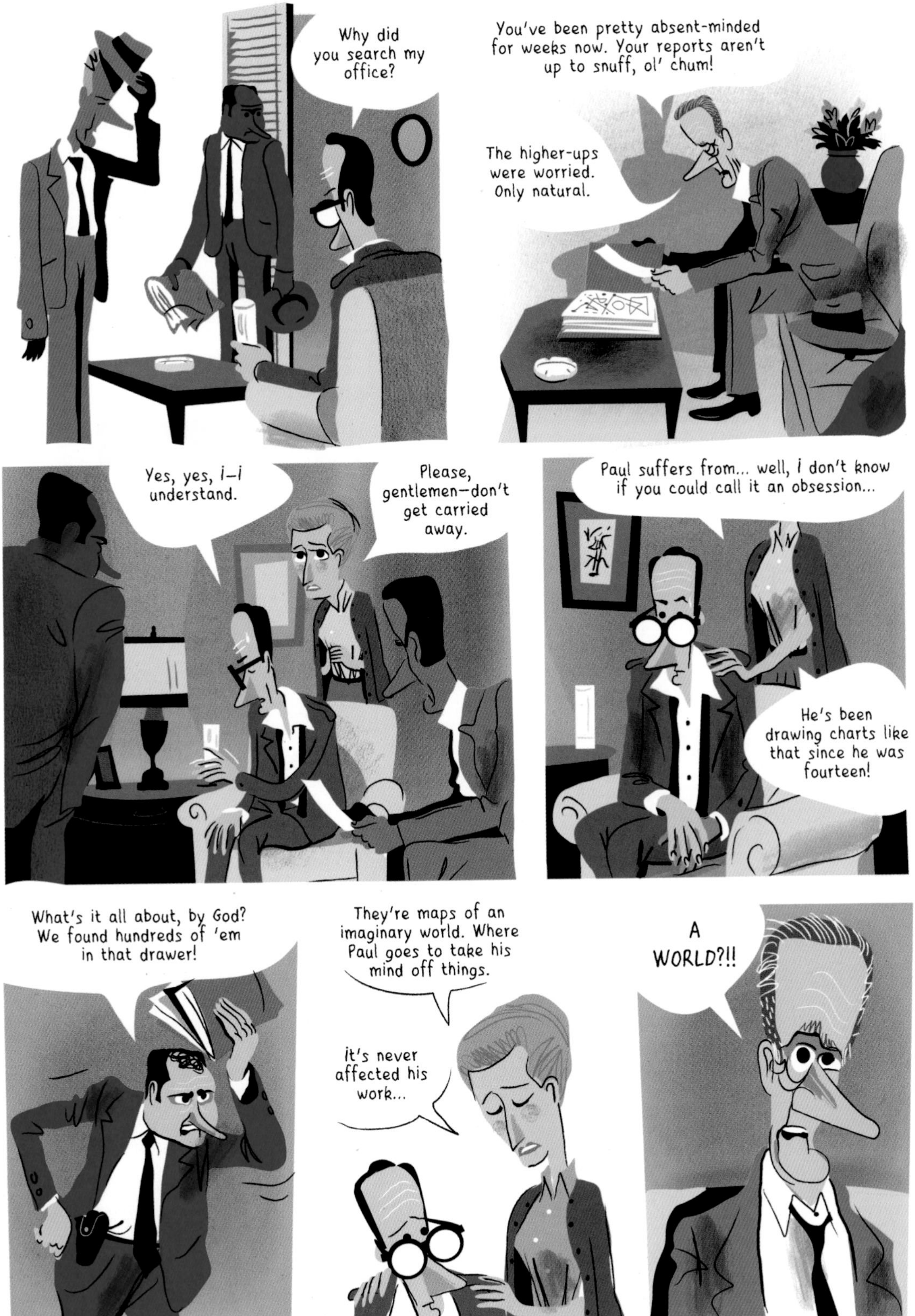
Why did you search my office?
You've been pretty absent-minded for weeks now. Your reports aren't up to snuff, ol' chum!
The higher-ups were worried. Only natural.
Yes, yes, I—I understand.
Please, gentlemen—don't get carried away.
Paul suffers from... well, I don't know if you could call it an obsession...
He's been drawing charts like that since he was fourteen!
What's it all about, by God? We found hundreds of 'em in that drawer!
They're maps of an imaginary world. Where Paul goes to take his mind off things.
It's never affected his work...
A WORLD?!!

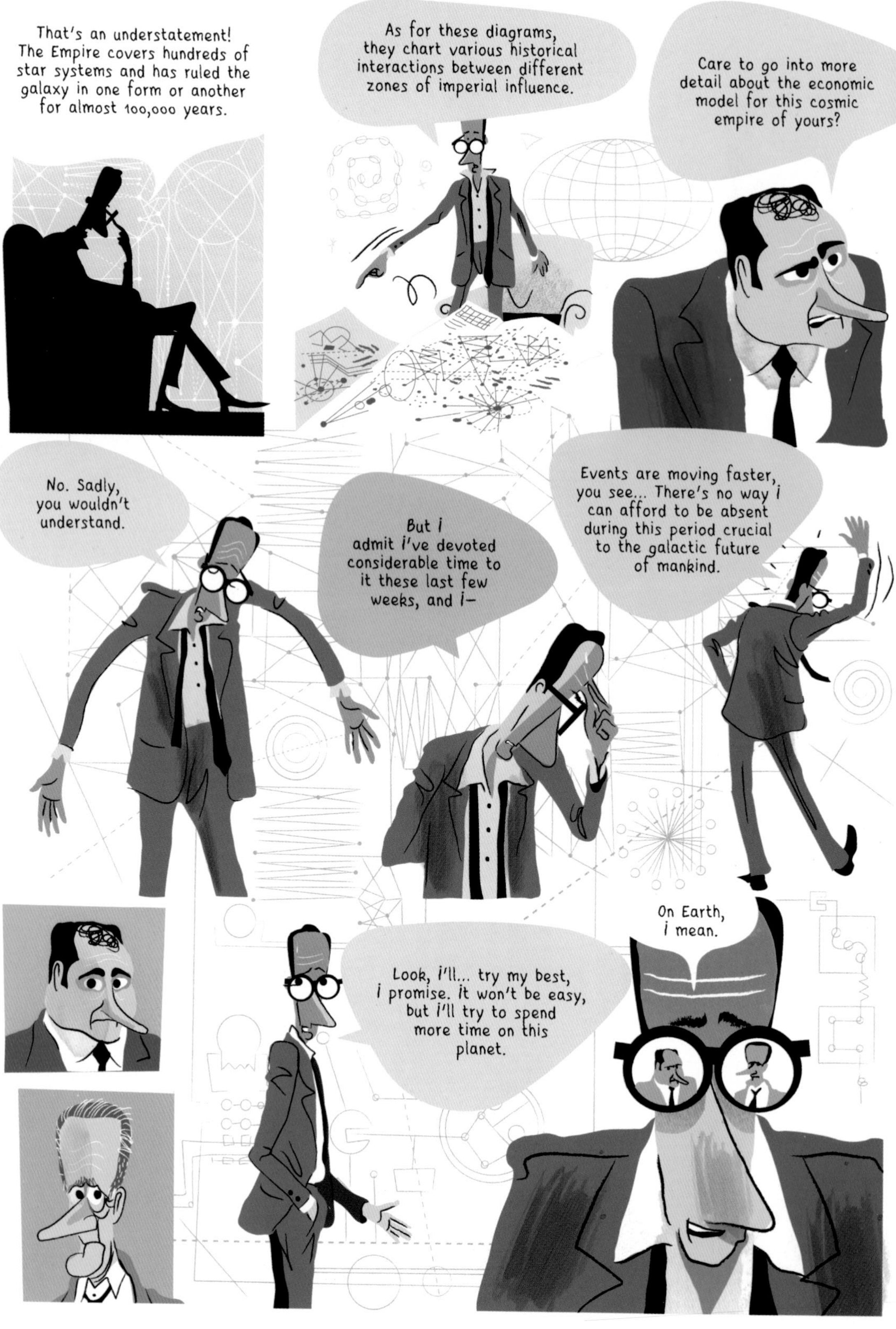

That's an understatement! The Empire covers hundreds of star systems and has ruled the galaxy in one form or another for almost 100,000 years.
As for these diagrams, they chart various historical interactions between different zones of imperial influence.
Care to go into more detail about the economic model for this cosmic empire of yours?
No. Sadly, you wouldn't understand.
But I admit I've devoted considerable time to it these last few weeks, and I–
Events are moving faster, you see... There's no way I can afford to be absent during this period crucial to the galactic future of mankind.
Look, I'll... try my best, I promise. It won't be easy, but I'll try to spend more time on this planet.
On Earth, I mean.

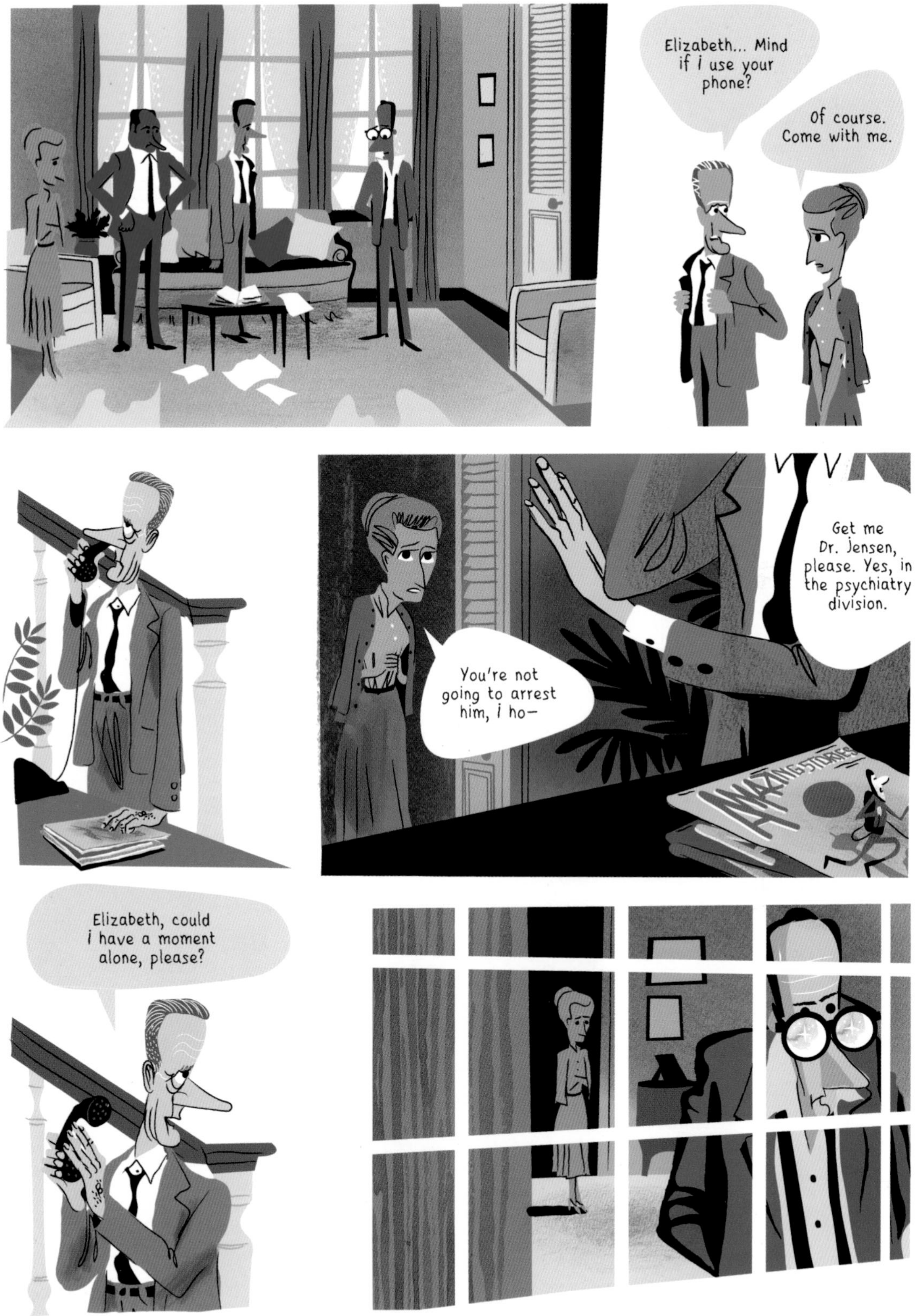
Elizabeth... Mind if i use your phone?
Of course. Come with me.
Get me Dr. Jensen, please. Yes, in the psychiatry division.
You're not going to arrest him, i ho—
AMAZING STORIES
Elizabeth, could i have a moment alone, please?

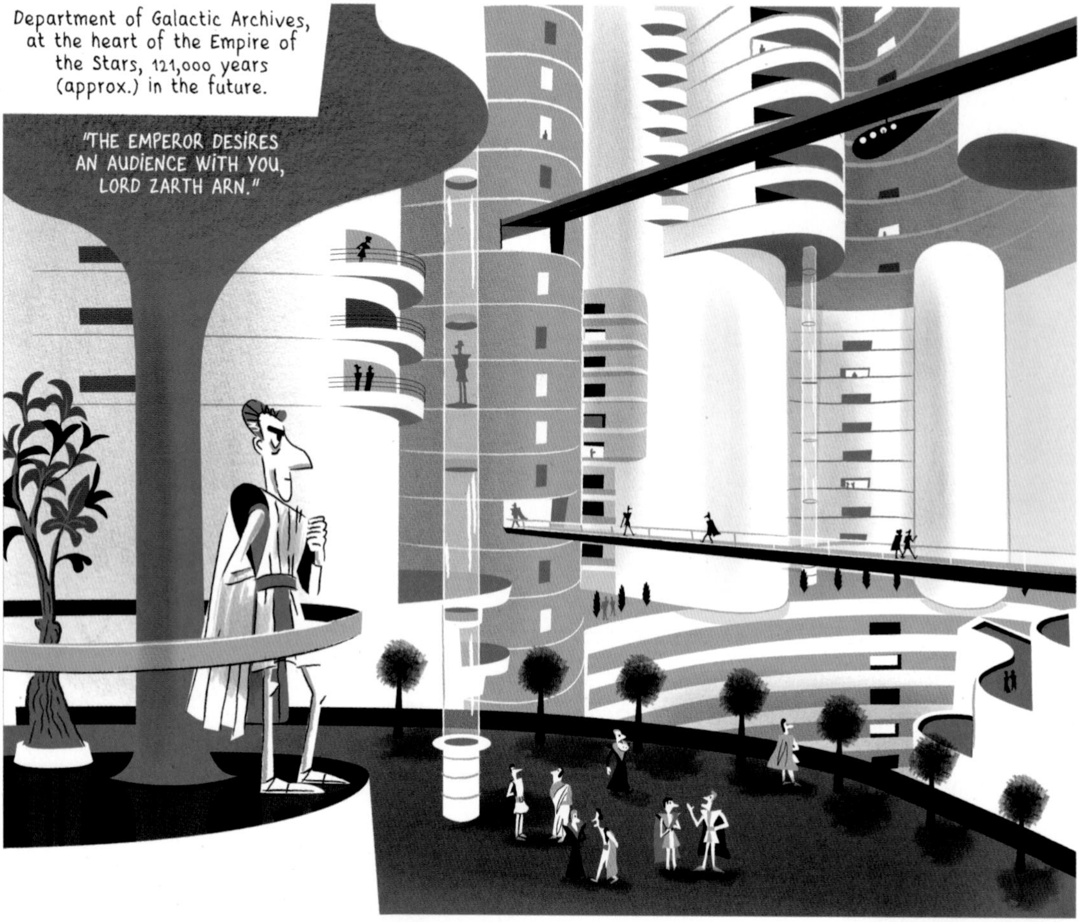
Department of Galactic Archives, at the heart of the Empire of the Stars, 121,000 years (approx.) in the future.
"THE EMPEROR DESIRES AN AUDIENCE WITH YOU, LORD ZARTH ARN."

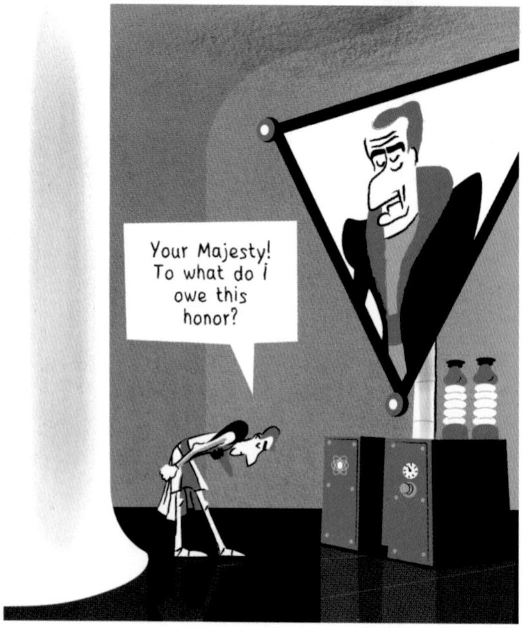
Your Majesty! To what do I owe this honor?

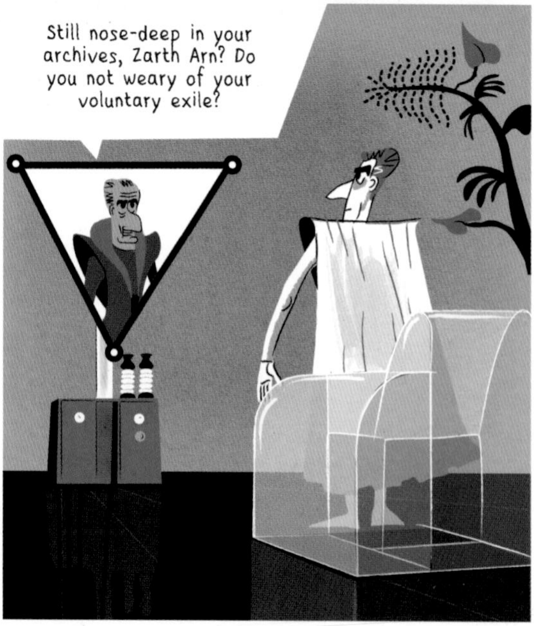
Still nose-deep in your archives, Zarth Arn? Do you not weary of your voluntary exile?

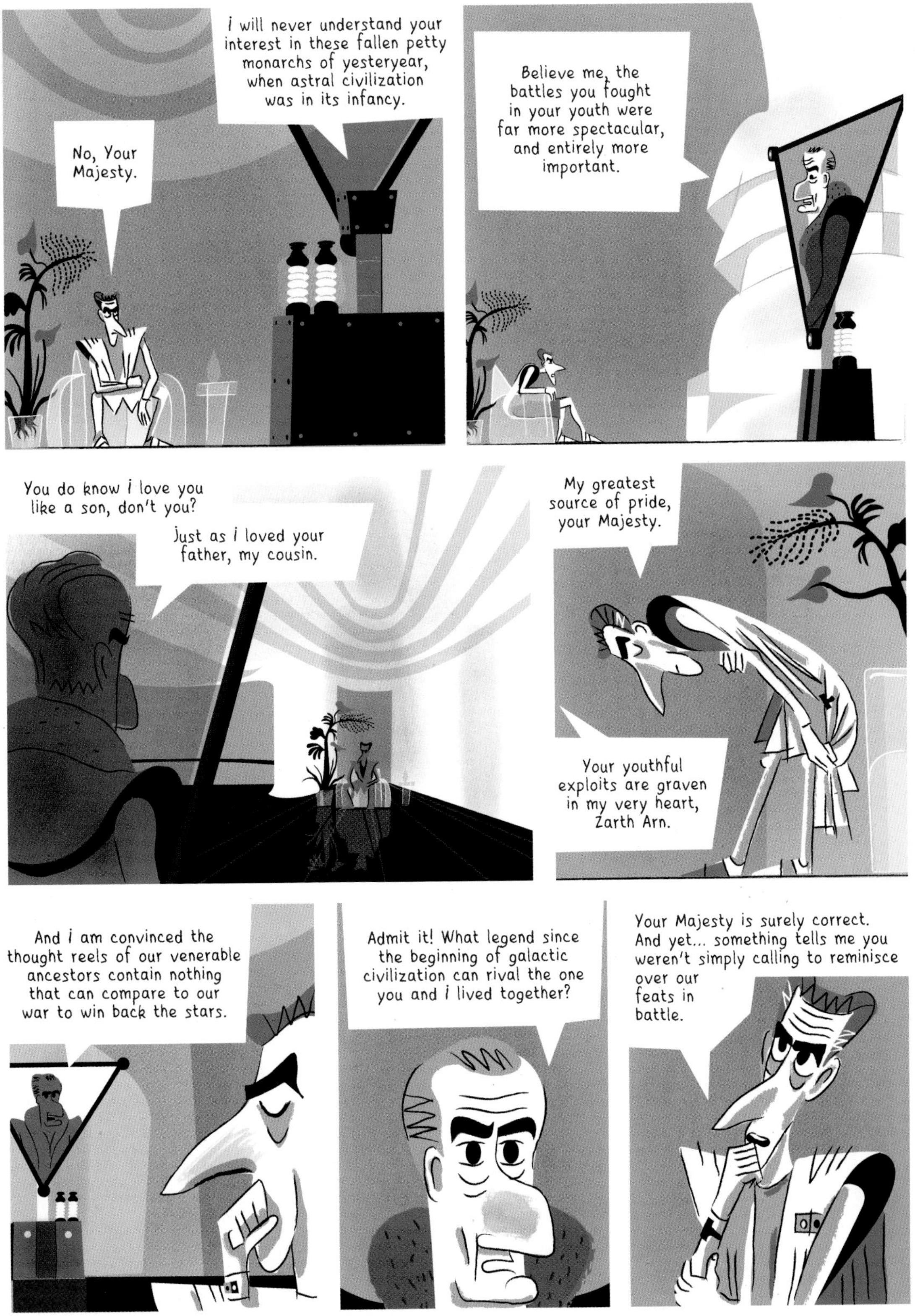
No, Your Majesty.
I will never understand your interest in these fallen petty monarchs of yesteryear, when astral civilization was in its infancy.
Believe me, the battles you fought in your youth were far more spectacular, and entirely more important.
You do know I love you like a son, don't you?
Just as I loved your father, my cousin.
My greatest source of pride, your Majesty.
Your youthful exploits are graven in my very heart, Zarth Arn.
And I am convinced the thought reels of our venerable ancestors contain nothing that can compare to our war to win back the stars.
Admit it! What legend since the beginning of galactic civilization can rival the one you and I lived together?
Your Majesty is surely correct. And yet... something tells me you weren't simply calling to reminisce over our feats in battle.

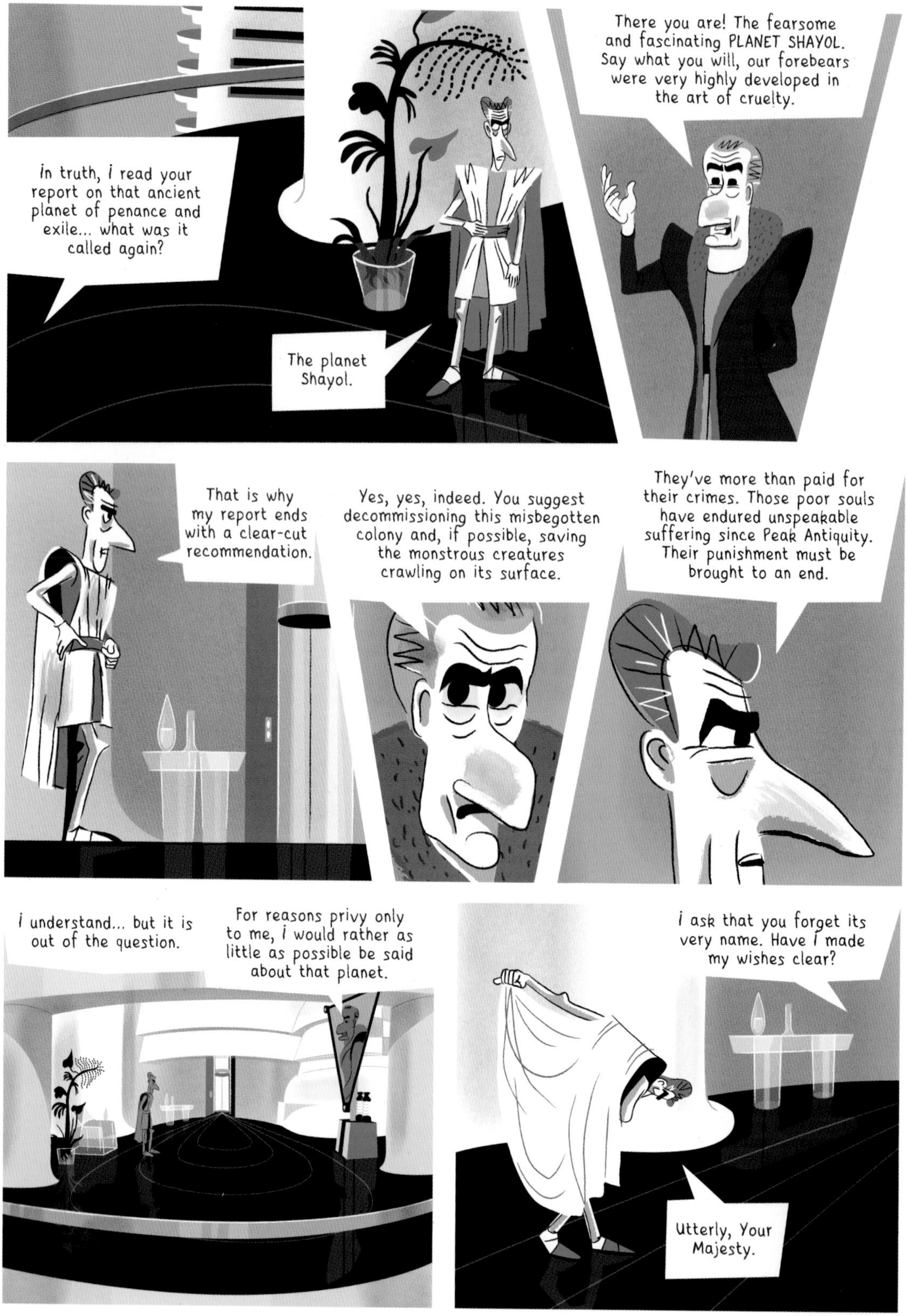
In truth, I read your report on that ancient planet of penance and exile... what was it called again?
The planet Shayol.
There you are! The fearsome and fascinating PLANET SHAYOL. Say what you will, our forebears were very highly developed in the art of cruelty.
That is why my report ends with a clear-cut recommendation.
Yes, yes, indeed. You suggest decommissioning this misbegotten colony and, if possible, saving the monstrous creatures crawling on its surface.
They've more than paid for their crimes. Those poor souls have endured unspeakable suffering since Peak Antiquity. Their punishment must be brought to an end.
I understand... but it is out of the question.
For reasons privy only to me, I would rather as little as possible be said about that planet.
I ask that you forget its very name. Have I made my wishes clear?
Utterly, Your Majesty.

Ah, my dear Paul...

...my confidant, my guardian angel!

What do you think of this latest development?

Tell me, since you read everything *i* do, over my shoulder.

Has some detail escaped me, in some forgotten corner of our beloved archives?

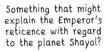

Something that might explain the Emperor's reticence with regard to the planet Shayol?

No, Zarth. *i* don't understand why the Emperor's worried.

Nor do *i*.

That ill-fated planet constitutes a moral problem, not a political one.

Have *i* touched some sensitive nerve?

35

Brussels. April 1, 1958

Paul... *i*'m having trouble wrapping my head around what you're telling us.

This imaginary world...

Do you really believe in it?

is it just some idle fantasy you've concocted, or the result of some—some—

Neurosis?

Who knows? Not even my psychiatrist ever managed to say for sure.

i walked him through every phase of my relationship with Zarth Arn, starting from our earliest telepathic encounter.

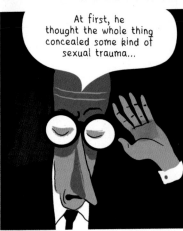

At first, he thought the whole thing concealed some kind of sexual trauma...

But when *i* described our battles, and then galactic history down to the last detail, a strange thing happened.

Dr. Jensen began to believe in the reality of my experience. He even wrote a famous article about it: "The Jet-Propelled Couch."

Hold on. Before you say any more, *i* need a glass of water.

36

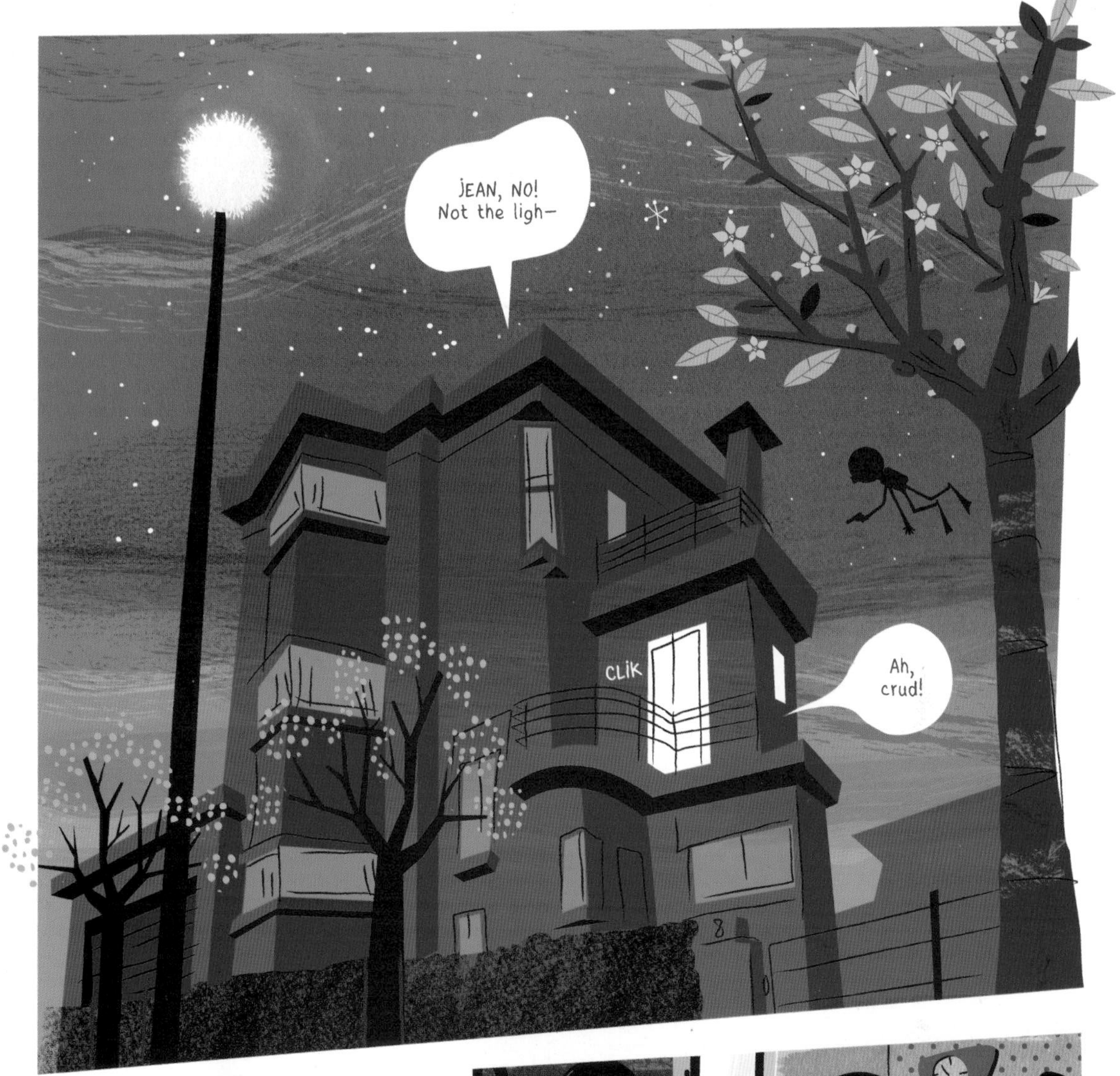
JEAN, NO! Not the ligh—
CLIK
Ah, crud!

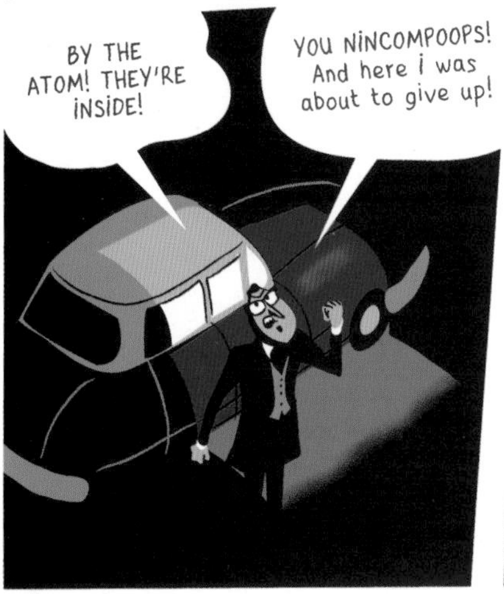
BY THE ATOM! THEY'RE INSIDE!
YOU NINCOMPOOPS! And here I was about to give up!

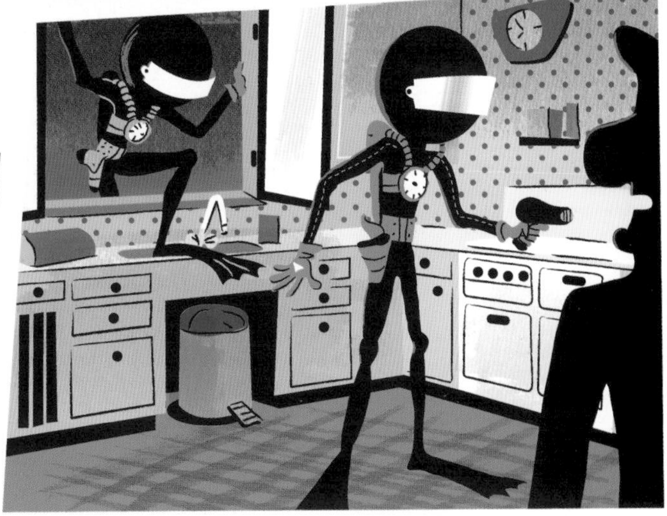

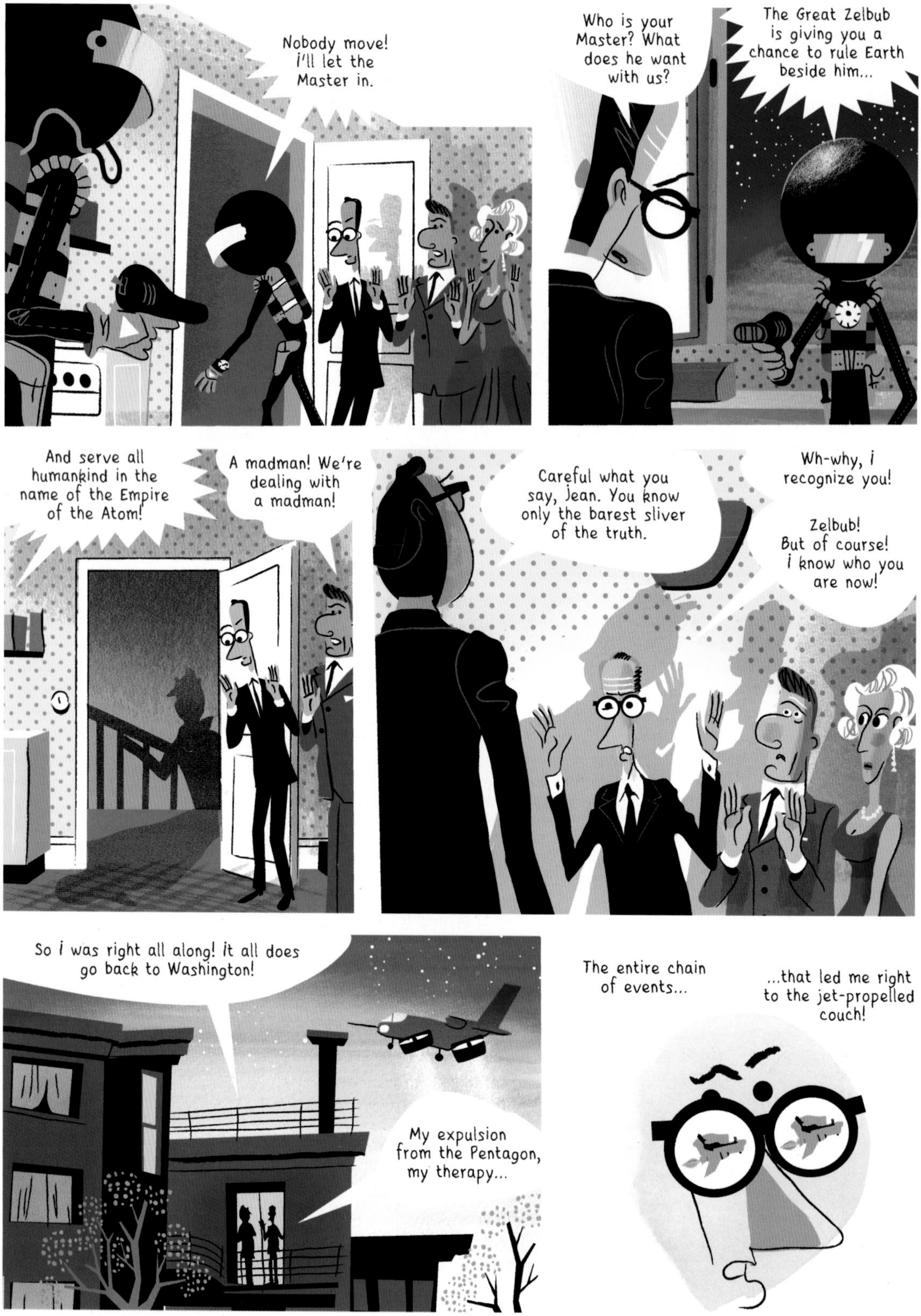
Nobody move! I'll let the Master in.
Who is your Master? What does he want with us?
The Great Zelbub is giving you a chance to rule Earth beside him...
And serve all humankind in the name of the Empire of the Atom!
A madman! We're dealing with a madman!
Careful what you say, Jean. You know only the barest sliver of the truth.
Wh-why, I recognize you!
Zelbub! But of course! I know who you are now!
So I was right all along! It all does go back to Washington!
My expulsion from the Pentagon, my therapy...
The entire chain of events...
...that led me right to the jet-propelled couch!

chapter 2

THE Jet-Propelled COUCH

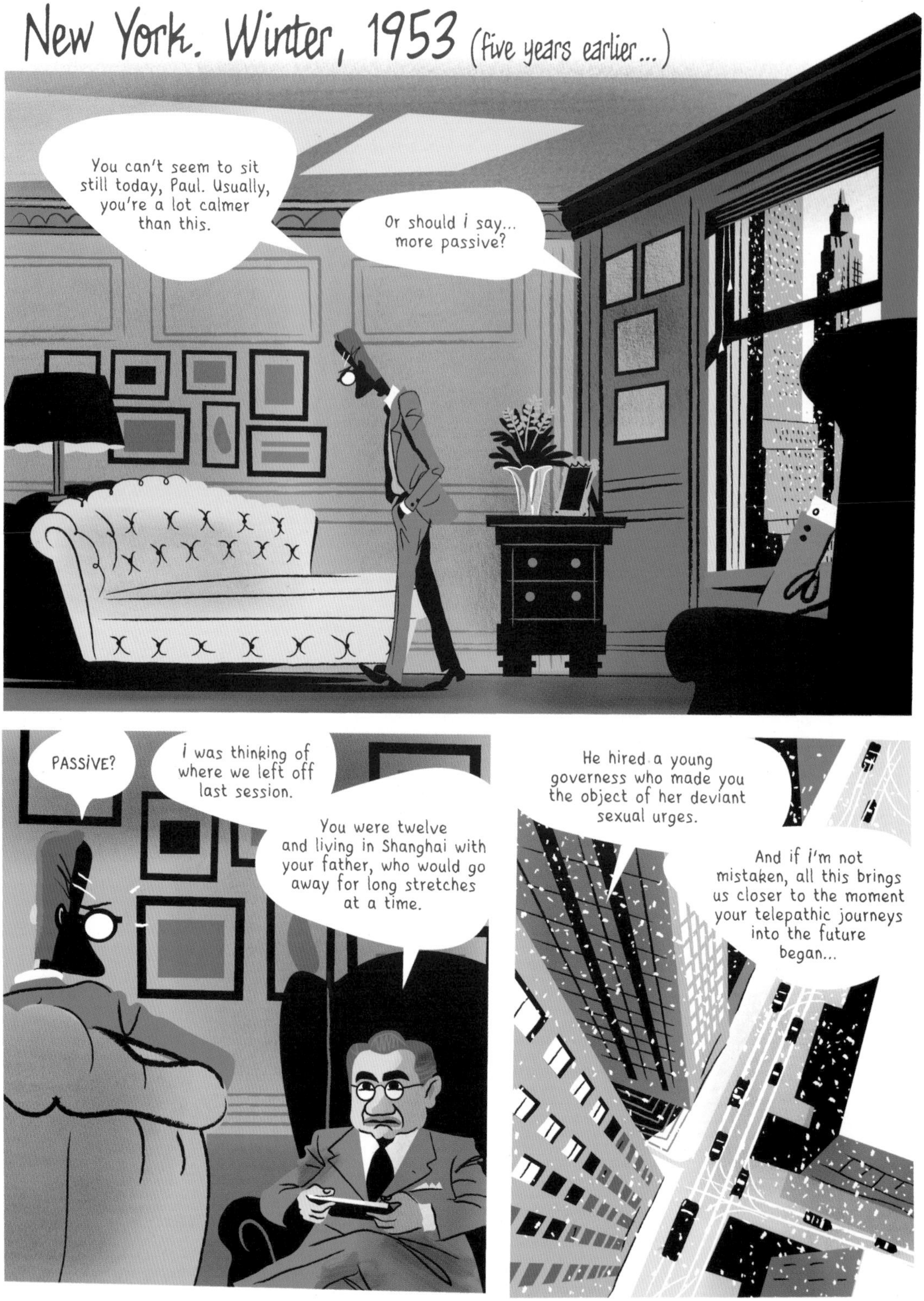
New York. Winter, 1953 (five years earlier...)
You can't seem to sit still today, Paul. Usually, you're a lot calmer than this.
Or should i say... more passive?
PASSIVE?
i was thinking of where we left off last session.
You were twelve and living in Shanghai with your father, who would go away for long stretches at a time.
He hired a young governess who made you the object of her deviant sexual urges.
And if i'm not mistaken, all this brings us closer to the moment your telepathic journeys into the future began...

Would you like to take it from the beginning again? And i exhort you not to leave out any details of this unusual early experience.

Every night, Sarah would come into my room.

She would undress, twisting and writhing, caressing herself in a scandalous fashion.

At first, i thought her visits were a form of sleepwalking.

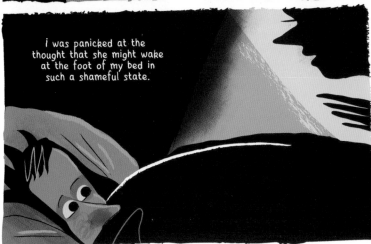

i was panicked at the thought that she might wake at the foot of my bed in such a shameful state.

One day, at breakfast, i broached the subject...

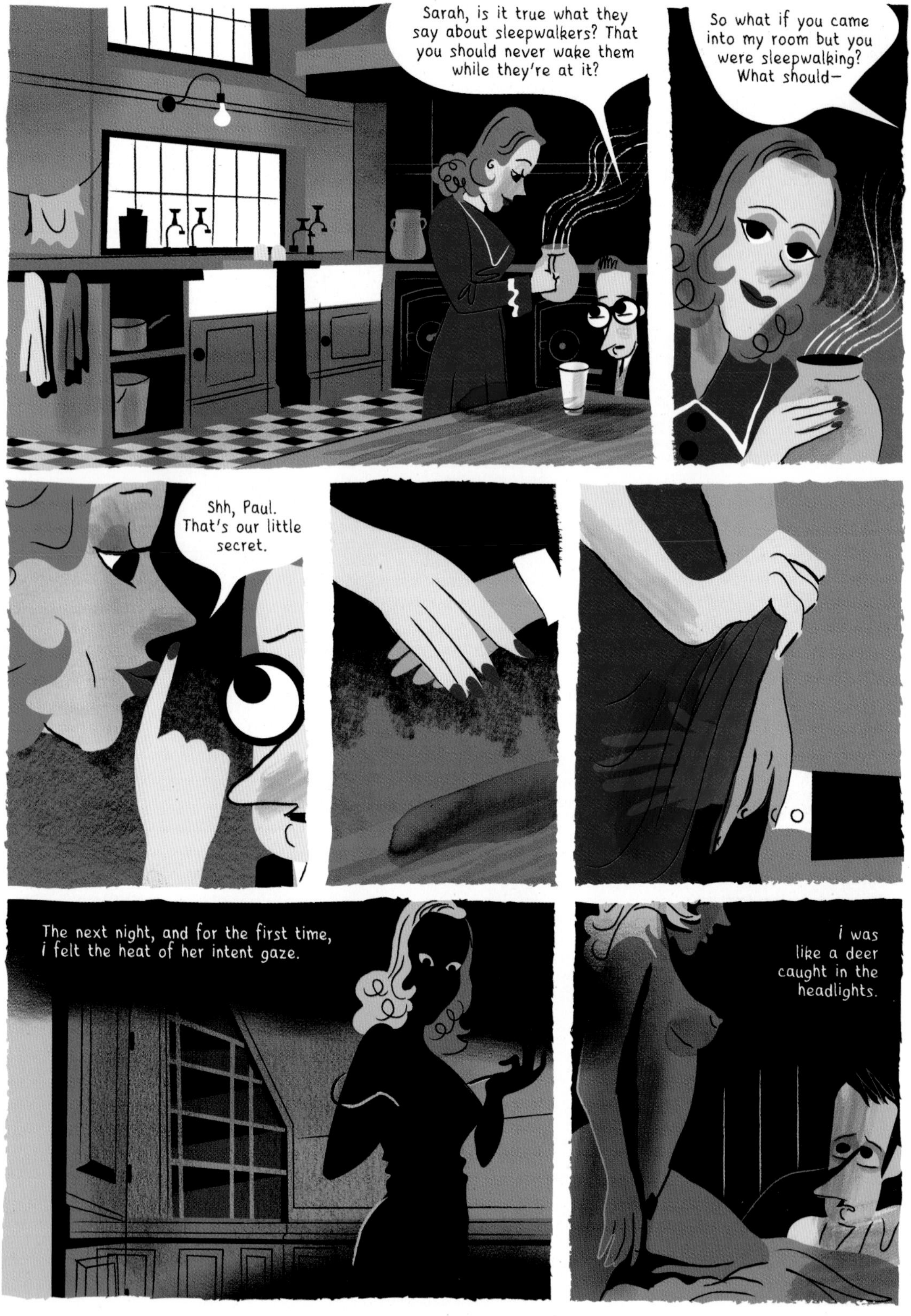

Sarah, is it true what they say about sleepwalkers? That you should never wake them while they're at it?
So what if you came into my room but you were sleepwalking? What should–
Shh, Paul. That's our little secret.
The next night, and for the first time, i felt the heat of her intent gaze.
i was like a deer caught in the headlights.

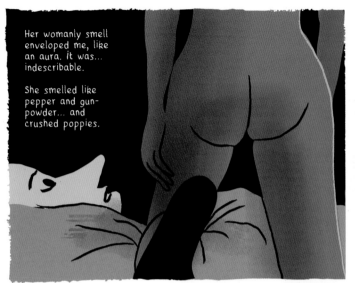

Her womanly smell enveloped me, like an aura. It was... indescribable.

She smelled like pepper and gun-powder... and crushed poppies.

Then nature played its part.

I couldn't help myself.

I tried to remain absolutely still. But my reaction was, shall we say... all too noticeable.

The news of my erection gave her great pleasure.

Was there an ejaculation?

Not that first time. But afterwards, I grew up fast.

While embarking on your first interstellar escapades at the same time!

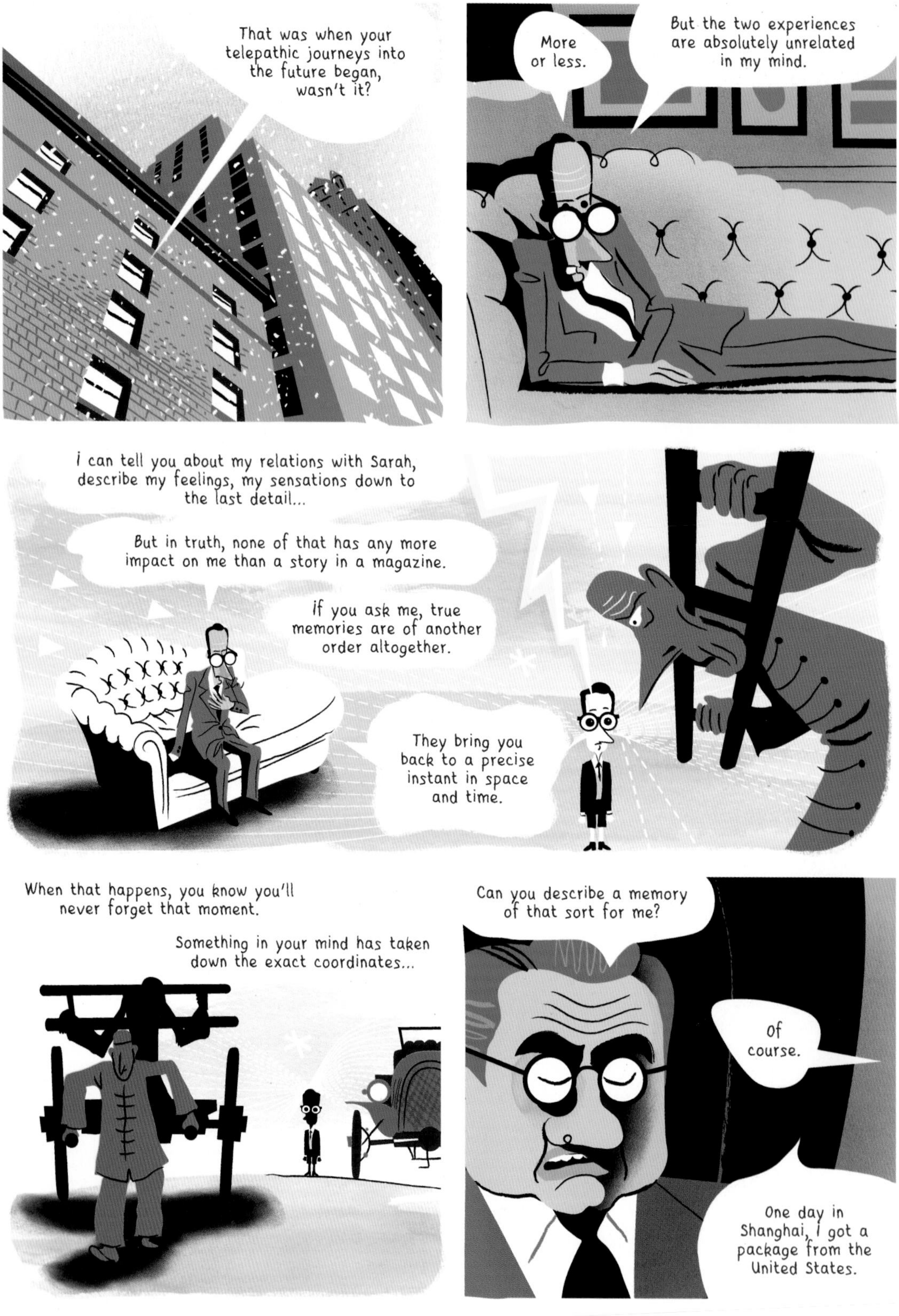
That was when your telepathic journeys into the future began, wasn't it?
More or less.
But the two experiences are absolutely unrelated in my mind.
I can tell you about my relations with Sarah, describe my feelings, my sensations down to the last detail...
But in truth, none of that has any more impact on me than a story in a magazine.
If you ask me, true memories are of another order altogether.
They bring you back to a precise instant in space and time.
When that happens, you know you'll never forget that moment.
Something in your mind has taken down the exact coordinates...
Can you describe a memory of that sort for me?
Of course.
One day in Shanghai, I got a package from the United States.

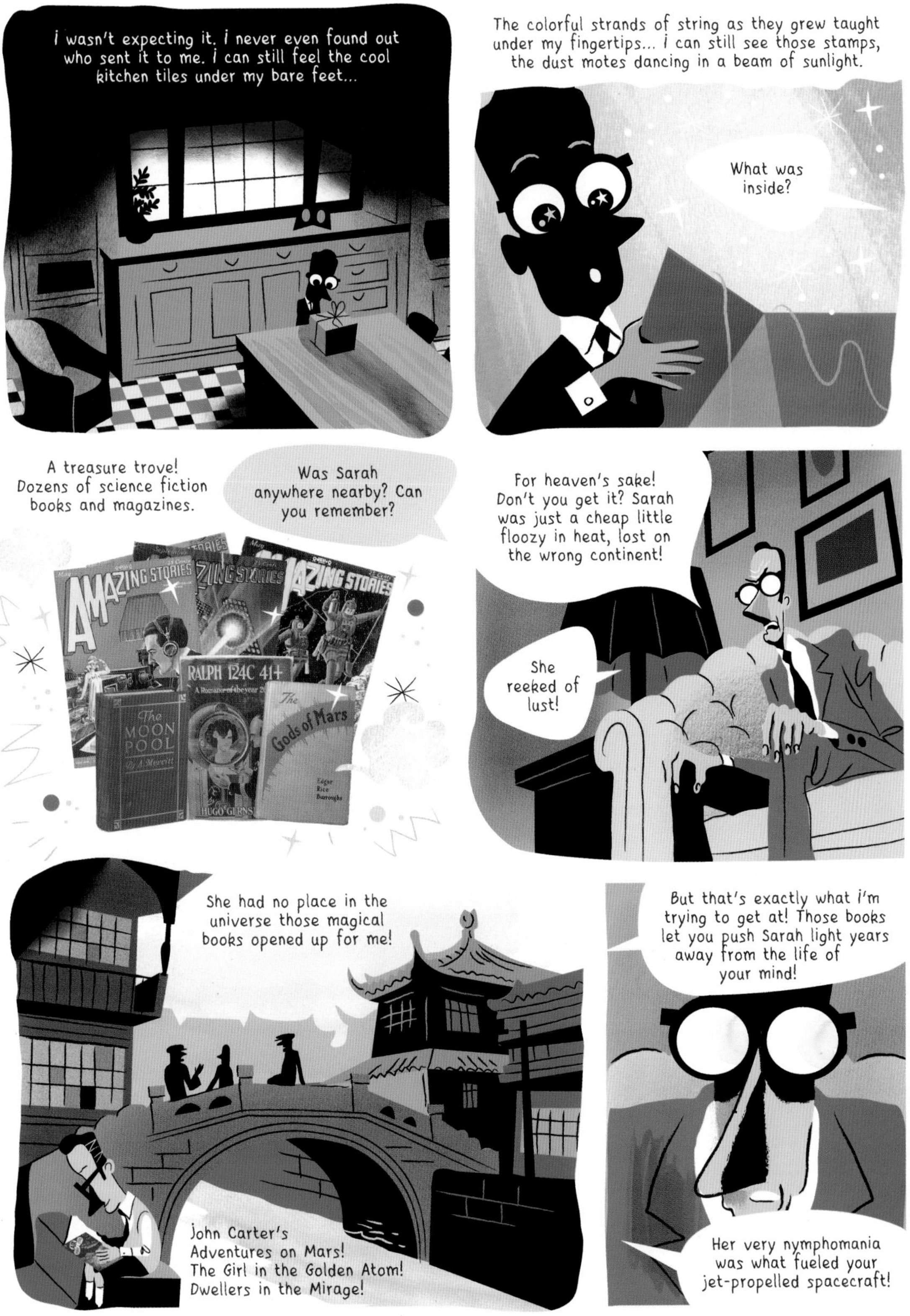
I wasn't expecting it. I never even found out who sent it to me. I can still feel the cool kitchen tiles under my bare feet...
The colorful strands of string as they grew taught under my fingertips... I can still see those stamps, the dust motes dancing in a beam of sunlight.
What was inside?
A treasure trove! Dozens of science fiction books and magazines.
Was Sarah anywhere nearby? Can you remember?
AMAZING STORIES
RALPH 124C 41+
The MOON POOL
The Gods of Mars
For heaven's sake! Don't you get it? Sarah was just a cheap little floozy in heat, lost on the wrong continent!
She reeked of lust!
She had no place in the universe those magical books opened up for me!
John Carter's Adventures on Mars! The Girl in the Golden Atom! Dwellers in the Mirage!
But that's exactly what I'm trying to get at! Those books let you push Sarah light years away from the life of your mind!
Her very nymphomania was what fueled your jet-propelled spacecraft!

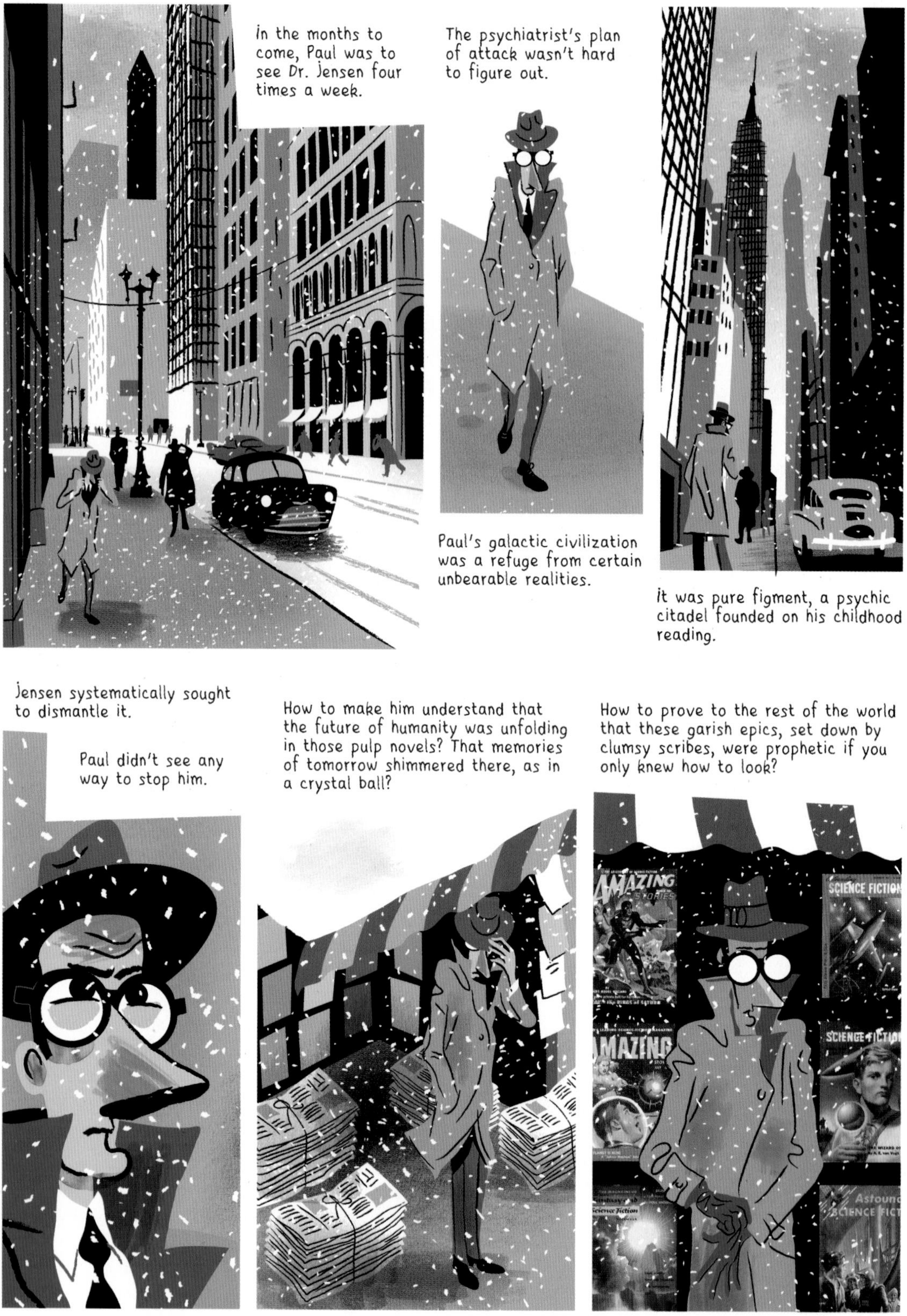
In the months to come, Paul was to see Dr. Jensen four times a week.
The psychiatrist's plan of attack wasn't hard to figure out.
Paul's galactic civilization was a refuge from certain unbearable realities.
It was pure figment, a psychic citadel founded on his childhood reading.
Jensen systematically sought to dismantle it.
Paul didn't see any way to stop him.
How to make him understand that the future of humanity was unfolding in those pulp novels? That memories of tomorrow shimmered there, as in a crystal ball?
How to prove to the rest of the world that these garish epics, set down by clumsy scribes, were prophetic if you only knew how to look?
AMAZING
SCIENCE FICTION
AMAZING
SCIENCE FICTION

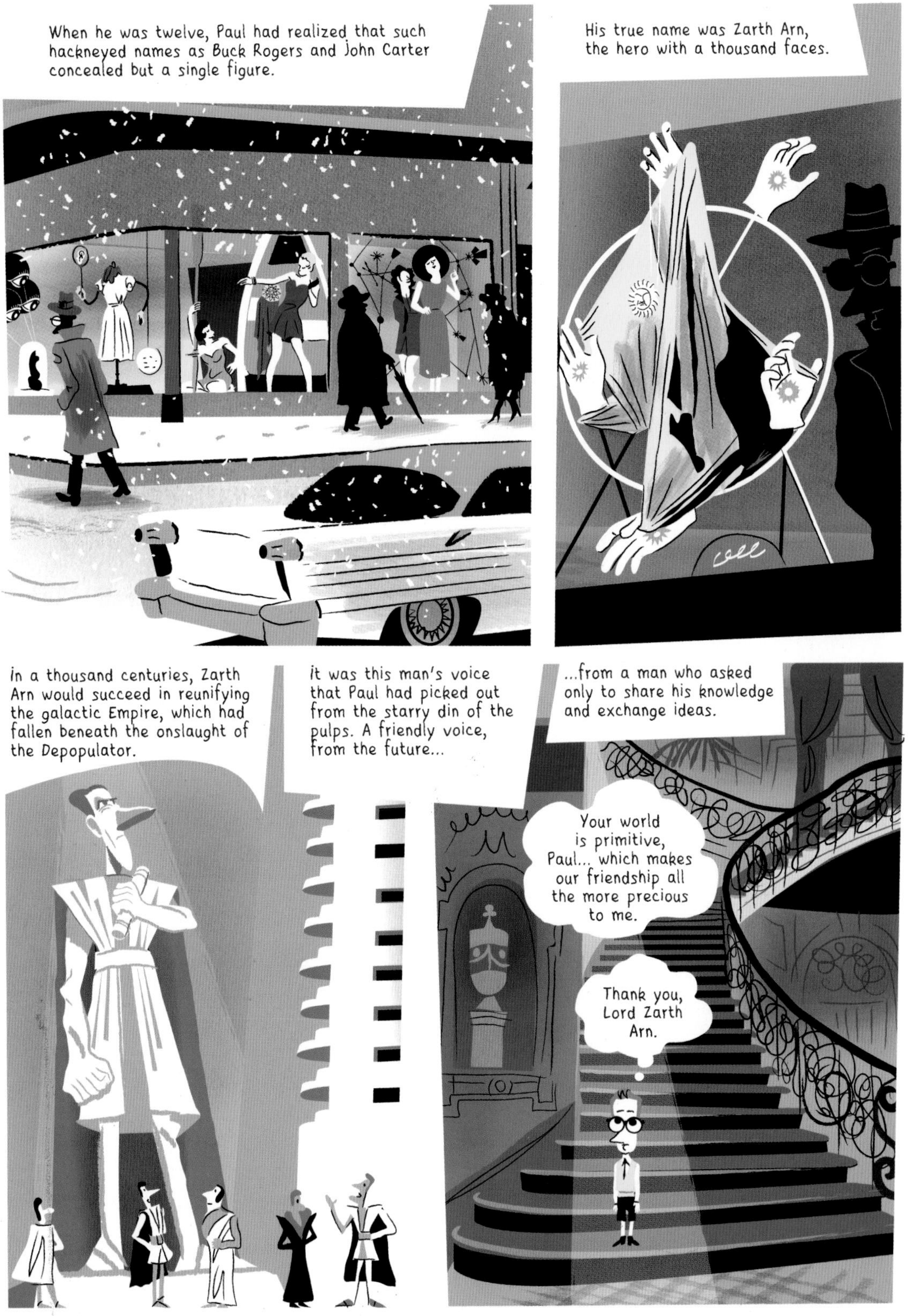
When he was twelve, Paul had realized that such hackneyed names as Buck Rogers and John Carter concealed but a single figure.
His true name was Zarth Arn, the hero with a thousand faces.
In a thousand centuries, Zarth Arn would succeed in reunifying the galactic Empire, which had fallen beneath the onslaught of the Depopulator.
It was this man's voice that Paul had picked out from the starry din of the pulps. A friendly voice, from the future...
...from a man who asked only to share his knowledge and exchange ideas.
Your world is primitive, Paul... which makes our friendship all the more precious to me.
Thank you, Lord Zarth Arn.

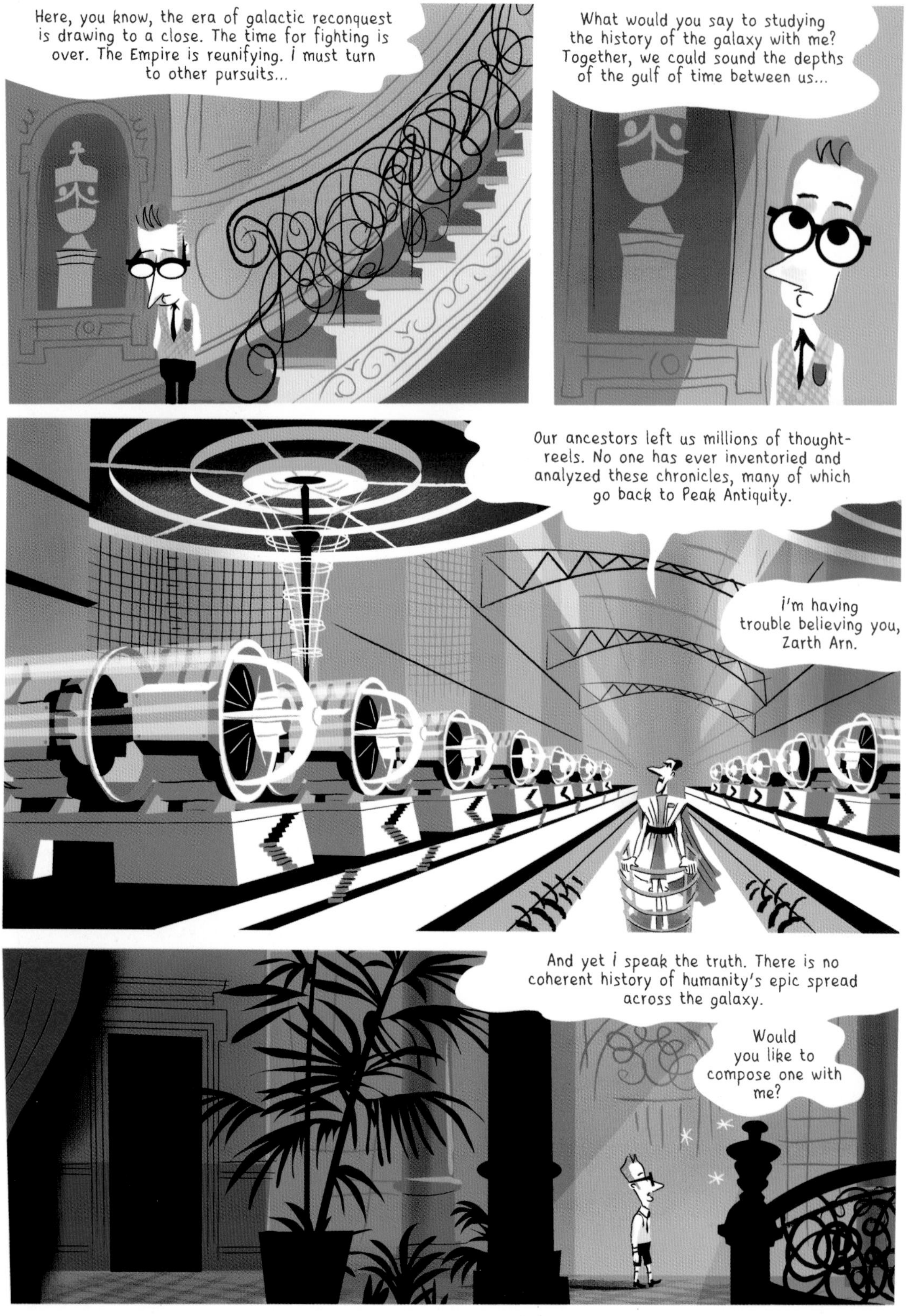

Here, you know, the era of galactic reconquest is drawing to a close. The time for fighting is over. The Empire is reunifying. I must turn to other pursuits...
What would you say to studying the history of the galaxy with me? Together, we could sound the depths of the gulf of time between us...
Our ancestors left us millions of thought-reels. No one has ever inventoried and analyzed these chronicles, many of which go back to Peak Antiquity.
I'm having trouble believing you, Zarth Arn.
And yet I speak the truth. There is no coherent history of humanity's epic spread across the galaxy.
Would you like to compose one with me?

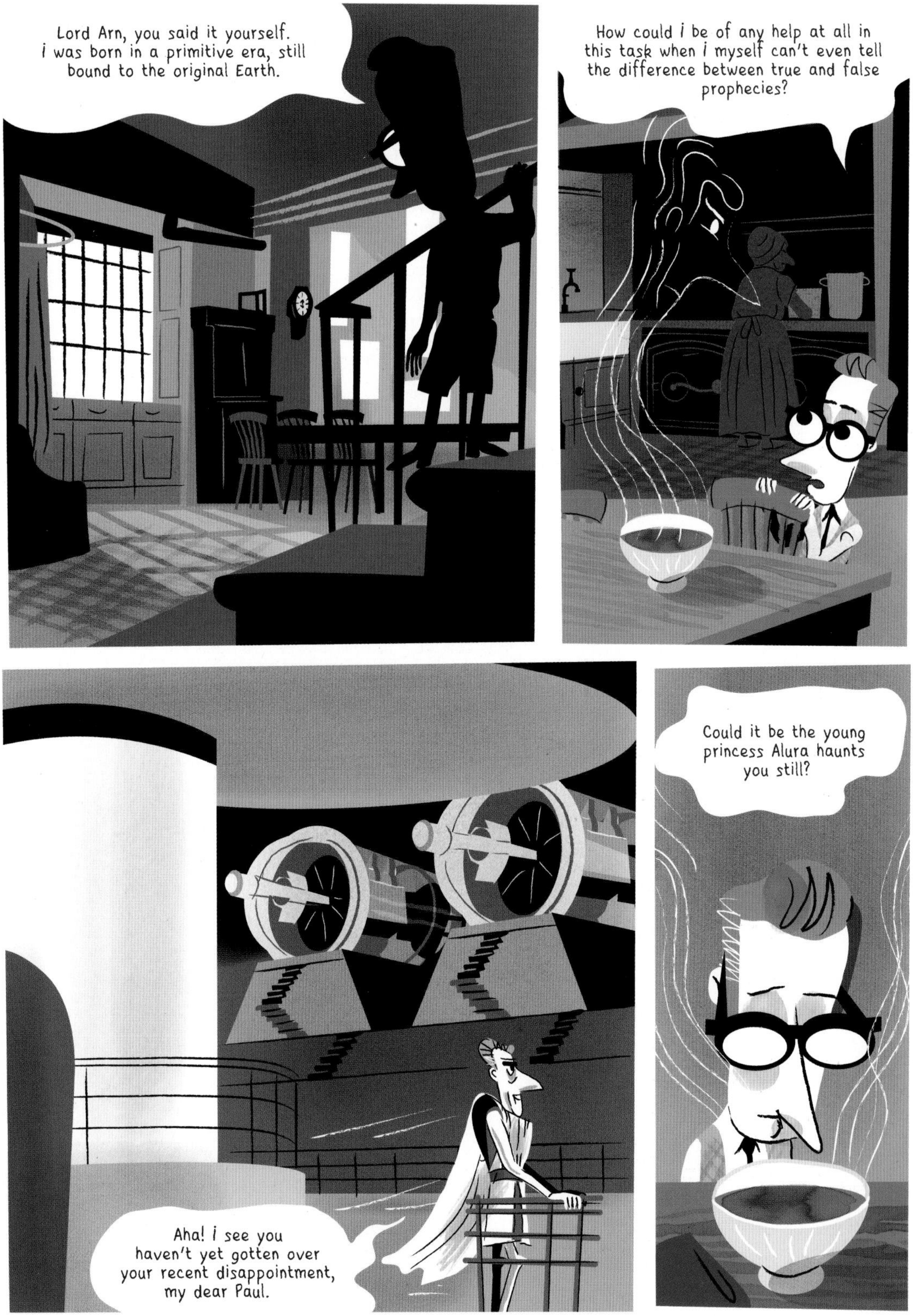
Lord Arn, you said it yourself. I was born in a primitive era, still bound to the original Earth.
How could I be of any help at all in this task when I myself can't even tell the difference between true and false prophecies?
Aha! I see you haven't yet gotten over your recent disappointment, my dear Paul.
Could it be the young princess Alura haunts you still?

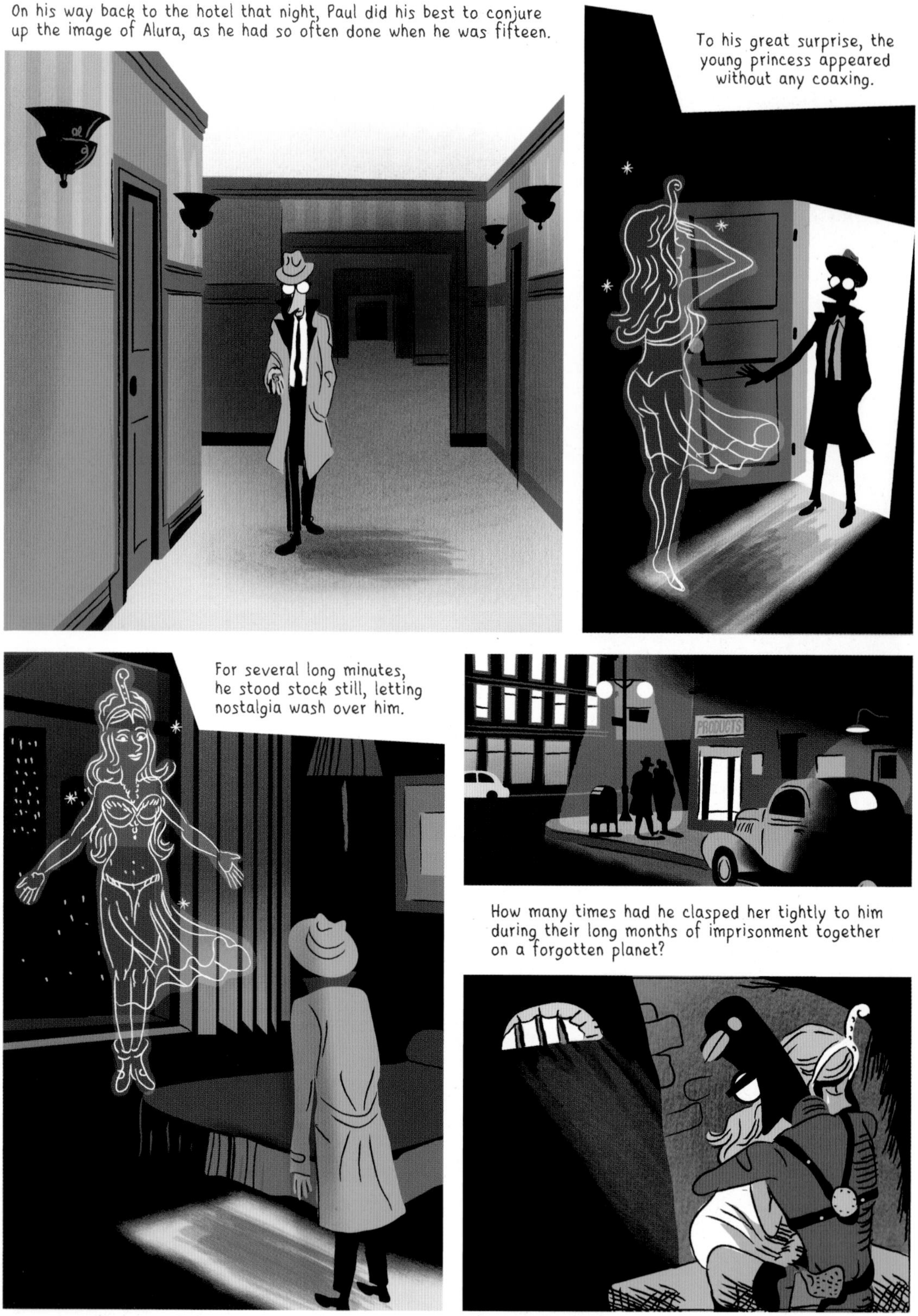
On his way back to the hotel that night, Paul did his best to conjure up the image of Alura, as he had so often done when he was fifteen.
To his great surprise, the young princess appeared without any coaxing.
For several long minutes, he stood stock still, letting nostalgia wash over him.
PRODUCTS
How many times had he clasped her tightly to him during their long months of imprisonment together on a forgotten planet?

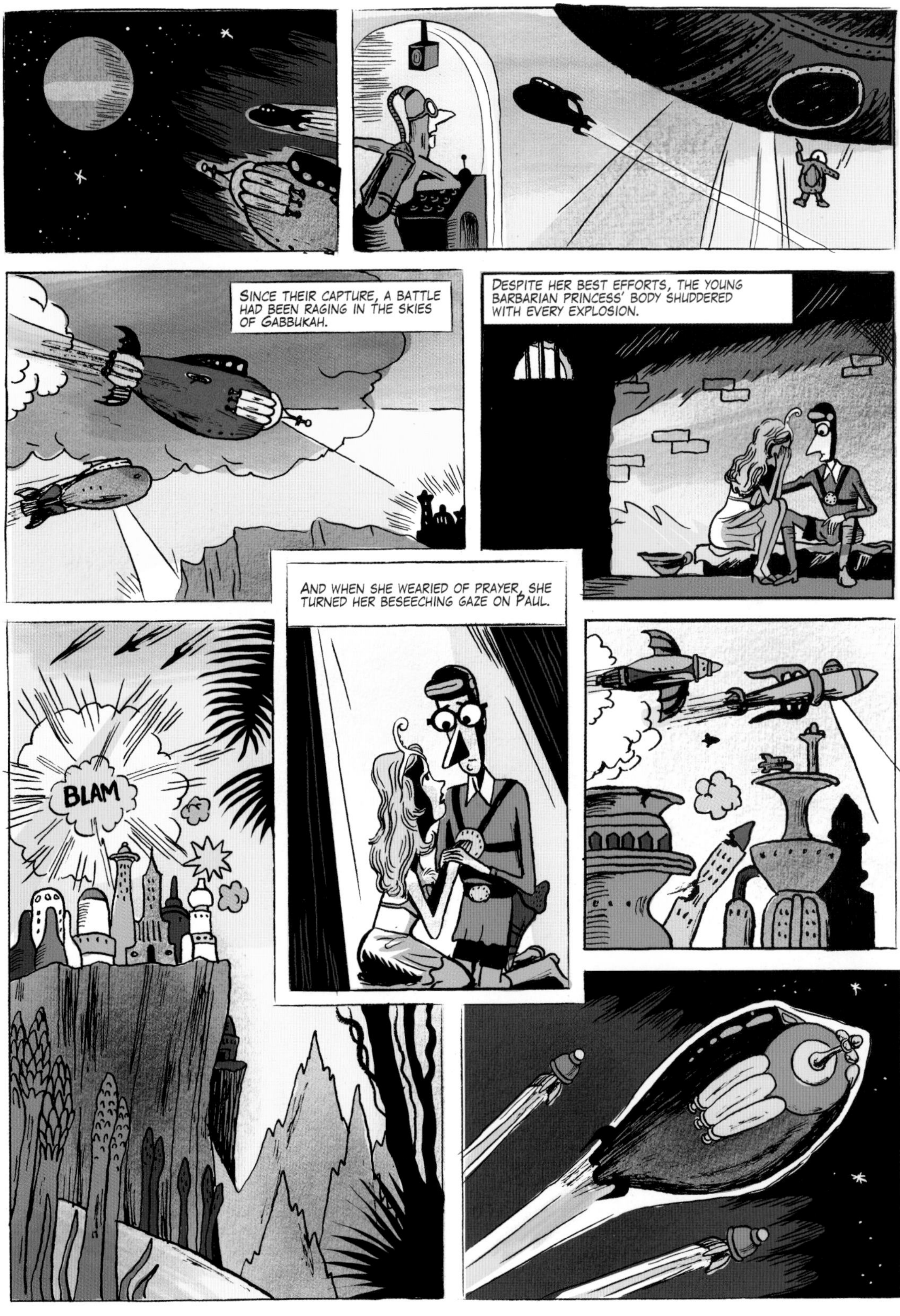

SINCE THEIR CAPTURE, A BATTLE HAD BEEN RAGING IN THE SKIES OF GABBUKAH.
DESPITE HER BEST EFFORTS, THE YOUNG BARBARIAN PRINCESS' BODY SHUDDERED WITH EVERY EXPLOSION.
BLAM
AND WHEN SHE WEARIED OF PRAYER, SHE TURNED HER BESEECHING GAZE ON PAUL.

HER WIDE EYES SHONE IN THE DARK. HE HAD NO WORDS FOR THE TENDERNESS HE FELT TOWARDS HER...

AT SUCH TIMES, HE WOULD SLIDE A SHELTERING ARM ABOUT HER FRAIL SHOULDERS, AND PRESS HIS LIPS TO HER BLONDE HAIR, WHICH SMELLED OF SAND AND STRAW...

Sadly, Alura was but a figment, and the battle of Gabbukah, a fiction.

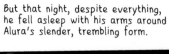

Neither had ever existed outside Paul's imagination.

But that night, despite everything, he fell asleep with his arms around Alura's slender, trembling form.

But even as he was sinking into sleep, a vague onrush of shame caught in his throat.

Zarth Arn had even teased him about the subject quite recently.

For the first time in a very long while, he felt the stirrings of an erection.

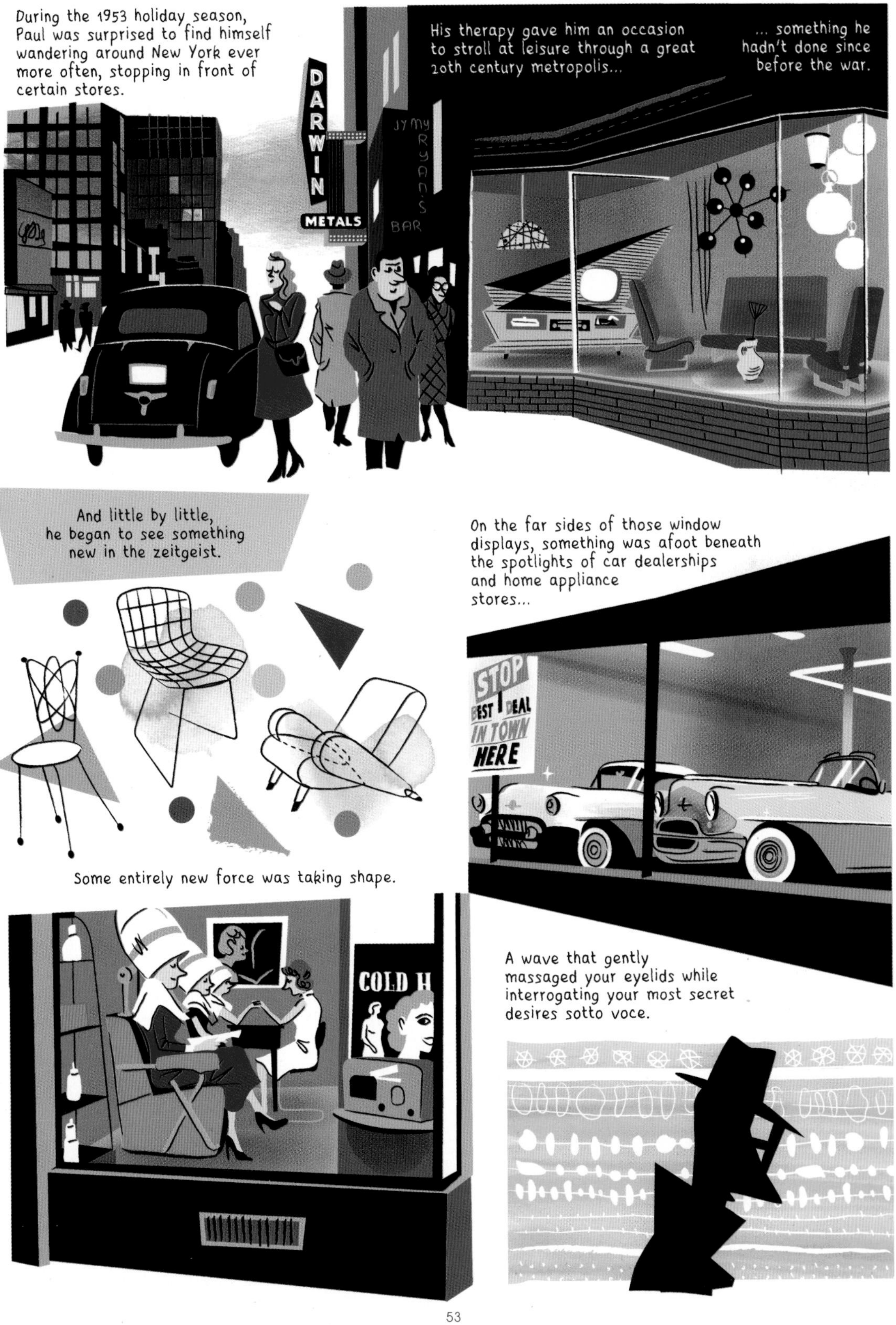
During the 1953 holiday season, Paul was surprised to find himself wandering around New York ever more often, stopping in front of certain stores.
DARWIN
METALS
BAR
His therapy gave him an occasion to stroll at leisure through a great 20th century metropolis...
... something he hadn't done since before the war.
And little by little, he began to see something new in the zeitgeist.
Some entirely new force was taking shape.
On the far sides of those window displays, something was afoot beneath the spotlights of car dealerships and home appliance stores...
STOP
IN TOWN
HERE
A wave that gently massaged your eyelids while interrogating your most secret desires sotto voce.

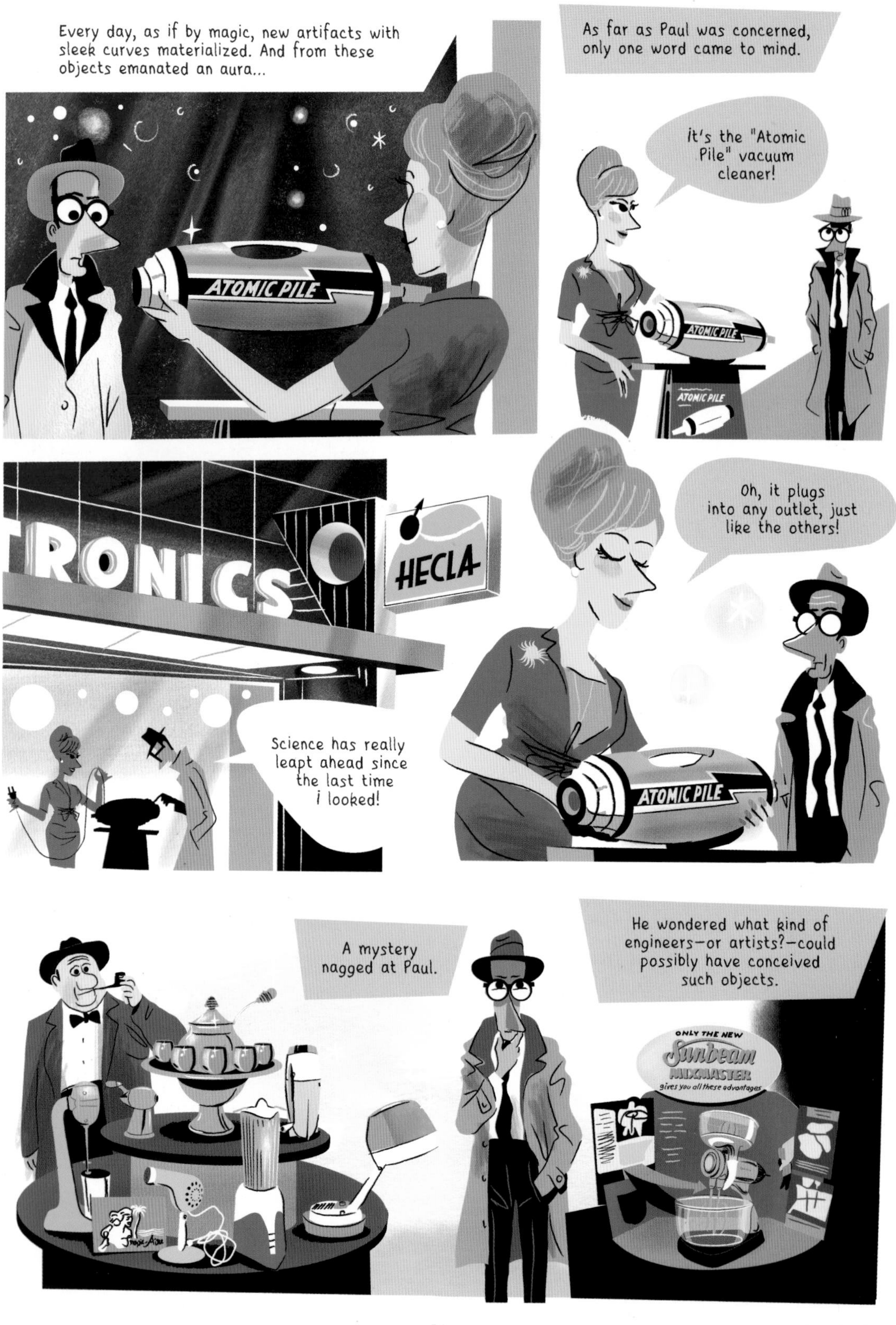
Every day, as if by magic, new artifacts with sleek curves materialized. And from these objects emanated an aura...
ATOMIC PILE
As far as Paul was concerned, only one word came to mind.
it's the "Atomic Pile" vacuum cleaner!
ATOMIC PILE
ATOMIC PILE
TRONICS
HECLA
Science has really leapt ahead since the last time i looked!
Oh, it plugs into any outlet, just like the others!
ATOMIC PILE
A mystery nagged at Paul.
He wondered what kind of engineers—or artists?—could possibly have conceived such objects.
ONLY THE NEW
Sunbeam
MIXMASTER
gives you all these advantages

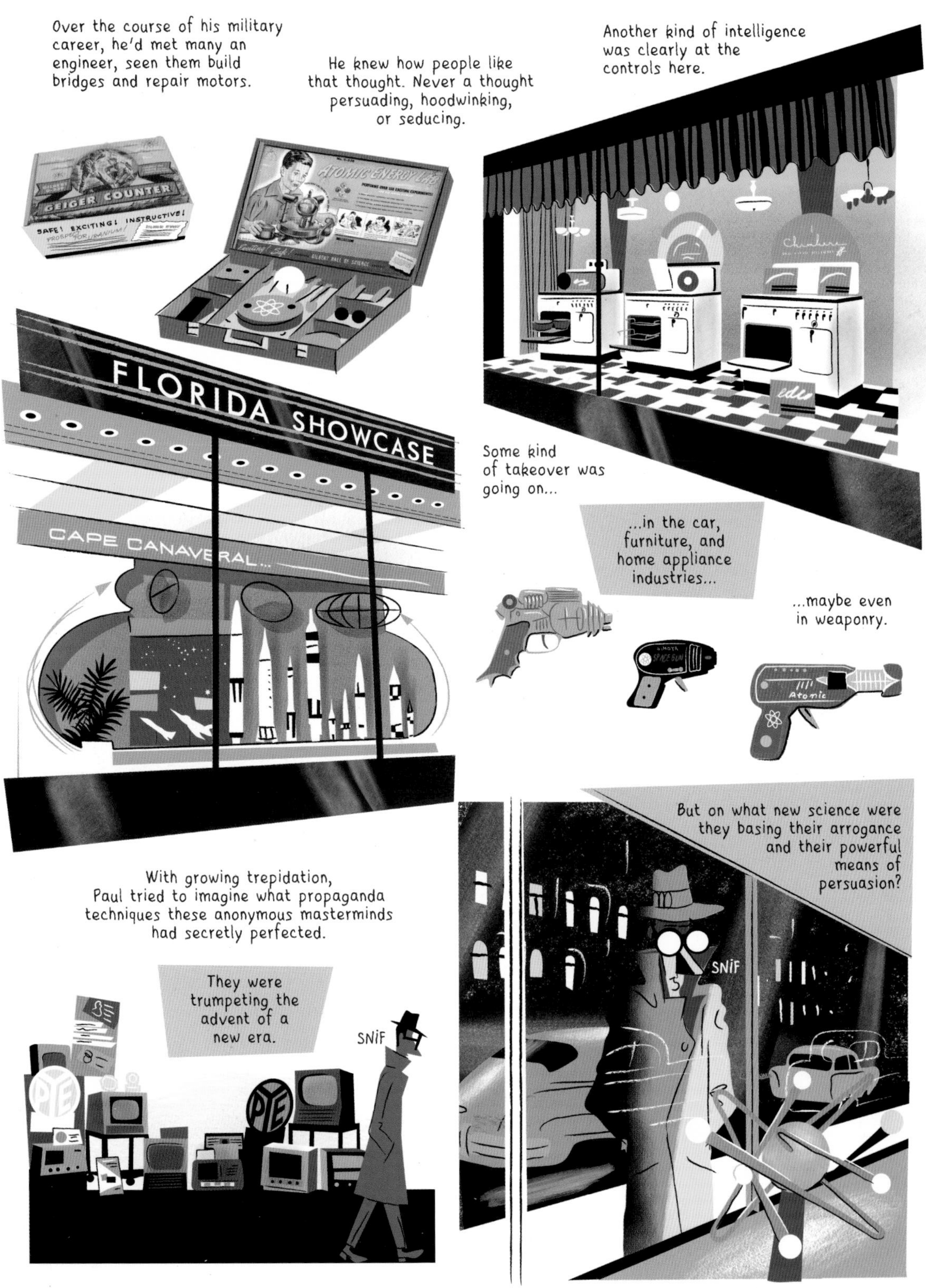
Over the course of his military career, he'd met many an engineer, seen them build bridges and repair motors.
GEIGER COUNTER
SAFE! EXCITING! INSTRUCTIVE!
PROSPECT FOR URANIUM!
He knew how people like that thought. Never a thought persuading, hoodwinking, or seducing.
ATOMIC ENERGY LAB
Another kind of intelligence was clearly at the controls here.
FLORIDA SHOWCASE
CAPE CANAVERAL...
Some kind of takeover was going on...
...in the car, furniture, and home appliance industries...
...maybe even in weaponry.
SPACE GUN
Atomic
With growing trepidation, Paul tried to imagine what propaganda techniques these anonymous masterminds had secretly perfected.
They were trumpeting the advent of a new era.
SNIF
PYE
PYE
But on what new science were they basing their arrogance and their powerful means of persuasion?
SNIF

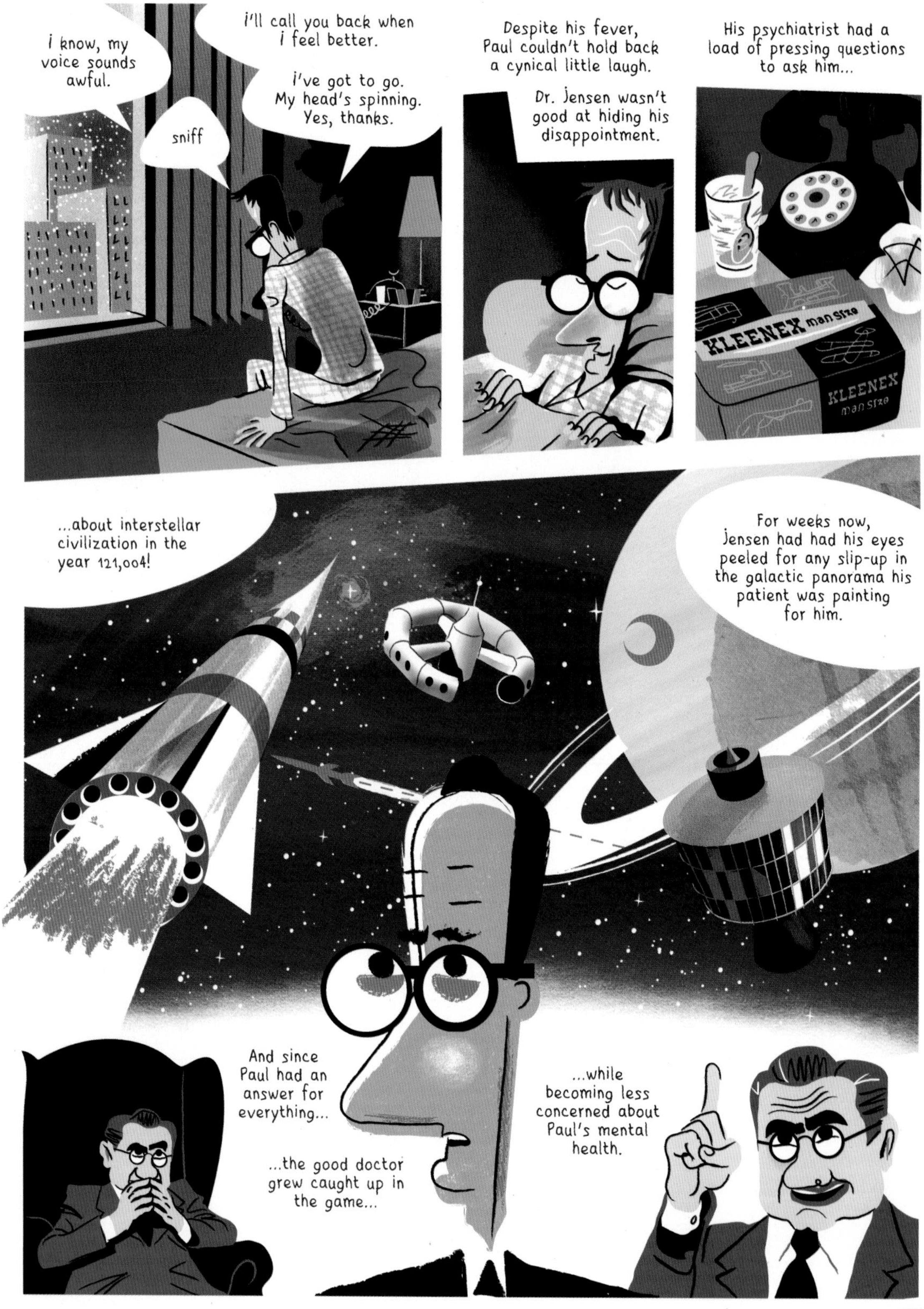
I know, my voice sounds awful.
sniff
I'll call you back when I feel better.
I've got to go. My head's spinning. Yes, thanks.
Despite his fever, Paul couldn't hold back a cynical little laugh.
Dr. Jensen wasn't good at hiding his disappointment.
His psychiatrist had a load of pressing questions to ask him...
KLEENEX man size
KLEENEX man size
...about interstellar civilization in the year 121,004!
For weeks now, Jensen had had his eyes peeled for any slip-up in the galactic panorama his patient was painting for him.
And since Paul had an answer for everything...
...the good doctor grew caught up in the game...
...while becoming less concerned about Paul's mental health.

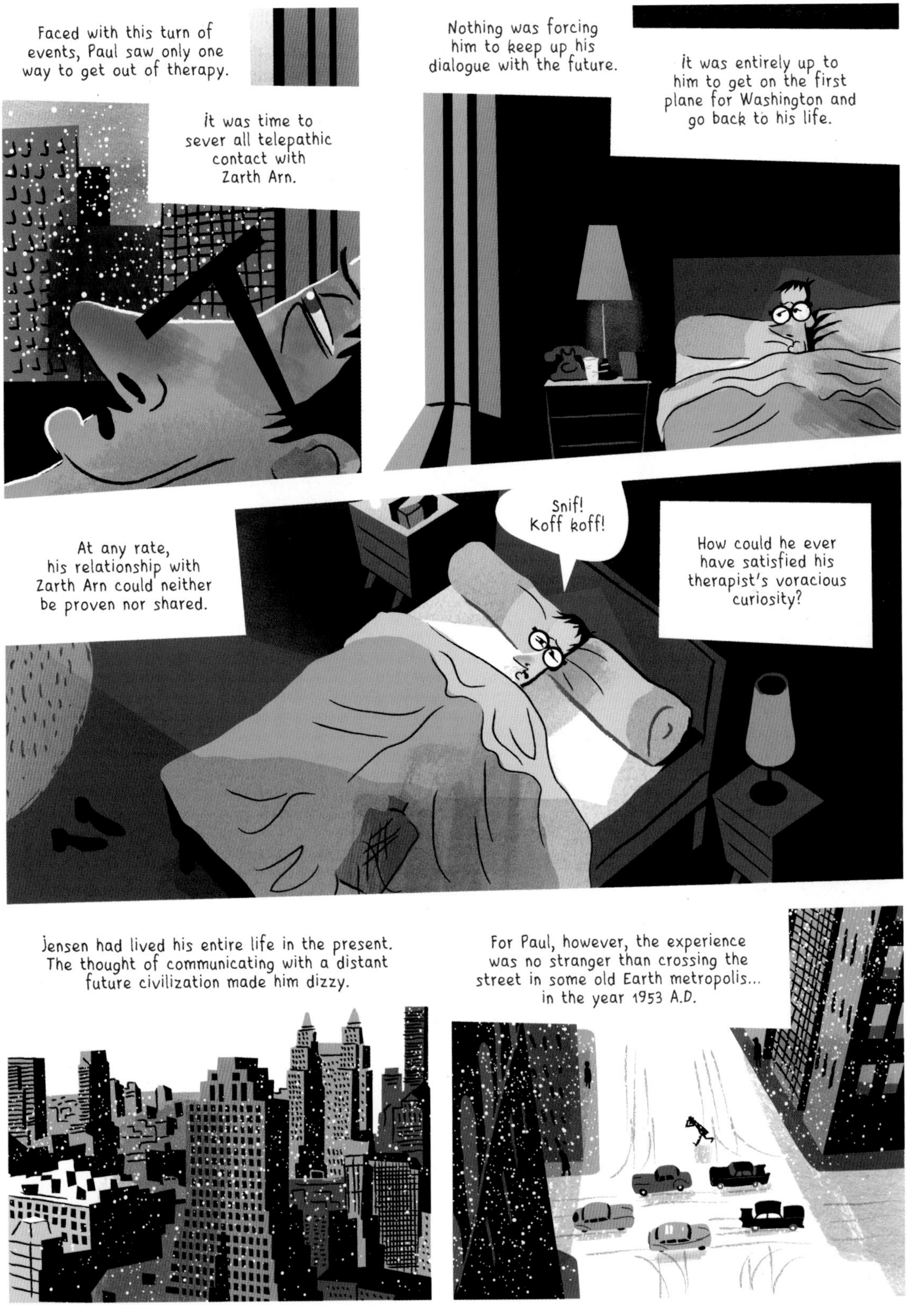
Faced with this turn of events, Paul saw only one way to get out of therapy.
It was time to sever all telepathic contact with Zarth Arn.
Nothing was forcing him to keep up his dialogue with the future.
It was entirely up to him to get on the first plane for Washington and go back to his life.
At any rate, his relationship with Zarth Arn could neither be proven nor shared.
Snif! Koff koff!
How could he ever have satisfied his therapist's voracious curiosity?
Jensen had lived his entire life in the present. The thought of communicating with a distant future civilization made him dizzy.
For Paul, however, the experience was no stranger than crossing the street in some old Earth metropolis... in the year 1953 A.D.

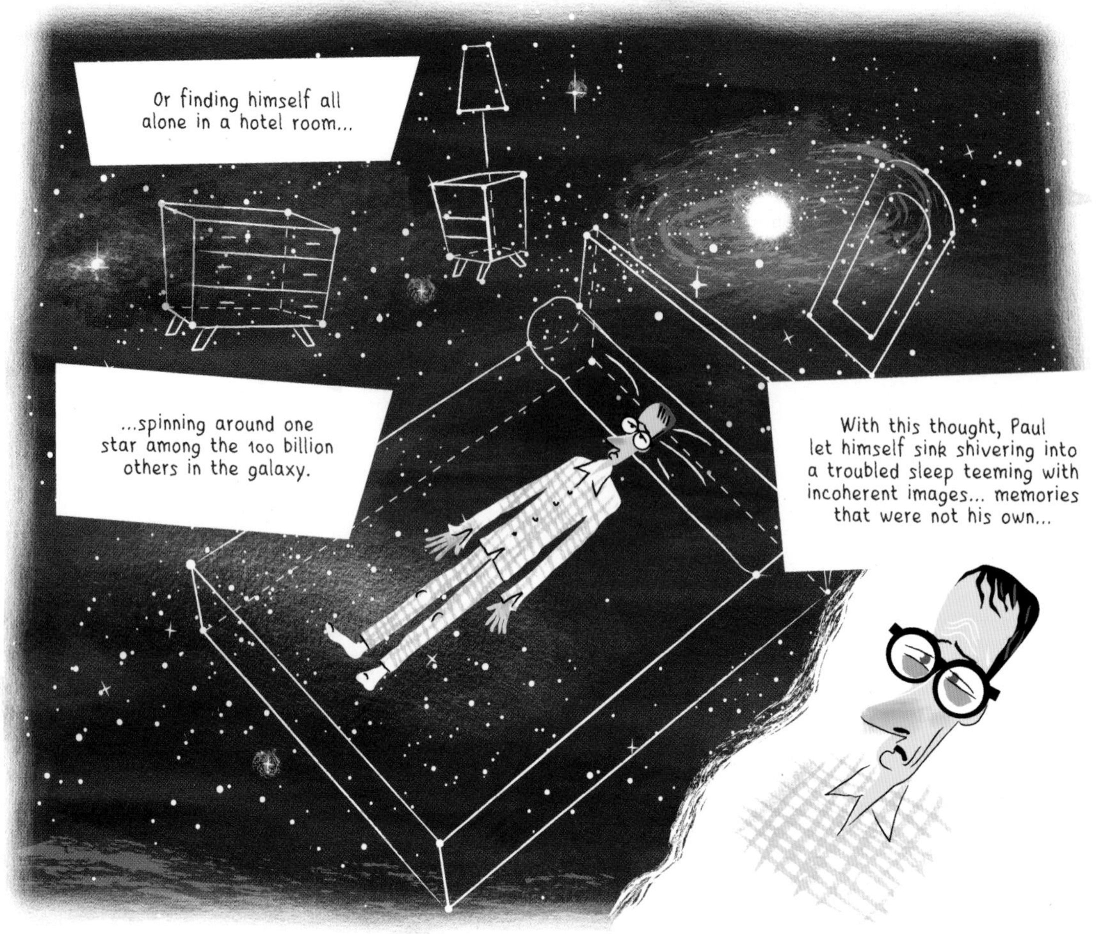
Or finding himself all alone in a hotel room...
...spinning around one star among the 100 billion others in the galaxy.
With this thought, Paul let himself sink shivering into a troubled sleep teeming with incoherent images... memories that were not his own...

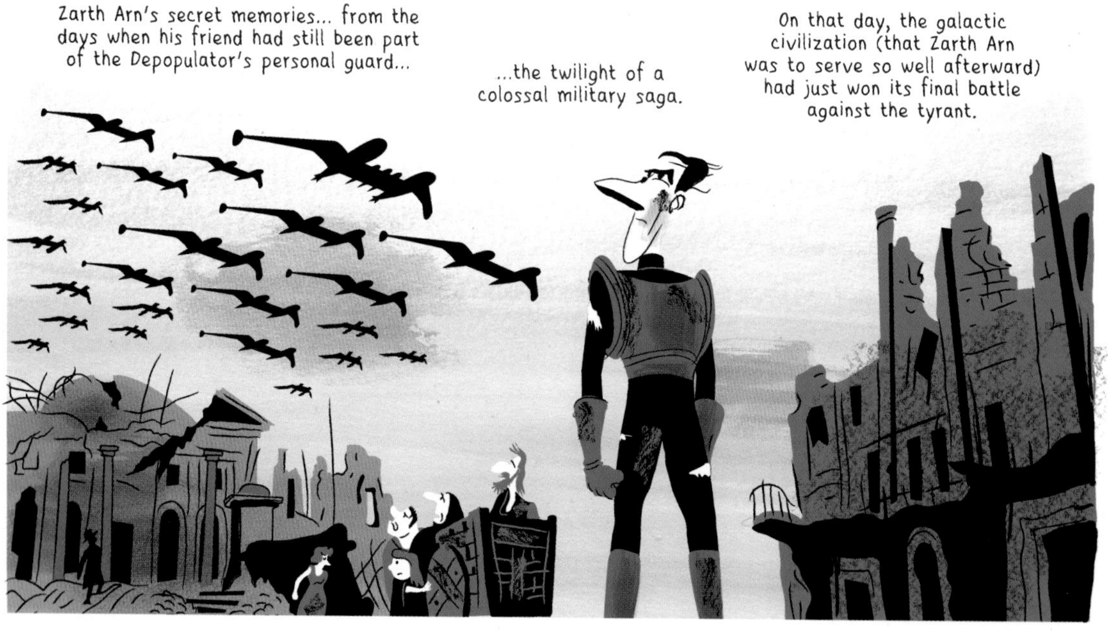
Zarth Arn's secret memories... from the days when his friend had still been part of the Depopulator's personal guard...
...the twilight of a colossal military saga.
On that day, the galactic civilization (that Zarth Arn was to serve so well afterward) had just won its final battle against the tyrant.

The Planet Ninjir. Year 110,895, in the future...

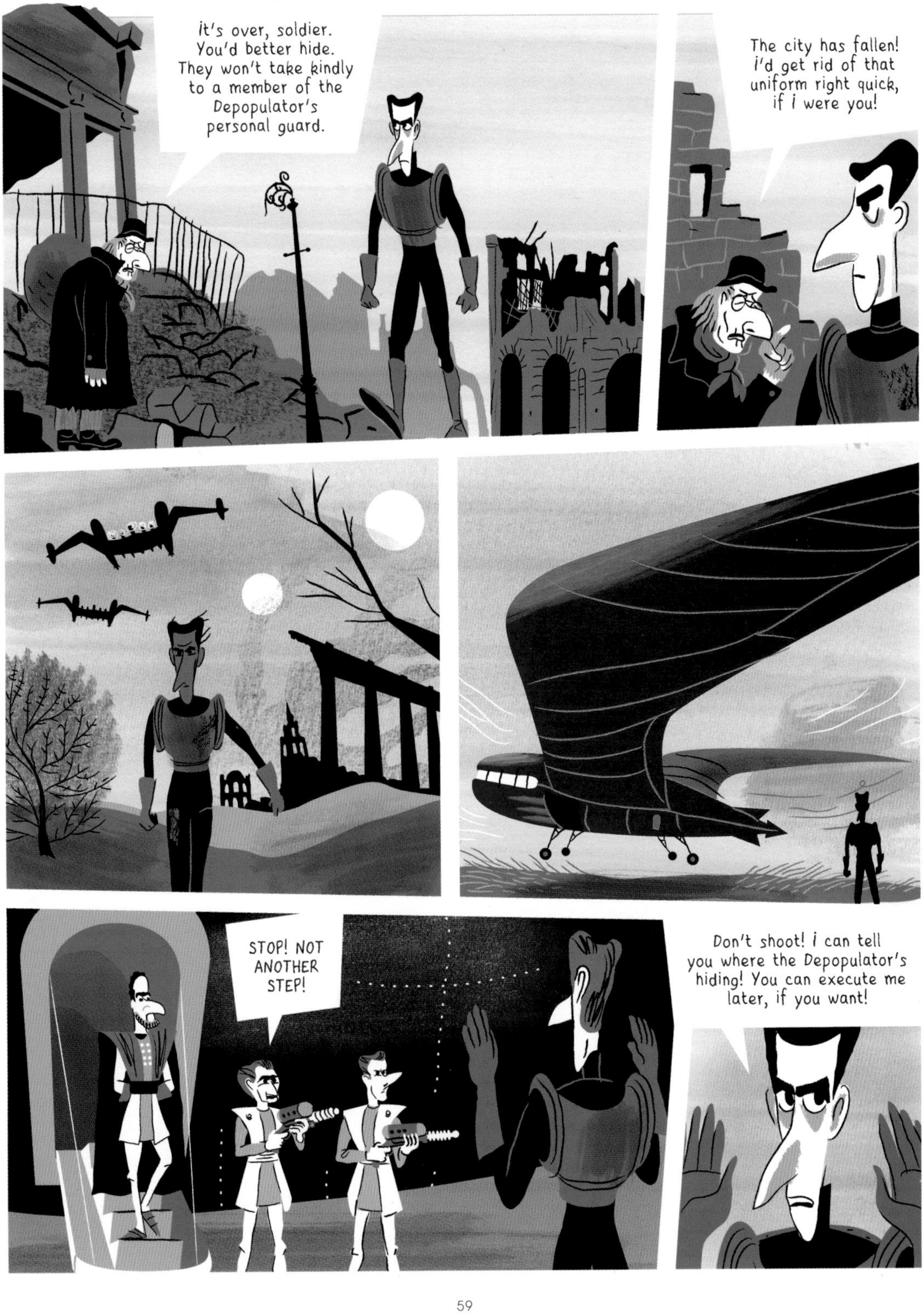

it's over, soldier. You'd better hide. They won't take kindly to a member of the Depopulator's personal guard.
The city has fallen! i'd get rid of that uniform right quick, if i were you!
STOP! NOT ANOTHER STEP!
Don't shoot! i can tell you where the Depopulator's hiding! You can execute me later, if you want!

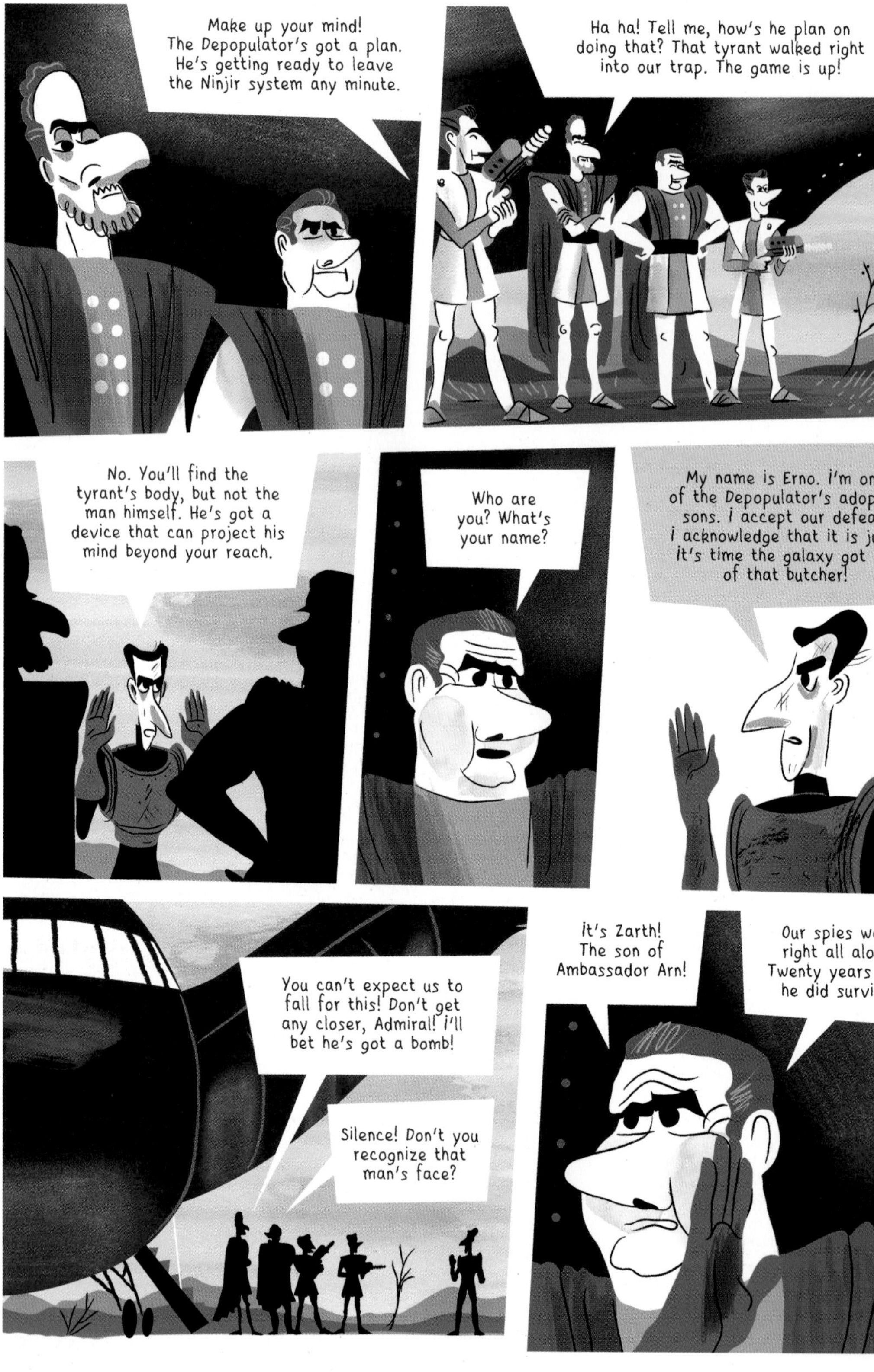
Make up your mind! The Depopulator's got a plan. He's getting ready to leave the Ninjir system any minute.
Ha ha! Tell me, how's he plan on doing that? That tyrant walked right into our trap. The game is up!
No. You'll find the tyrant's body, but not the man himself. He's got a device that can project his mind beyond your reach.
Who are you? What's your name?
My name is Erno. I'm one of the Depopulator's adopted sons. I accept our defeat. I acknowledge that it is just. It's time the galaxy got rid of that butcher!
You can't expect us to fall for this! Don't get any closer, Admiral! I'll bet he's got a bomb!
Silence! Don't you recognize that man's face?
It's Zarth! The son of Ambassador Arn!
Our spies were right all along! Twenty years ago, he did survive!

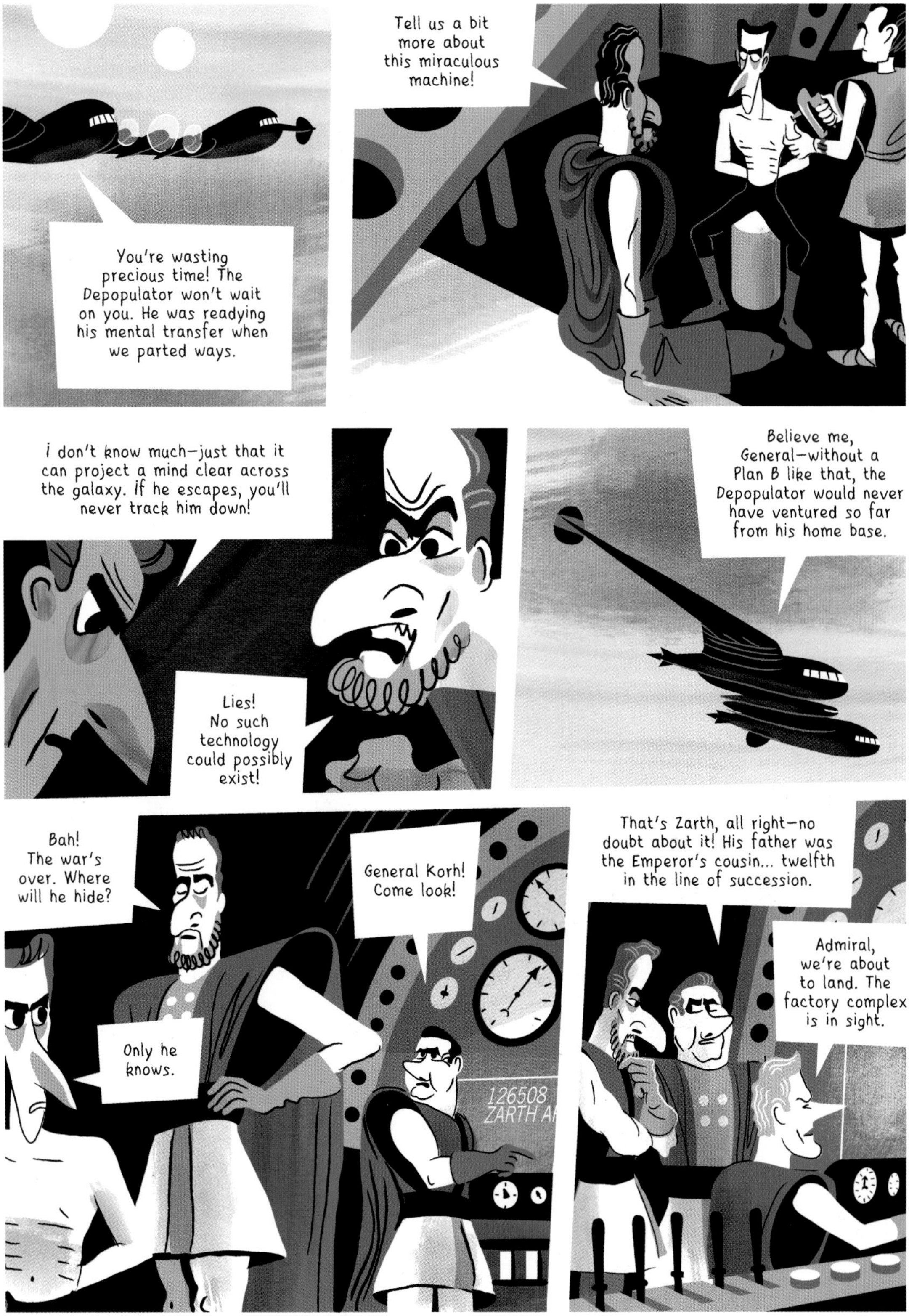
You're wasting precious time! The Depopulator won't wait on you. He was readying his mental transfer when we parted ways.
Tell us a bit more about this miraculous machine!
I don't know much—just that it can project a mind clear across the galaxy. If he escapes, you'll never track him down!
Lies! No such technology could possibly exist!
Believe me, General—without a Plan B like that, the Depopulator would never have ventured so far from his home base.
Bah! The war's over. Where will he hide?
Only he knows.
General Korh! Come look!
126508
ZARTH A
That's Zarth, all right—no doubt about it! His father was the Emperor's cousin... twelfth in the line of succession.
Admiral, we're about to land. The factory complex is in sight.

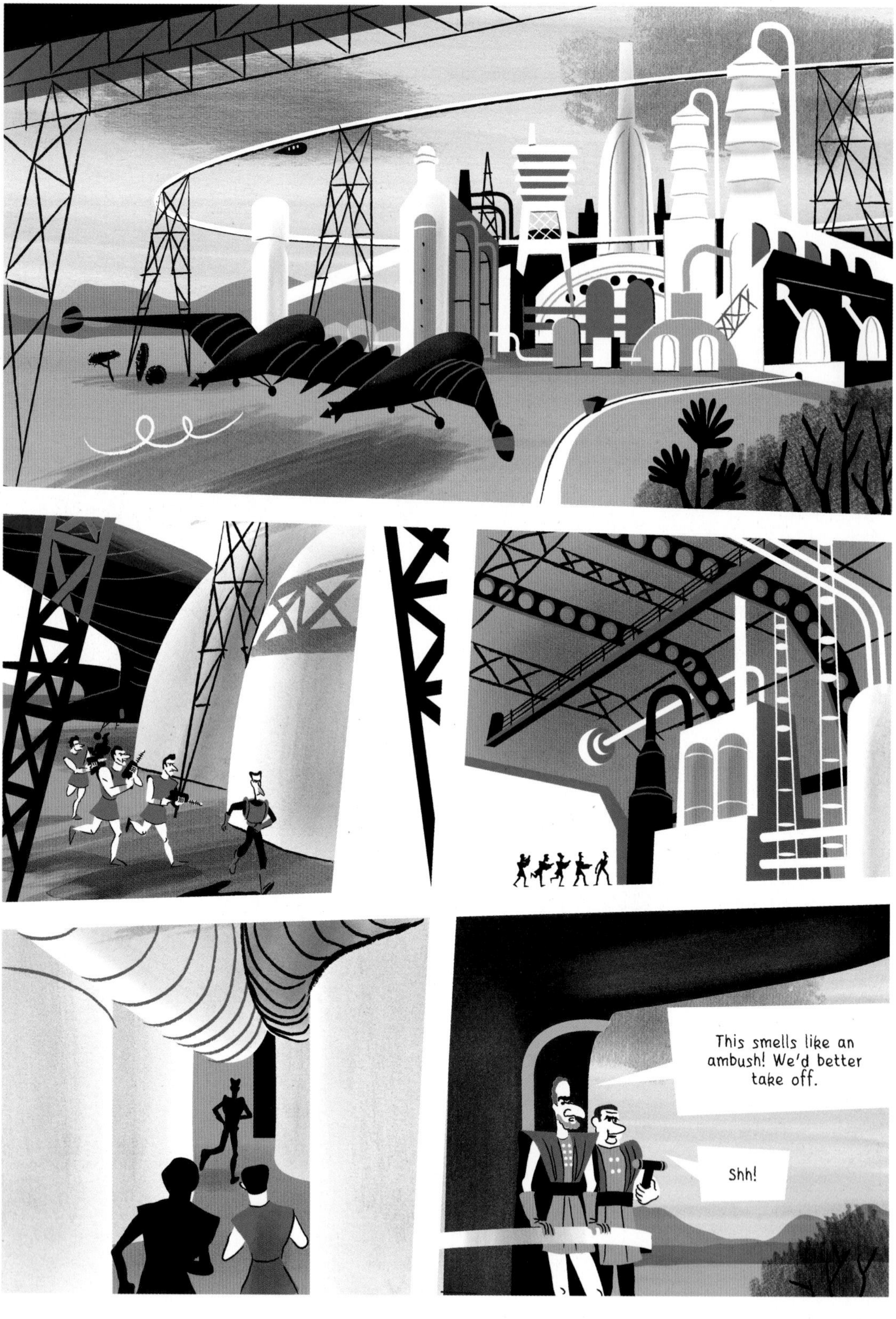
This smells like an ambush! We'd better take off.
Shh!

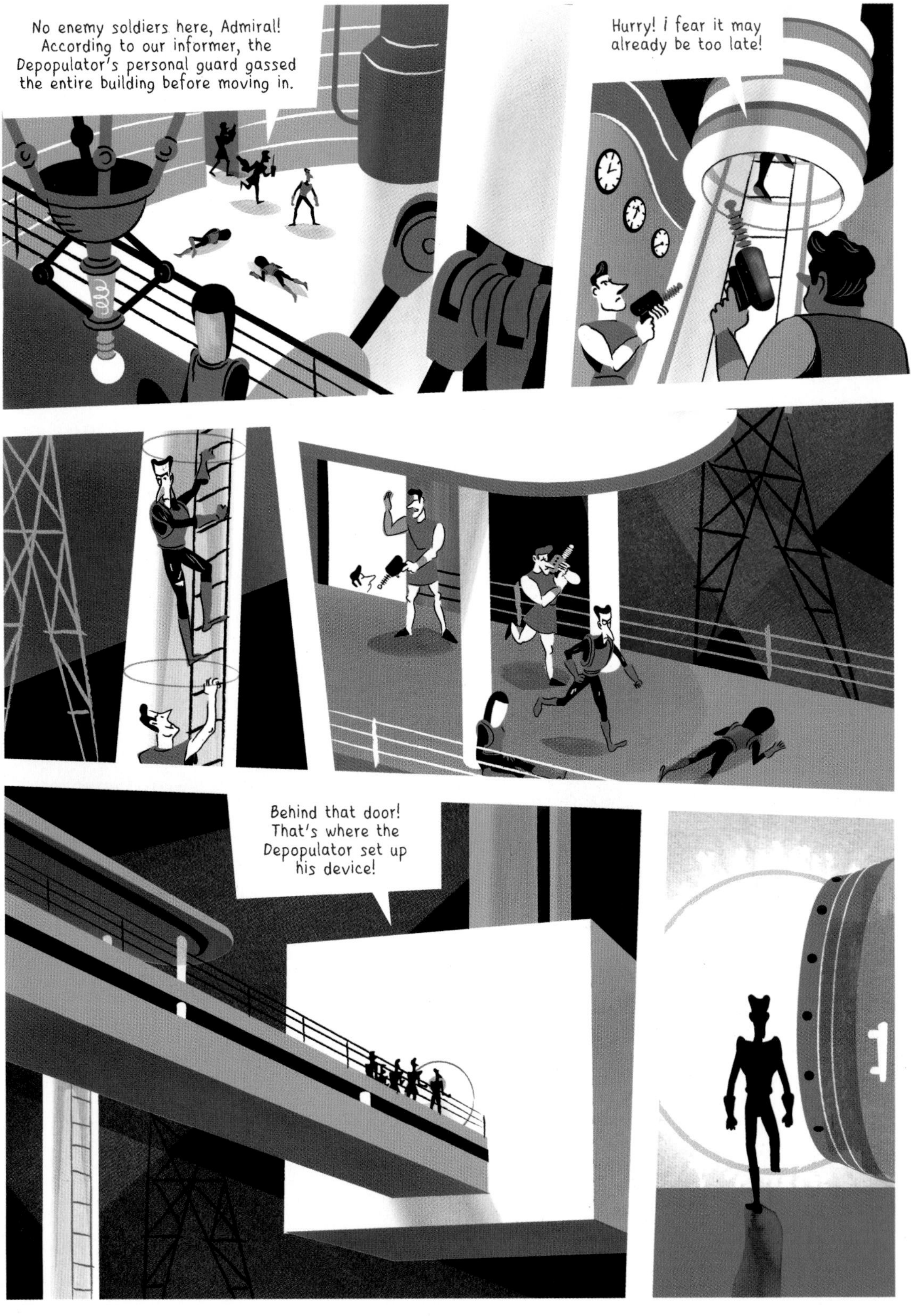
No enemy soldiers here, Admiral! According to our informer, the Depopulator's personal guard gassed the entire building before moving in.
Hurry! i fear it may already be too late!
Behind that door! That's where the Depopulator set up his device!

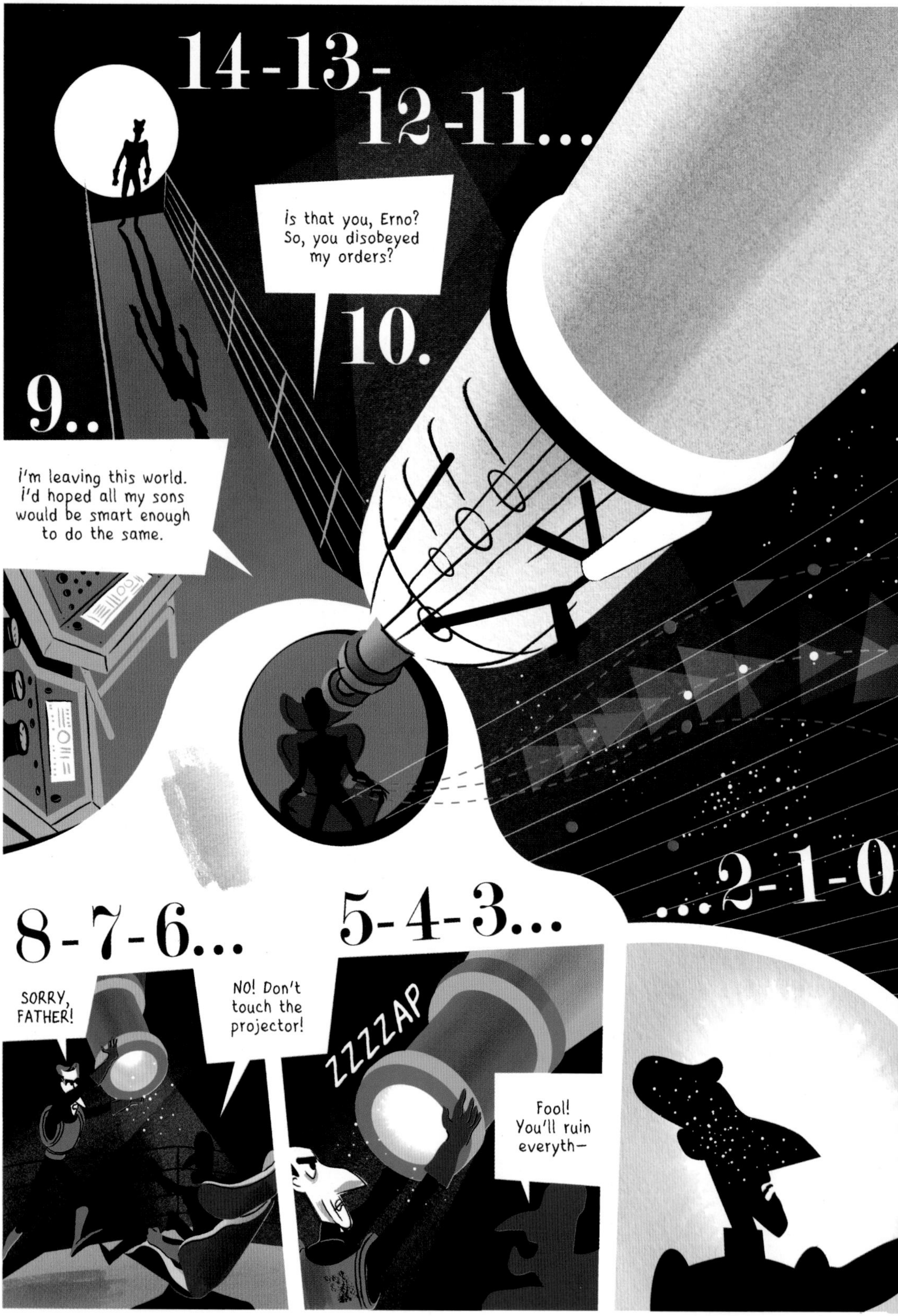
14-13-12-11...
Is that you, Erno? So, you disobeyed my orders?
10.
9..
I'm leaving this world. I'd hoped all my sons would be smart enough to do the same.
8-7-6...
5-4-3...
...2-1-0
SORRY, FATHER!
NO! Don't touch the projector!
ZZZZAP
Fool! You'll ruin everyth—

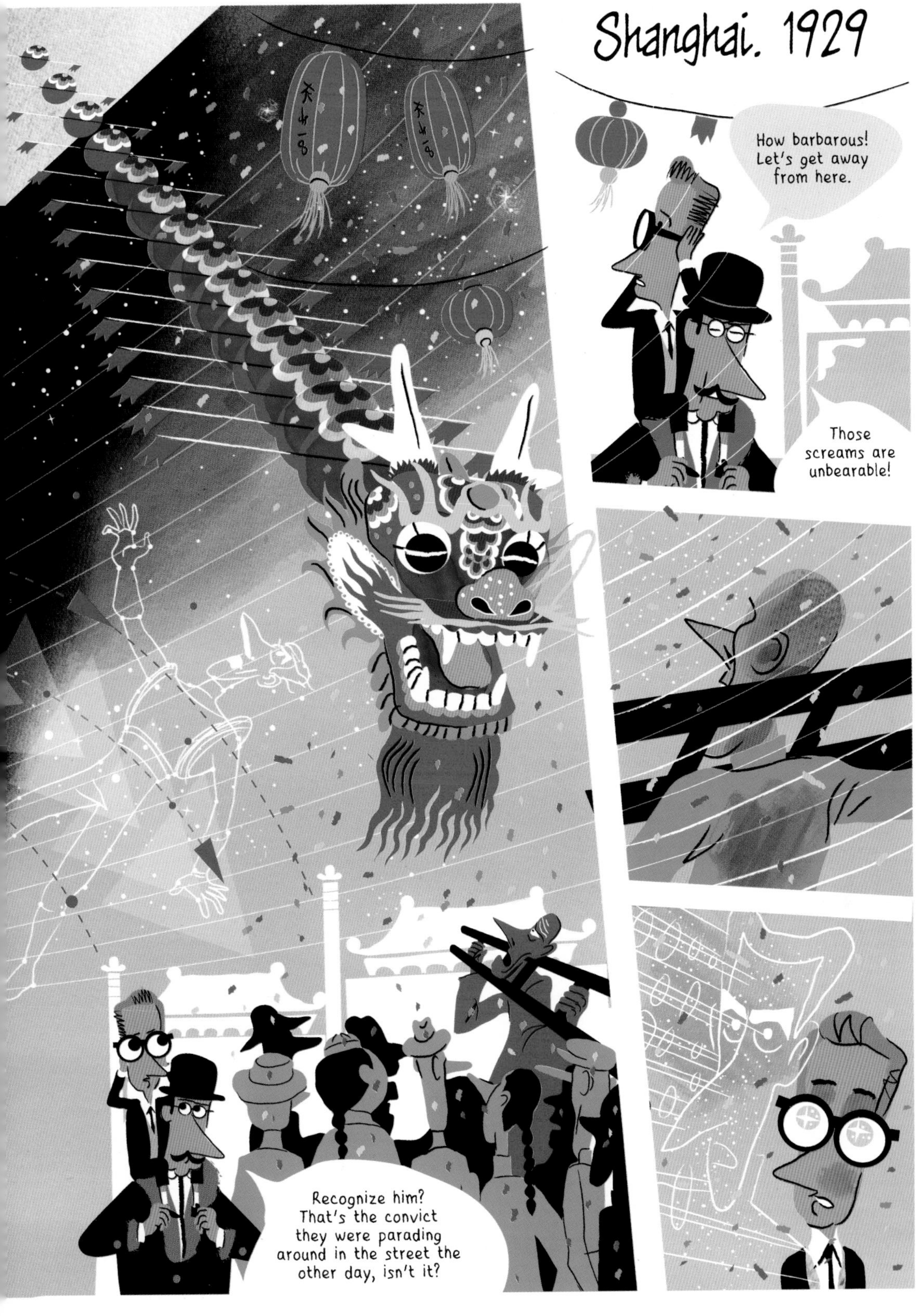
Shanghai. 1929
How barbarous! Let's get away from here.
Those screams are unbearable!
Recognize him? That's the convict they were parading around in the street the other day, isn't it?

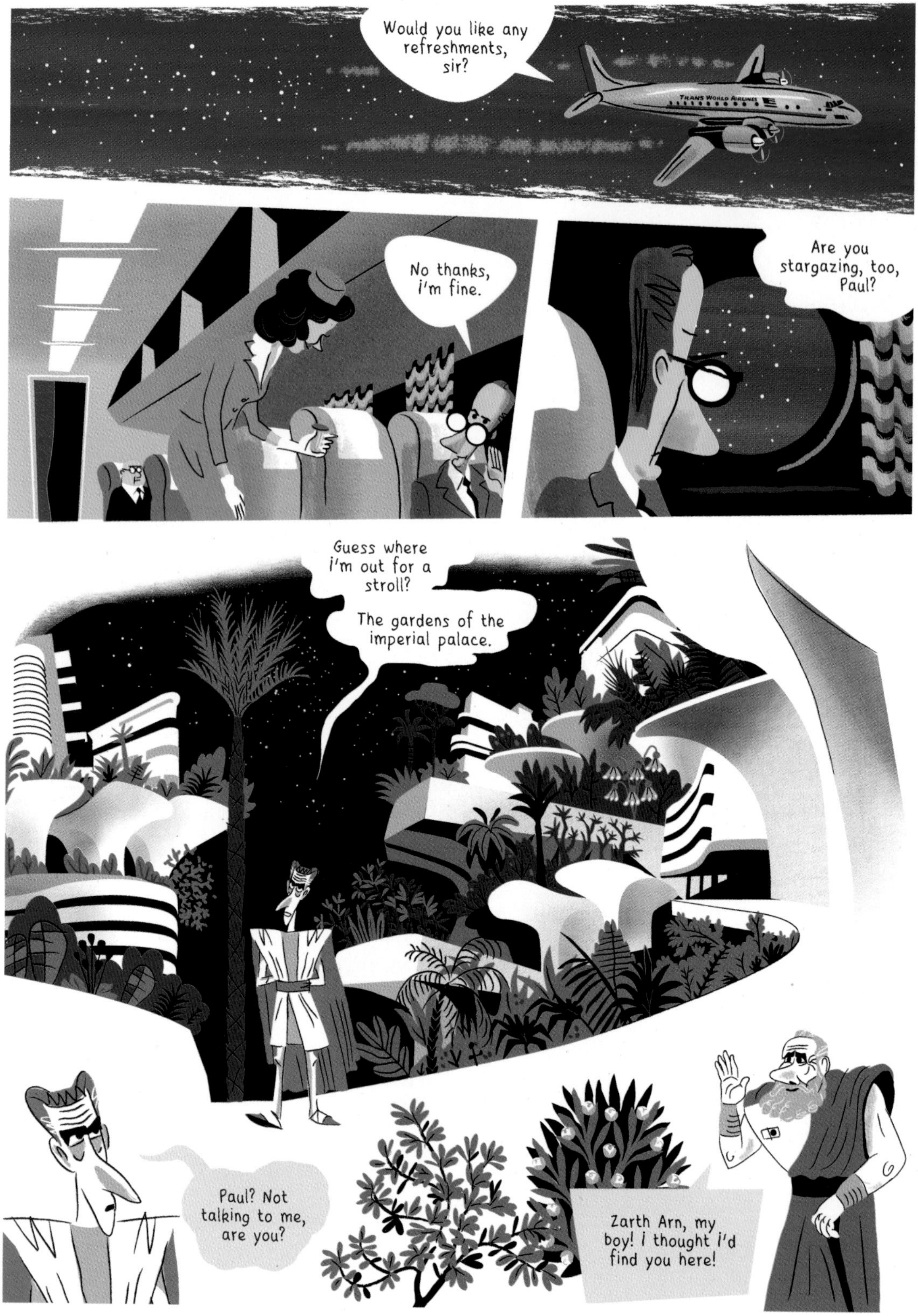
Would you like any refreshments, sir?
No thanks, i'm fine.
Are you stargazing, too, Paul?
Guess where i'm out for a stroll?
The gardens of the imperial palace.
Paul? Not talking to me, are you?
Zarth Arn, my boy! i thought i'd find you here!

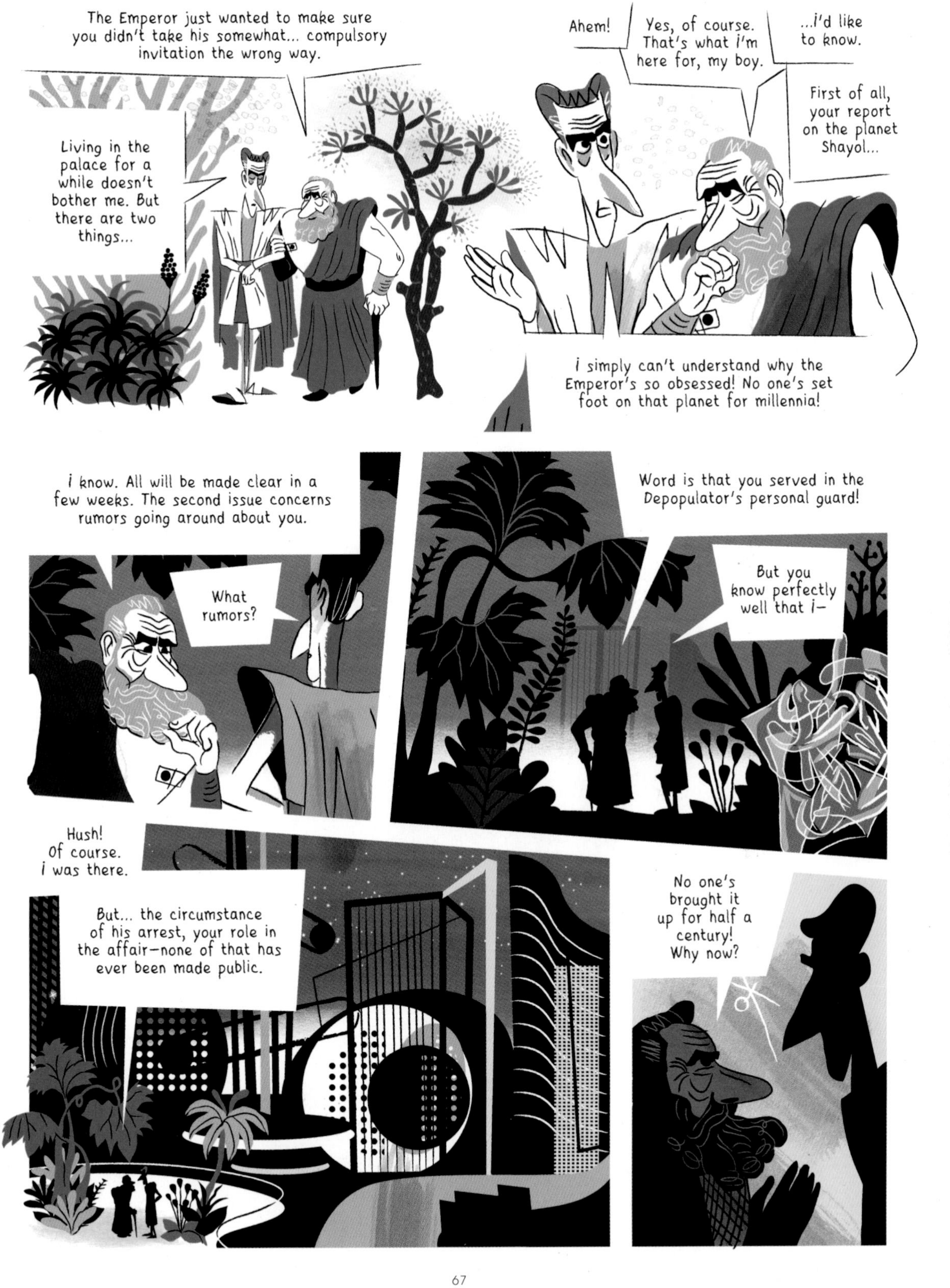
The Emperor just wanted to make sure you didn't take his somewhat... compulsory invitation the wrong way.
Living in the palace for a while doesn't bother me. But there are two things...
Ahem!
Yes, of course. That's what I'm here for, my boy.
...I'd like to know.
First of all, your report on the planet Shayol...
I simply can't understand why the Emperor's so obsessed! No one's set foot on that planet for millennia!
I know. All will be made clear in a few weeks. The second issue concerns rumors going around about you.
What rumors?
Word is that you served in the Depopulator's personal guard!
But you know perfectly well that I–
Hush! Of course. I was there.
But... the circumstance of his arrest, your role in the affair–none of that has ever been made public.
No one's brought it up for half a century! Why now?

What's the Depopulator got to do with the planet Shayol?

Oho ho ho!

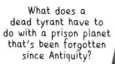

He's been dead for fifty years. His ashes were scattered in space.

What does a dead tyrant have to do with a prison planet that's been forgotten since Antiquity?

Patience, Zarth Arn. All will soon be revealed.

Come see me whenever you'd like.

i've left express orders. My door is open to you at any hour of the day or night.

it's over, darling. Everything's fine. i'm better now.

a BRAIN-storm in Vermont

Washington, 1956 (Three years later...)

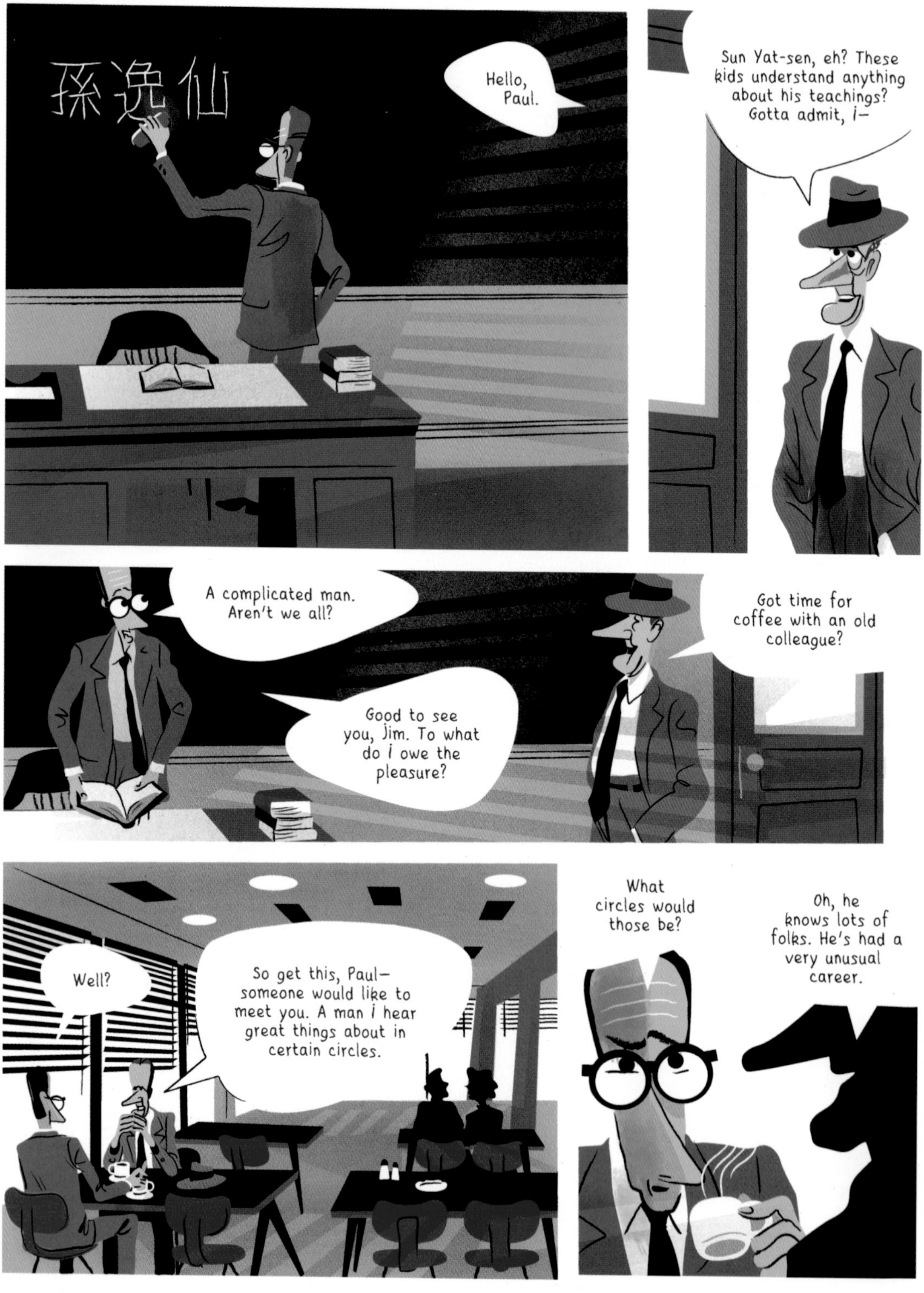
孫逸仙
Hello, Paul.
Sun Yat-sen, eh? These kids understand anything about his teachings? Gotta admit, I—
A complicated man. Aren't we all?
Good to see you, Jim. To what do I owe the pleasure?
Got time for coffee with an old colleague?
Well?
So get this, Paul— someone would like to meet you. A man I hear great things about in certain circles.
What circles would those be?
Oh, he knows lots of folks. He's had a very unusual career.

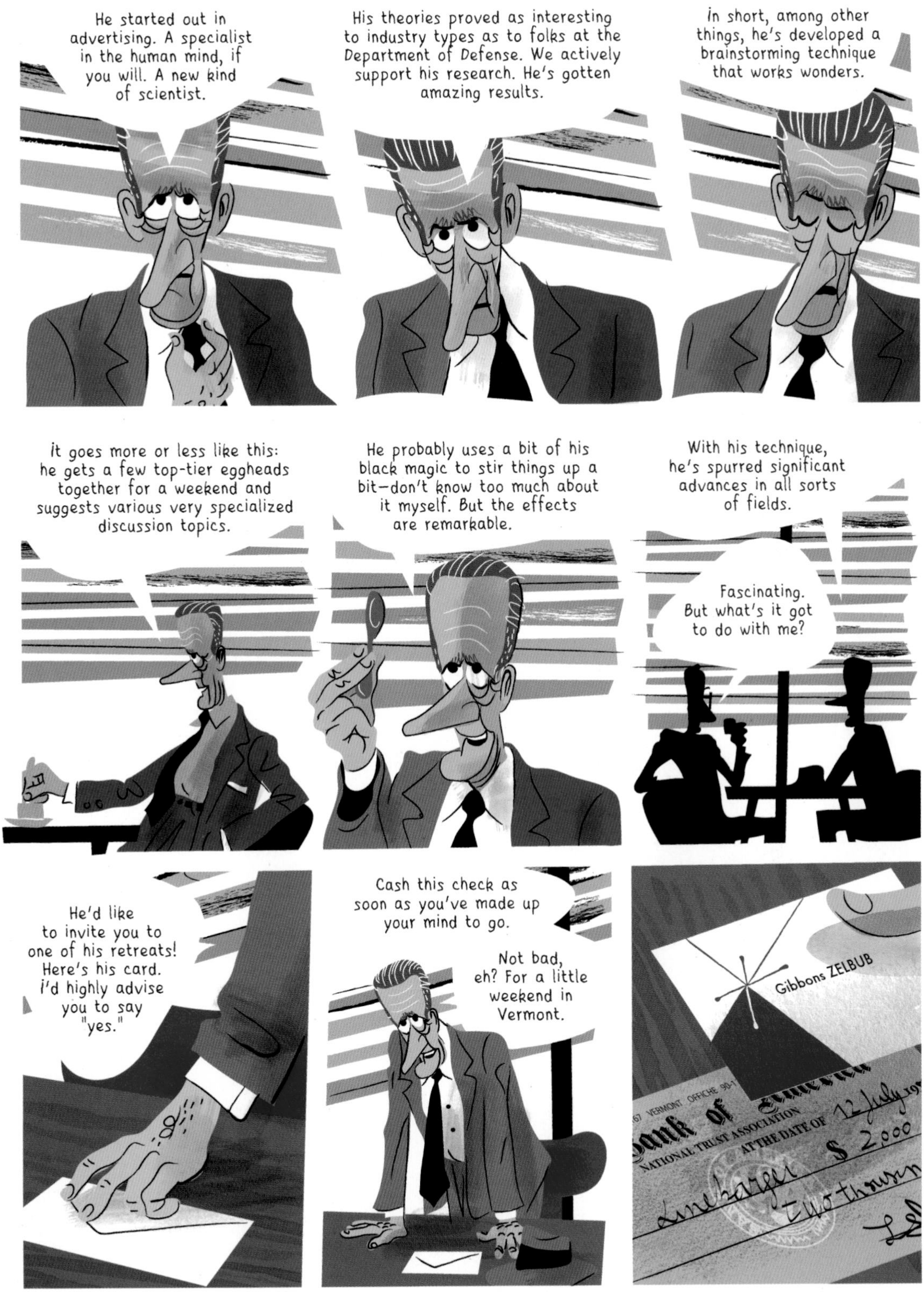

He started out in advertising. A specialist in the human mind, if you will. A new kind of scientist.
His theories proved as interesting to industry types as to folks at the Department of Defense. We actively support his research. He's gotten amazing results.
In short, among other things, he's developed a brainstorming technique that works wonders.
It goes more or less like this: he gets a few top-tier eggheads together for a weekend and suggests various very specialized discussion topics.
He probably uses a bit of his black magic to stir things up a bit—don't know too much about it myself. But the effects are remarkable.
With his technique, he's spurred significant advances in all sorts of fields.
Fascinating. But what's it got to do with me?
He'd like to invite you to one of his retreats! Here's his card. I'd highly advise you to say "yes."
Cash this check as soon as you've made up your mind to go.
Not bad, eh? For a little weekend in Vermont.
Gibbons ZELBUB
VERMONT OFFICHE 90-1
Bank of
NATIONAL TRUST ASSOCIATION
AT THE DATE OF 12 July
$ 2,000

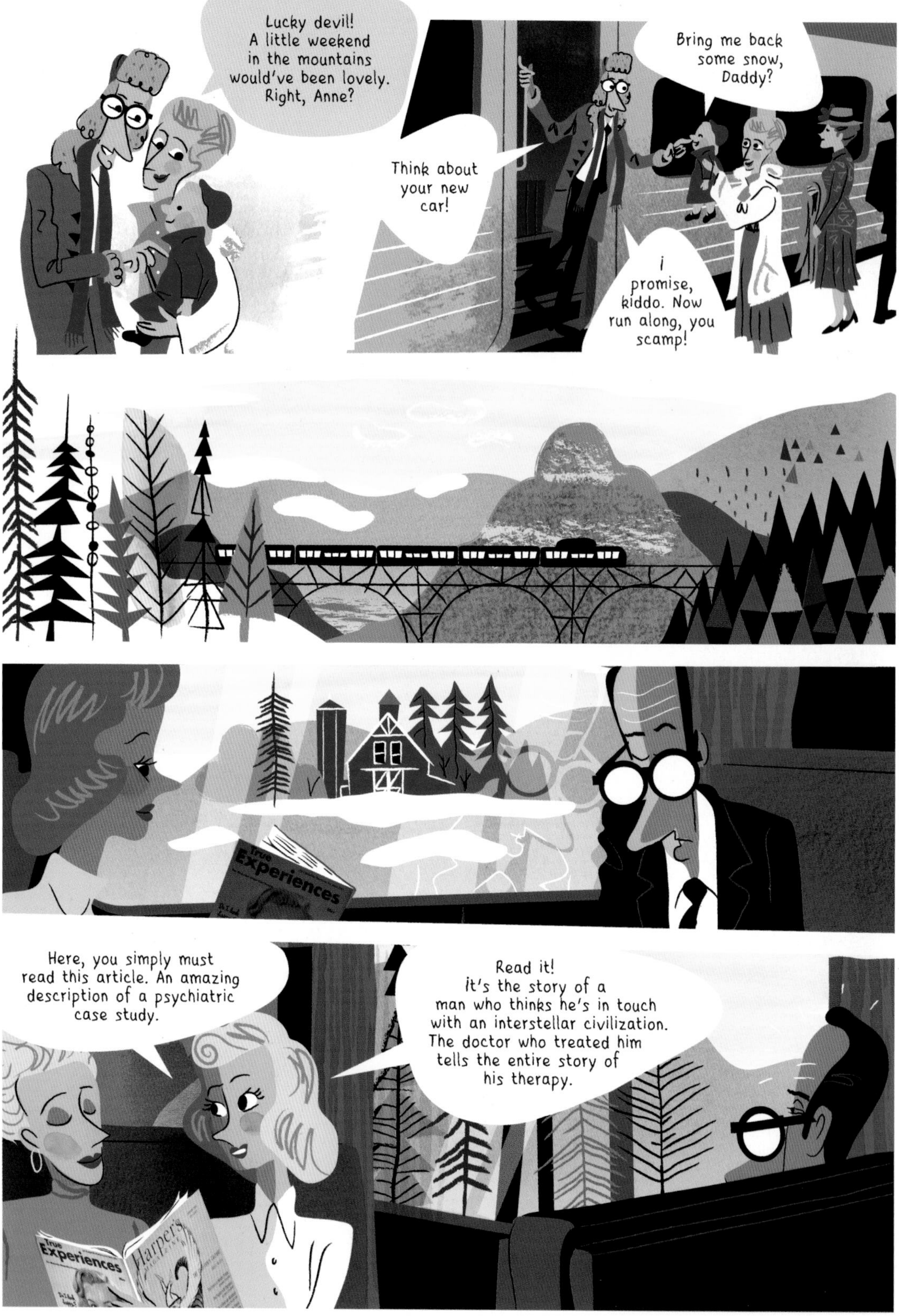
Lucky devil! A little weekend in the mountains would've been lovely. Right, Anne?
Think about your new car!
Bring me back some snow, Daddy?
I promise, kiddo. Now run along, you scamp!
True Experiences
Here, you simply must read this article. An amazing description of a psychiatric case study.
Read it! It's the story of a man who thinks he's in touch with an interstellar civilization. The doctor who treated him tells the entire story of his therapy.
True Experiences
Harper's

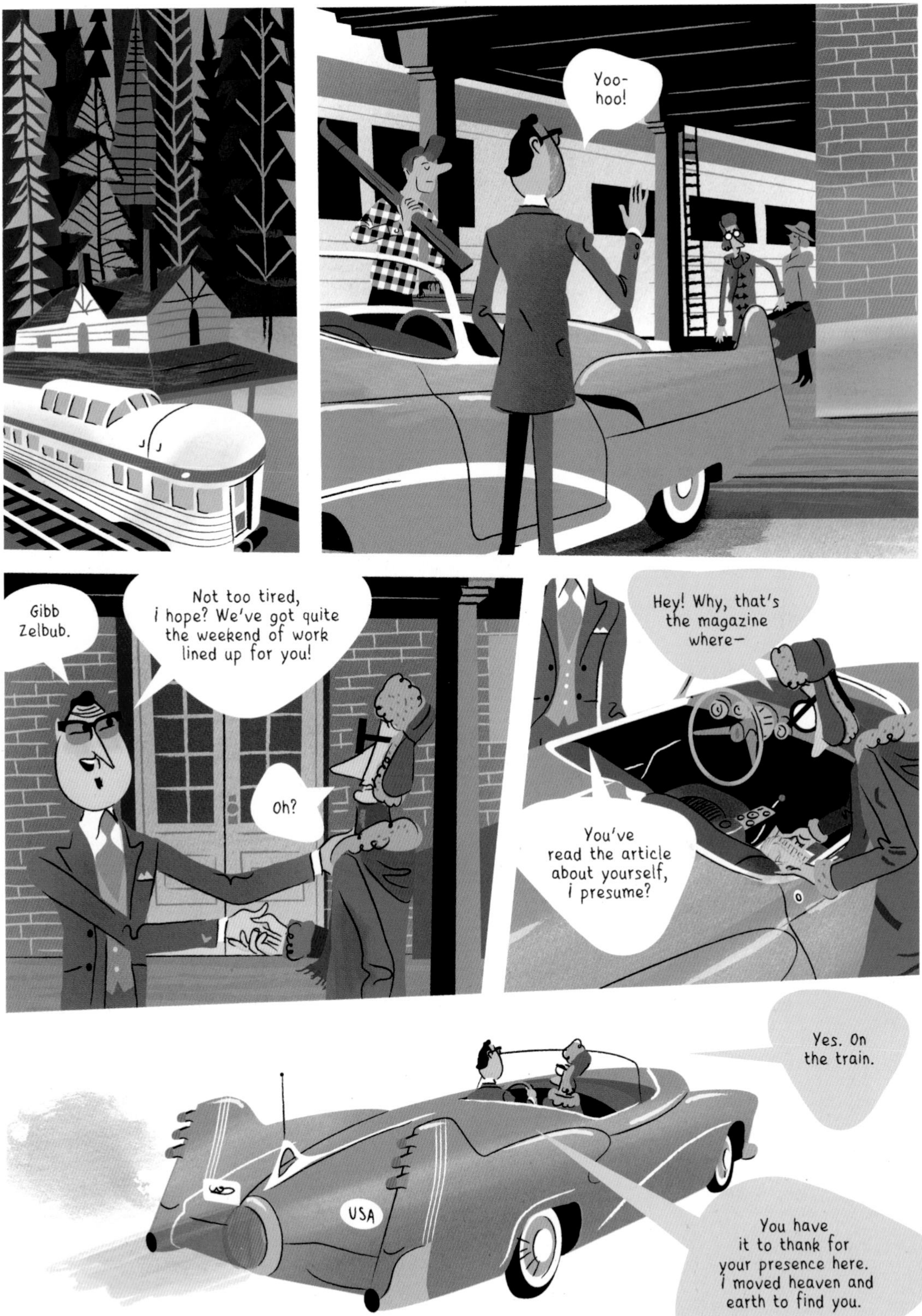

Yoo-
hoo!
Gibb
Zelbub.
Not too tired, i hope? We've got quite the weekend of work lined up for you!
Oh?
Hey! Why, that's the magazine where–
You've read the article about yourself, i presume?
Yes. On the train.
You have it to thank for your presence here. i moved heaven and earth to find you.

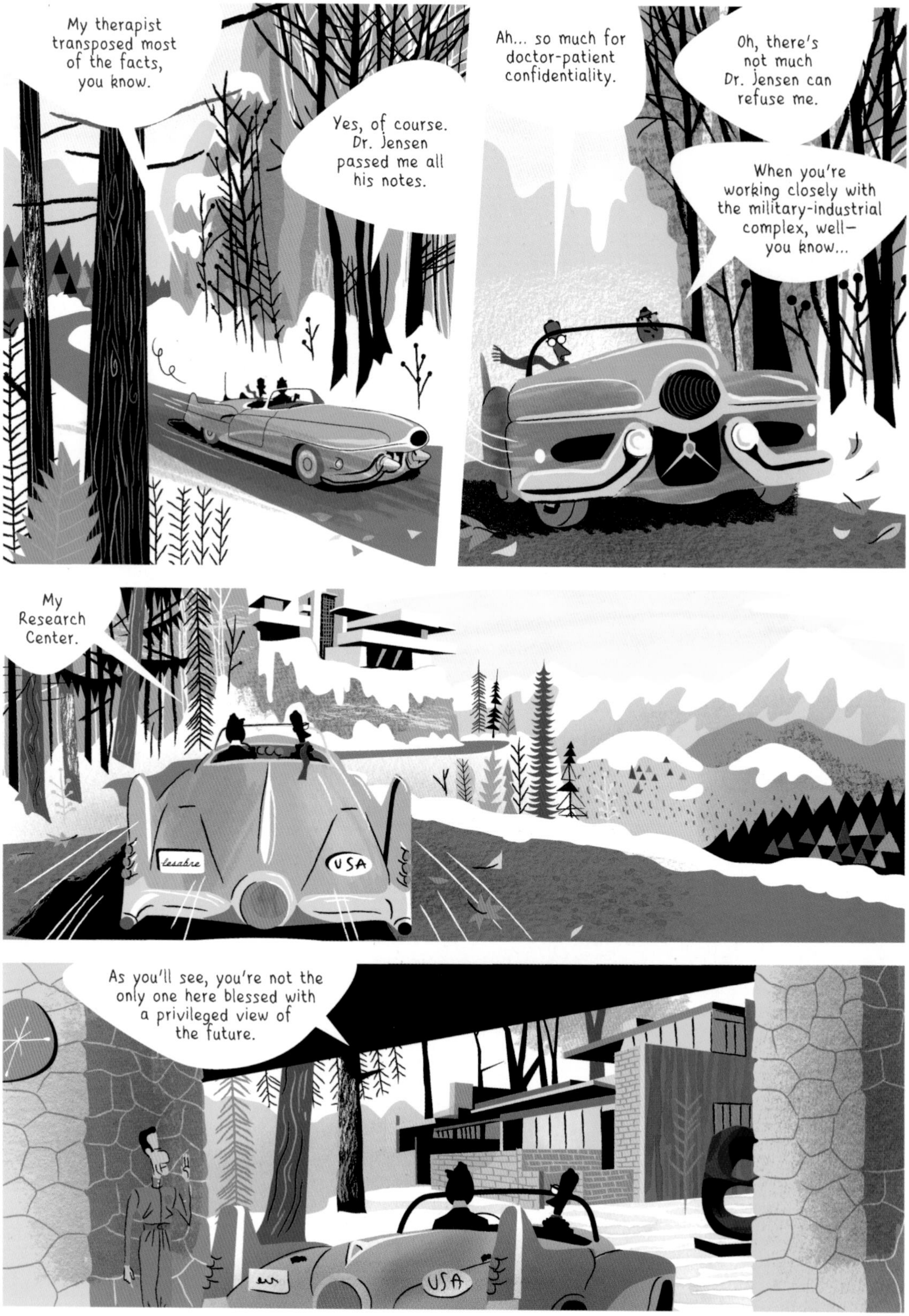
My therapist transposed most of the facts, you know.
Yes, of course. Dr. Jensen passed me all his notes.
Ah... so much for doctor-patient confidentiality.
Oh, there's not much Dr. Jensen can refuse me.
When you're working closely with the military-industrial complex, well— you know...
My Research Center.
USA
As you'll see, you're not the only one here blessed with a privileged view of the future.
USA

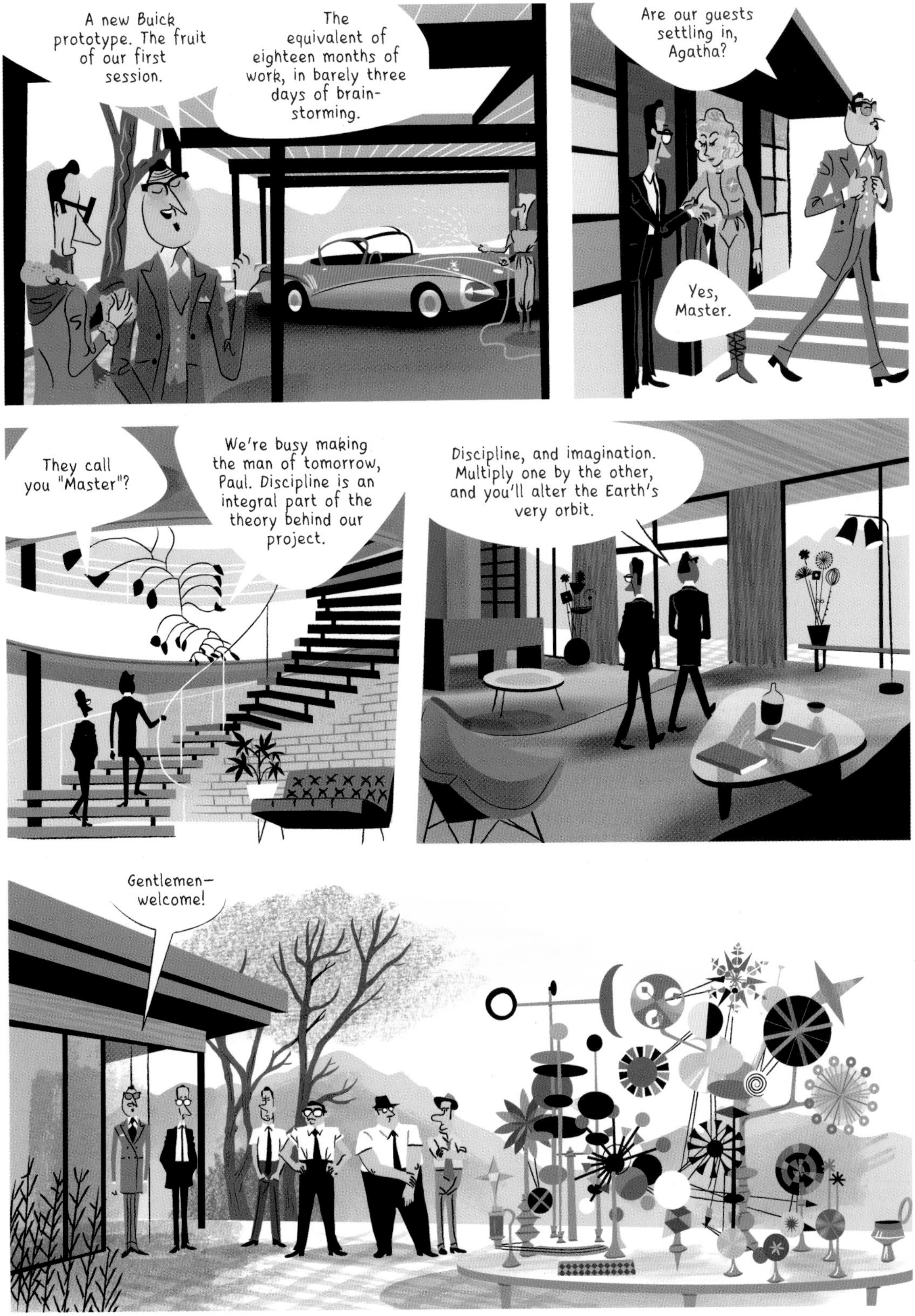
A new Buick prototype. The fruit of our first session.
The equivalent of eighteen months of work, in barely three days of brain-storming.
Are our guests settling in, Agatha?
Yes, Master.
They call you "Master"?
We're busy making the man of tomorrow, Paul. Discipline is an integral part of the theory behind our project.
Discipline, and imagination. Multiply one by the other, and you'll alter the Earth's very orbit.
Gentlemen—welcome!

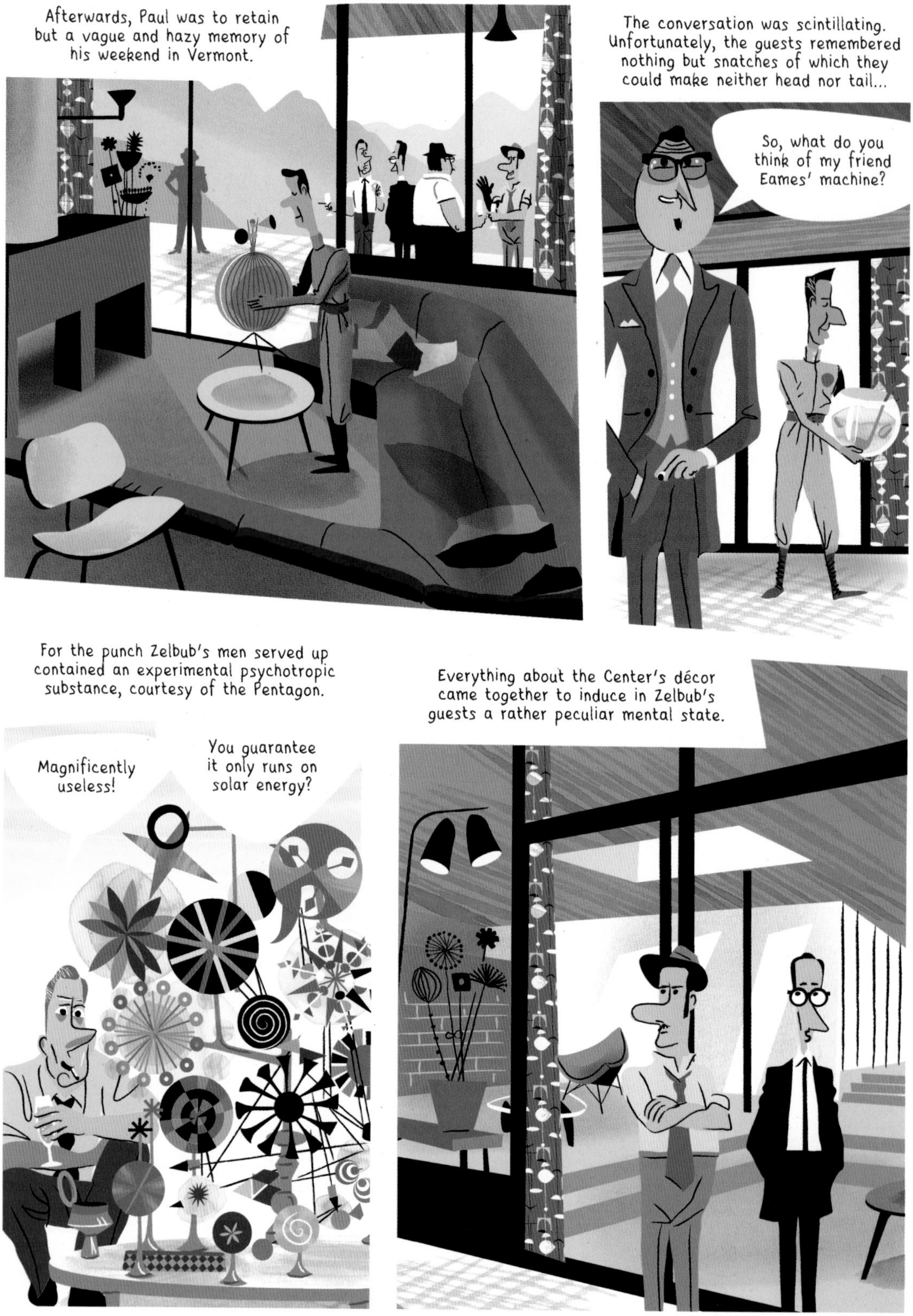
Afterwards, Paul was to retain but a vague and hazy memory of his weekend in Vermont.
The conversation was scintillating. Unfortunately, the guests remembered nothing but snatches of which they could make neither head nor tail...
So, what do you think of my friend Eames' machine?
For the punch Zelbub's men served up contained an experimental psychotropic substance, courtesy of the Pentagon.
Magnificently useless!
You guarantee it only runs on solar energy?
Everything about the Center's décor came together to induce in Zelbub's guests a rather peculiar mental state.

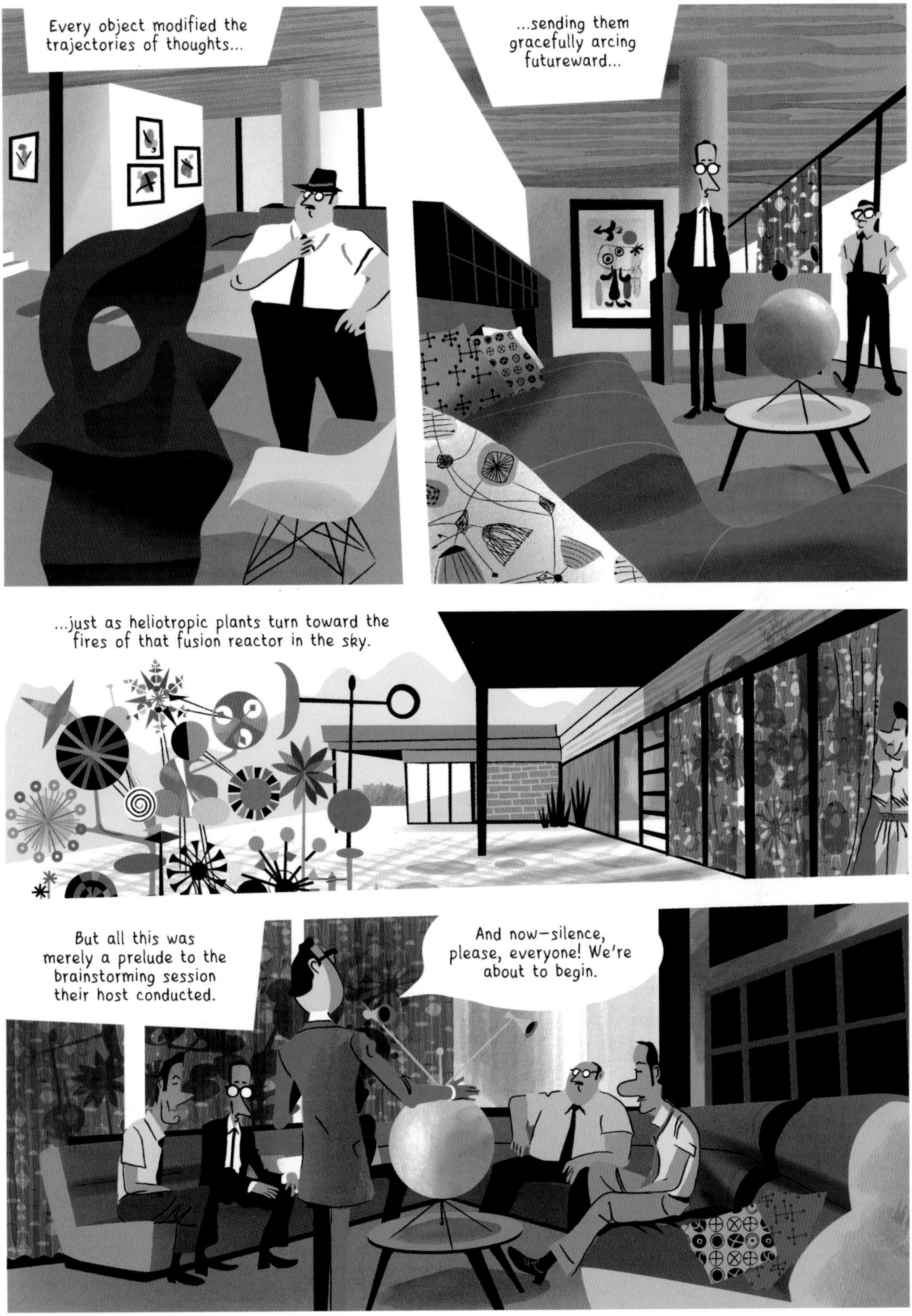
Every object modified the trajectories of thoughts...
...sending them gracefully arcing futureward...
...just as heliotropic plants turn toward the fires of that fusion reactor in the sky.
But all this was merely a prelude to the brainstorming session their host conducted.
And now—silence, please, everyone! We're about to begin.

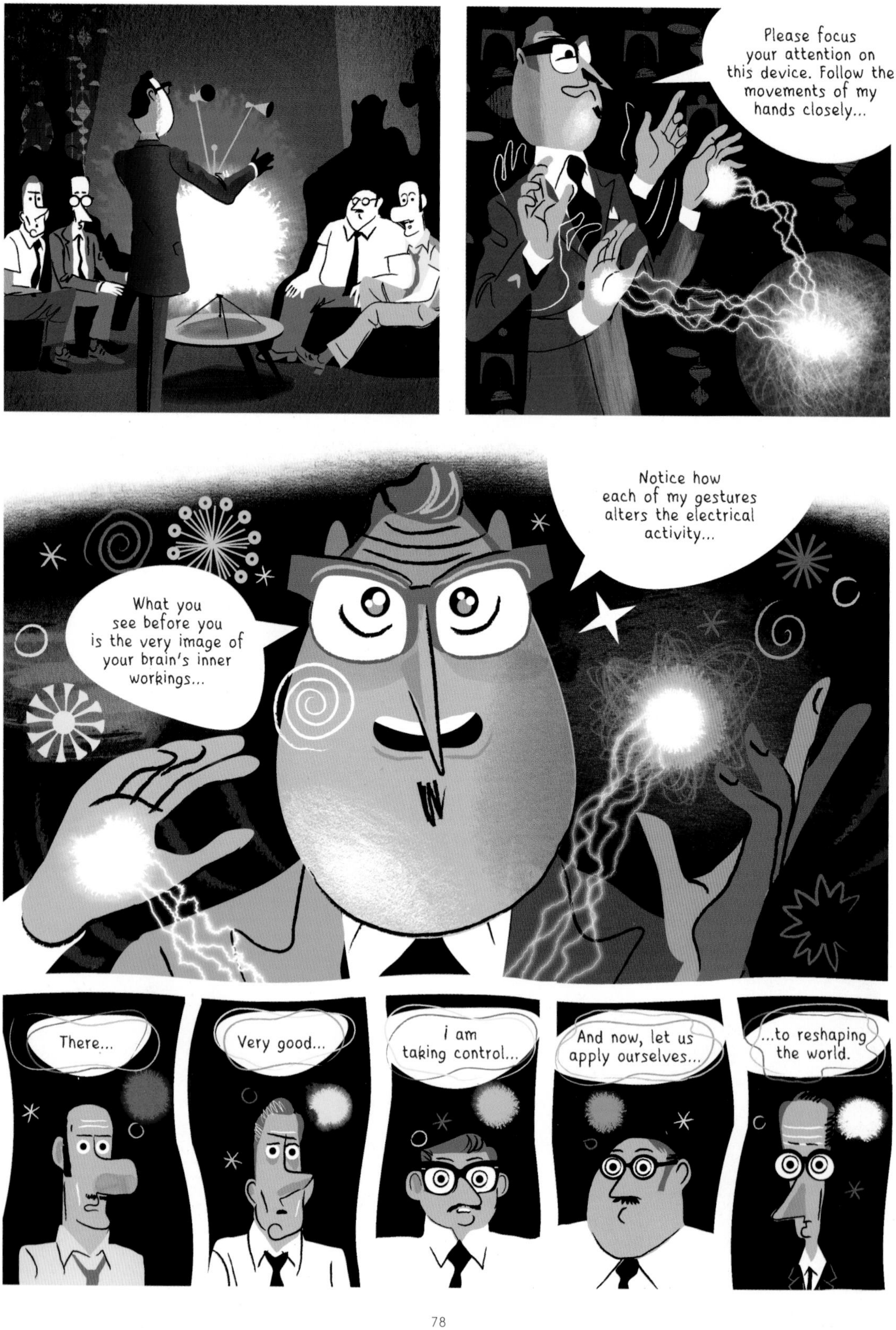
Please focus your attention on this device. Follow the movements of my hands closely...
Notice how each of my gestures alters the electrical activity...
What you see before you is the very image of your brain's inner workings...
There...
Very good...
I am taking control...
And now, let us apply ourselves...
...to reshaping the world.

A few hours later...

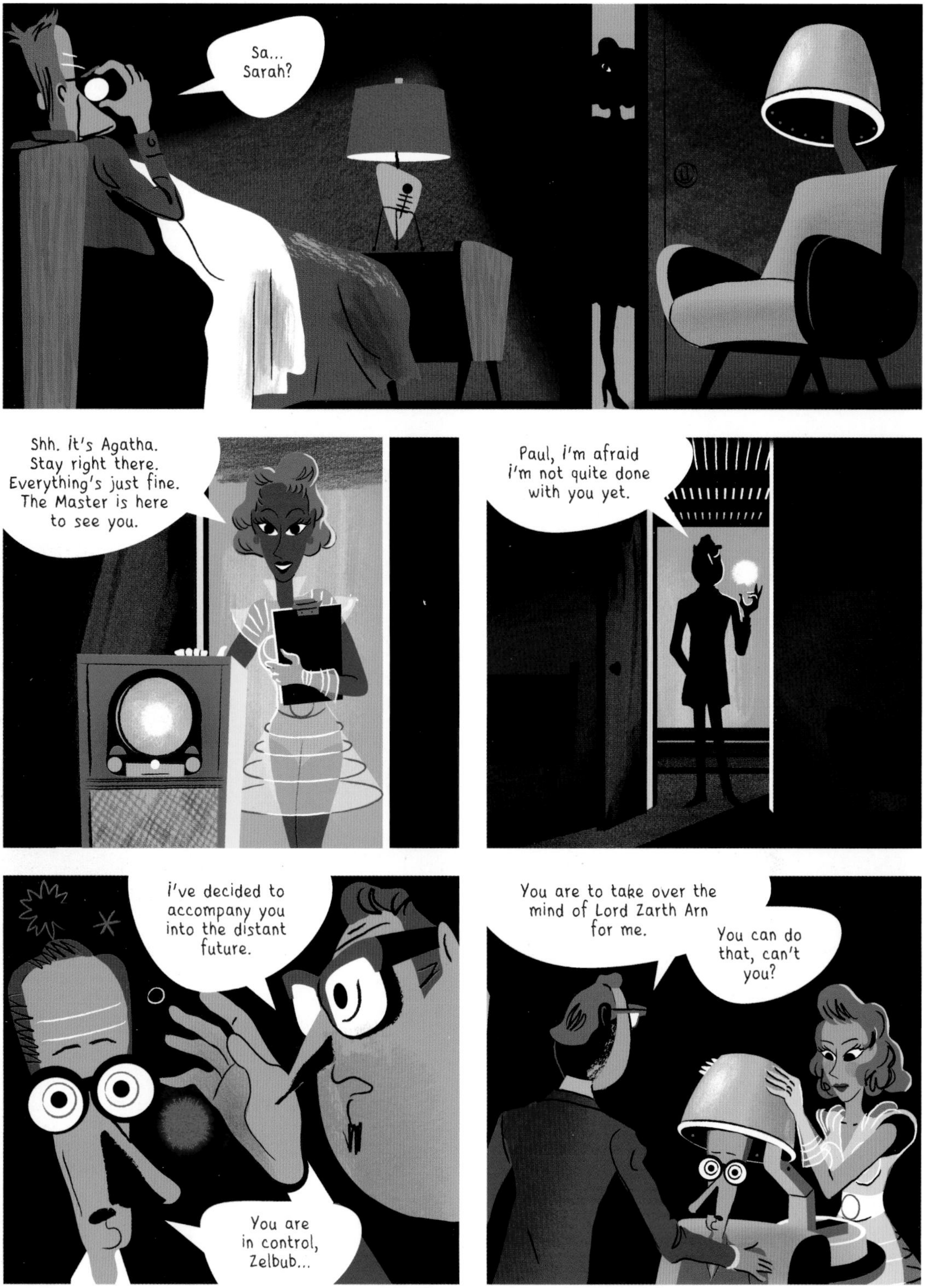
Sa... Sarah?
Shh. It's Agatha. Stay right there. Everything's just fine. The Master is here to see you.
Paul, I'm afraid I'm not quite done with you yet.
I've decided to accompany you into the distant future.
You are in control, Zelbub...
You are to take over the mind of Lord Zarth Arn for me.
You can do that, can't you?

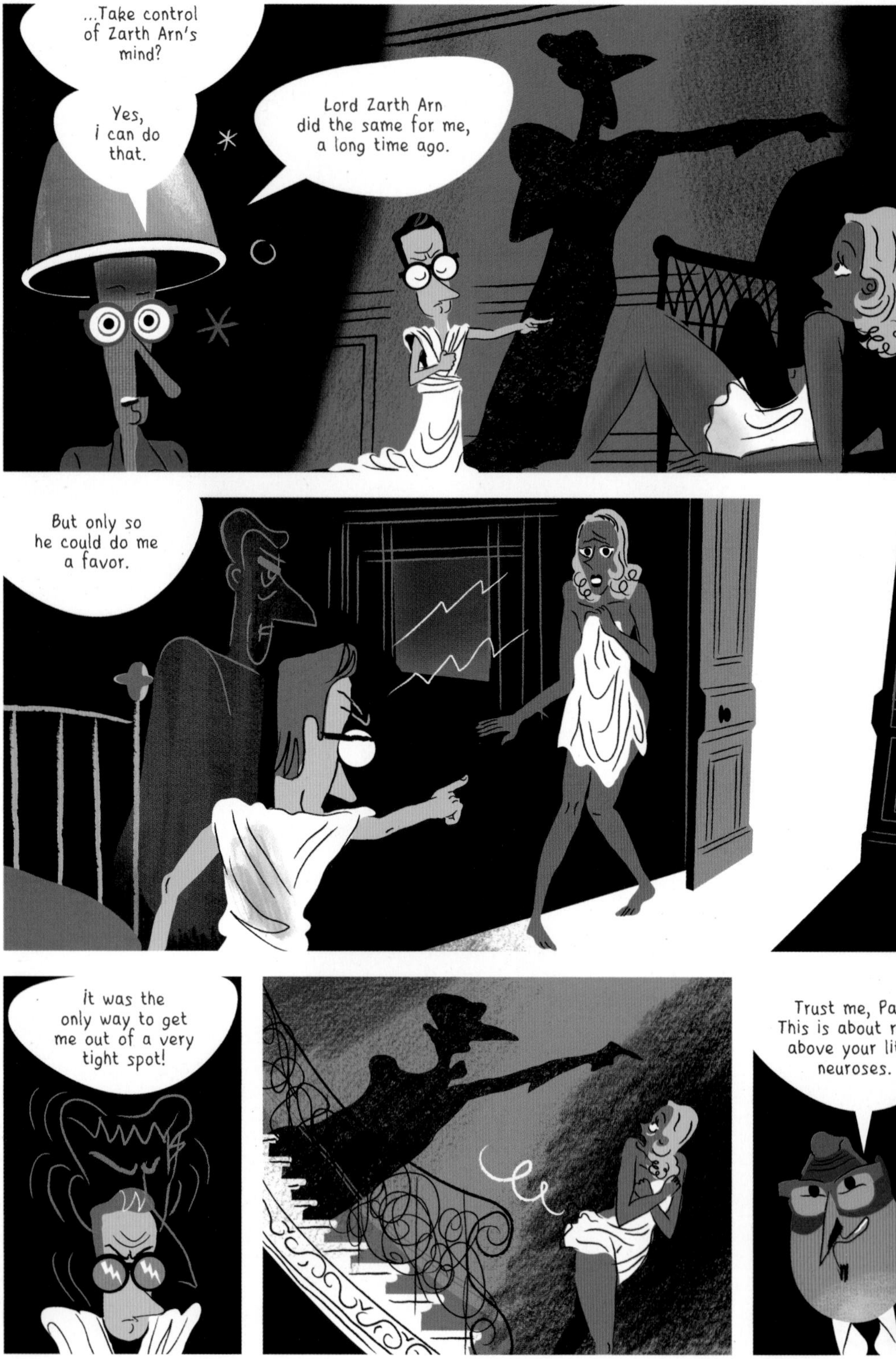
...Take control of Zarth Arn's mind?
Yes, I can do that.
Lord Zarth Arn did the same for me, a long time ago.
But only so he could do me a favor.
It was the only way to get me out of a very tight spot!
Trust me, Paul. This is about rising above your little neuroses.

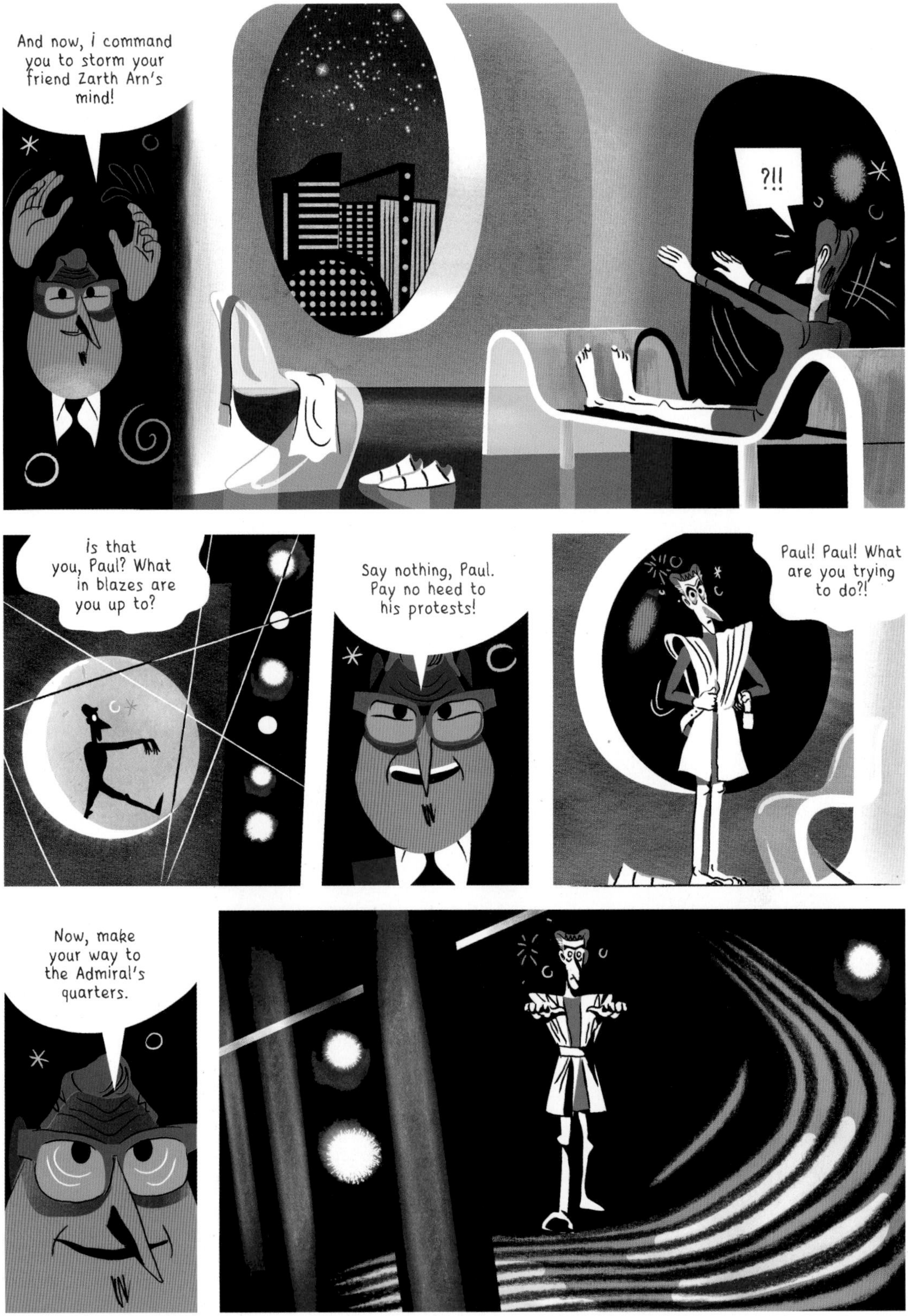
And now, i command you to storm your friend Zarth Arn's mind!
?!!
is that you, Paul? What in blazes are you up to?
Say nothing, Paul. Pay no heed to his protests!
Paul! Paul! What are you trying to do?!
Now, make your way to the Admiral's quarters.

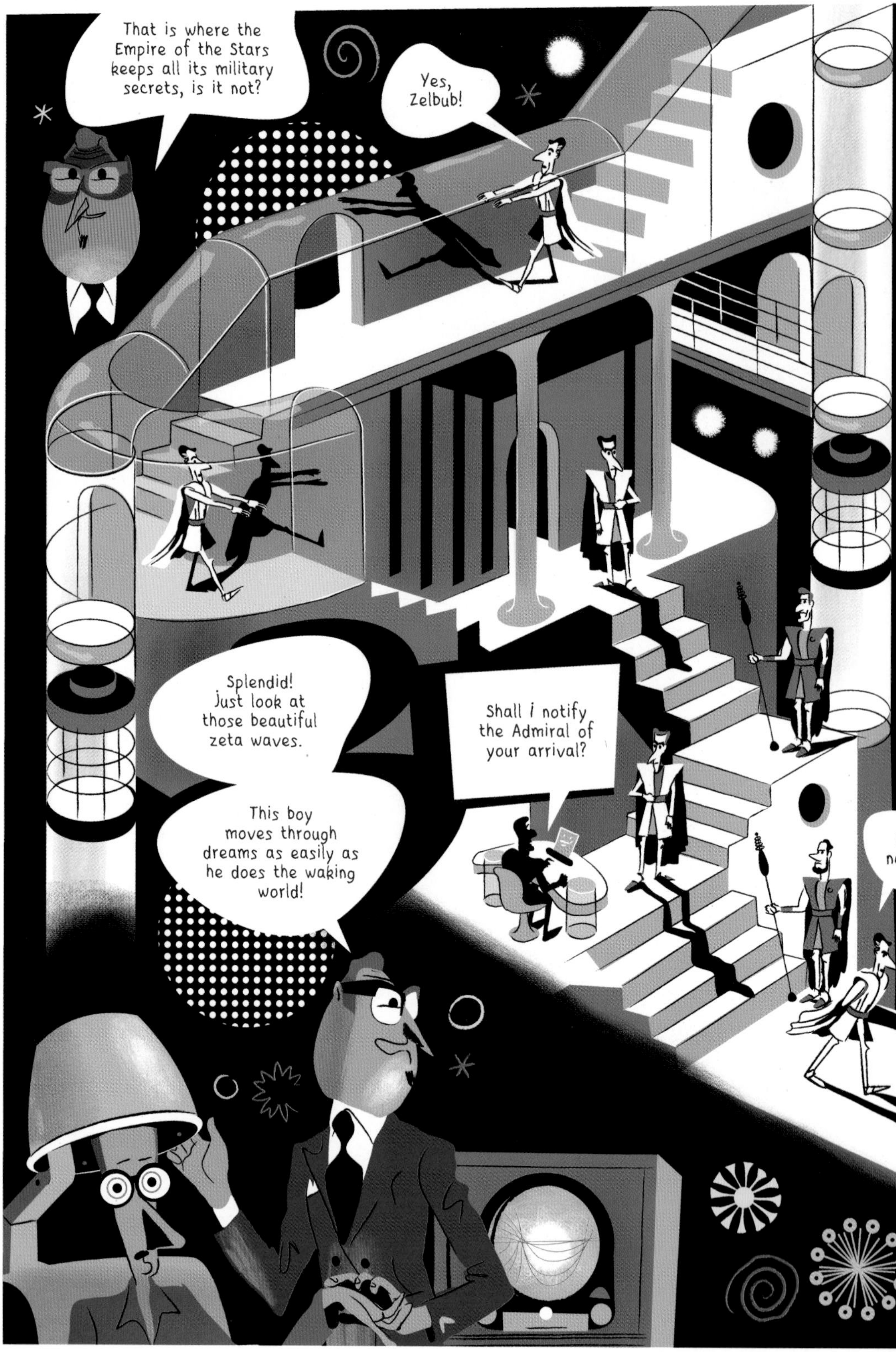
That is where the Empire of the Stars keeps all its military secrets, is it not?
Yes, Zelbub!
Splendid! Just look at those beautiful zeta waves.
This boy moves through dreams as easily as he does the waking world!
Shall I notify the Admiral of your arrival?
No need.

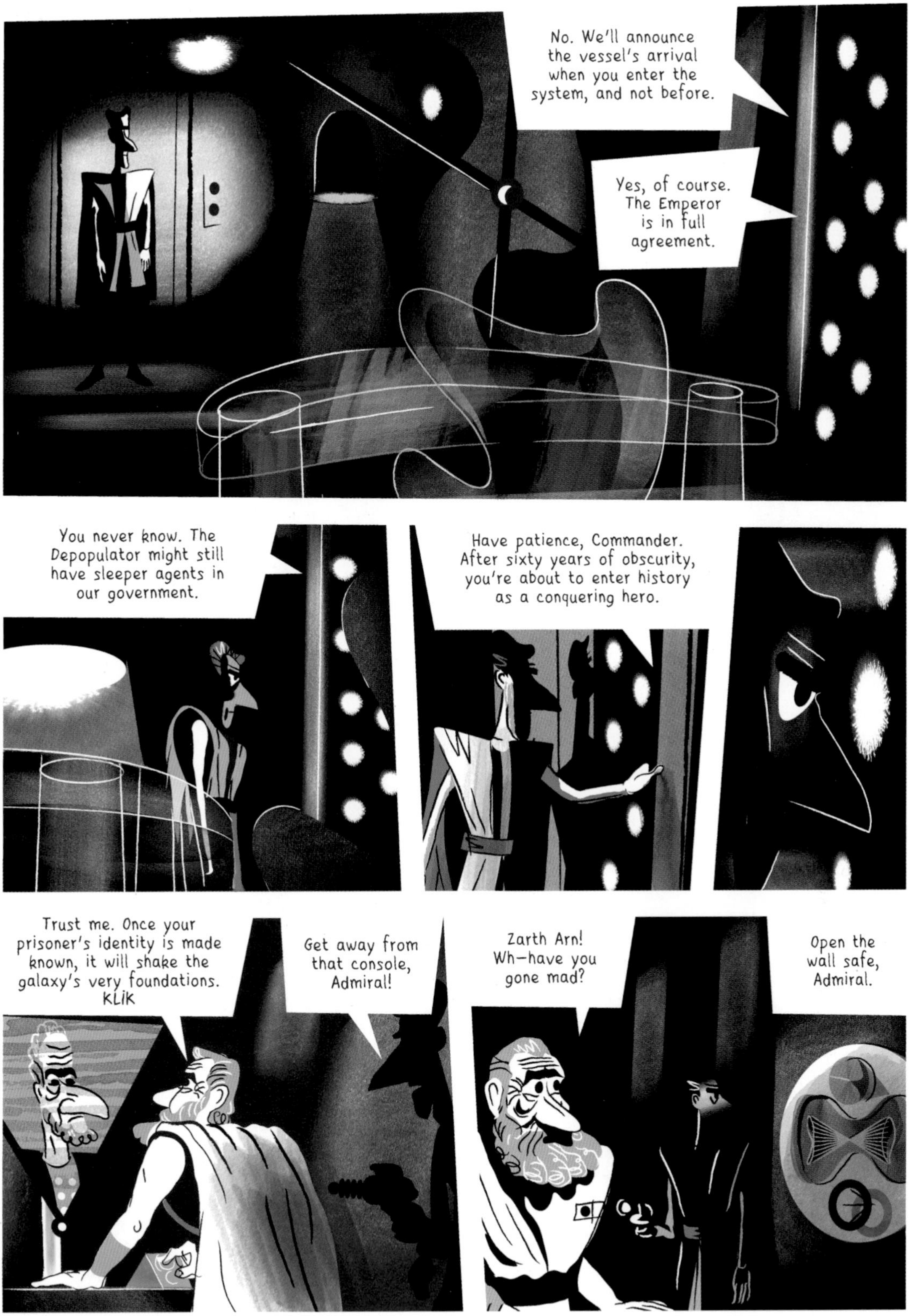
No. We'll announce the vessel's arrival when you enter the system, and not before.
Yes, of course. The Emperor is in full agreement.
You never know. The Depopulator might still have sleeper agents in our government.
Have patience, Commander. After sixty years of obscurity, you're about to enter history as a conquering hero.
Trust me. Once your prisoner's identity is made known, it will shake the galaxy's very foundations.
KLIK
Get away from that console, Admiral!
Zarth Arn! Wh—have you gone mad?
Open the wall safe, Admiral.

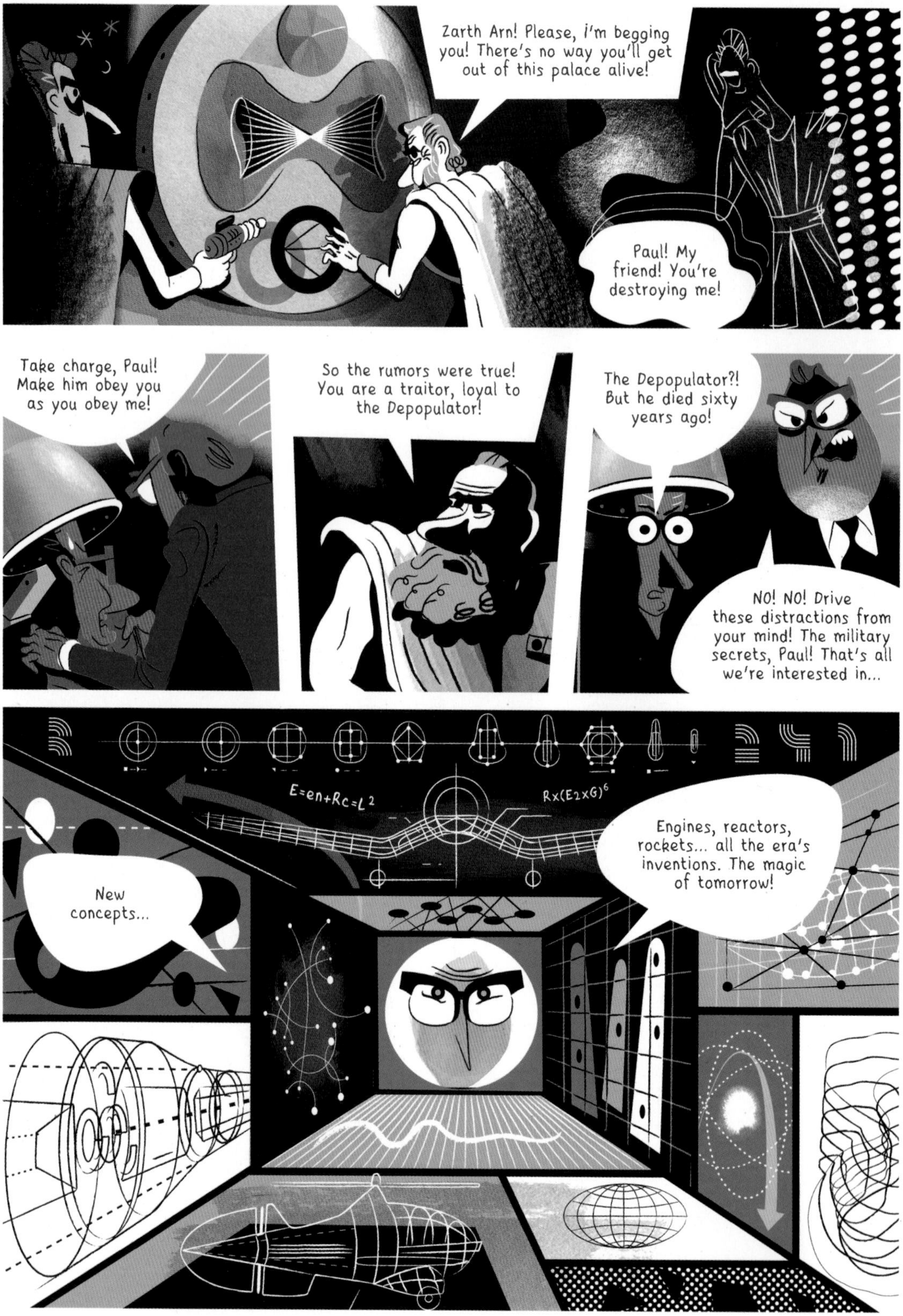
Zarth Arn! Please, i'm begging you! There's no way you'll get out of this palace alive!
Paul! My friend! You're destroying me!
Take charge, Paul! Make him obey you as you obey me!
So the rumors were true! You are a traitor, loyal to the Depopulator!
The Depopulator?! But he died sixty years ago!
NO! NO! Drive these distractions from your mind! The military secrets, Paul! That's all we're interested in...
E=en+Rc=L²
Rx(E2xG)⁶
New concepts...
Engines, reactors, rockets... all the era's inventions. The magic of tomorrow!

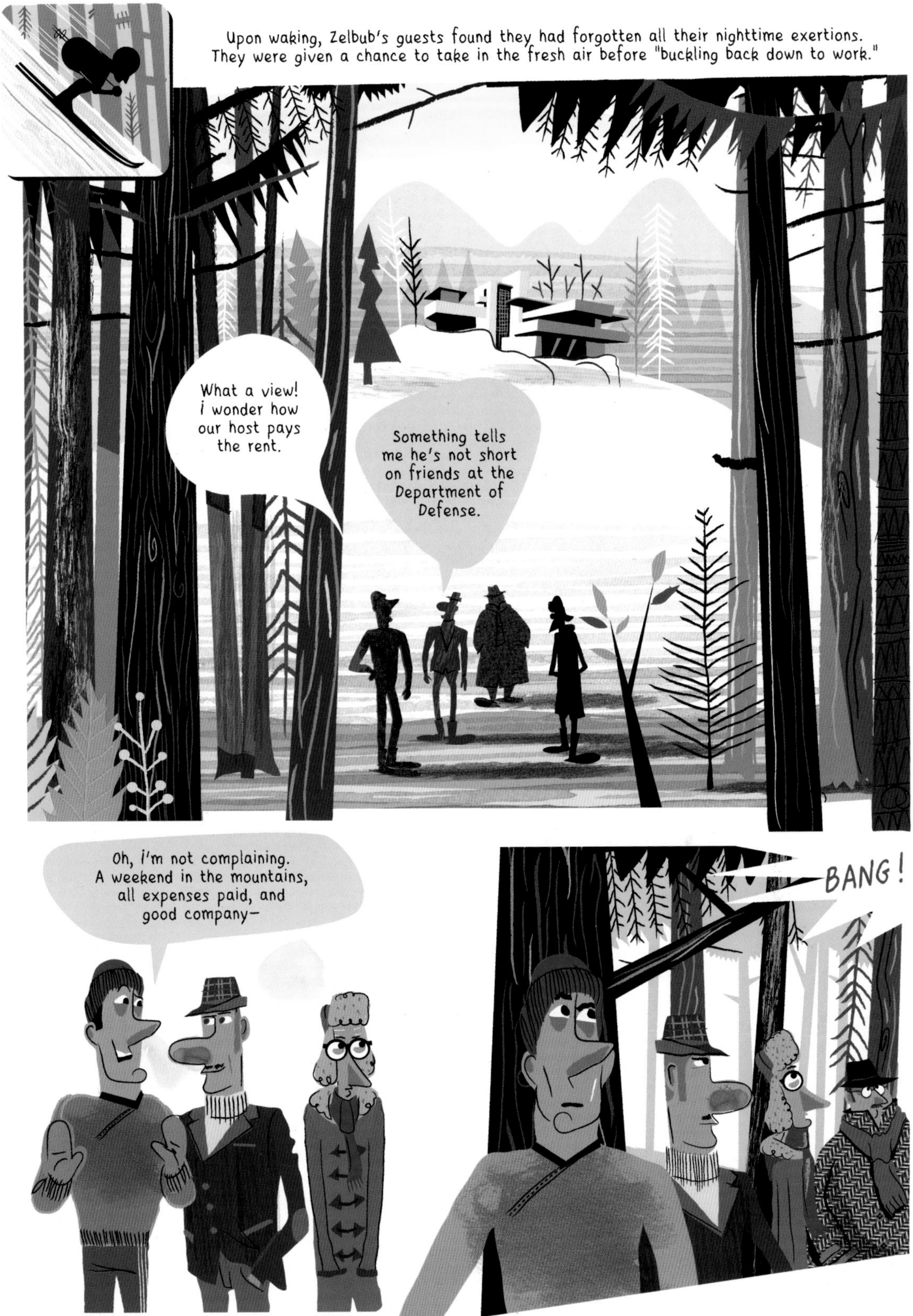
Upon waking, Zelbub's guests found they had forgotten all their nighttime exertions. They were given a chance to take in the fresh air before "buckling back down to work."
What a view! I wonder how our host pays the rent.
Something tells me he's not short on friends at the Department of Defense.
Oh, I'm not complaining. A weekend in the mountains, all expenses paid, and good company—
BANG!

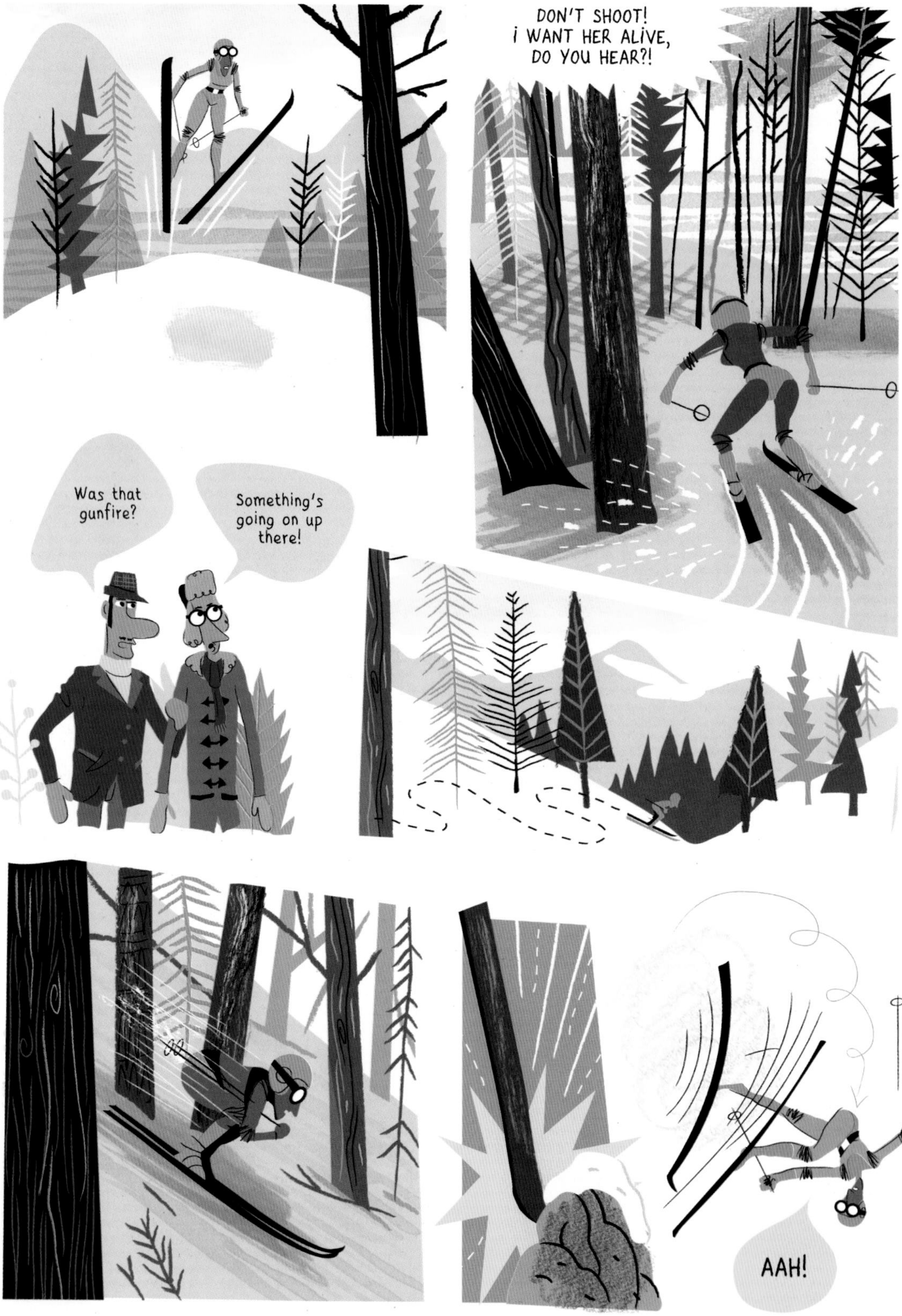
DON'T SHOOT!
I WANT HER ALIVE,
DO YOU HEAR?!
Was that gunfire?
Something's going on up there!
AAH!

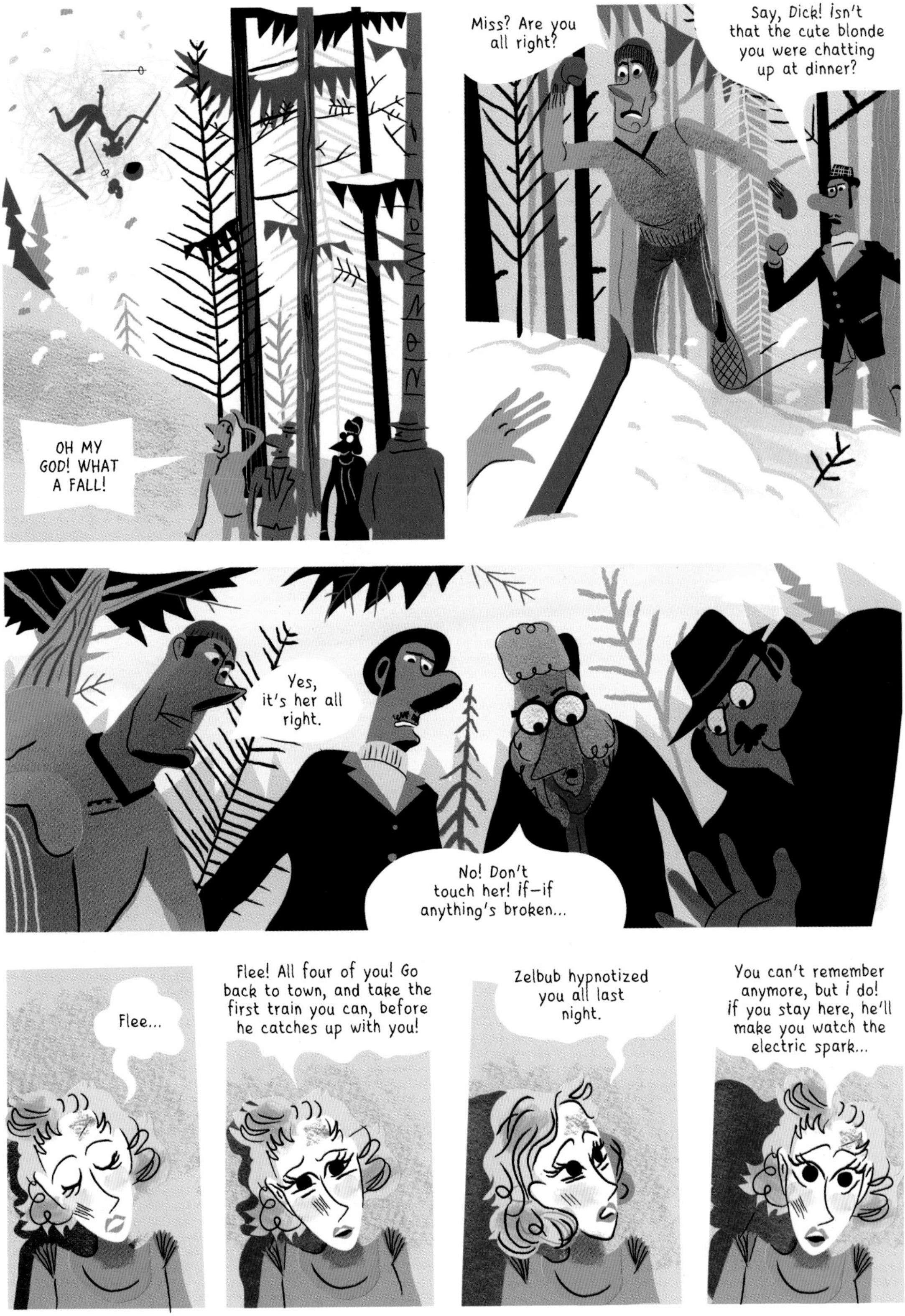
OH MY GOD! WHAT A FALL!
Miss? Are you all right?
Say, Dick! isn't that the cute blonde you were chatting up at dinner?
Yes, it's her all right.
No! Don't touch her! if—if anything's broken...
Flee...
Flee! All four of you! Go back to town, and take the first train you can, before he catches up with you!
Zelbub hypnotized you all last night.
You can't remember anymore, but i do! if you stay here, he'll make you watch the electric spark...

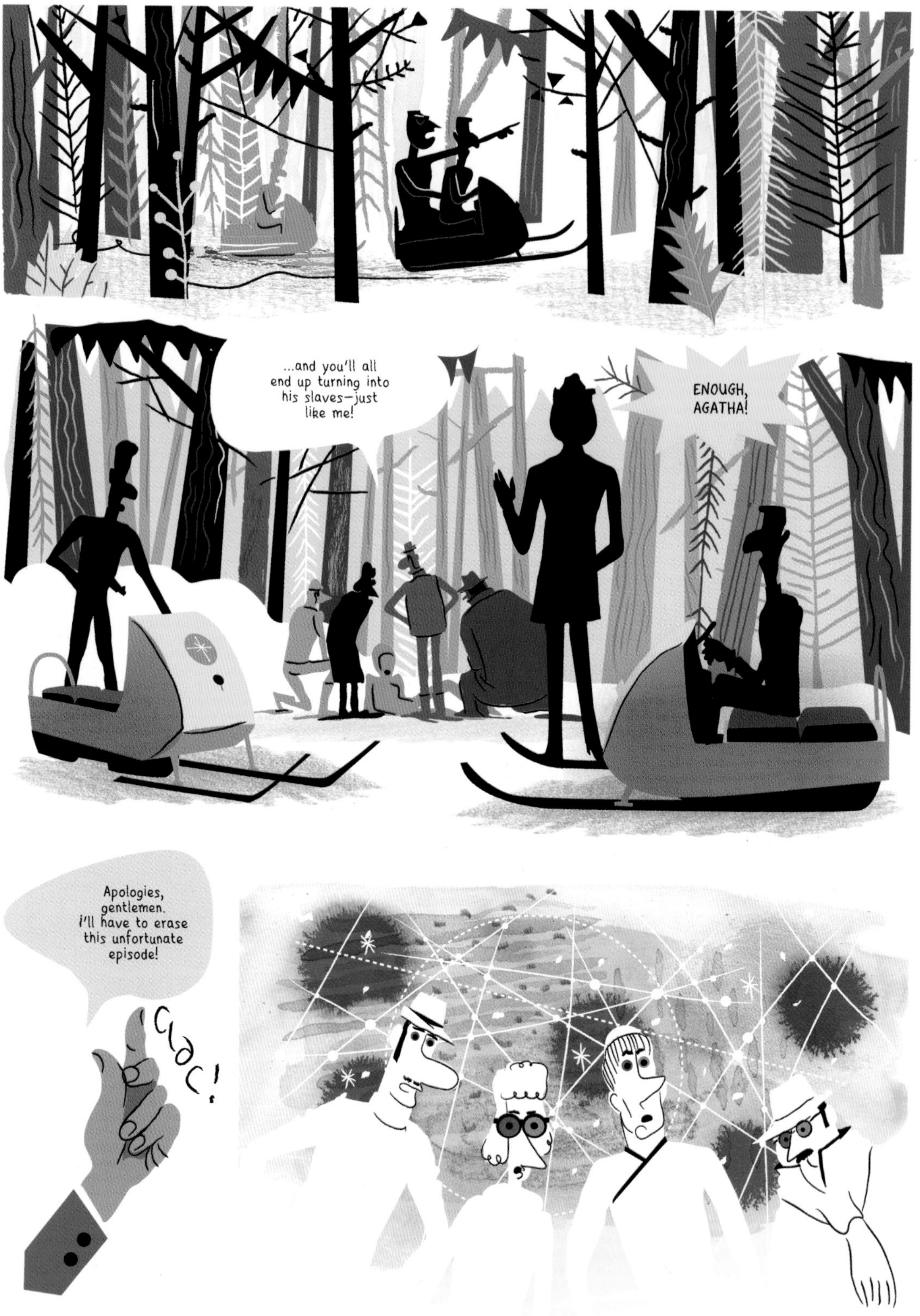
...and you'll all end up turning into his slaves—just like me!
ENOUGH, AGATHA!
Apologies, gentlemen. i'll have to erase this unfortunate episode!
CLAC!

chapter 4

THE TRIUMPH OF ZELBUB

Washington. March, 1958 (two years later...)

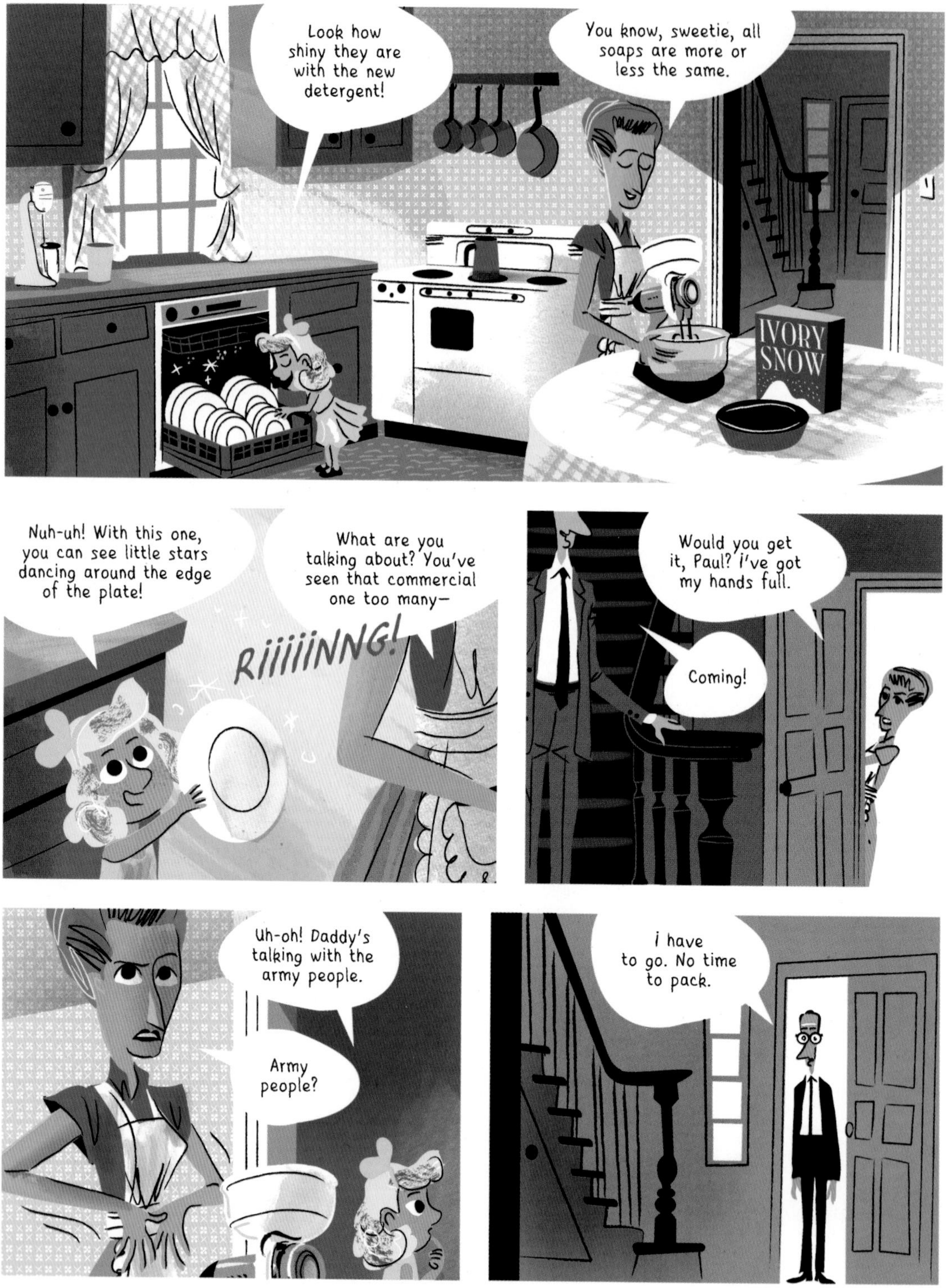
Look how shiny they are with the new detergent!
You know, sweetie, all soaps are more or less the same.
IVORY SNOW
Nuh-uh! With this one, you can see little stars dancing around the edge of the plate!
What are you talking about? You've seen that commercial one too many—
RIIIIINNG!
Would you get it, Paul? I've got my hands full.
Coming!
Uh-oh! Daddy's talking with the army people.
Army people?
I have to go. No time to pack.

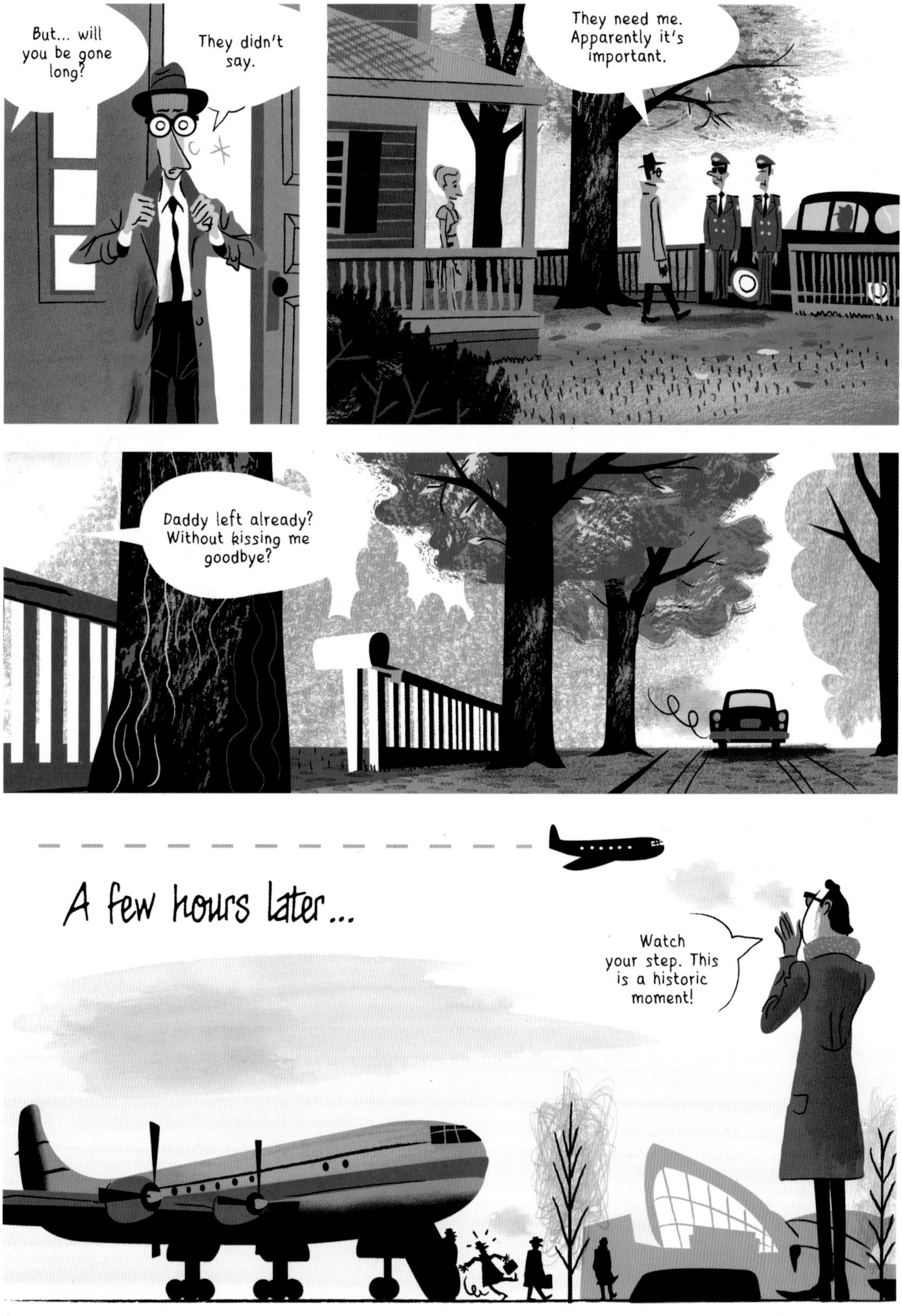
But... will you be gone long?
They didn't say.
They need me. Apparently it's important.
Daddy left already? Without kissing me goodbye?
A few hours later...
Watch your step. This is a historic moment!

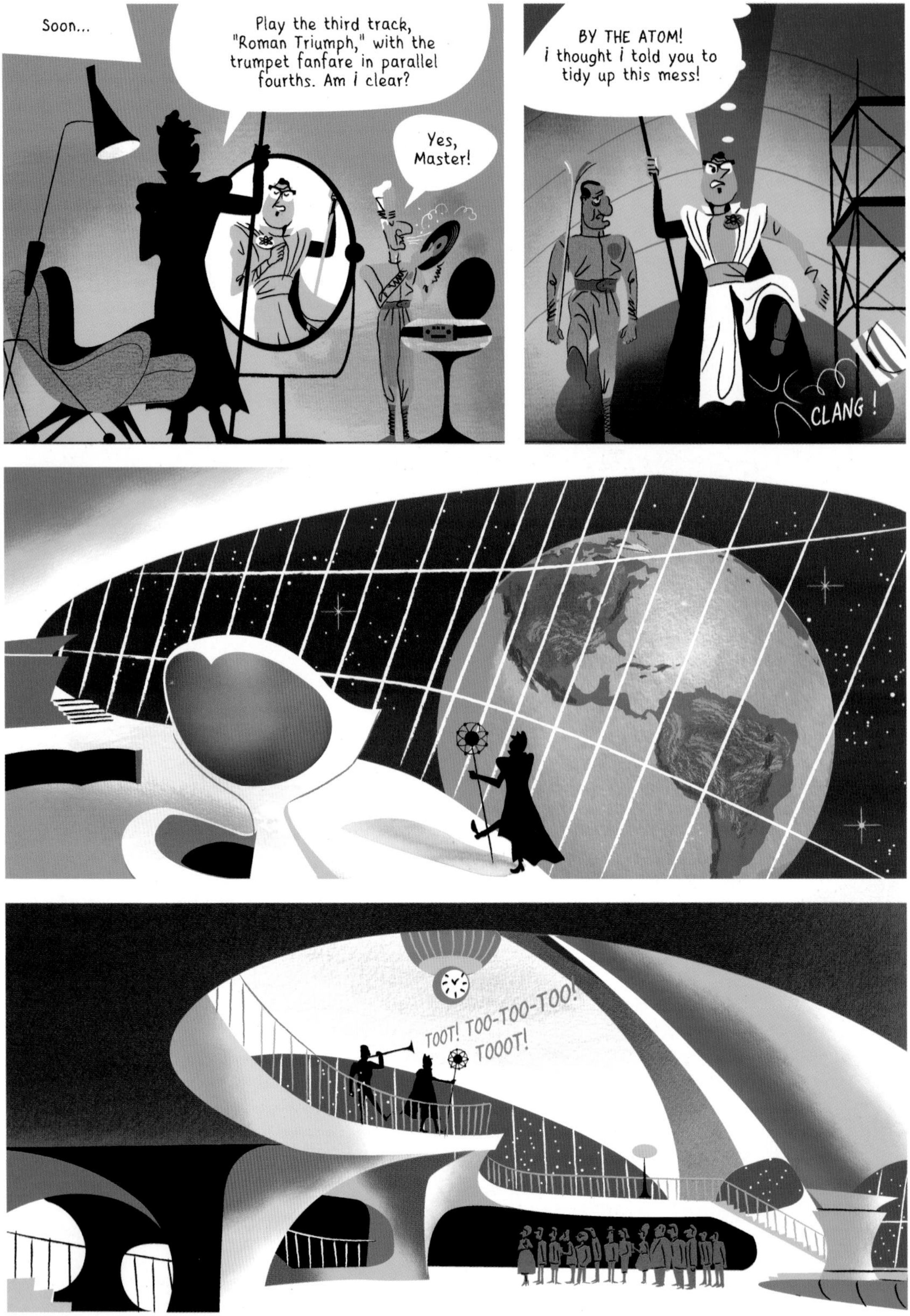
Soon...
Play the third track, "Roman Triumph," with the trumpet fanfare in parallel fourths. Am i clear?
Yes, Master!
BY THE ATOM! i thought i told you to tidy up this mess!
CLANG!
TOOT! TOO-TOO-TOO! TOOOT!

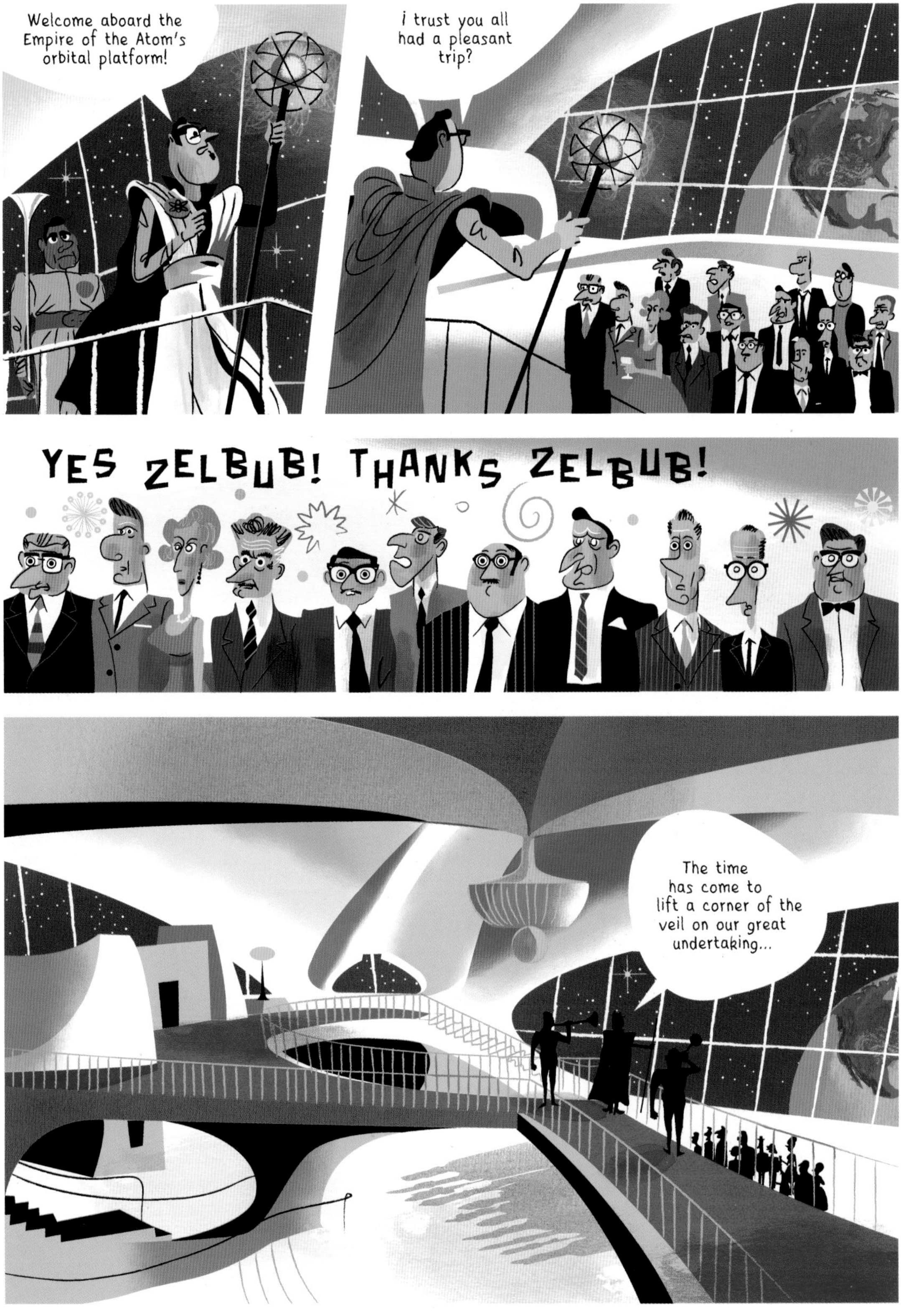
Welcome aboard the Empire of the Atom's orbital platform!
I trust you all had a pleasant trip?
YES ZELBUB! THANKS ZELBUB!
The time has come to lift a corner of the veil on our great undertaking...

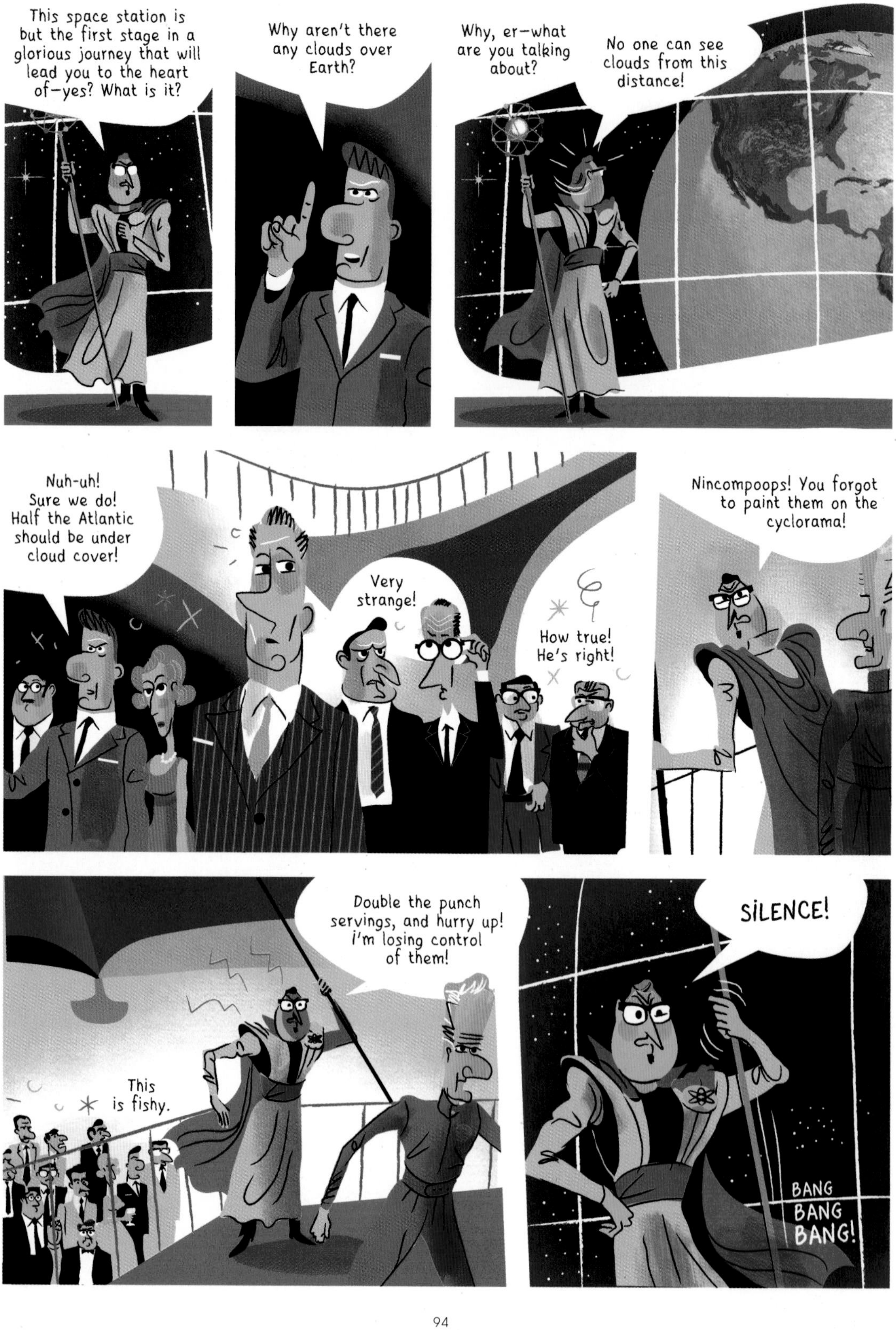

This space station is but the first stage in a glorious journey that will lead you to the heart of—yes? What is it?
Why aren't there any clouds over Earth?
Why, er—what are you talking about?
No one can see clouds from this distance!
Nuh-uh! Sure we do! Half the Atlantic should be under cloud cover!
Very strange!
How true! He's right!
Nincompoops! You forgot to paint them on the cyclorama!
Double the punch servings, and hurry up! i'm losing control of them!
This is fishy.
SiLENCE!
BANG
BANG
BANG!

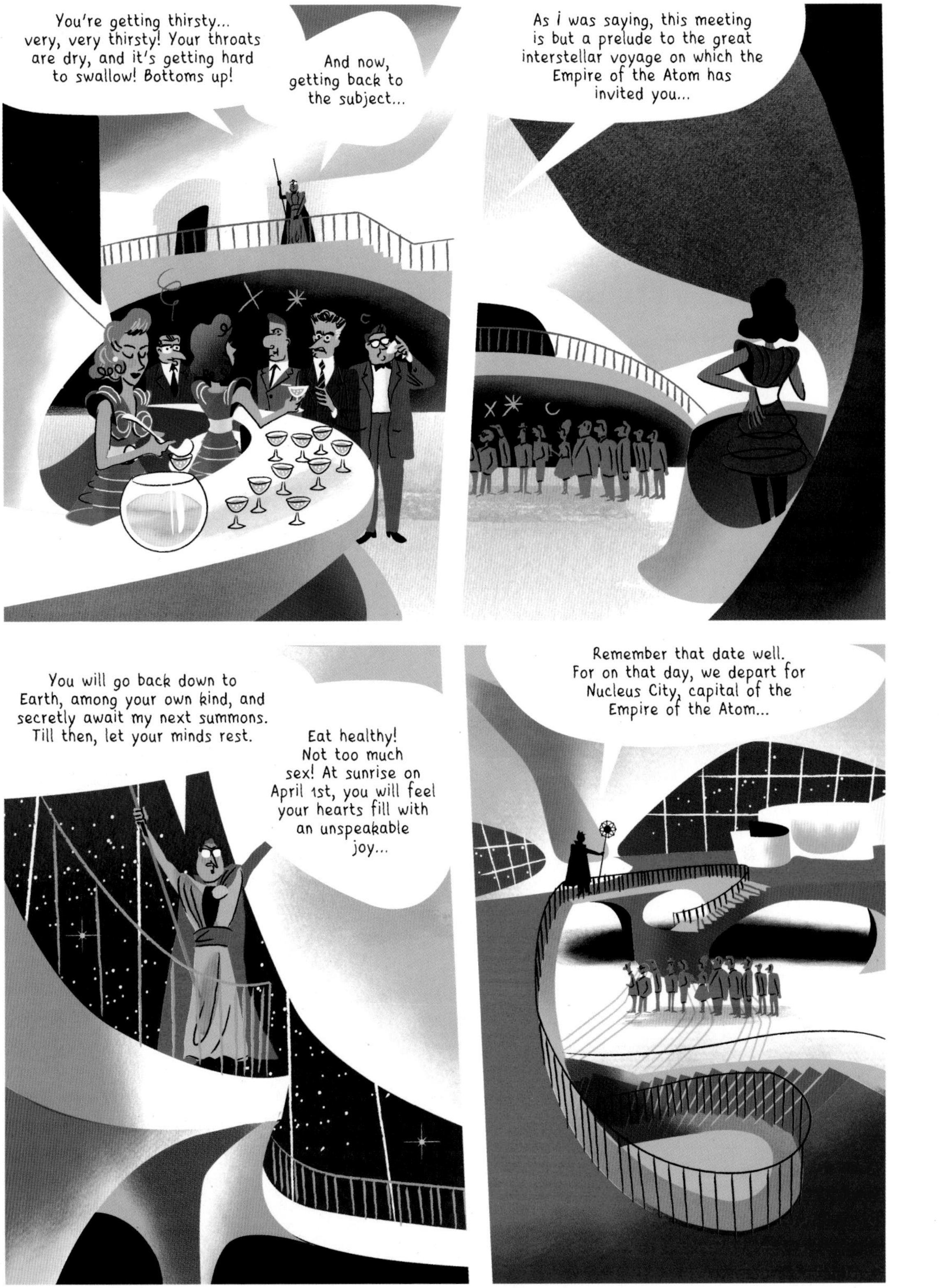
You're getting thirsty... very, very thirsty! Your throats are dry, and it's getting hard to swallow! Bottoms up!
And now, getting back to the subject...
As i was saying, this meeting is but a prelude to the great interstellar voyage on which the Empire of the Atom has invited you...
You will go back down to Earth, among your own kind, and secretly await my next summons. Till then, let your minds rest.
Eat healthy! Not too much sex! At sunrise on April 1st, you will feel your hearts fill with an unspeakable joy...
Remember that date well. For on that day, we depart for Nucleus City, capital of the Empire of the Atom...

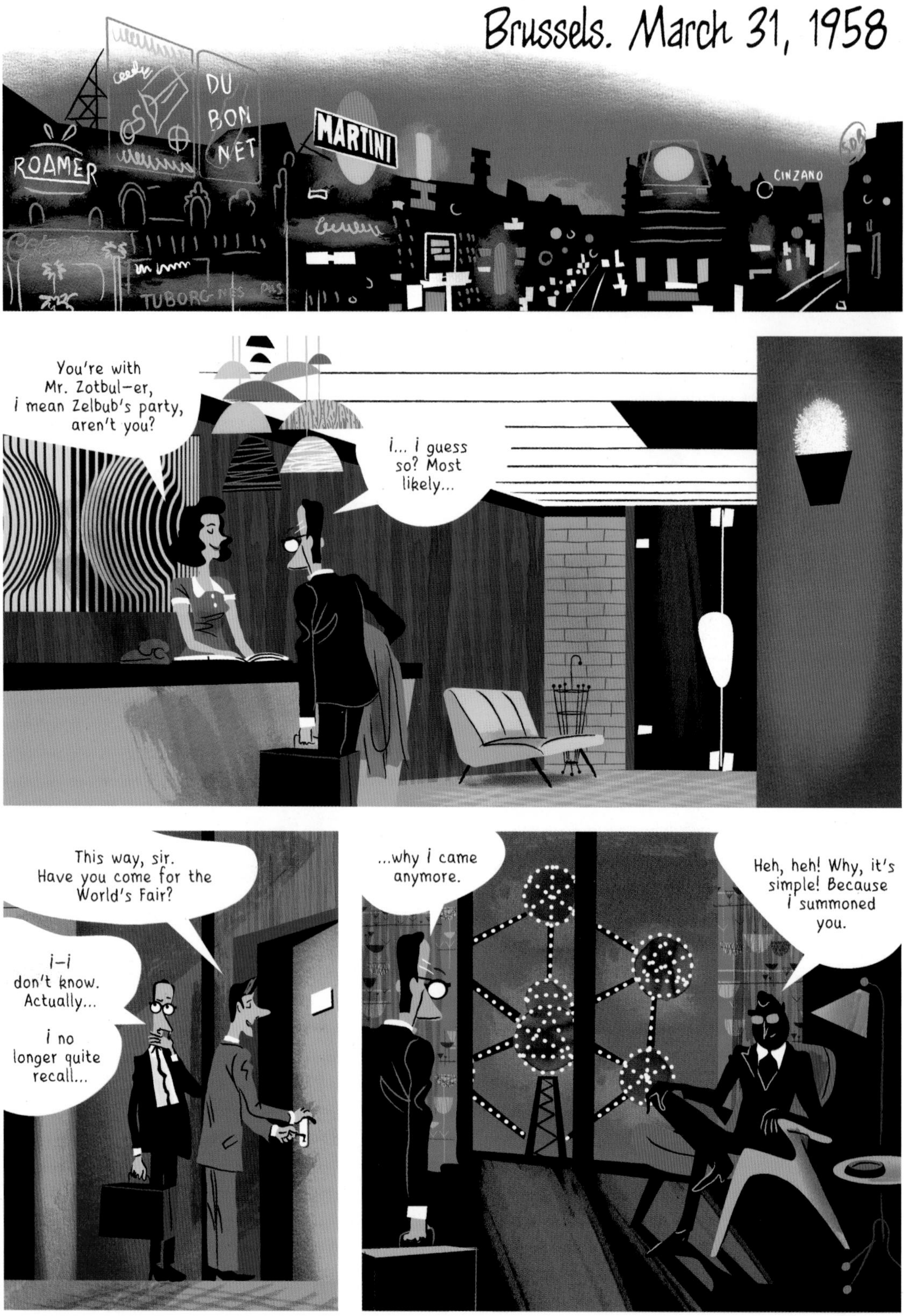
Brussels. March 31, 1958
ROAMER
DU BON NET
MARTINI
CINZANO
TUBORG
You're with Mr. Zotbul–er, i mean Zelbub's party, aren't you?
i... i guess so? Most likely...
This way, sir. Have you come for the World's Fair?
i–i don't know. Actually...
i no longer quite recall...
...why i came anymore.
Heh, heh! Why, it's simple! Because i summoned you.

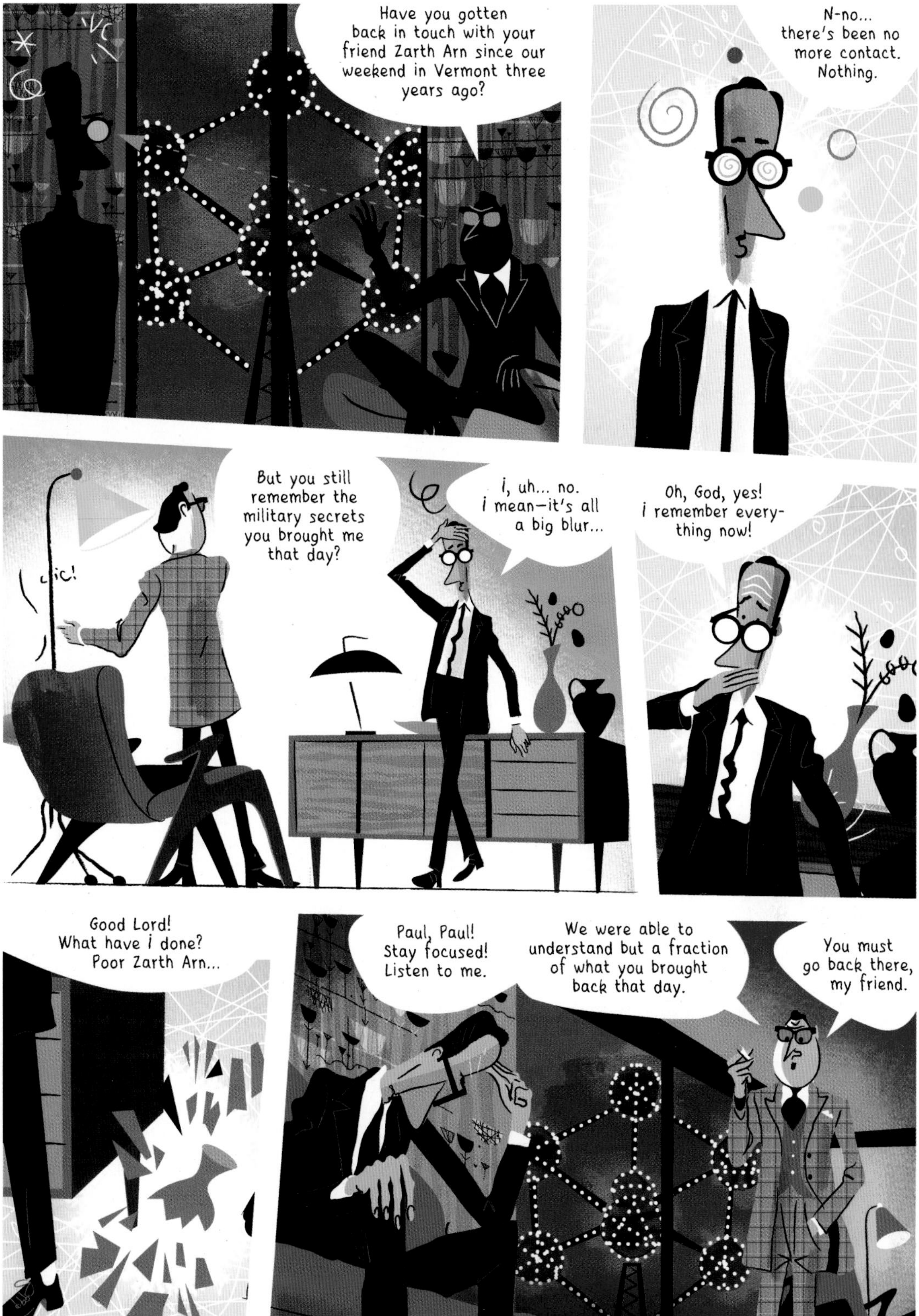
Have you gotten back in touch with your friend Zarth Arn since our weekend in Vermont three years ago?
N-no... there's been no more contact. Nothing.
clic!
But you still remember the military secrets you brought me that day?
i, uh... no. i mean—it's all a big blur...
Oh, God, yes! i remember everything now!
Good Lord! What have i done? Poor Zarth Arn...
Paul, Paul! Stay focused! Listen to me.
We were able to understand but a fraction of what you brought back that day.
You must go back there, my friend.

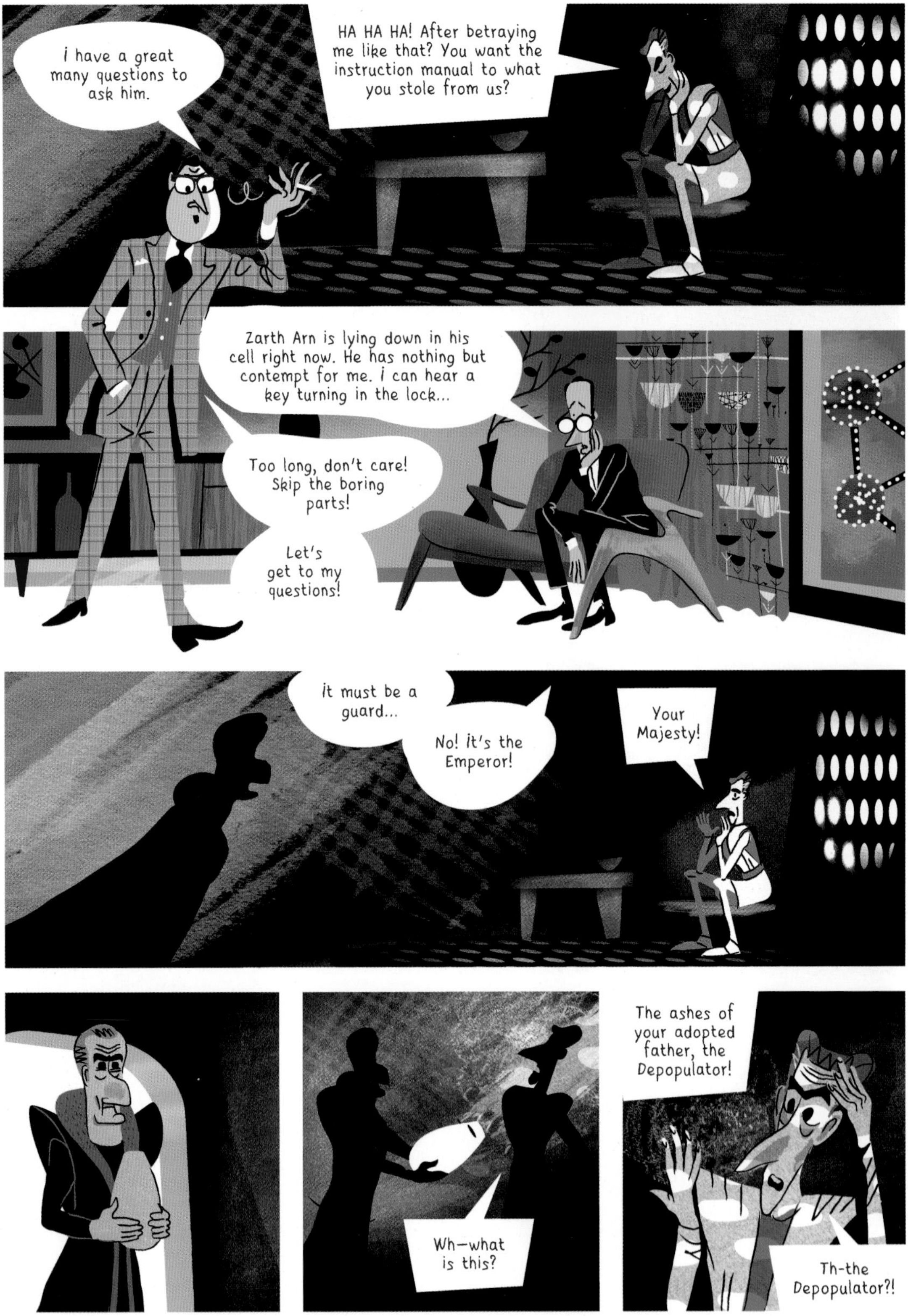

i have a great many questions to ask him.
HA HA HA! After betraying me like that? You want the instruction manual to what you stole from us?
Zarth Arn is lying down in his cell right now. He has nothing but contempt for me. i can hear a key turning in the lock...
Too long, don't care! Skip the boring parts!
Let's get to my questions!
it must be a guard...
No! it's the Emperor!
Your Majesty!
Wh—what is this?
The ashes of your adopted father, the Depopulator!
Th-the Depopulator?!

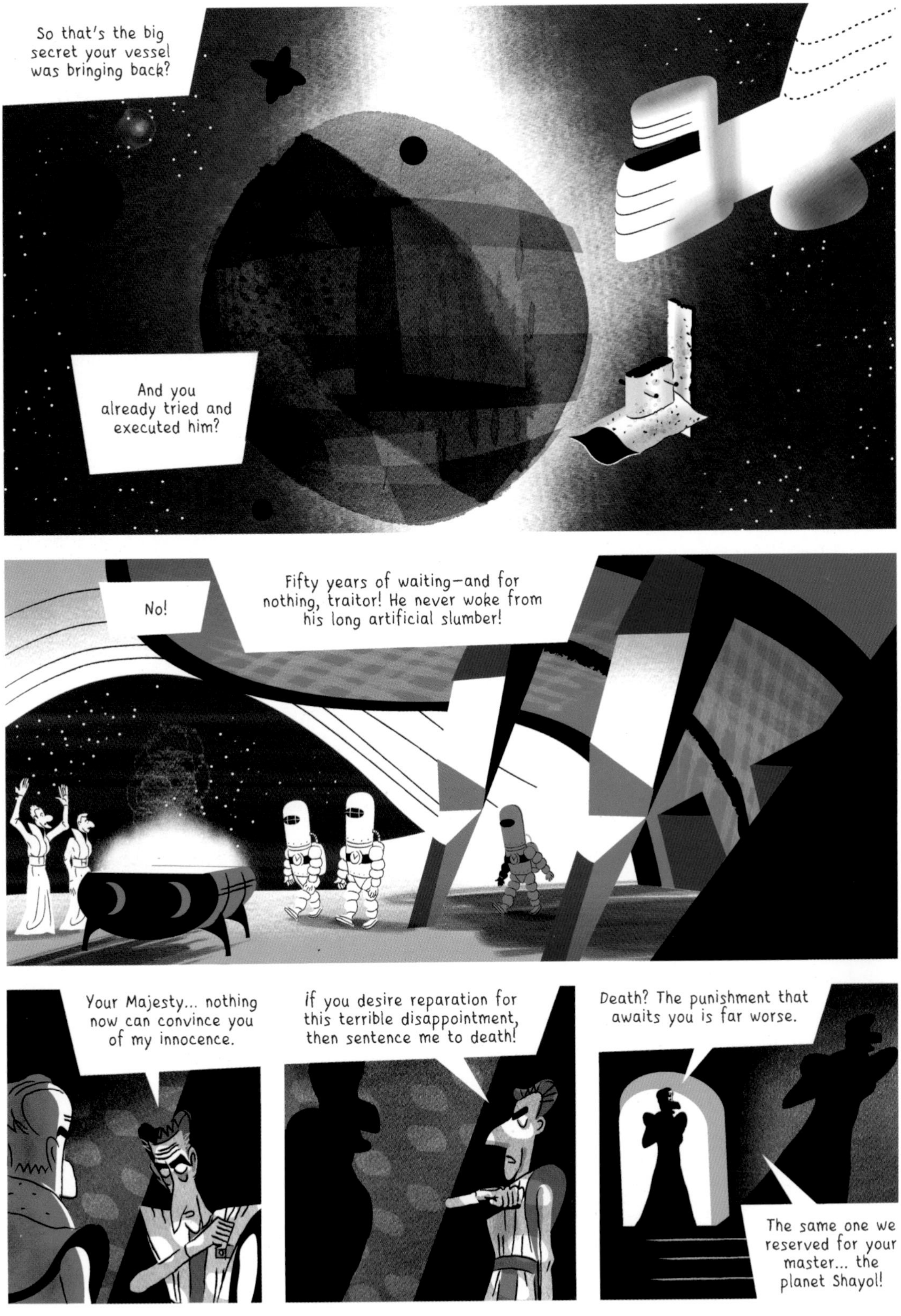
So that's the big secret your vessel was bringing back?
And you already tried and executed him?
No!
Fifty years of waiting—and for nothing, traitor! He never woke from his long artificial slumber!
Your Majesty... nothing now can convince you of my innocence.
If you desire reparation for this terrible disappointment, then sentence me to death!
Death? The punishment that awaits you is far worse.
The same one we reserved for your master... the planet Shayol!

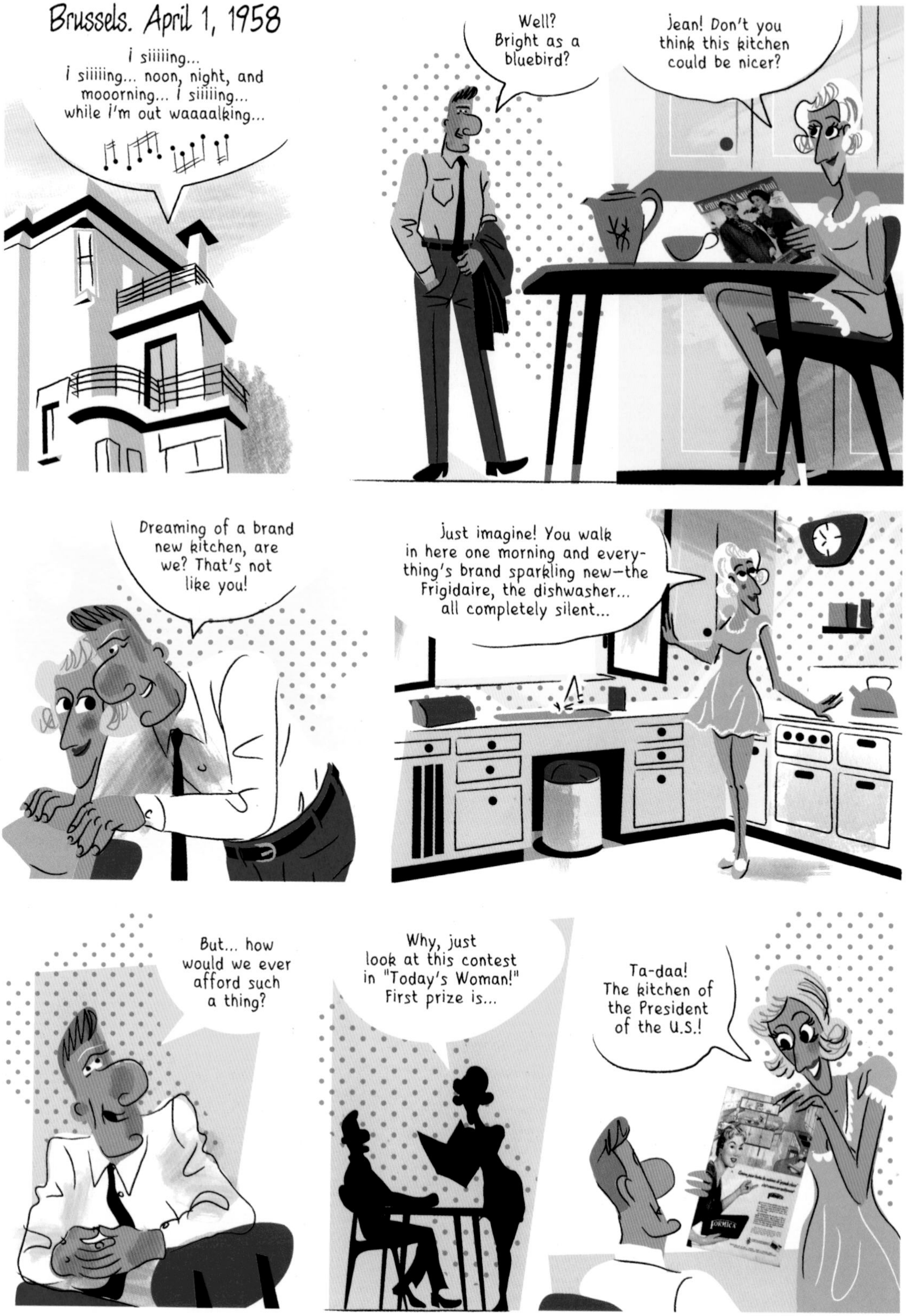
Brussels. April 1, 1958
I siiiiing... I siiiiing... noon, night, and mooorning... I siiiing... while I'm out waaaalking...
Well? Bright as a bluebird?
Jean! Don't you think this kitchen could be nicer?
Dreaming of a brand new kitchen, are we? That's not like you!
Just imagine! You walk in here one morning and every-thing's brand sparkling new—the Frigidaire, the dishwasher... all completely silent...
But... how would we ever afford such a thing?
Why, just look at this contest in "Today's Woman!" First prize is...
Ta-daa! The kitchen of the President of the U.S.!

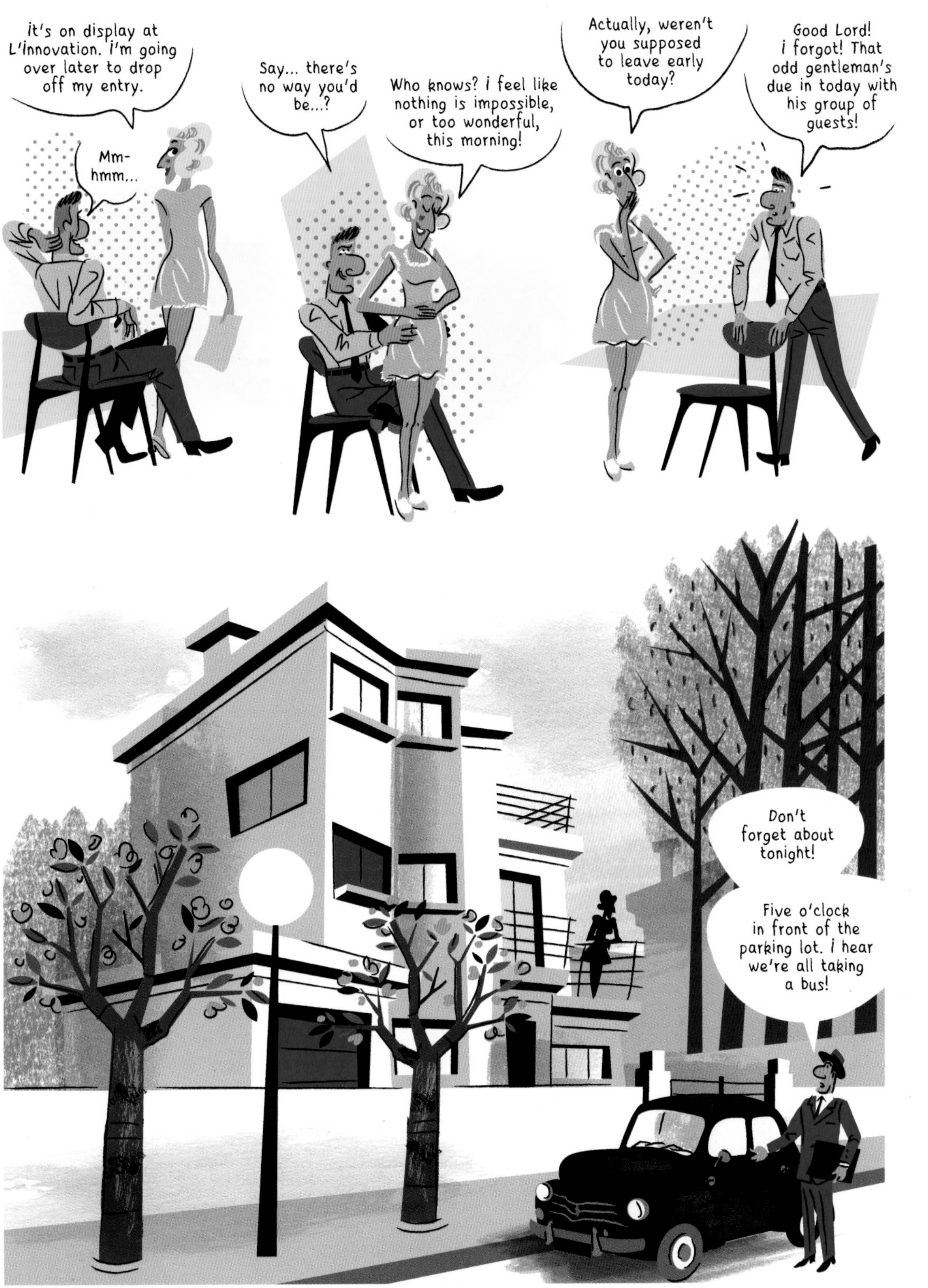
it's on display at L'innovation. i'm going over later to drop off my entry.
Mm-hmm...
Say... there's no way you'd be...?
Who knows? i feel like nothing is impossible, or too wonderful, this morning!
Actually, weren't you supposed to leave early today?
Good Lord! i forgot! That odd gentleman's due in today with his group of guests!
Don't forget about tonight!
Five o'clock in front of the parking lot. i hear we're all taking a bus!

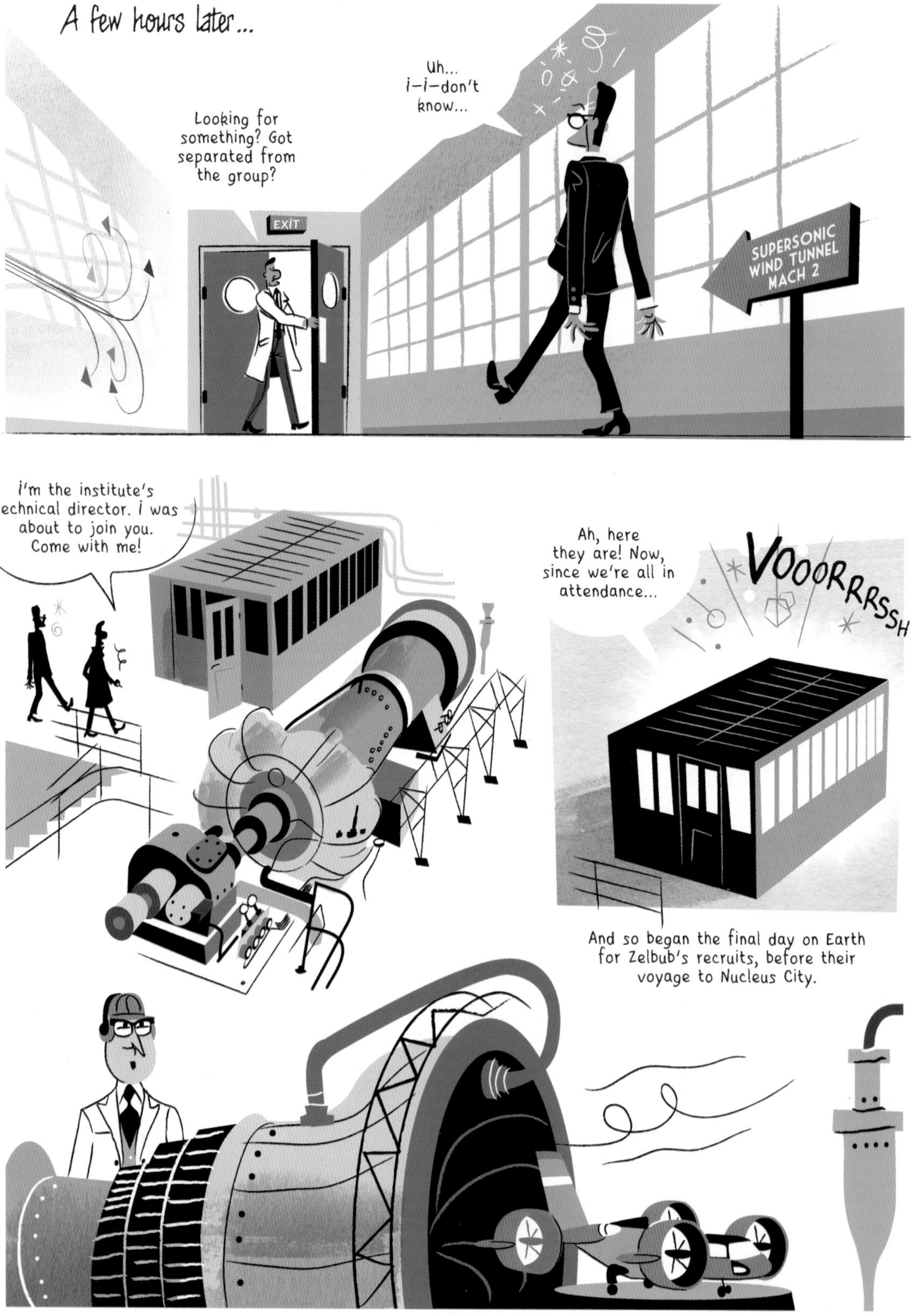
A few hours later...
Looking for something? Got separated from the group?
Uh... i-i-don't know...
EXIT
SUPERSONIC WIND TUNNEL MACH 2
i'm the institute's technical director. i was about to join you. Come with me!
Ah, here they are! Now, since we're all in attendance...
VOOORRRSSH
And so began the final day on Earth for Zelbub's recruits, before their voyage to Nucleus City.

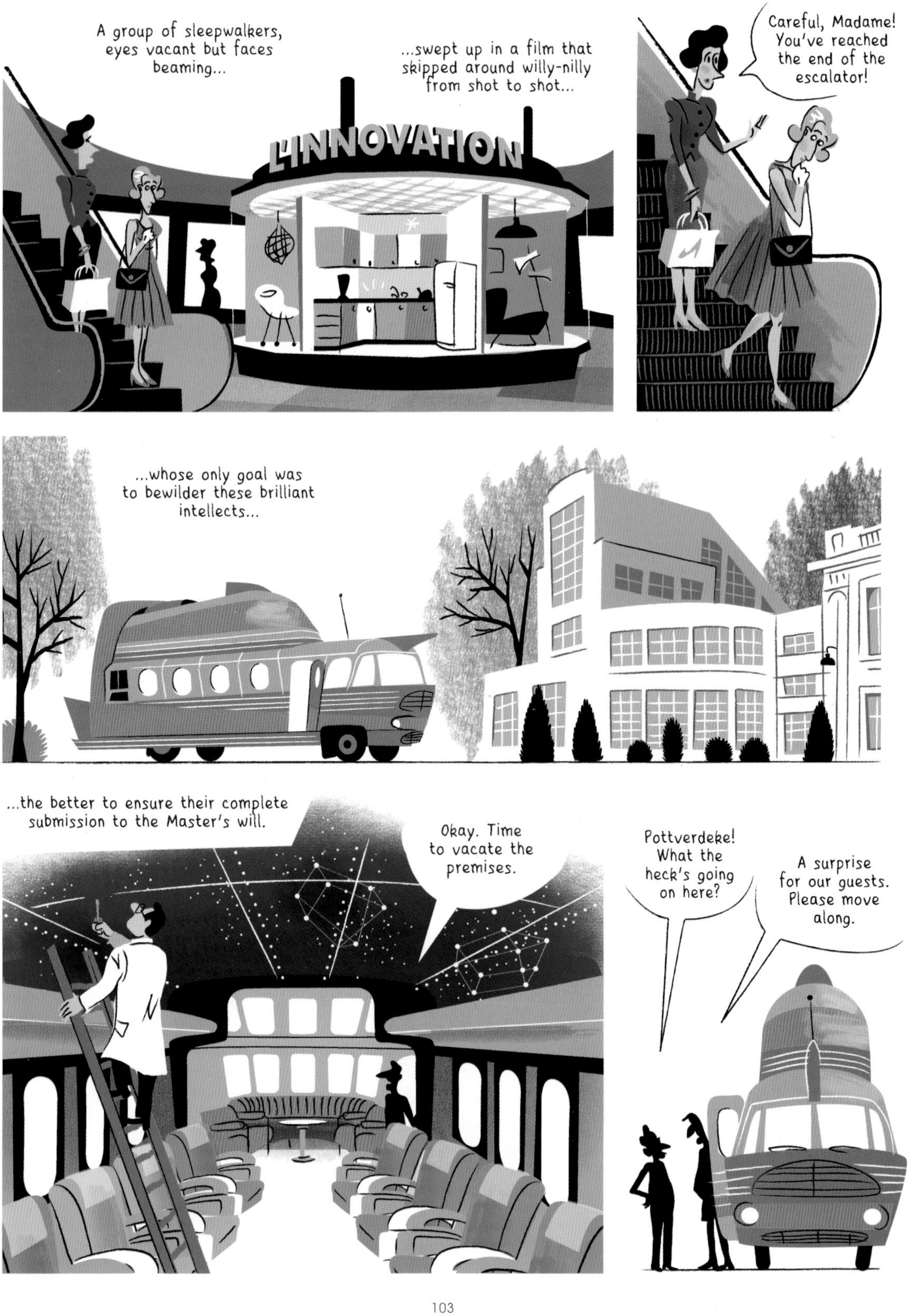
A group of sleepwalkers, eyes vacant but faces beaming...
...swept up in a film that skipped around willy-nilly from shot to shot...
L'INNOVATION
Careful, Madame! You've reached the end of the escalator!
...whose only goal was to bewilder these brilliant intellects...
...the better to ensure their complete submission to the Master's will.
Okay. Time to vacate the premises.
Pottverdeke! What the heck's going on here?
A surprise for our guests. Please move along.

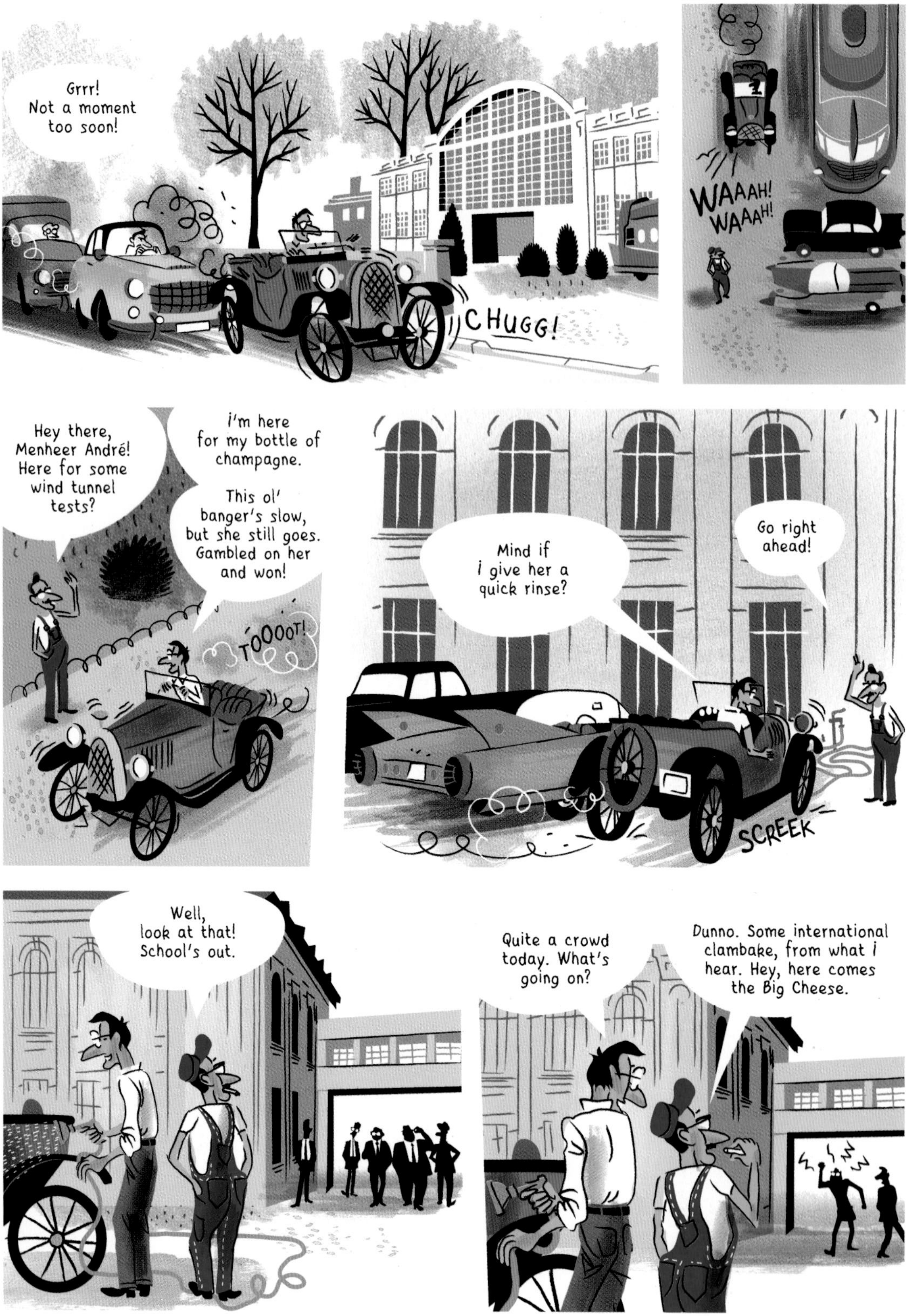
Grrr! Not a moment too soon!
CHUGG!
WAAAH! WAAAH!
Hey there, Menheer André! Here for some wind tunnel tests?
i'm here for my bottle of champagne.
This ol' banger's slow, but she still goes. Gambled on her and won!
TOOOOT!
Mind if i give her a quick rinse?
Go right ahead!
SCREEK
Well, look at that! School's out.
Quite a crowd today. What's going on?
Dunno. Some international clambake, from what i hear. Hey, here comes the Big Cheese.

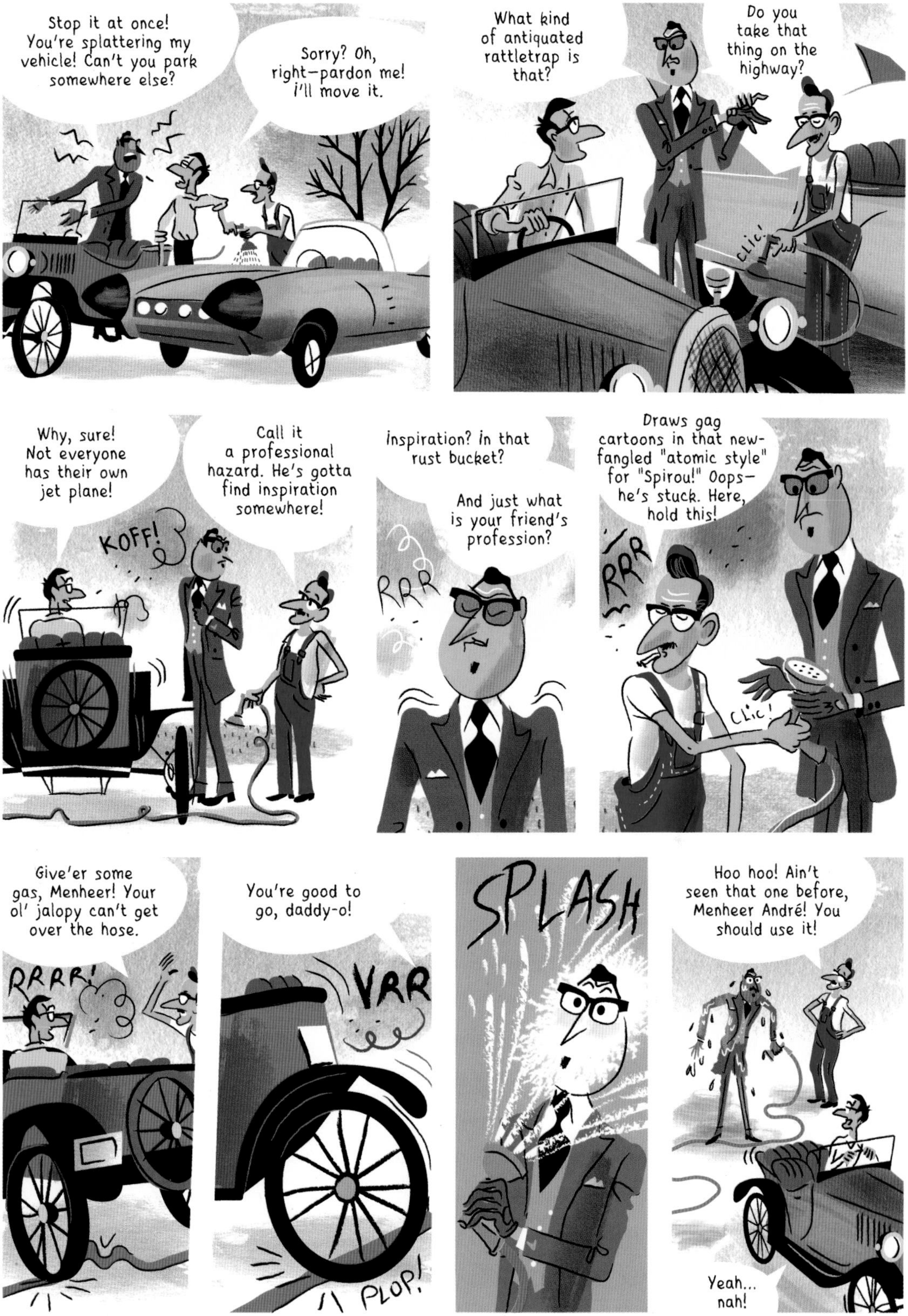
Stop it at once! You're splattering my vehicle! Can't you park somewhere else?
Sorry? Oh, right—pardon me! I'll move it.
What kind of antiquated rattletrap is that?
Do you take that thing on the highway?
CLIC!
Why, sure! Not everyone has their own jet plane!
Call it a professional hazard. He's gotta find inspiration somewhere!
KOFF!
Inspiration? In that rust bucket?
And just what is your friend's profession?
RRR
Draws gag cartoons in that new-fangled "atomic style" for "Spirou!" Oops—he's stuck. Here, hold this!
RRR
CLIC!
Give'er some gas, Menheer! Your ol' jalopy can't get over the hose.
RRRR!
You're good to go, daddy-o!
VRR
PLOP!
SPLASH
Hoo hoo! Ain't seen that one before, Menheer André! You should use it!
Yeah... nah!

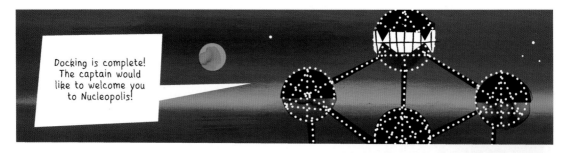

Docking is complete! The captain would like to welcome you to Nucleopolis!

In just a few minutes, the Empire of the Atom will be ready to receive you in the interstellar capital of peace and progress.

Oh my God! Look at that!

Extra-ordinary!

Nucleopolis? Have we really arrived?

You will be able to tour the administrative heart of the city and marvel at its ideals of science and technology.

And now, your attention, please!

Drink the punch in one gulp. It's the perfect cocktail of vitamins—you'll see!

ZZZZEEEP!

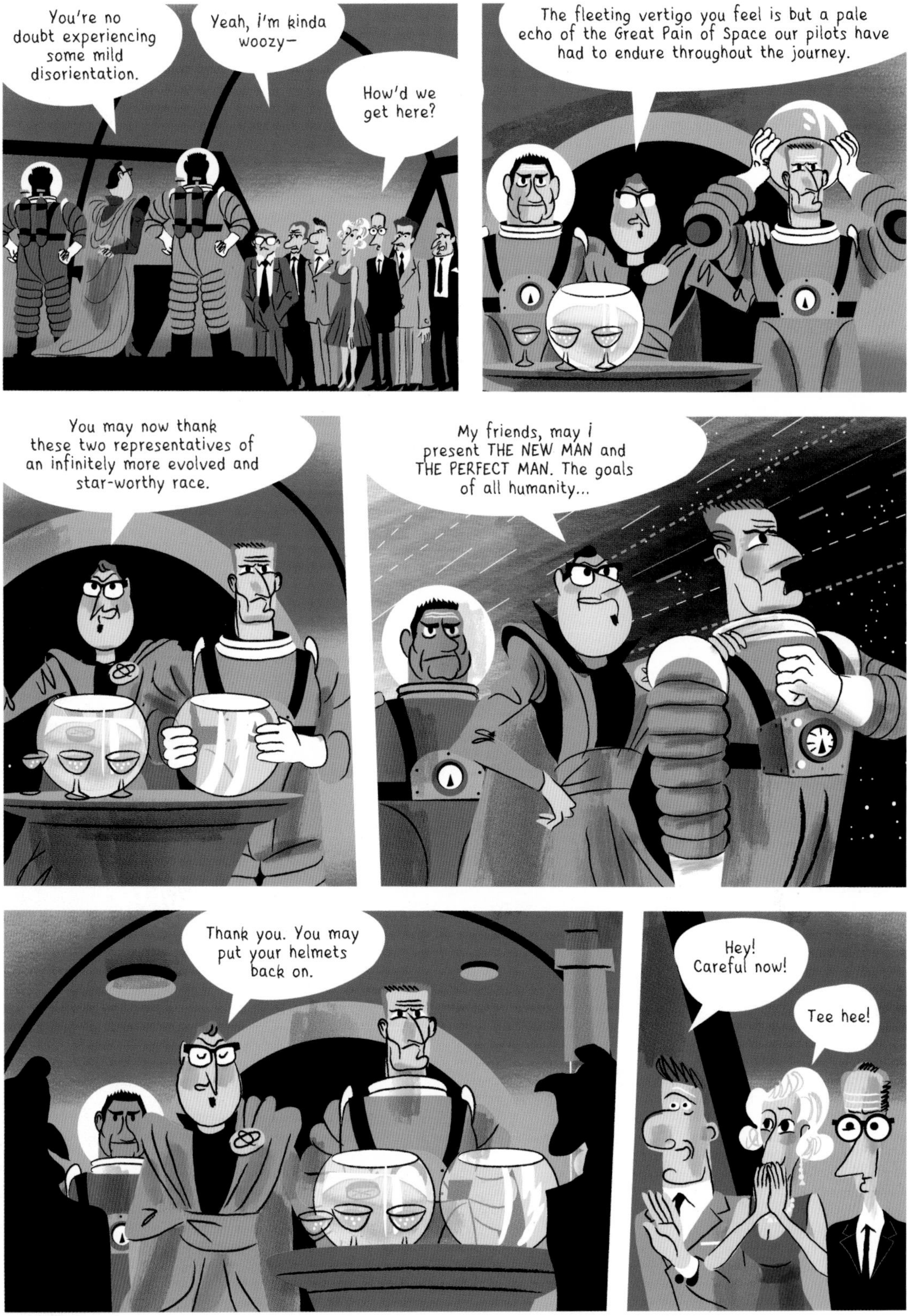

You're no doubt experiencing some mild disorientation.
Yeah, i'm kinda woozy–
How'd we get here?
The fleeting vertigo you feel is but a pale echo of the Great Pain of Space our pilots have had to endure throughout the journey.
You may now thank these two representatives of an infinitely more evolved and star-worthy race.
My friends, may i present THE NEW MAN and THE PERFECT MAN. The goals of all humanity...
Thank you. You may put your helmets back on.
Hey! Careful now!
Tee hee!

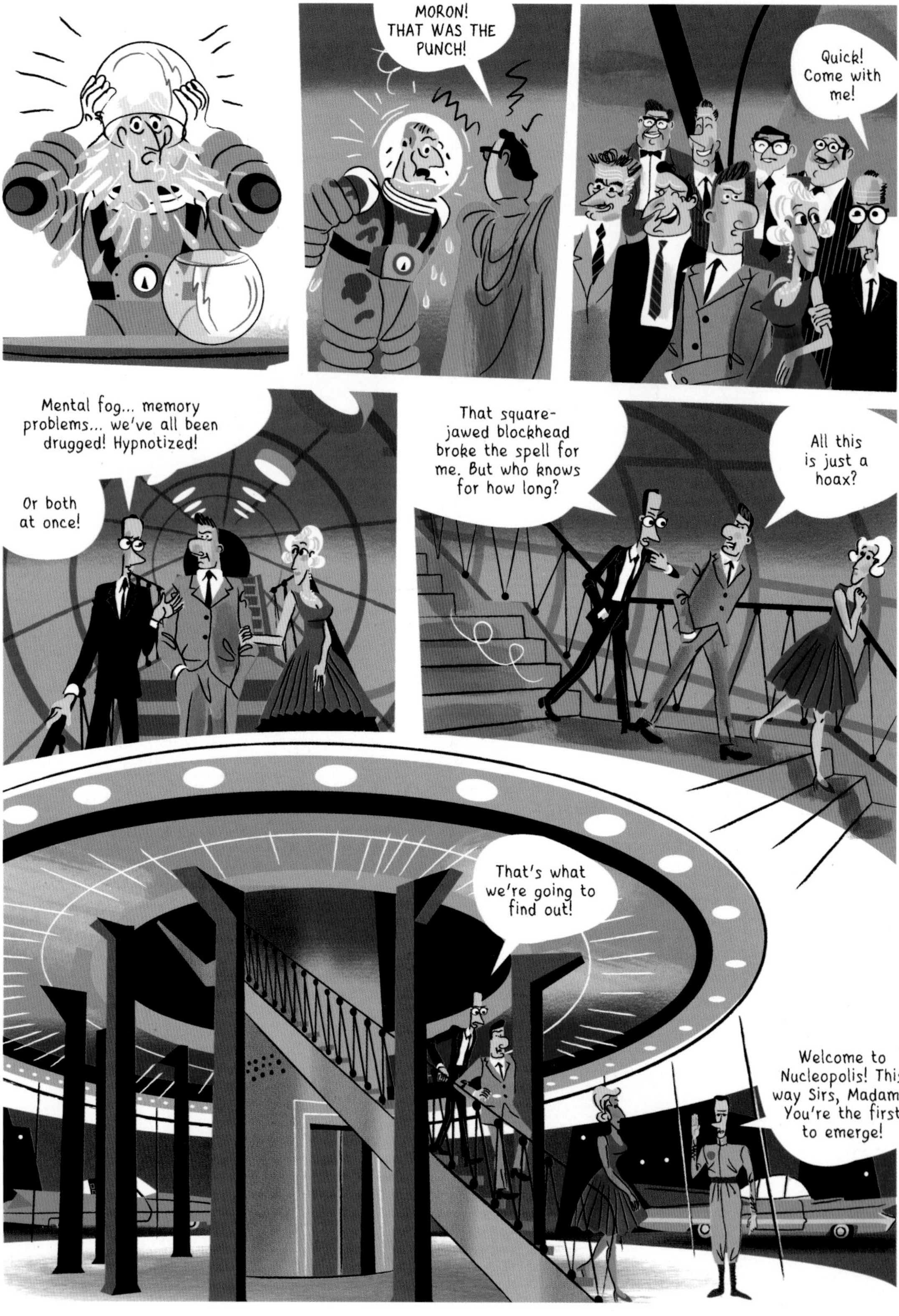
MORON! THAT WAS THE PUNCH!
Quick! Come with me!
Mental fog... memory problems... we've all been drugged! Hypnotized!
Or both at once!
That square-jawed blockhead broke the spell for me. But who knows for how long?
All this is just a hoax?
That's what we're going to find out!
Welcome to Nucleopolis! This way Sirs, Madame. You're the first to emerge!

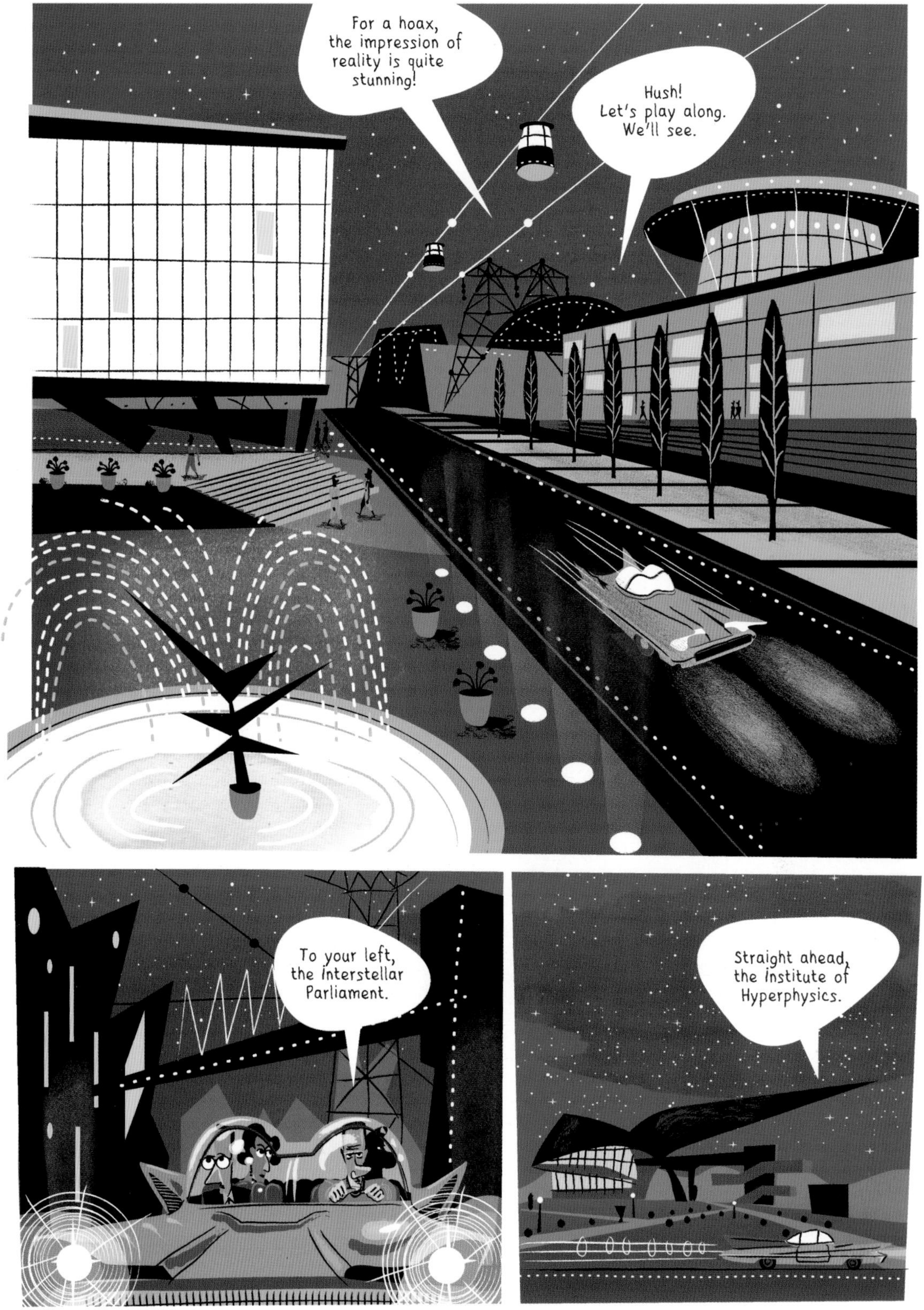
For a hoax, the impression of reality is quite stunning!
Hush! Let's play along. We'll see.
To your left, the Interstellar Parliament.
Straight ahead, the Institute of Hyperphysics.

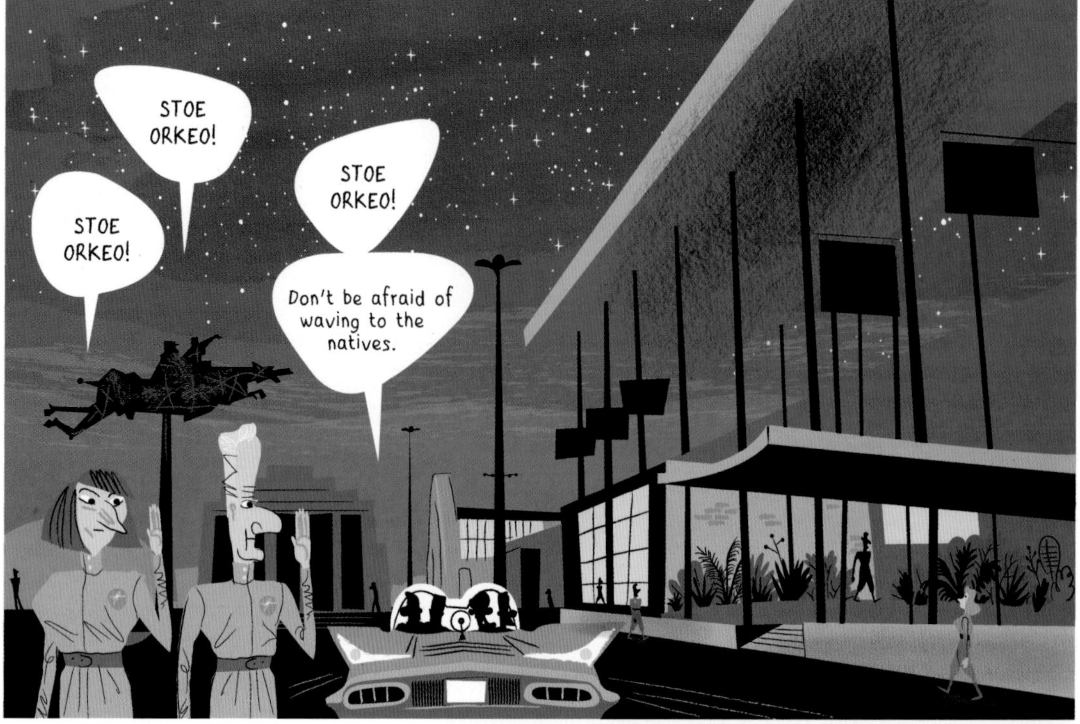
STOE ORKEO!
STOE ORKEO!
STOE ORKEO!
Don't be afraid of waving to the natives.

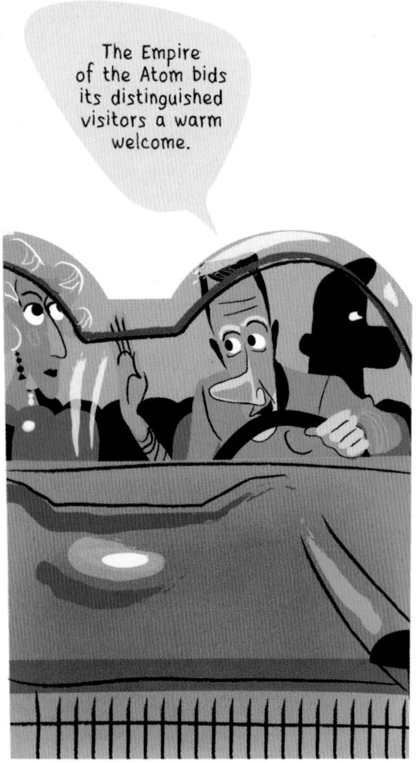
The Empire of the Atom bids its distinguished visitors a warm welcome.

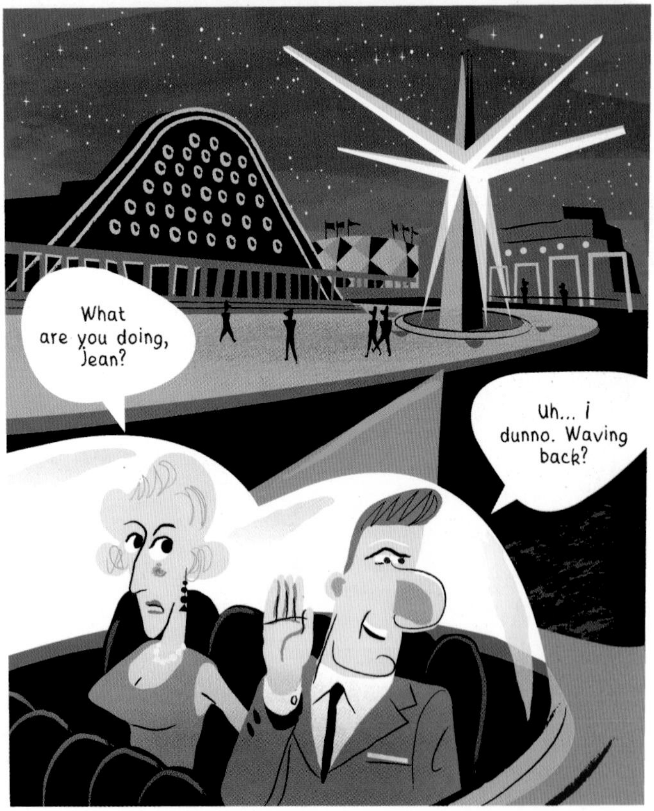
What are you doing, Jean?
Uh... I dunno. Waving back?

STOE ORKEO!
STOE ORKEO!
Who are all these people? And what is this city called?
Why—NUCLEUS CITY, naturally! And now our tour is coming to an end. We're back where we started.
The Temple to Lucretia, the beating atomic heart of the Empire of Zelb—
WATCH OUT!

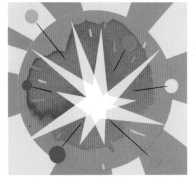

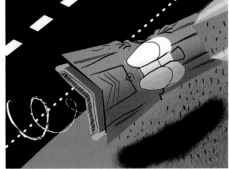

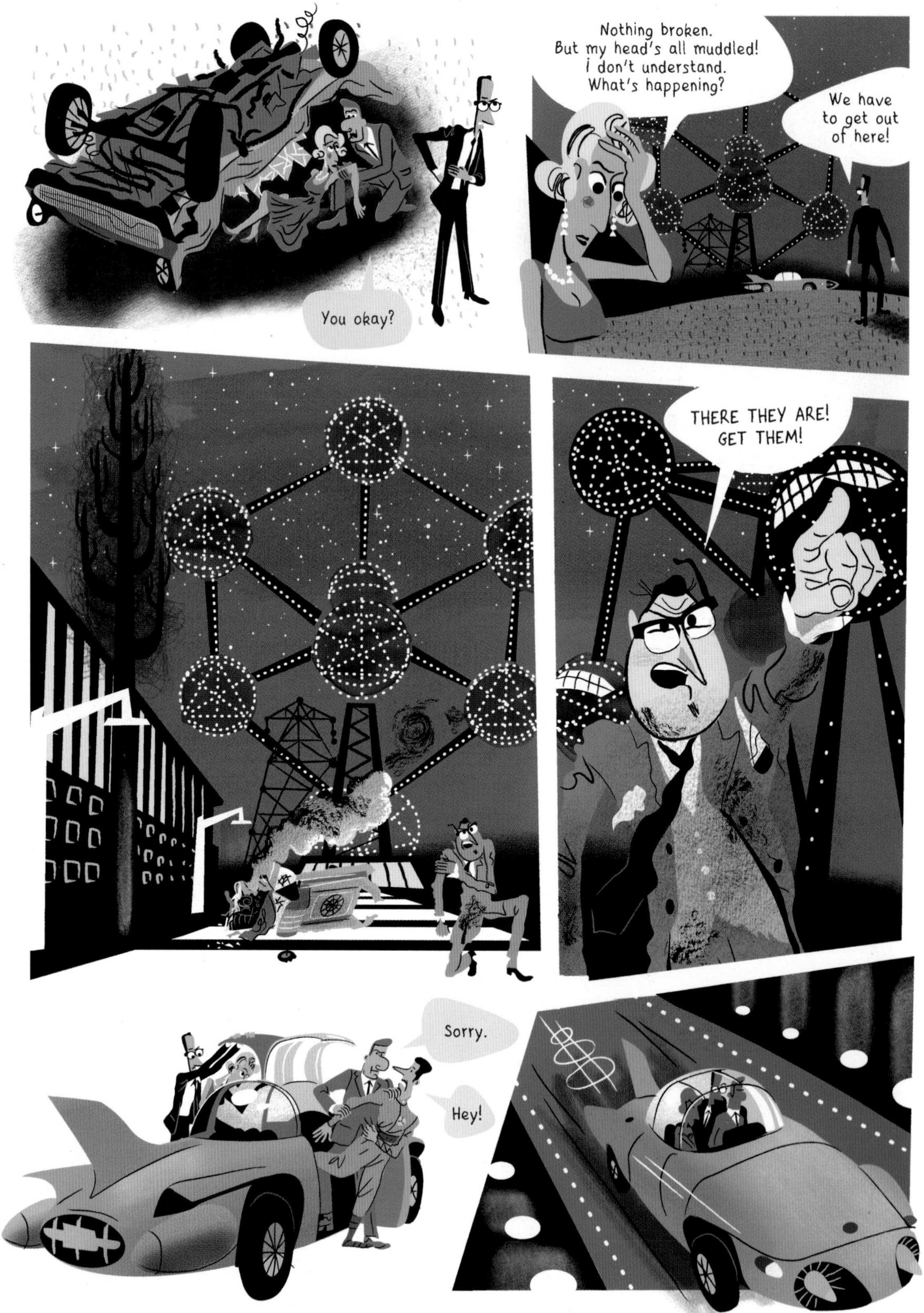
You okay?
Nothing broken. But my head's all muddled! I don't understand. What's happening?
We have to get out of here!
THERE THEY ARE! GET THEM!
Sorry.
Hey!

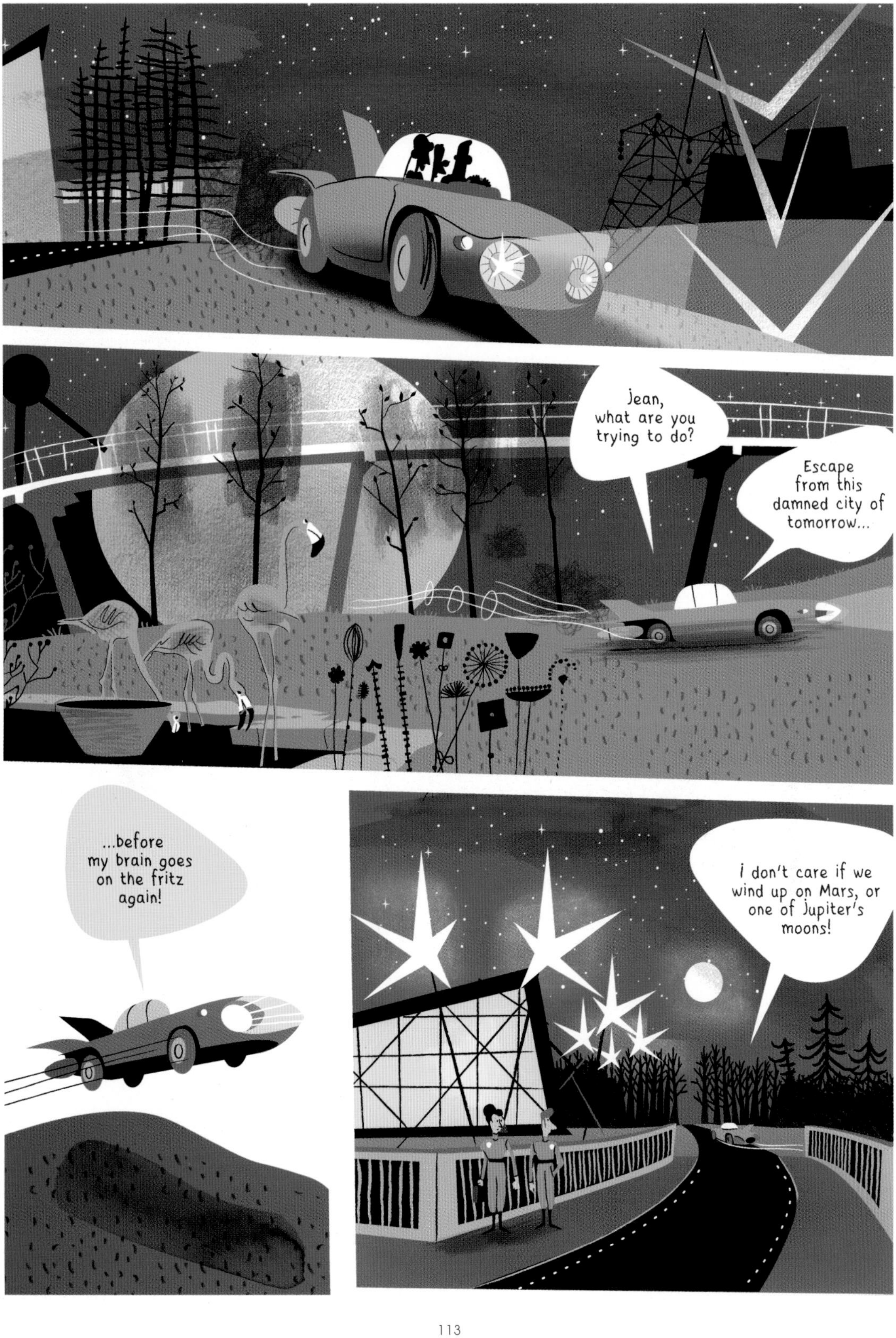

Jean, what are you trying to do?
Escape from this damned city of tomorrow...
...before my brain goes on the fritz again!
I don't care if we wind up on Mars, or one of Jupiter's moons!

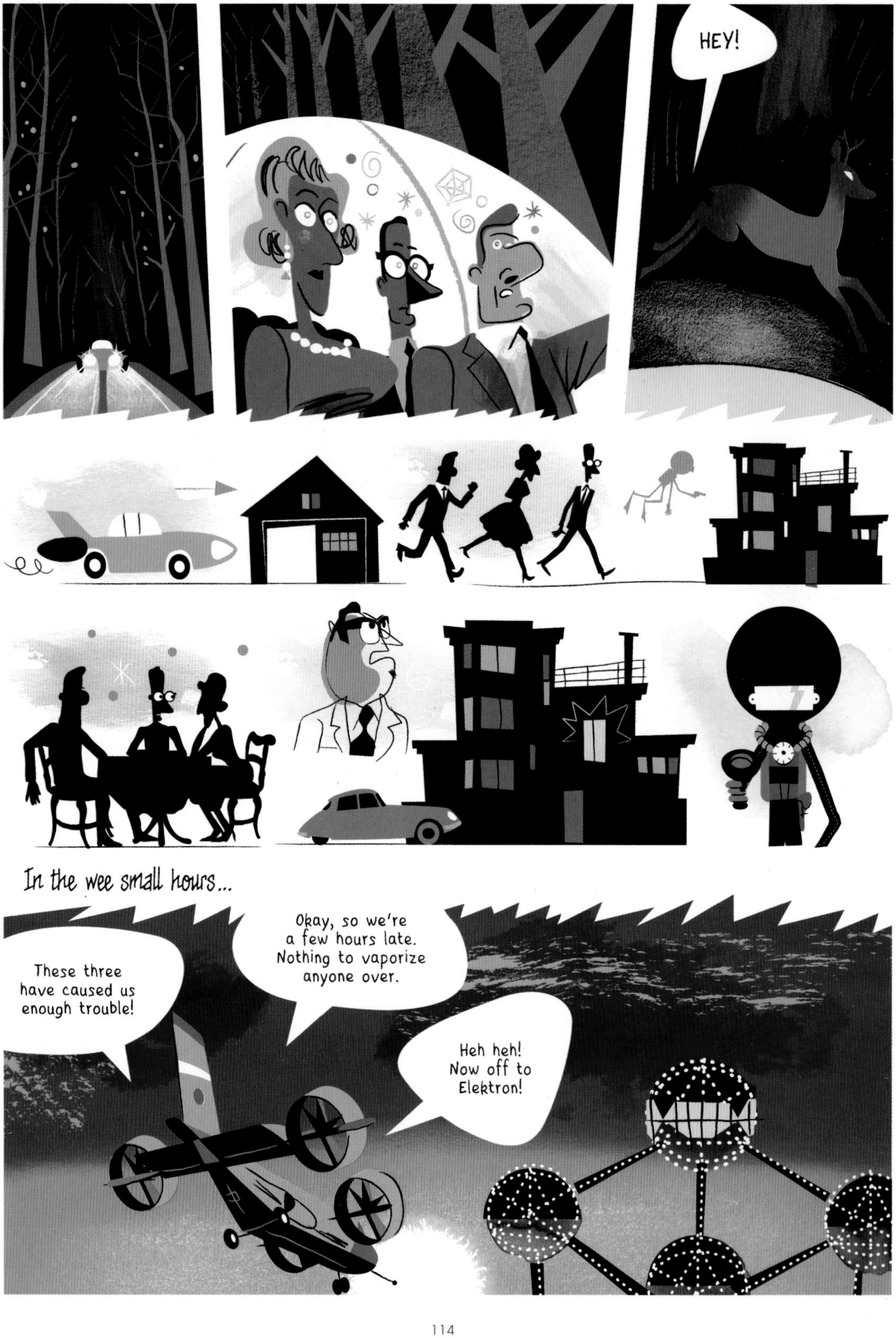
HEY!
In the wee small hours...
These three have caused us enough trouble!
Okay, so we're a few hours late. Nothing to vaporize anyone over.
Heh heh! Now off to Elektron!

chapter 5

THE PLANET SHAYOL

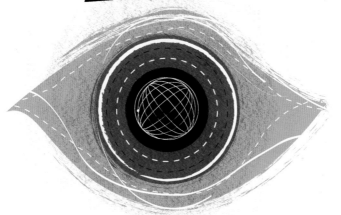

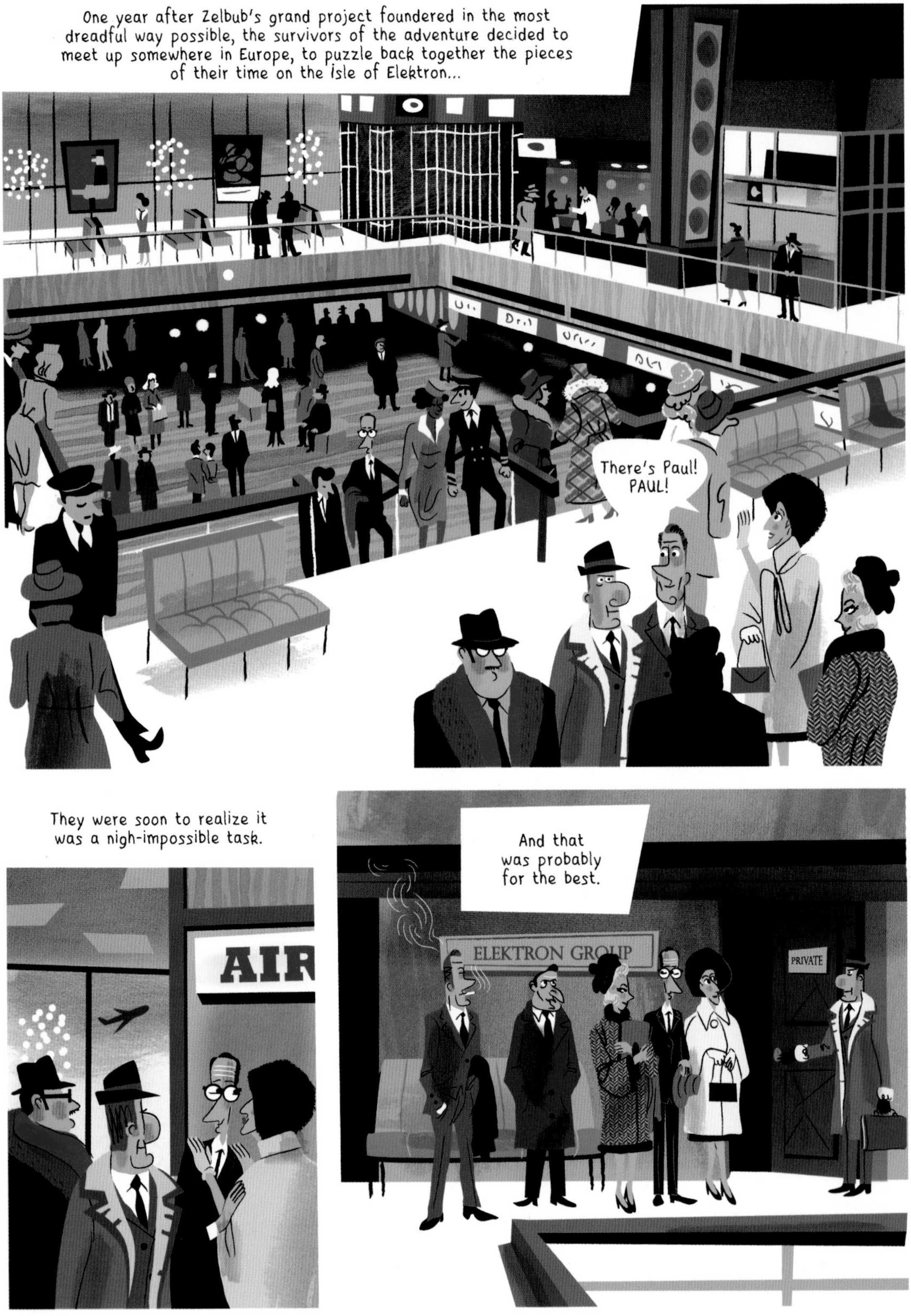
One year after Zelbub's grand project foundered in the most dreadful way possible, the survivors of the adventure decided to meet up somewhere in Europe, to puzzle back together the pieces of their time on the Isle of Elektron...
There's Paul! PAUL!
They were soon to realize it was a nigh-impossible task.
AIR
And that was probably for the best.
ELEKTRON GROUP
PRIVATE

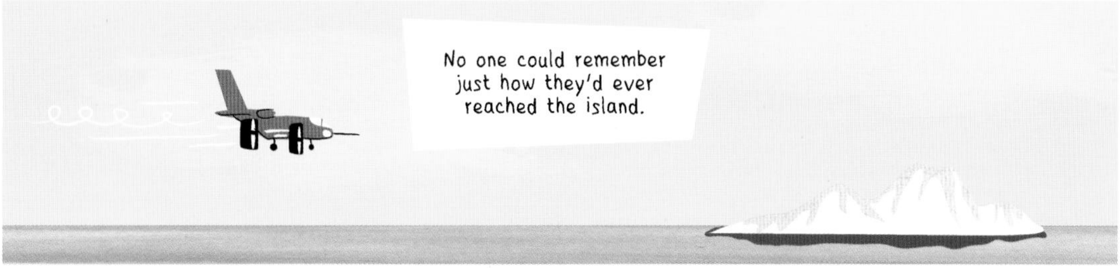
No one could remember
just how they'd ever
reached the island.

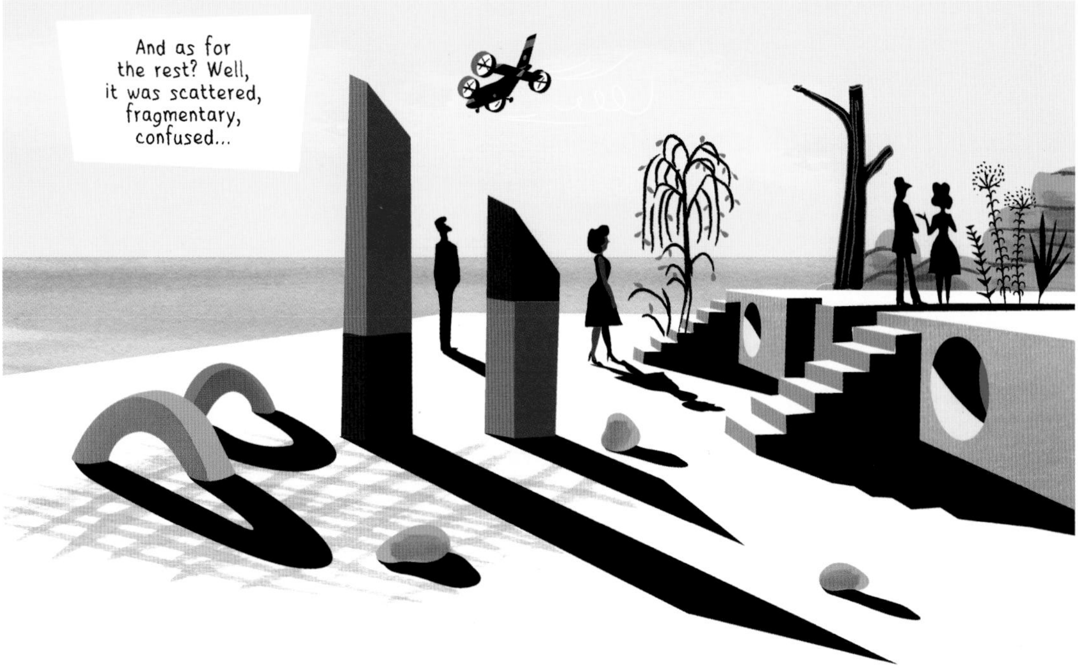
And as for
the rest? Well,
it was scattered,
fragmentary,
confused...

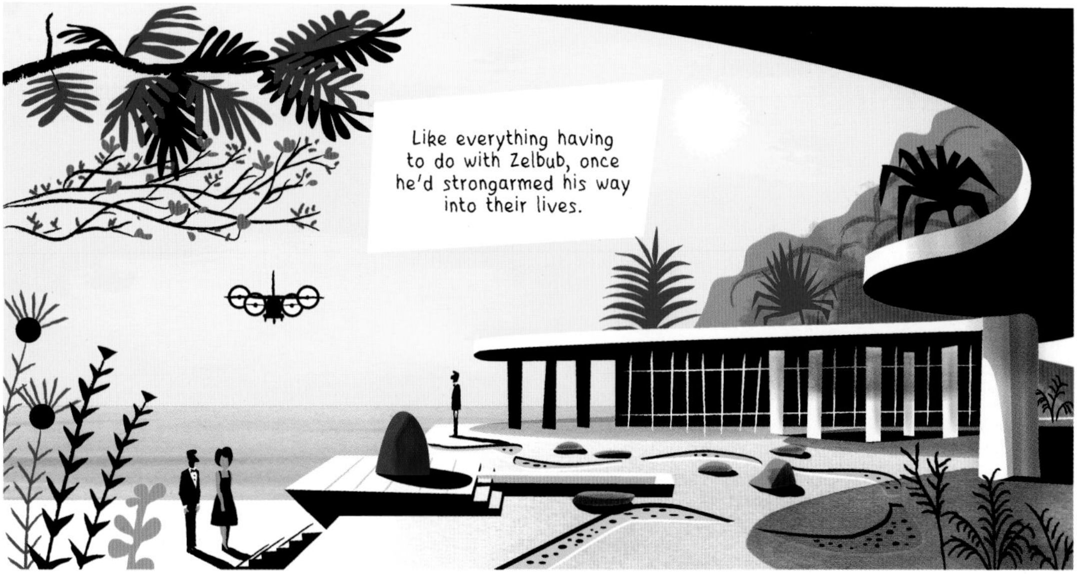
Like everything having
to do with Zelbub, once
he'd strongarmed his way
into their lives.

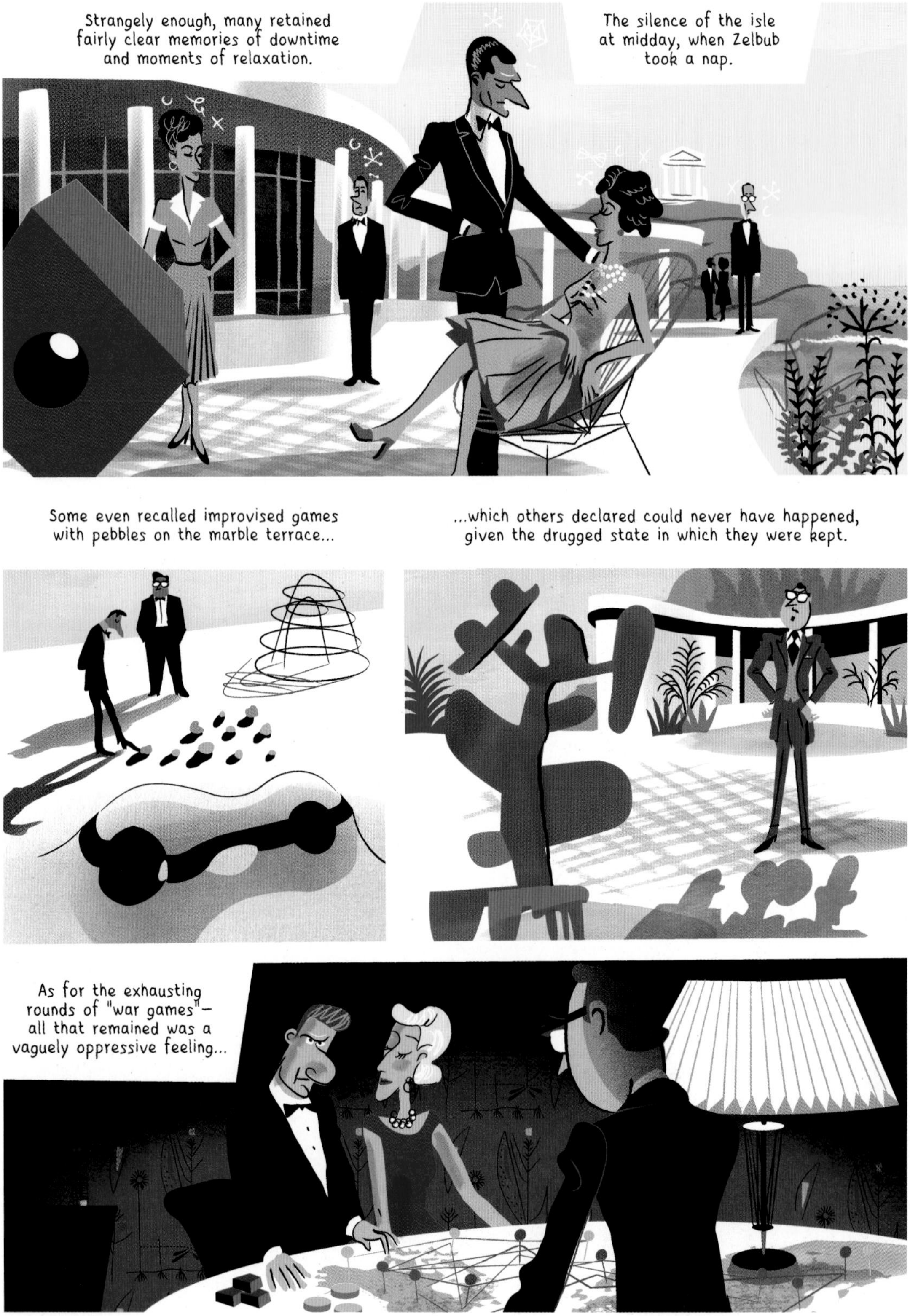
Strangely enough, many retained fairly clear memories of downtime and moments of relaxation.
The silence of the isle at midday, when Zelbub took a nap.
Some even recalled improvised games with pebbles on the marble terrace...
...which others declared could never have happened, given the drugged state in which they were kept.
As for the exhausting rounds of "war games"— all that remained was a vaguely oppressive feeling...

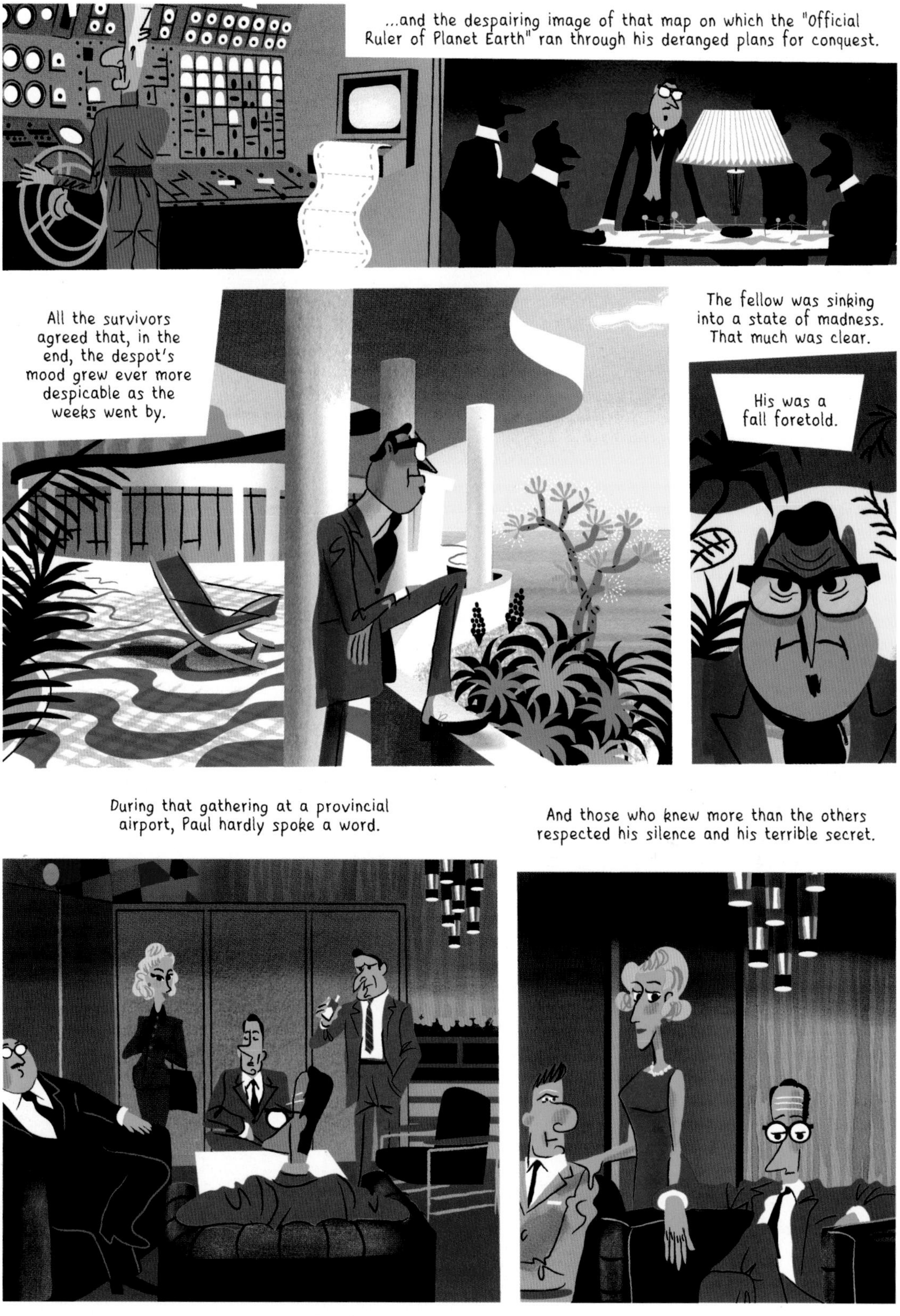
...and the despairing image of that map on which the "Official Ruler of Planet Earth" ran through his deranged plans for conquest.
All the survivors agreed that, in the end, the despot's mood grew ever more despicable as the weeks went by.
The fellow was sinking into a state of madness. That much was clear.
His was a fall foretold.
During that gathering at a provincial airport, Paul hardly spoke a word.
And those who knew more than the others respected his silence and his terrible secret.

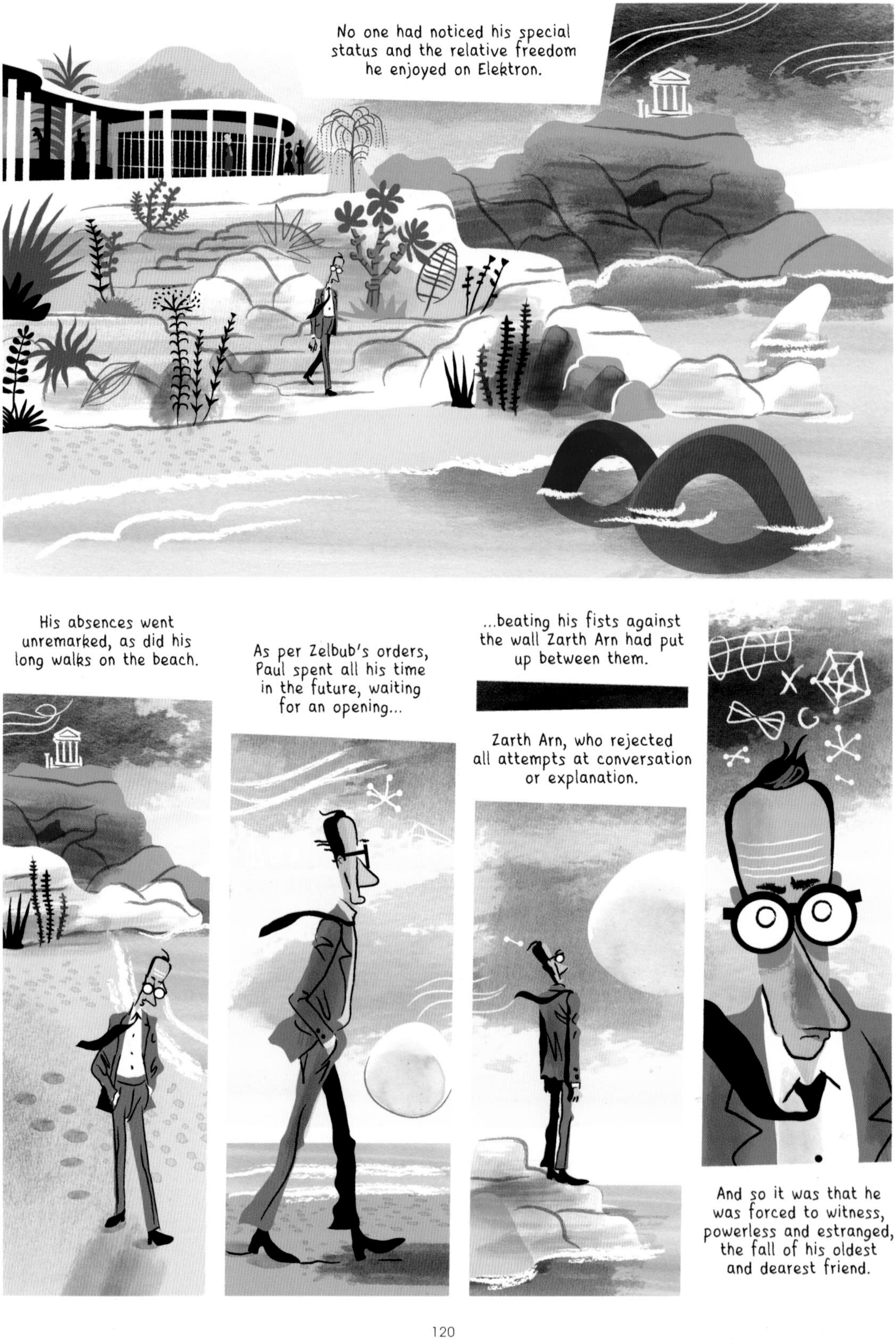
No one had noticed his special status and the relative freedom he enjoyed on Elektron.
His absences went unremarked, as did his long walks on the beach.
As per Zelbub's orders, Paul spent all his time in the future, waiting for an opening...
...beating his fists against the wall Zarth Arn had put up between them.
Zarth Arn, who rejected all attempts at conversation or explanation.
And so it was that he was forced to witness, powerless and estranged, the fall of his oldest and dearest friend.

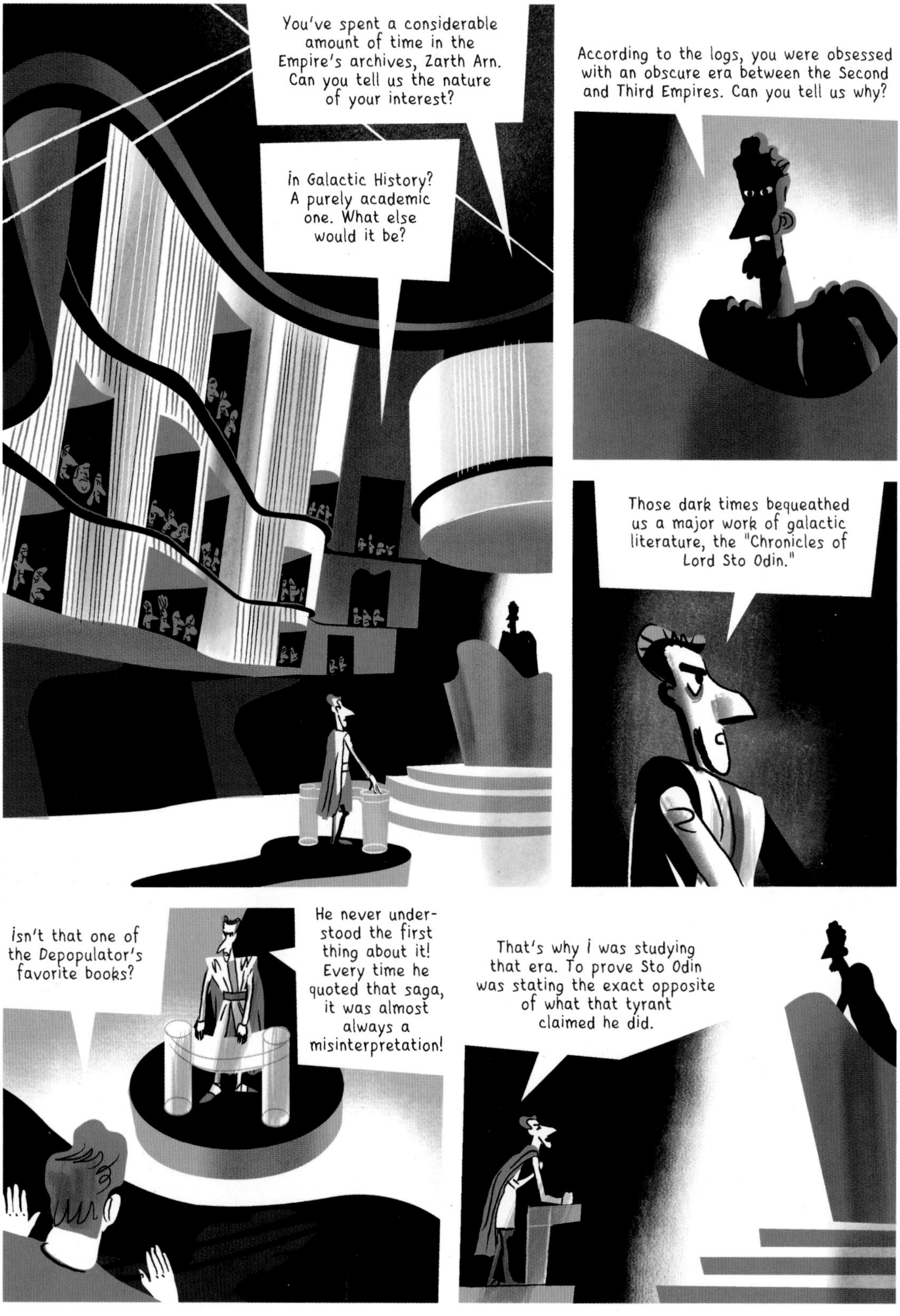
You've spent a considerable amount of time in the Empire's archives, Zarth Arn. Can you tell us the nature of your interest?
in Galactic History? A purely academic one. What else would it be?
According to the logs, you were obsessed with an obscure era between the Second and Third Empires. Can you tell us why?
Those dark times bequeathed us a major work of galactic literature, the "Chronicles of Lord Sto Odin."
isn't that one of the Depopulator's favorite books?
He never understood the first thing about it! Every time he quoted that saga, it was almost always a misinterpretation!
That's why i was studying that era. To prove Sto Odin was stating the exact opposite of what that tyrant claimed he did.

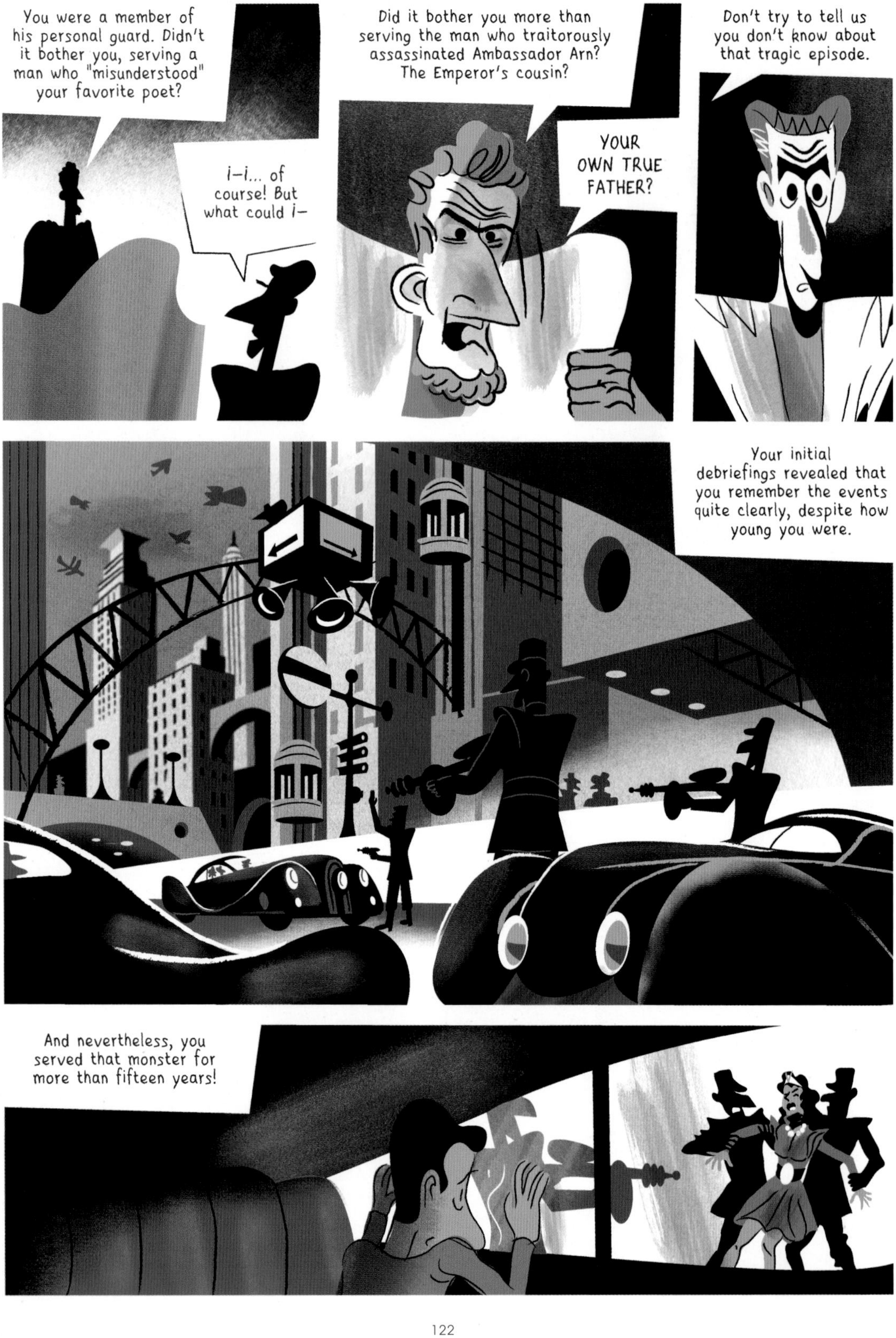
You were a member of his personal guard. Didn't it bother you, serving a man who "misunderstood" your favorite poet?
I-I... of course! But what could I-
Did it bother you more than serving the man who traitorously assassinated Ambassador Arn? The Emperor's cousin?
YOUR OWN TRUE FATHER?
Don't try to tell us you don't know about that tragic episode.
Your initial debriefings revealed that you remember the events quite clearly, despite how young you were.
And nevertheless, you served that monster for more than fifteen years!

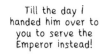

Till the day i handed him over to you to serve the Emperor instead!

Devoting myself body and soul to restoring the Pax Galactica!

i've heard enough!

Zarth Arn, an eternity of suffering awaits you on the Planet Shayol!

Take the convict to the Astroport. His sentence begins immediately. It is the Emperor's will!

Shayol...

ZARTH ARN! MY POOR FRIEND! WHAT HAVE i DONE?

???

BOING!

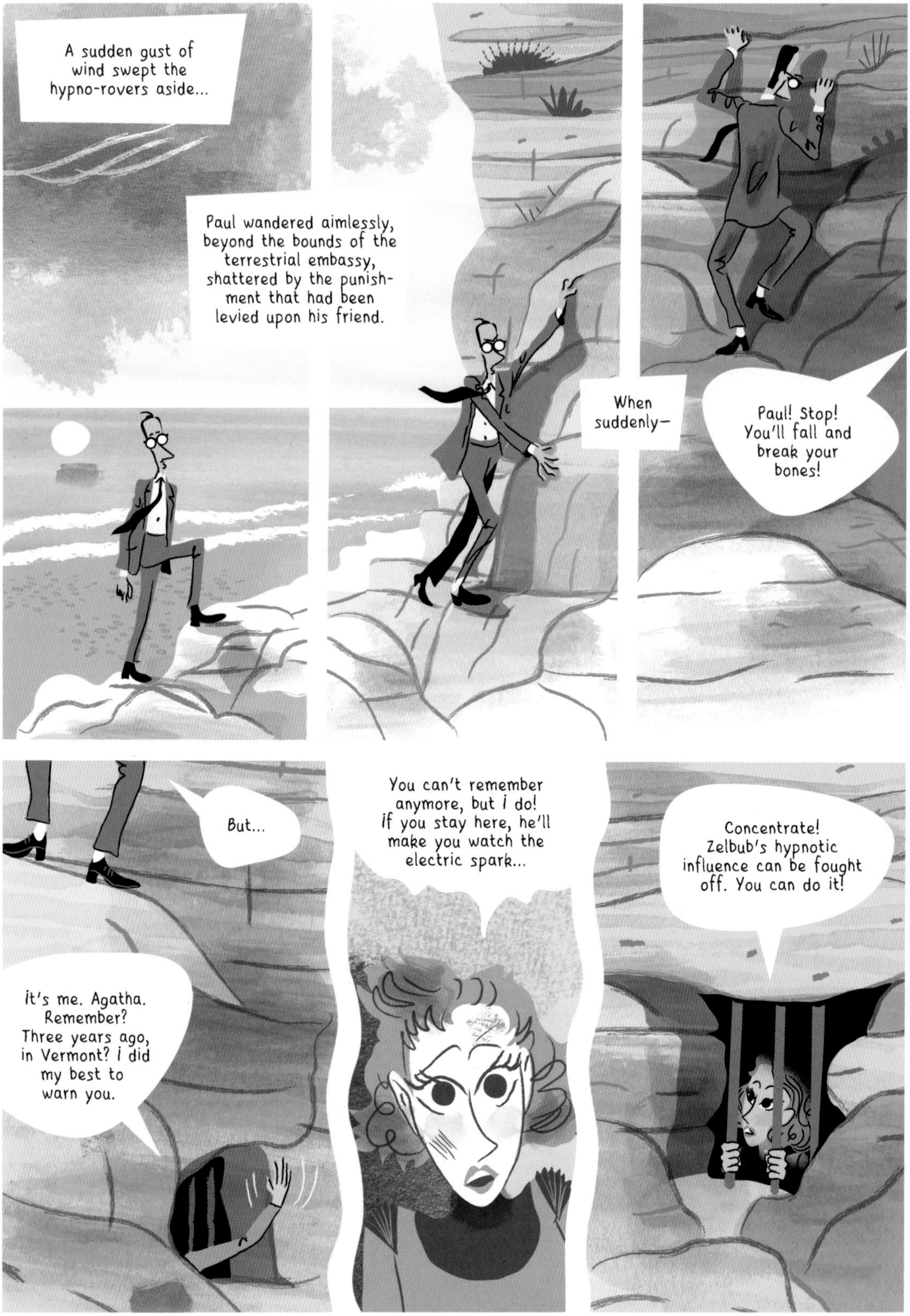

A sudden gust of wind swept the hypno-rovers aside...
Paul wandered aimlessly, beyond the bounds of the terrestrial embassy, shattered by the punishment that had been levied upon his friend.
When suddenly—
Paul! Stop! You'll fall and break your bones!
But...
It's me. Agatha. Remember? Three years ago, in Vermont? I did my best to warn you.
You can't remember anymore, but I do! If you stay here, he'll make you watch the electric spark...
Concentrate! Zelbub's hypnotic influence can be fought off. You can do it!

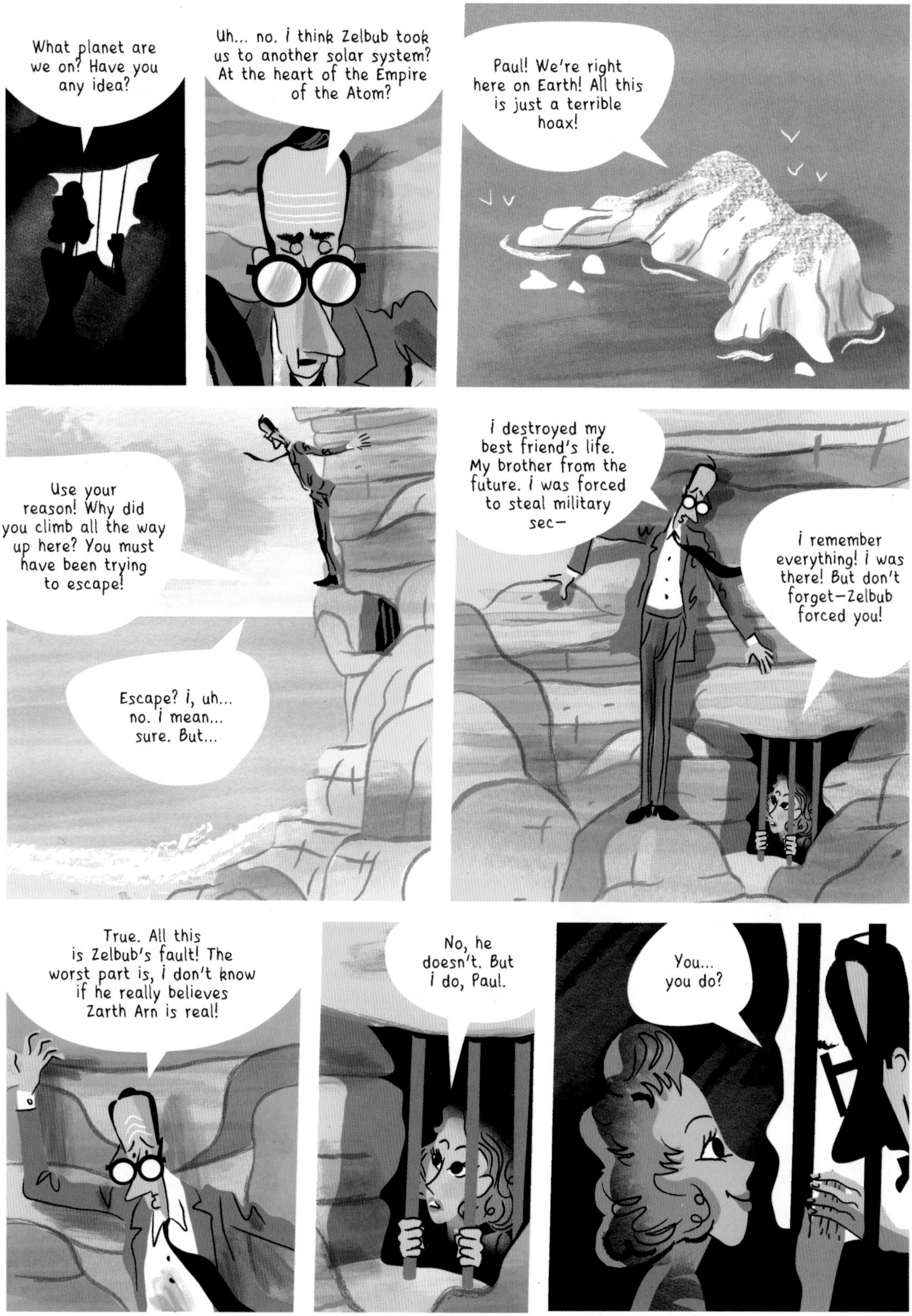
What planet are we on? Have you any idea?
Uh... no. I think Zelbub took us to another solar system? At the heart of the Empire of the Atom?
Paul! We're right here on Earth! All this is just a terrible hoax!
Use your reason! Why did you climb all the way up here? You must have been trying to escape!
Escape? I, uh... no. I mean... sure. But...
I destroyed my best friend's life. My brother from the future. I was forced to steal military sec–
I remember everything! I was there! But don't forget—Zelbub forced you!
True. All this is Zelbub's fault! The worst part is, I don't know if he really believes Zarth Arn is real!
No, he doesn't. But I do, Paul.
You... you do?

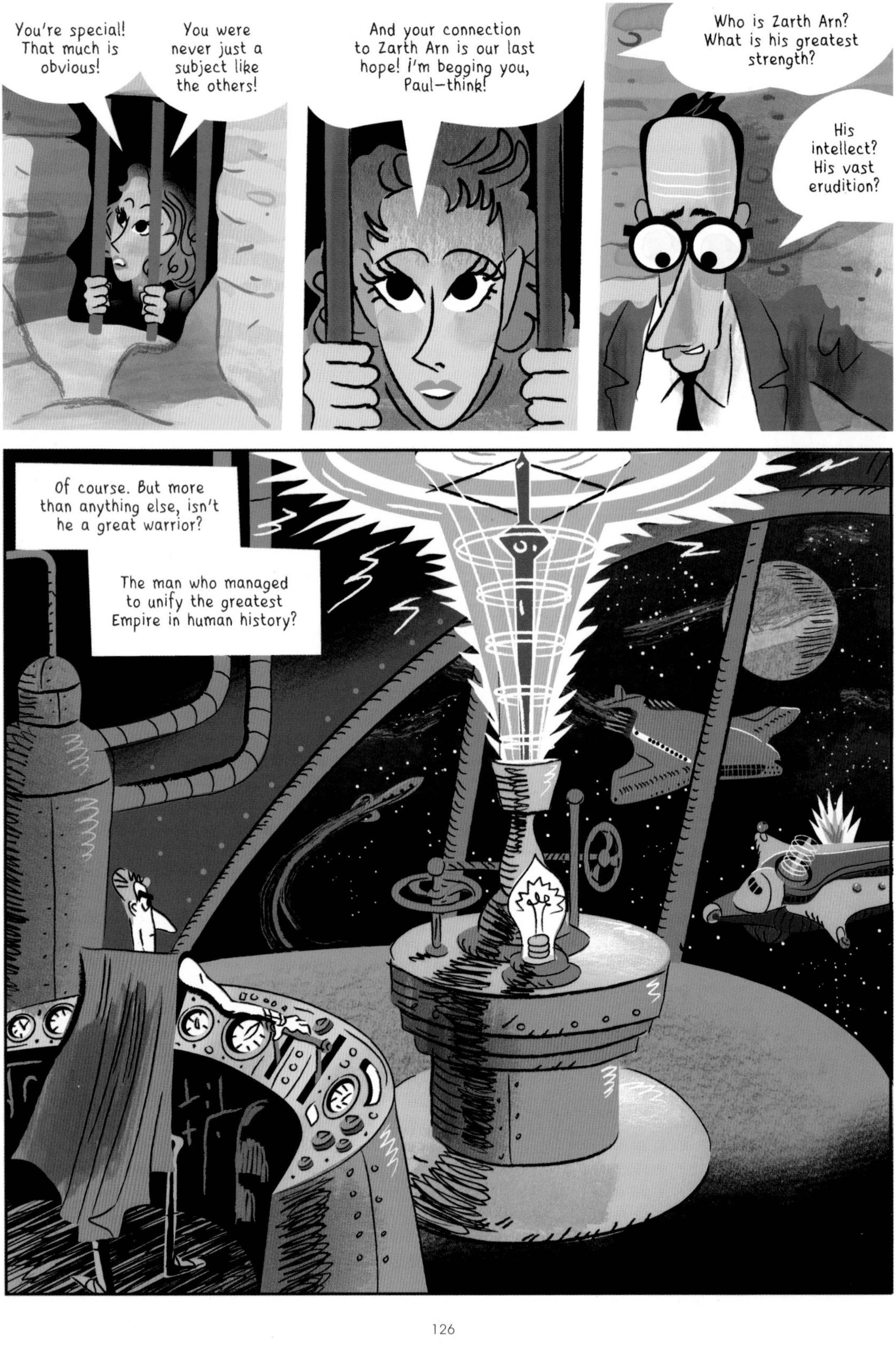

You're special! That much is obvious!
You were never just a subject like the others!
And your connection to Zarth Arn is our last hope! I'm begging you, Paul—think!
Who is Zarth Arn? What is his greatest strength?
His intellect? His vast erudition?
Of course. But more than anything else, isn't he a great warrior?
The man who managed to unify the greatest Empire in human history?

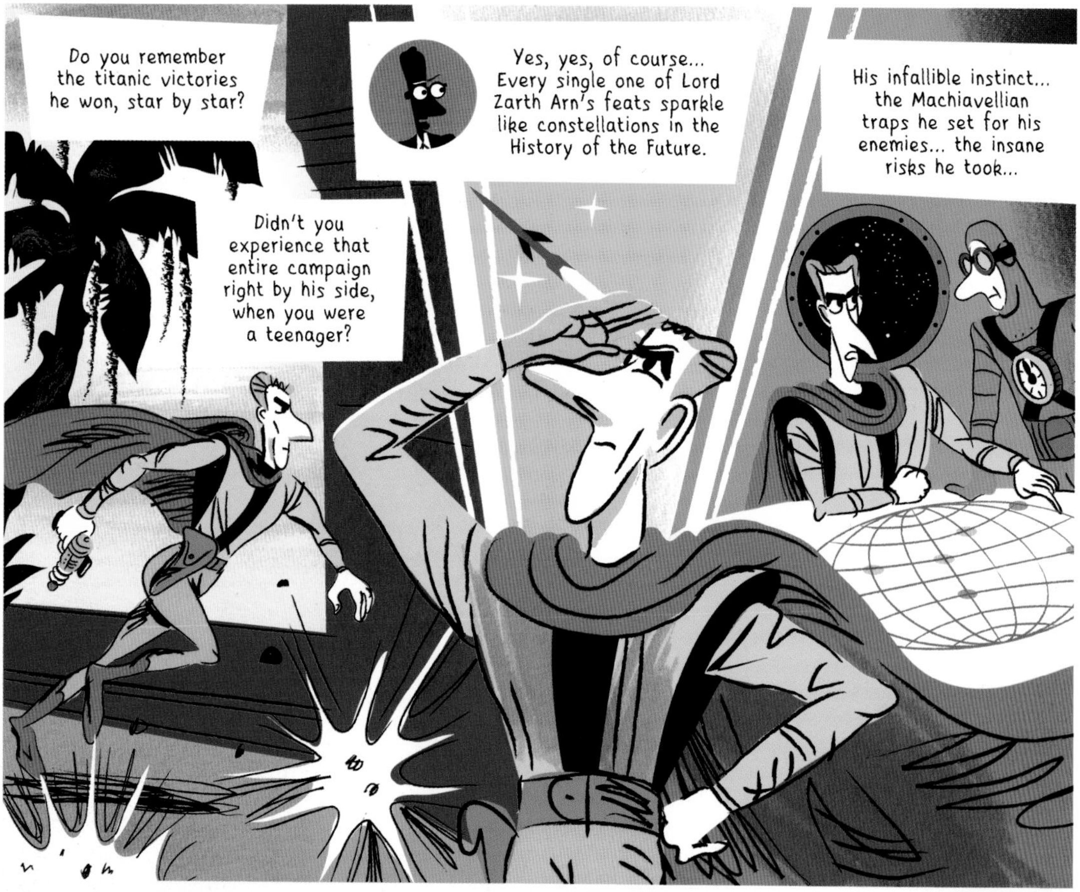
Do you remember the titanic victories he won, star by star?
Yes, yes, of course... Every single one of Lord Zarth Arn's feats sparkle like constellations in the History of the Future.
His infallible instinct... the Machiavellian traps he set for his enemies... the insane risks he took...
Didn't you experience that entire campaign right by his side, when you were a teenager?

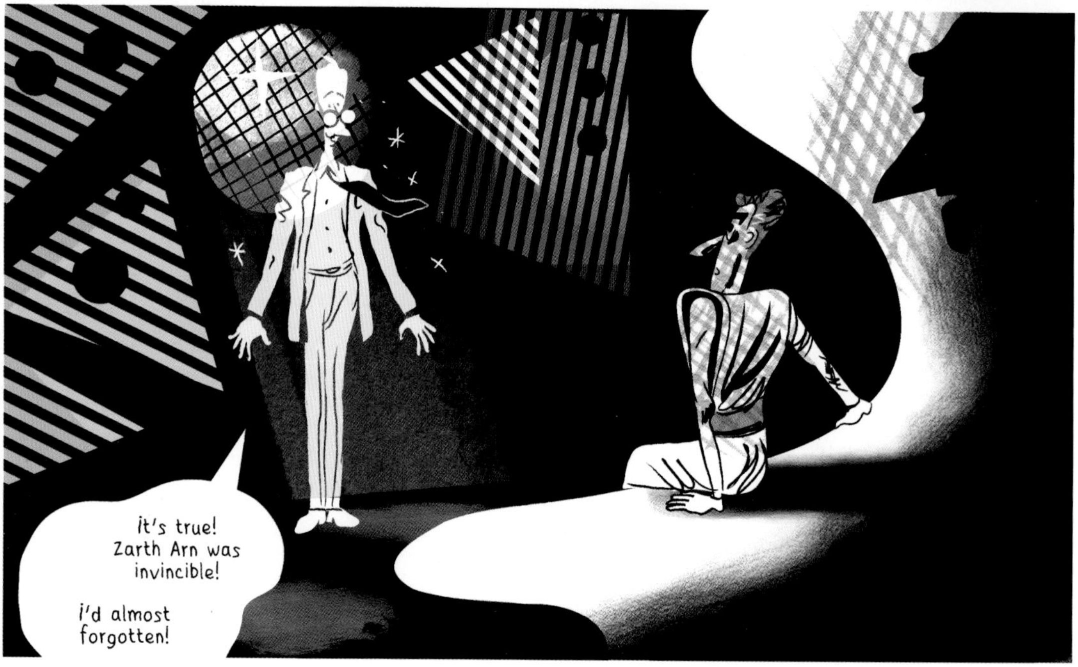
It's true! Zarth Arn was invincible!
I'd almost forgotten!

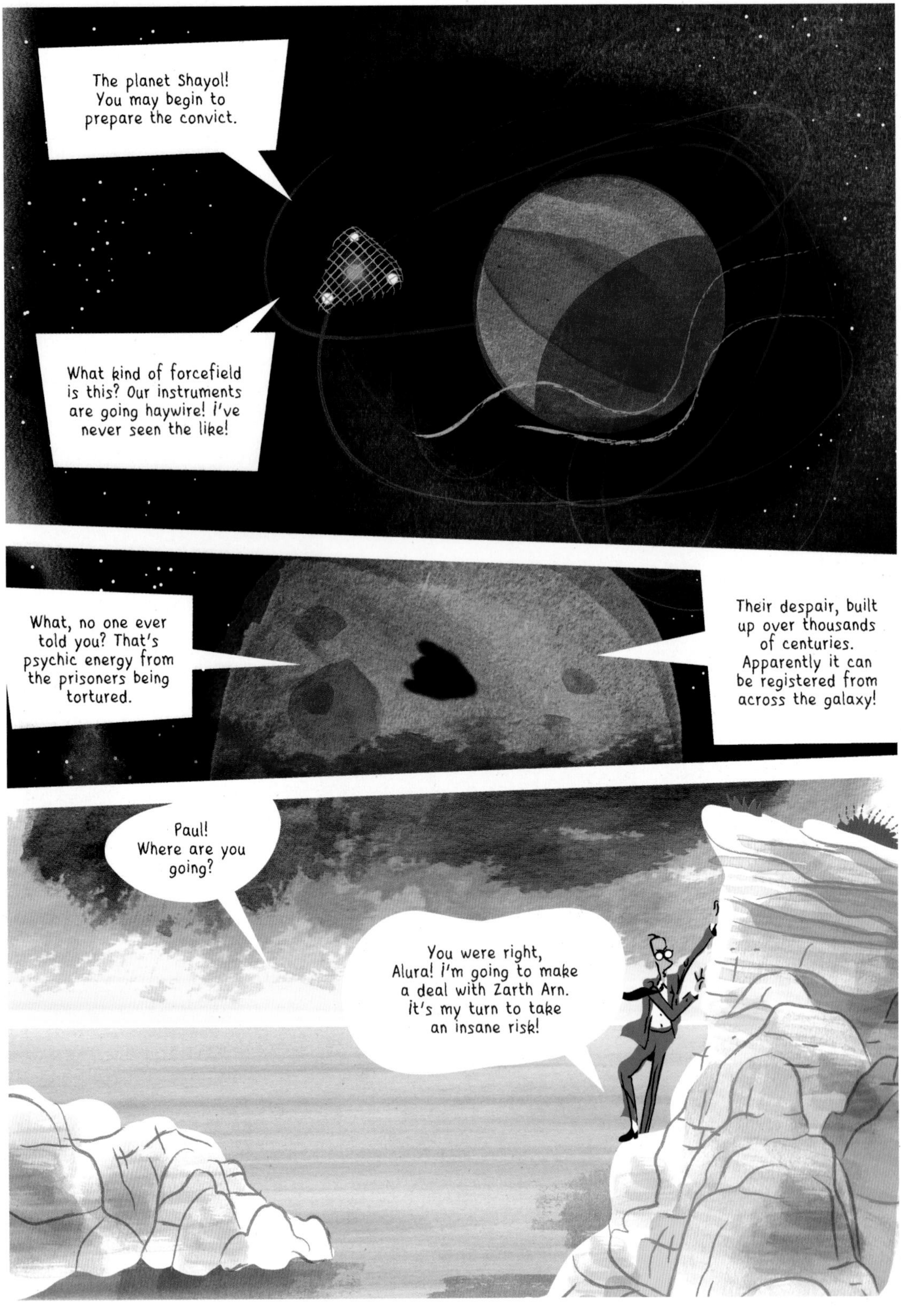
The planet Shayol! You may begin to prepare the convict.
What kind of forcefield is this? Our instruments are going haywire! I've never seen the like!
What, no one ever told you? That's psychic energy from the prisoners being tortured.
Their despair, built up over thousands of centuries. Apparently it can be registered from across the galaxy!
Paul! Where are you going?
You were right, Alura! I'm going to make a deal with Zarth Arn. It's my turn to take an insane risk!

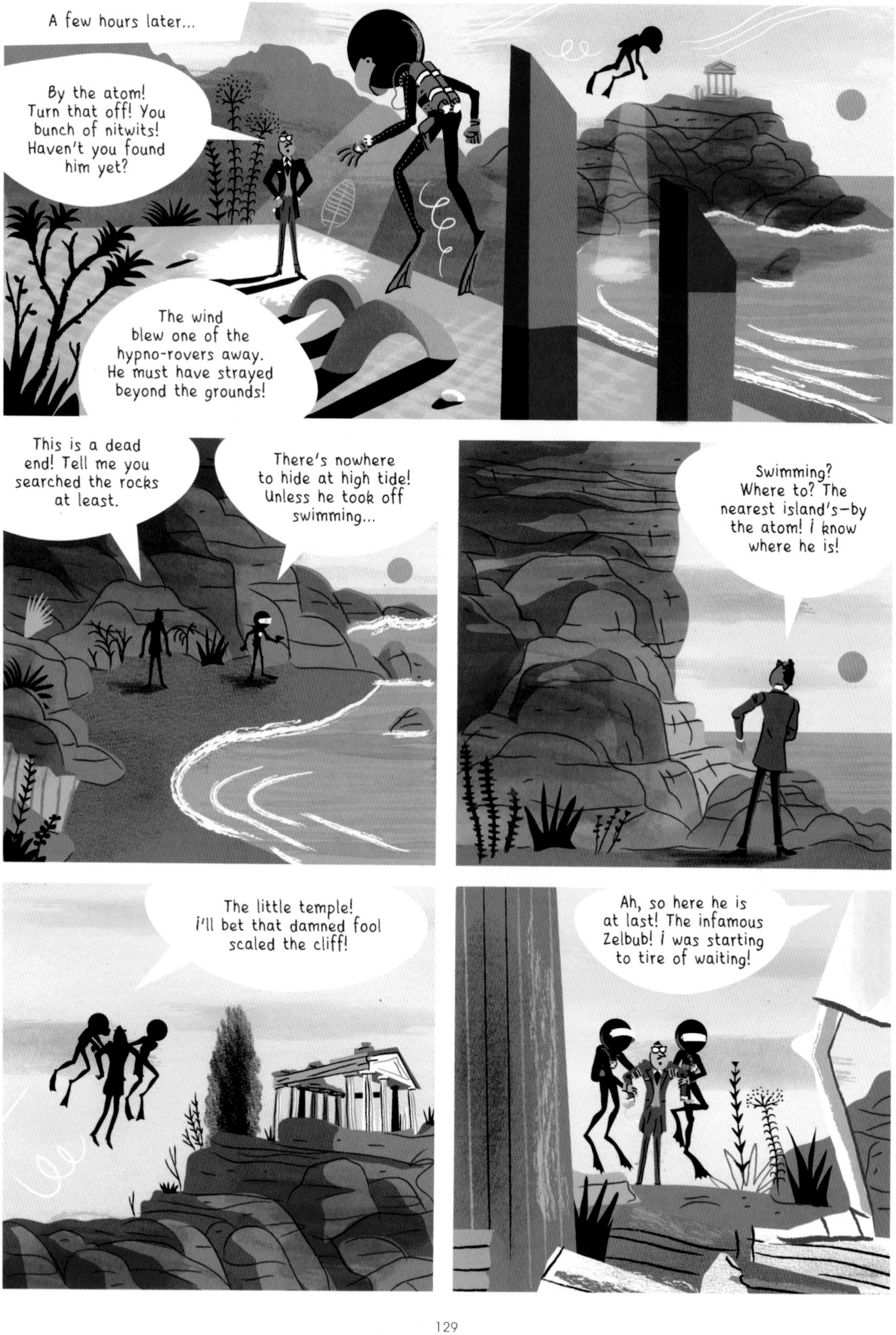
A few hours later...
By the atom! Turn that off! You bunch of nitwits! Haven't you found him yet?
The wind blew one of the hypno-rovers away. He must have strayed beyond the grounds!
This is a dead end! Tell me you searched the rocks at least.
There's nowhere to hide at high tide! Unless he took off swimming...
Swimming? Where to? The nearest island's—by the atom! I know where he is!
The little temple! I'll bet that damned fool scaled the cliff!
Ah, so here he is at last! The infamous Zelbub! I was starting to tire of waiting!

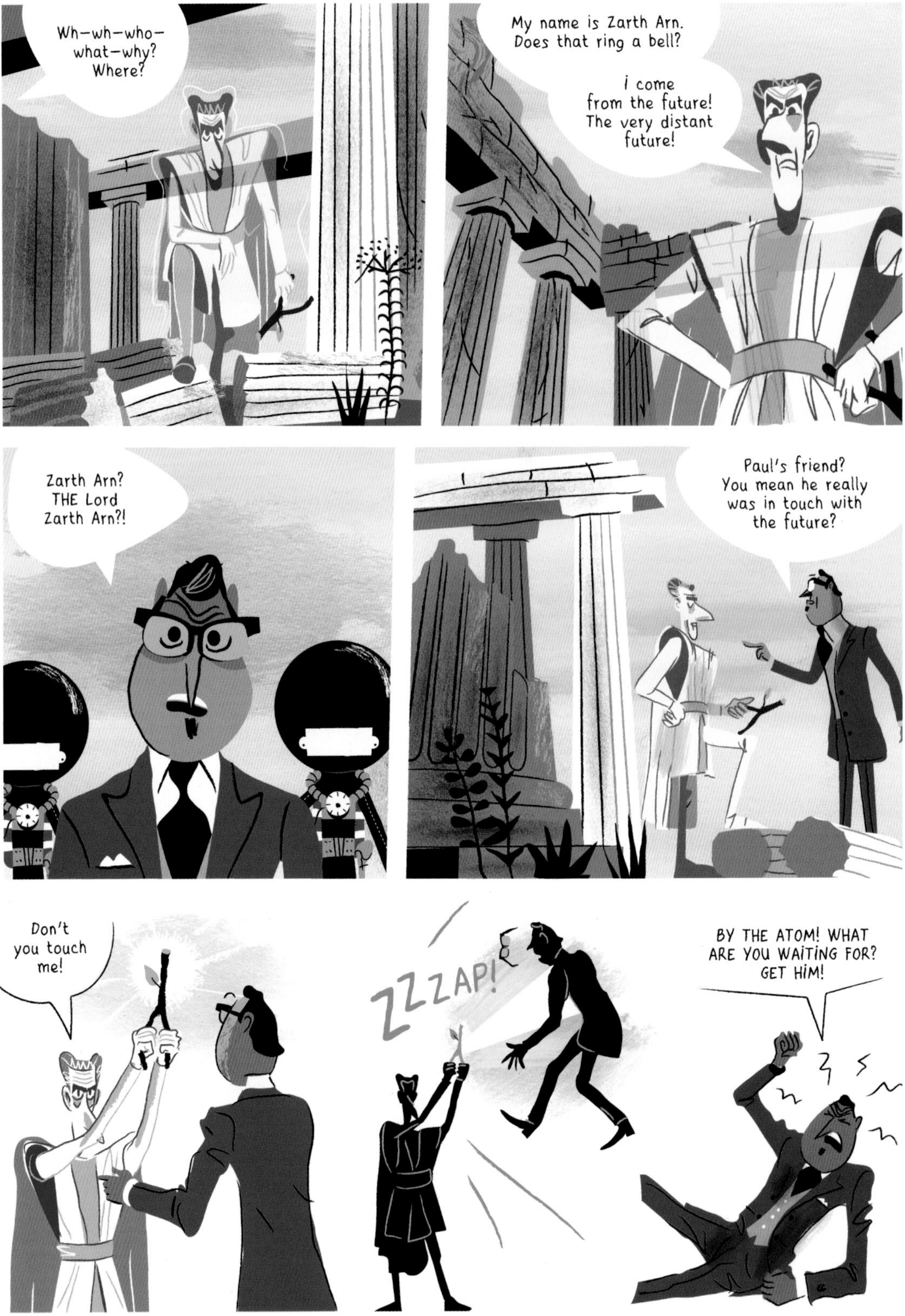
Wh-wh-who-
what-why?
Where?
My name is Zarth Arn.
Does that ring a bell?
i come
from the future!
The very distant
future!
Zarth Arn?
THE Lord
Zarth Arn?!
Paul's friend?
You mean he really
was in touch with
the future?
Don't
you touch
me!
ZZZAP!
BY THE ATOM! WHAT
ARE YOU WAITING FOR?
GET HIM!

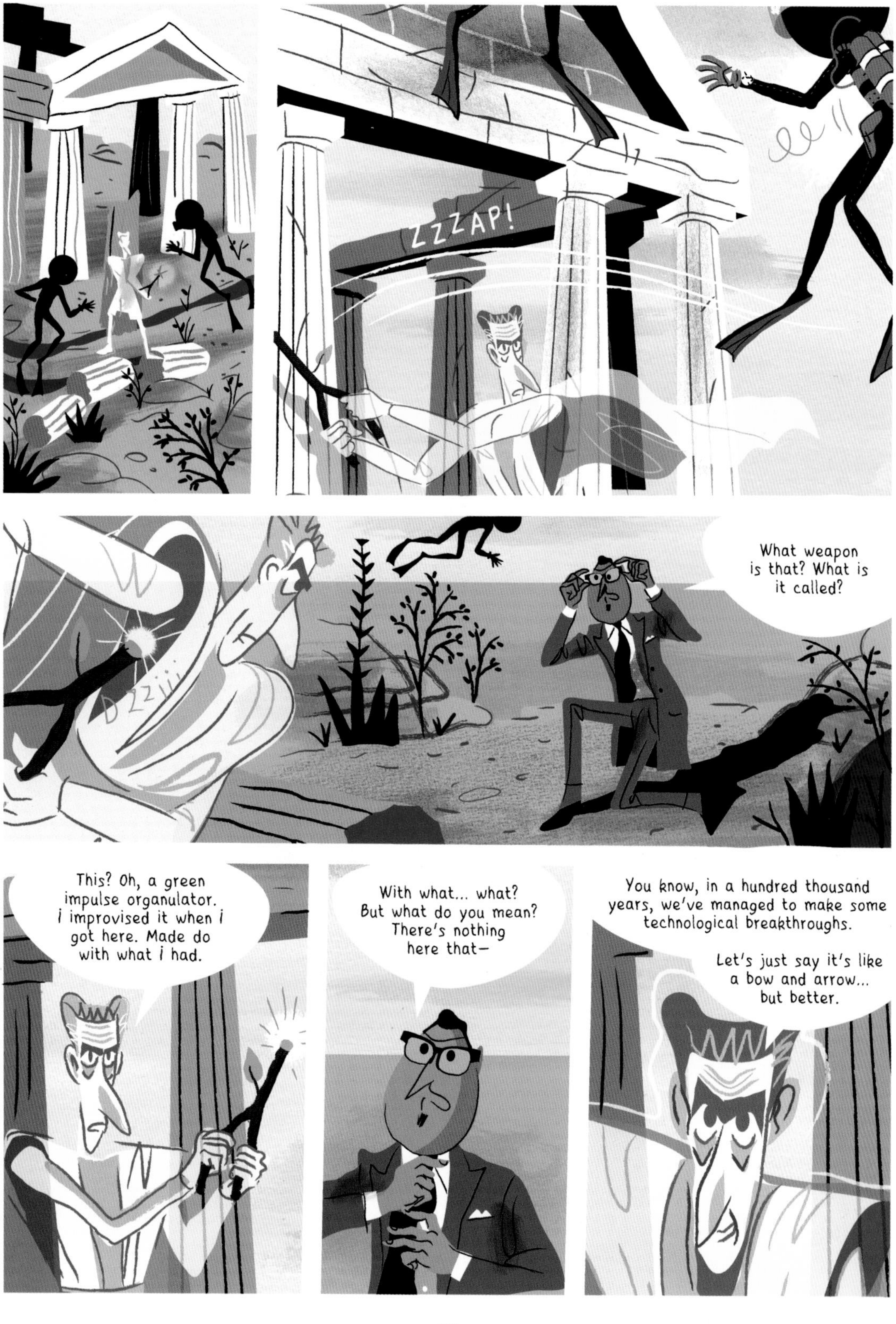

ZZZAP!
DZZiii
What weapon is that? What is it called?
This? Oh, a green impulse organulator. i improvised it when i got here. Made do with what i had.
With what... what? But what do you mean? There's nothing here that—
You know, in a hundred thousand years, we've managed to make some technological breakthroughs.
Let's just say it's like a bow and arrow... but better.

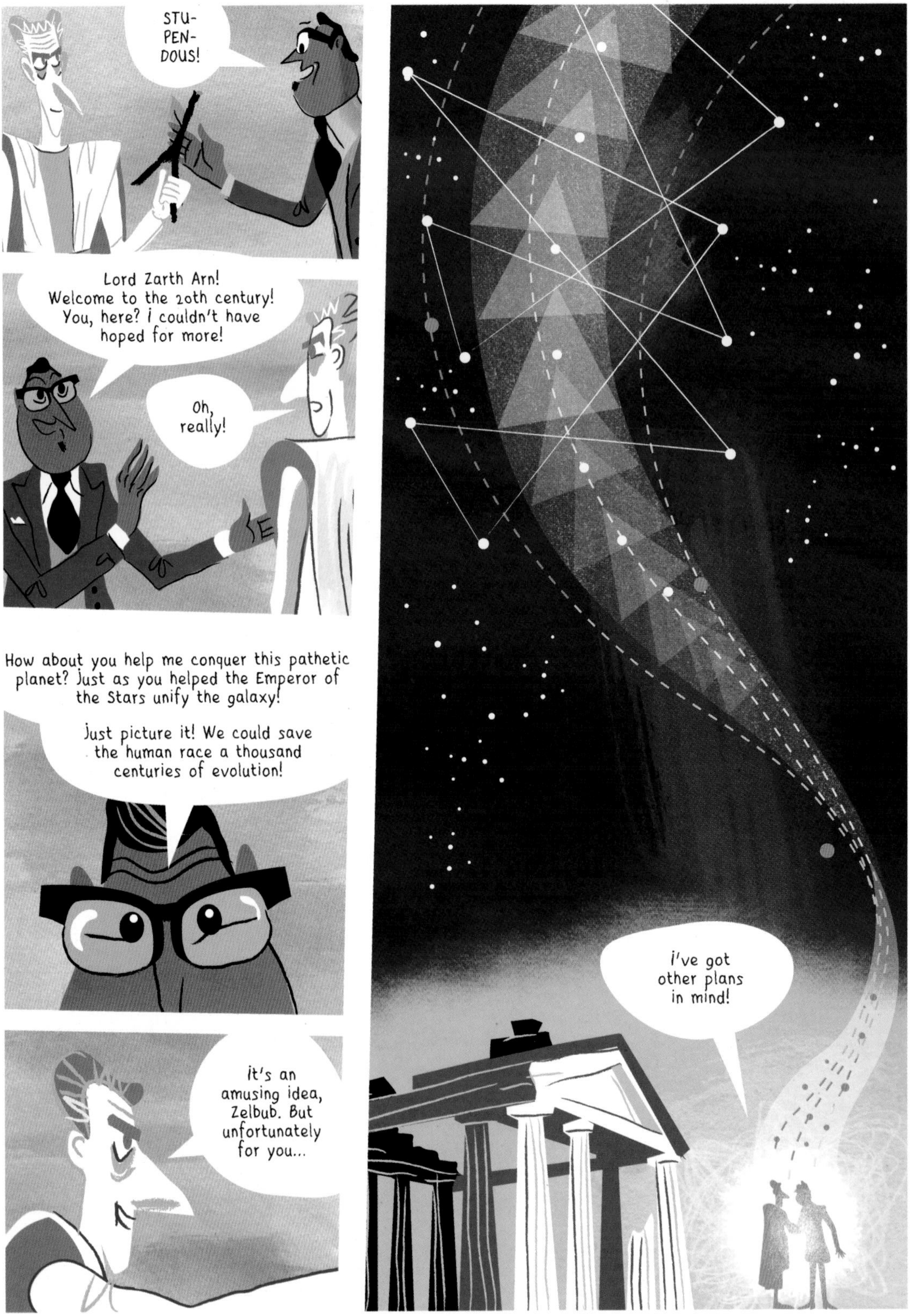
STU-PEN-DOUS!
Lord Zarth Arn! Welcome to the 20th century! You, here? I couldn't have hoped for more!
Oh, really!
How about you help me conquer this pathetic planet? Just as you helped the Emperor of the Stars unify the galaxy!
Just picture it! We could save the human race a thousand centuries of evolution!
It's an amusing idea, Zelbub. But unfortunately for you...
I've got other plans in mind!

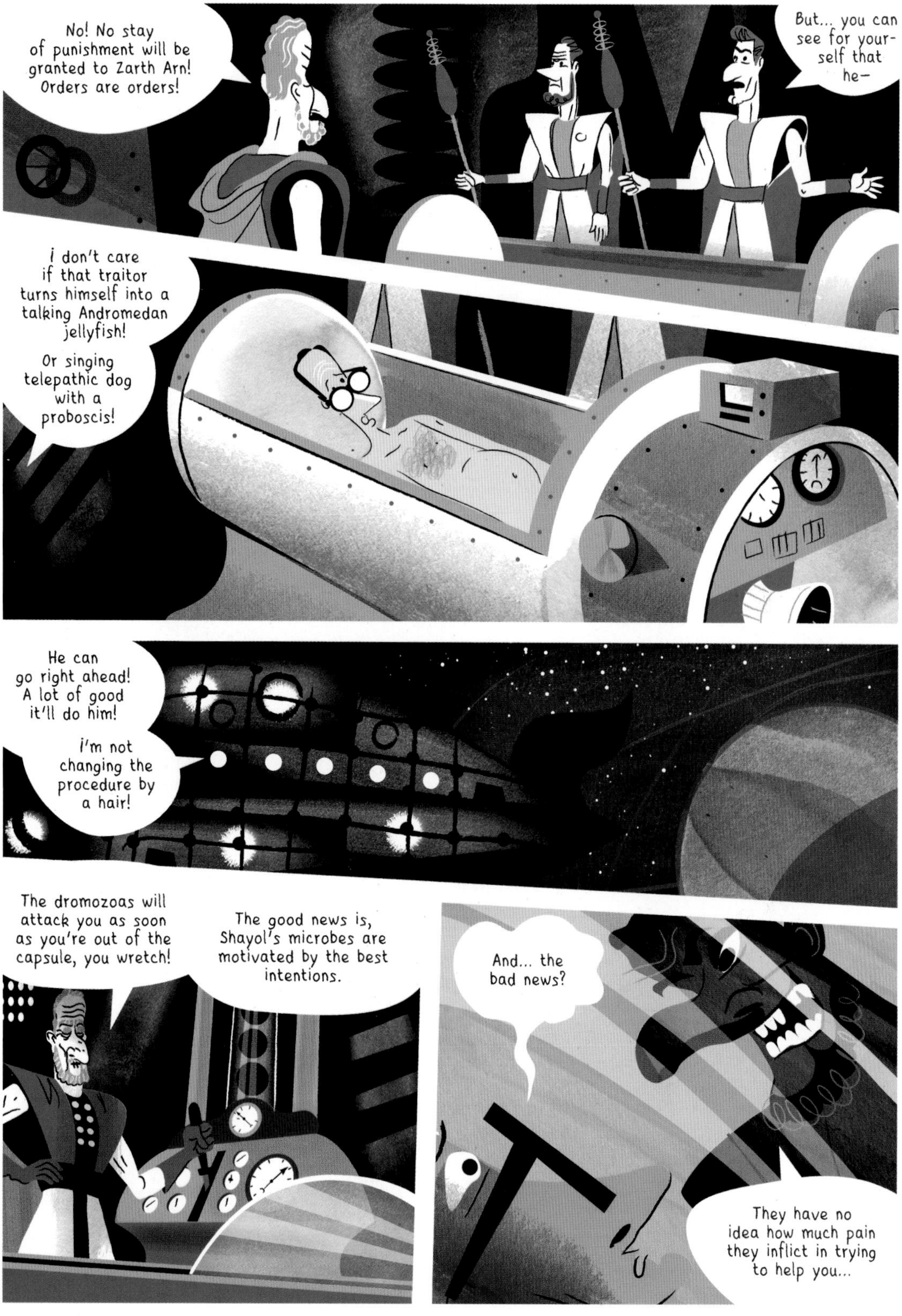
No! No stay of punishment will be granted to Zarth Arn! Orders are orders!
But... you can see for yourself that he—
i don't care if that traitor turns himself into a talking Andromedan jellyfish!
Or singing telepathic dog with a proboscis!
He can go right ahead! A lot of good it'll do him!
i'm not changing the procedure by a hair!
The dromozoas will attack you as soon as you're out of the capsule, you wretch!
The good news is, Shayol's microbes are motivated by the best intentions.
And... the bad news?
They have no idea how much pain they inflict in trying to help you...

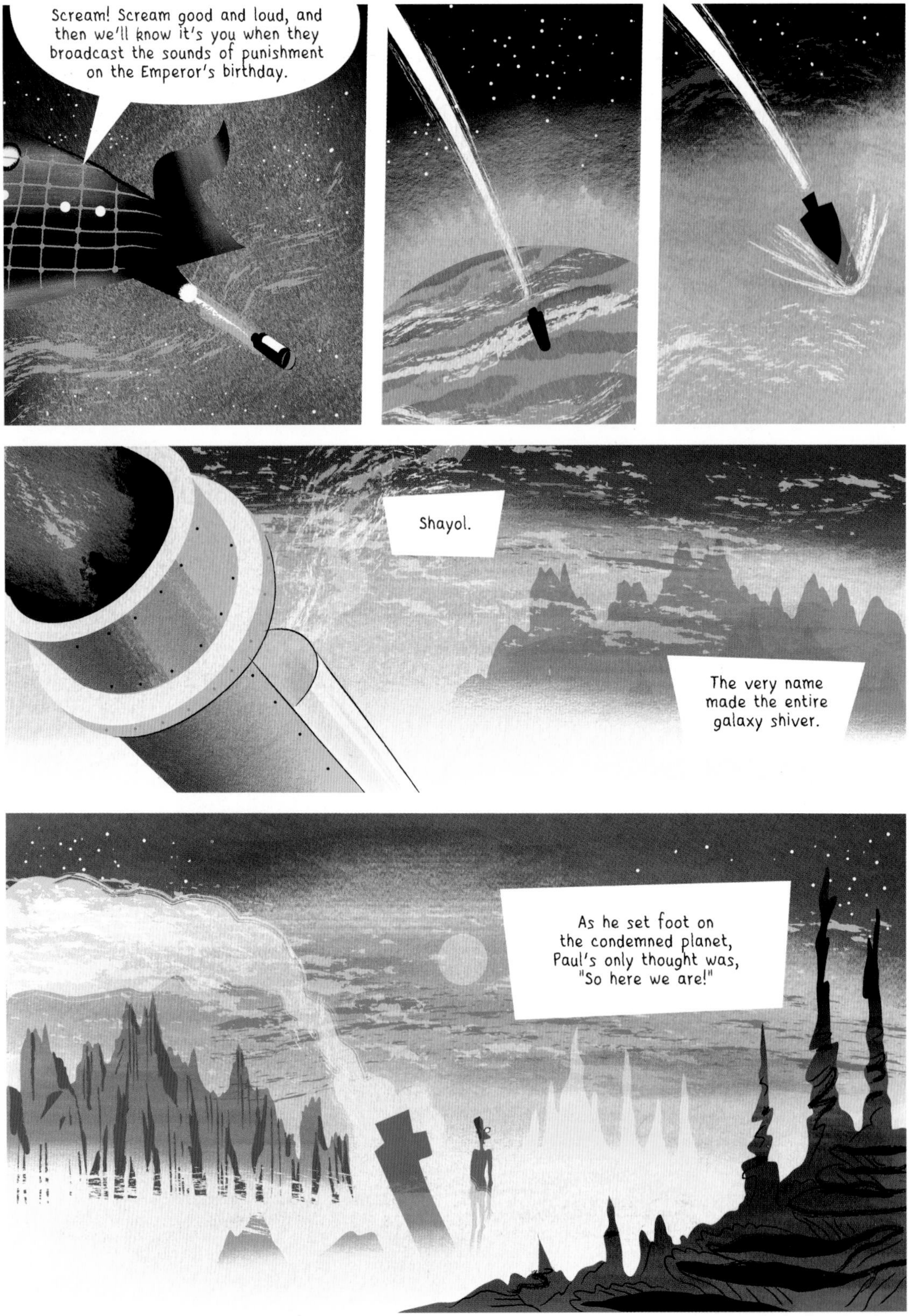
Scream! Scream good and loud, and then we'll know it's you when they broadcast the sounds of punishment on the Emperor's birthday.
Shayol.
The very name made the entire galaxy shiver.
As he set foot on the condemned planet, Paul's only thought was, "So here we are!"

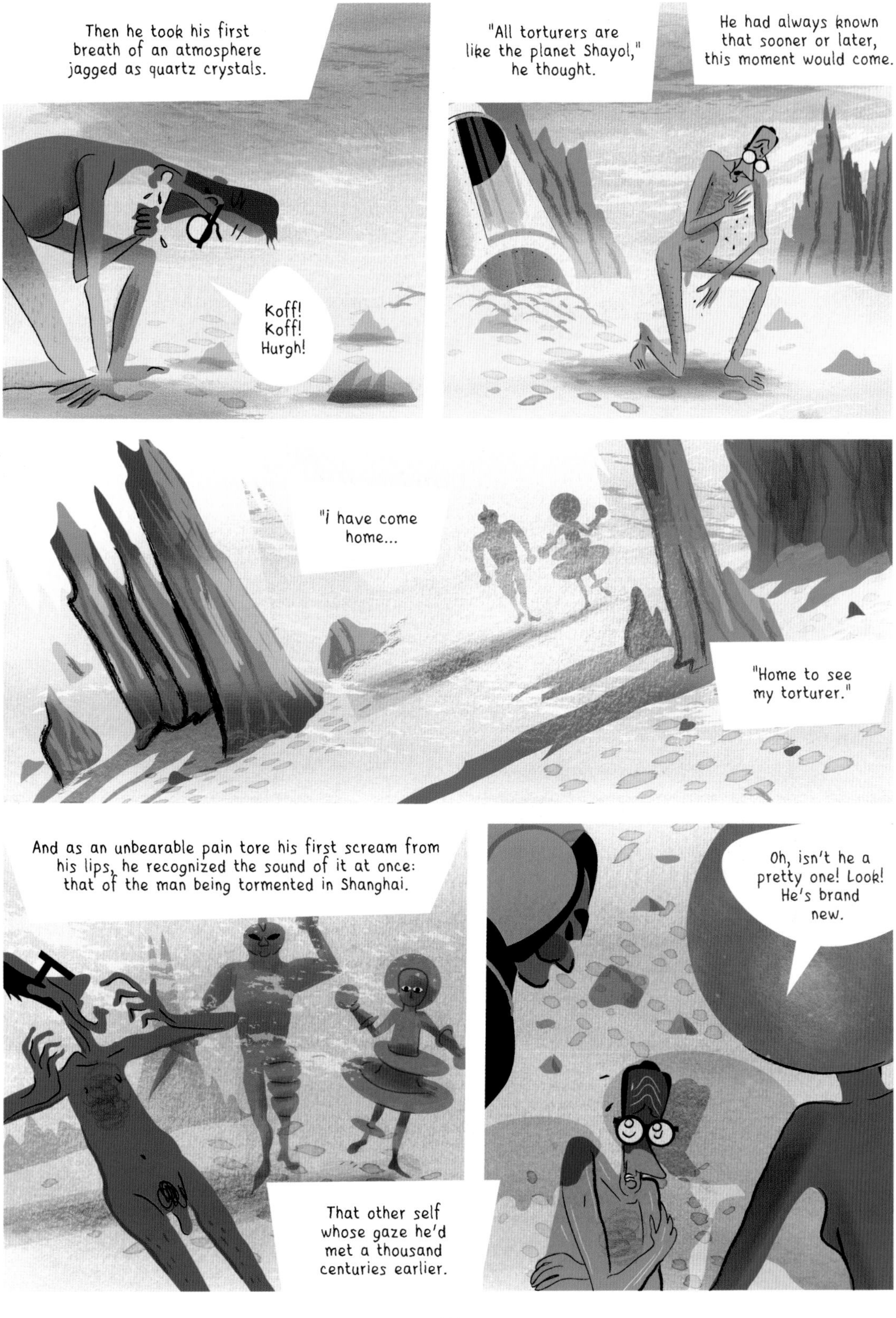
Then he took his first breath of an atmosphere jagged as quartz crystals.
Koff! Koff! Hurgh!
"All torturers are like the planet Shayol," he thought.
He had always known that sooner or later, this moment would come.
"I have come home...
"Home to see my torturer."
And as an unbearable pain tore his first scream from his lips, he recognized the sound of it at once: that of the man being tormented in Shanghai.
That other self whose gaze he'd met a thousand centuries earlier.
Oh, isn't he a pretty one! Look! He's brand new.

The dromozoa noticed at once.

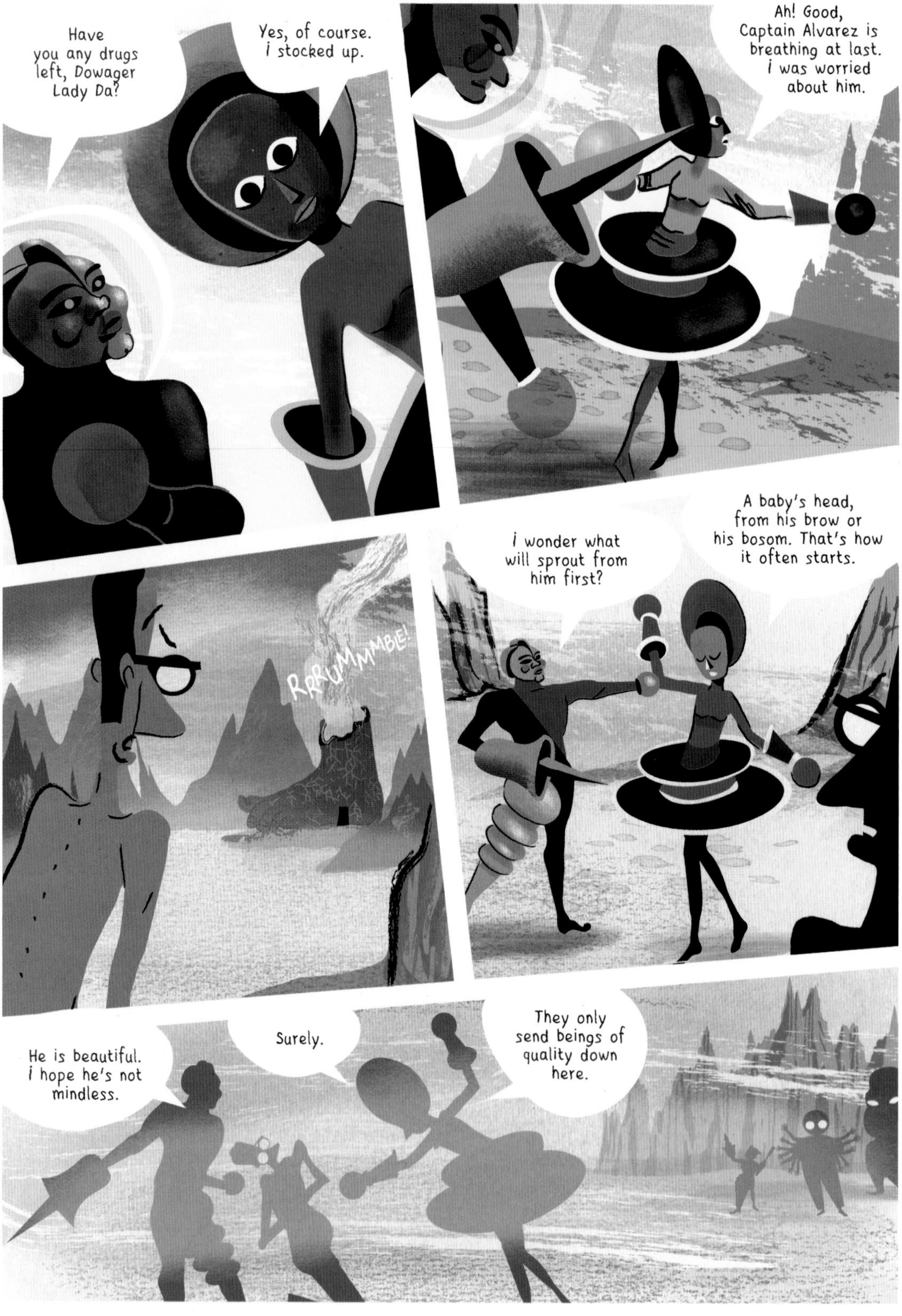
Have you any drugs left, Dowager Lady Da?
Yes, of course. i stocked up.
Ah! Good, Captain Alvarez is breathing at last. i was worried about him.
RRRUMMMBLE!
i wonder what will sprout from him first?
A baby's head, from his brow or his bosom. That's how it often starts.
He is beautiful. i hope he's not mindless.
Surely.
They only send beings of quality down here.

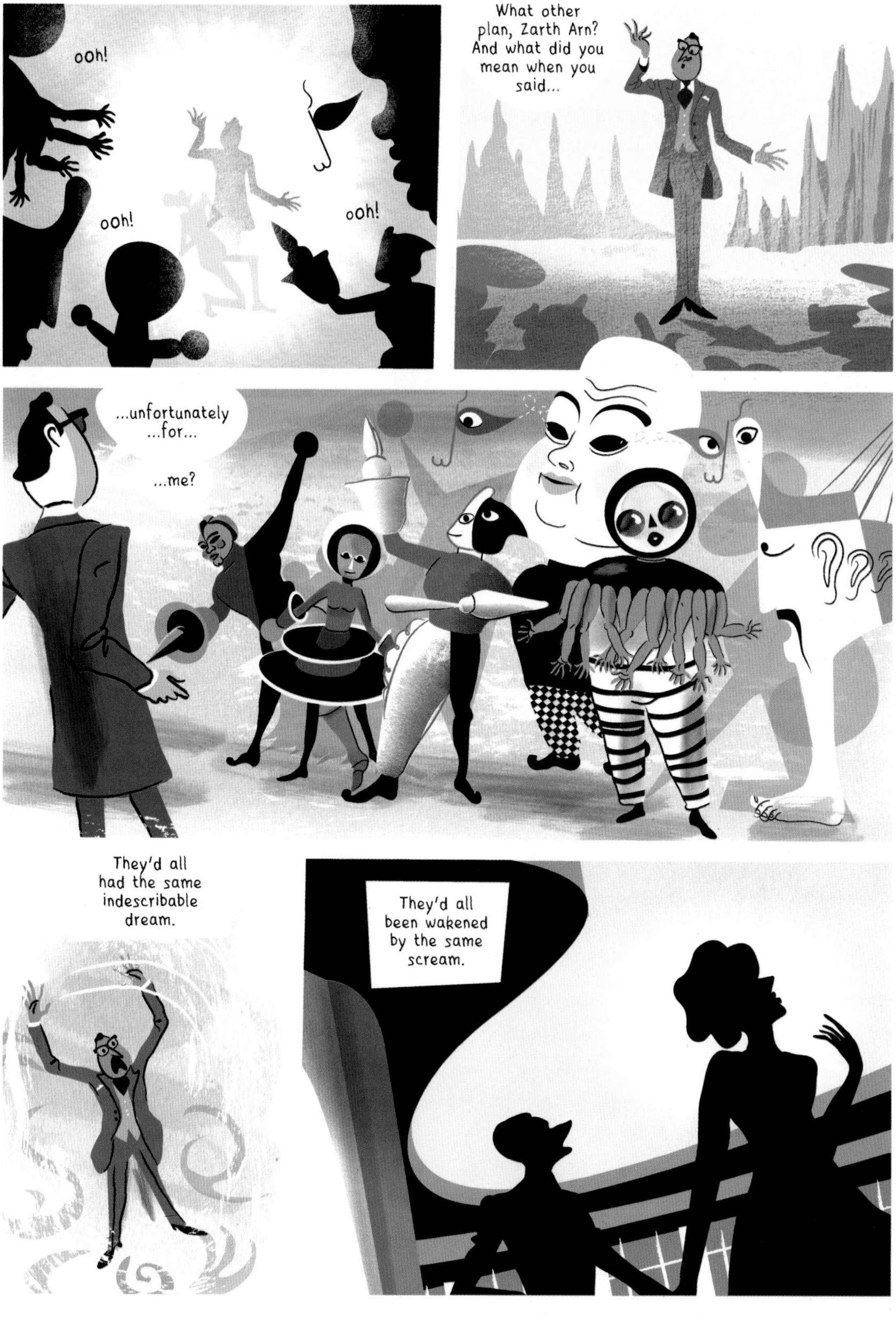
ooh!
ooh!
ooh!
What other plan, Zarth Arn? And what did you mean when you said...
...unfortunately ...for...
...me?
They'd all had the same indescribable dream.
They'd all been wakened by the same scream.

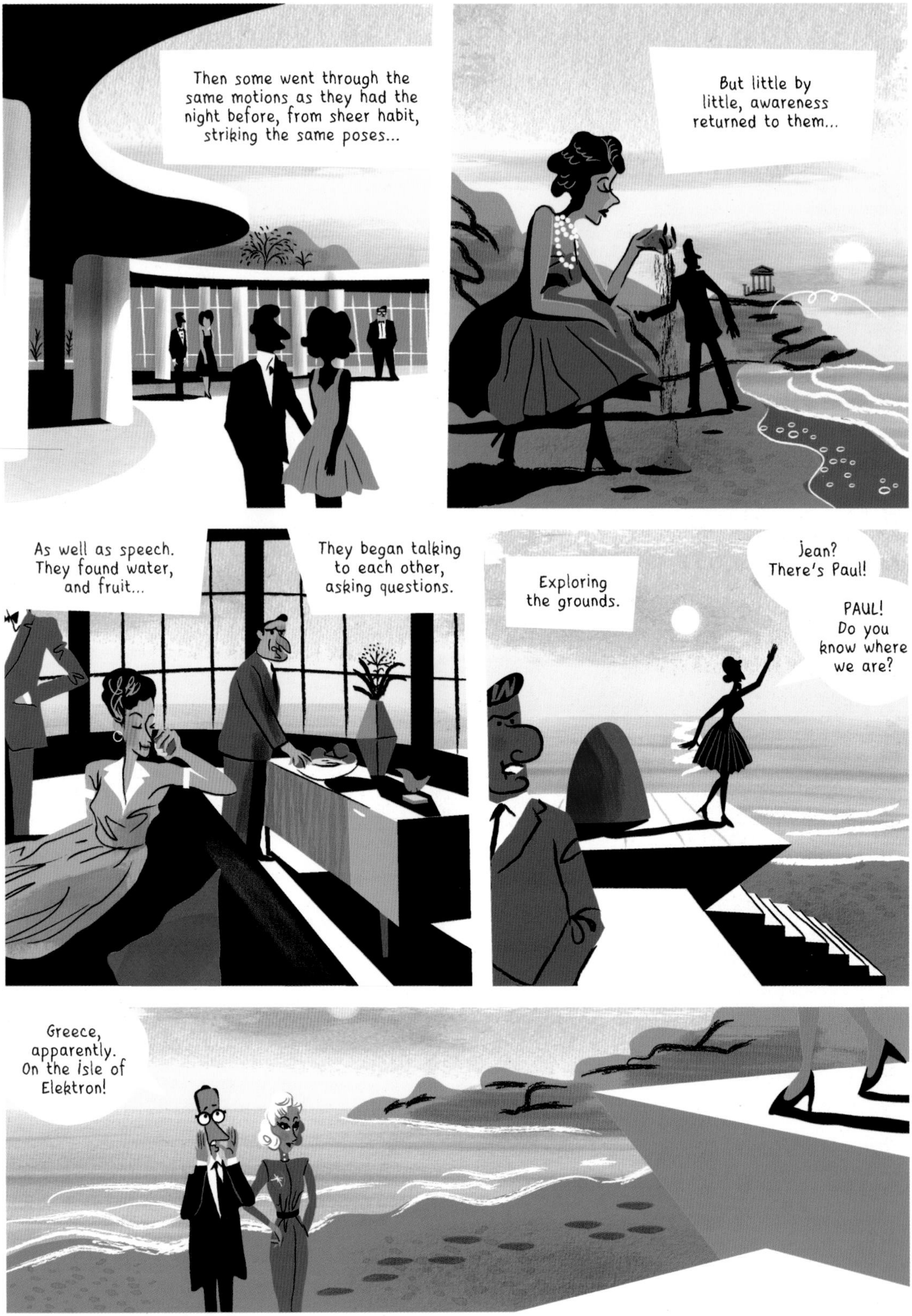

Then some went through the same motions as they had the night before, from sheer habit, striking the same poses...
But little by little, awareness returned to them...
As well as speech. They found water, and fruit...
They began talking to each other, asking questions.
Exploring the grounds.
Jean? There's Paul!
PAUL! Do you know where we are?
Greece, apparently. On the isle of Elektron!

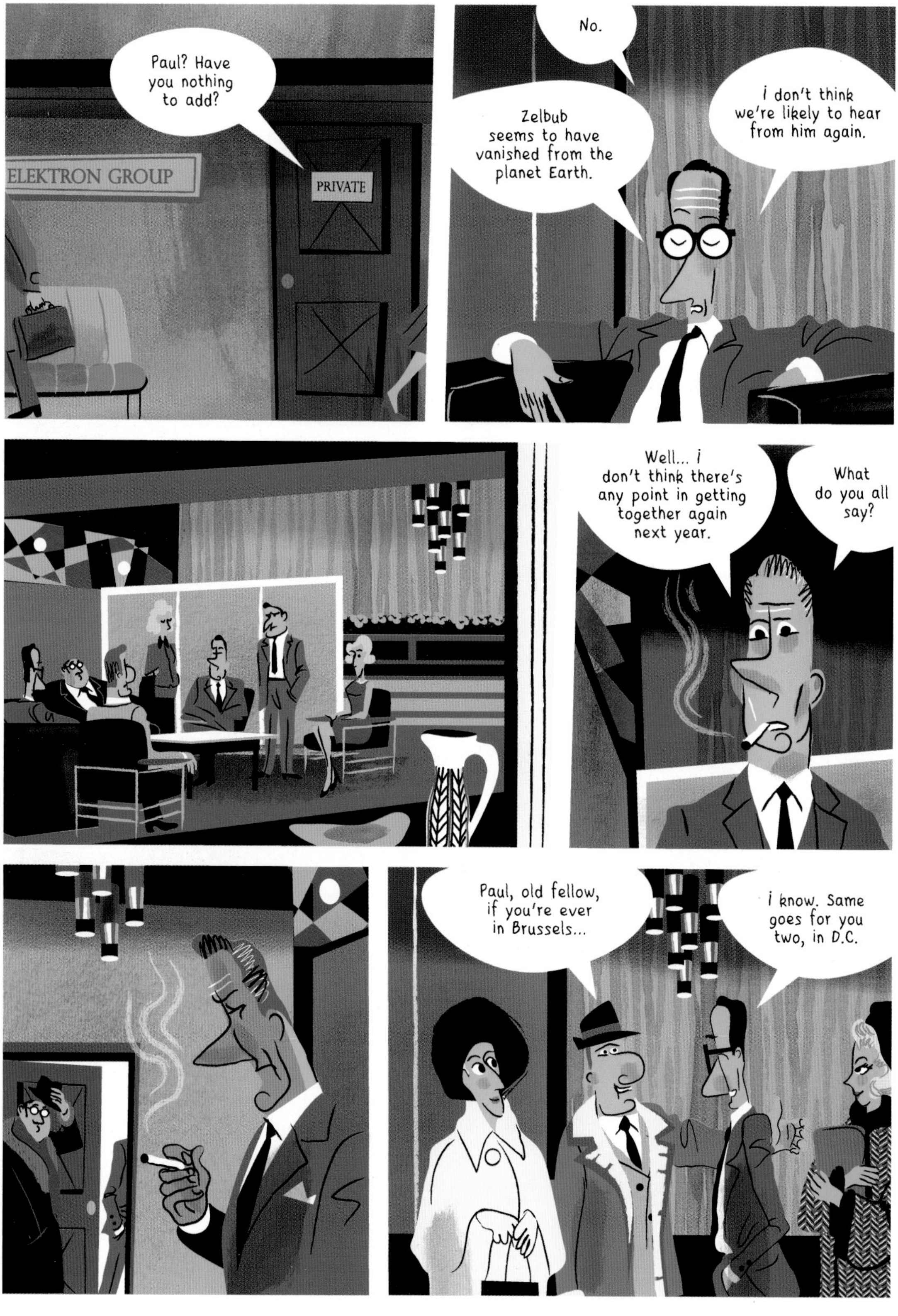
Paul? Have you nothing to add?
ELEKTRON GROUP
PRIVATE
No.
Zelbub seems to have vanished from the planet Earth.
I don't think we're likely to hear from him again.
Well... I don't think there's any point in getting together again next year.
What do you all say?
Paul, old fellow, if you're ever in Brussels...
I know. Same goes for you two, in D.C.

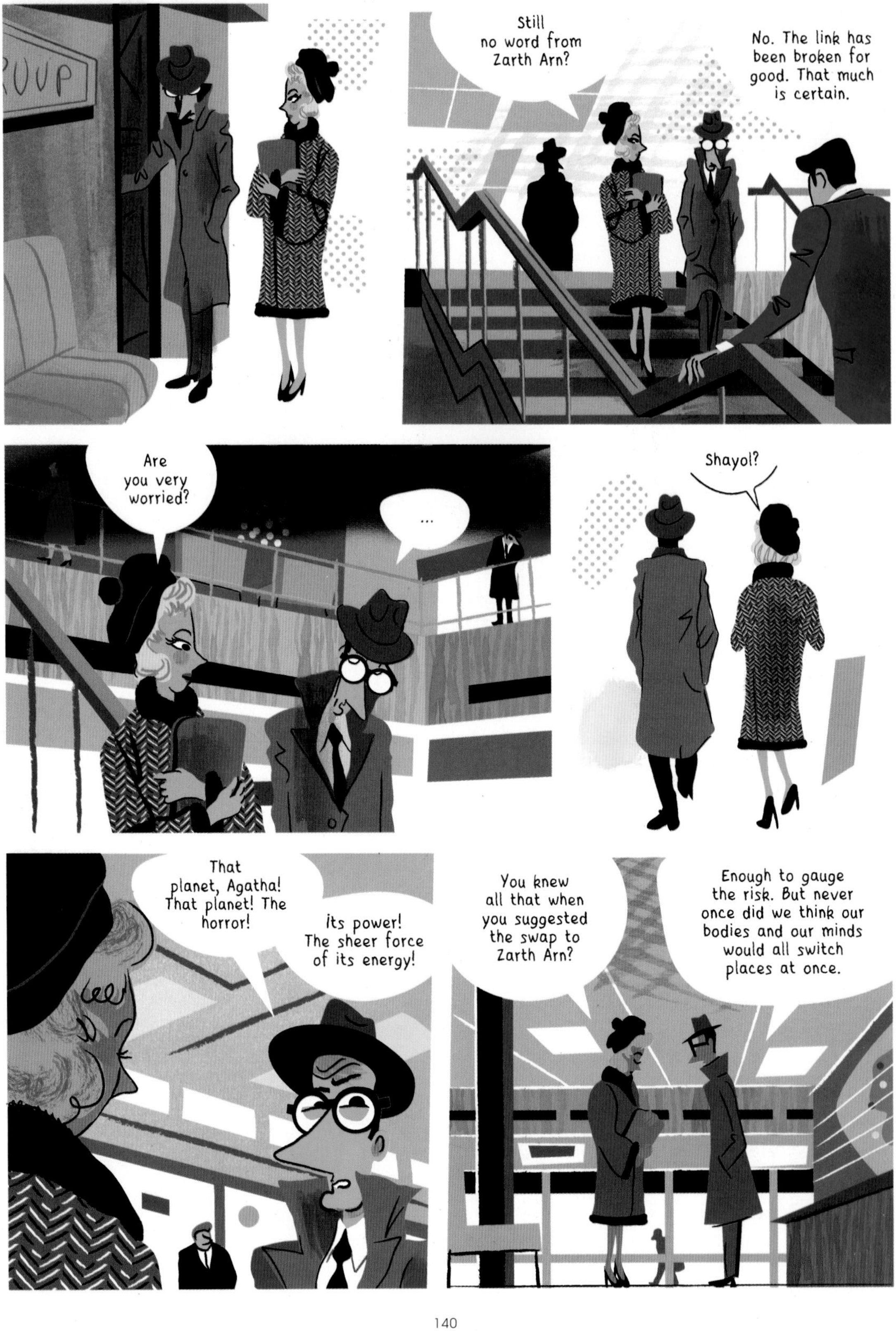
RUUP
Still no word from Zarth Arn?
No. The link has been broken for good. That much is certain.
Are you very worried?
...
Shayol?
That planet, Agatha! That planet! The horror!
Its power! The sheer force of its energy!
You knew all that when you suggested the swap to Zarth Arn?
Enough to gauge the risk. But never once did we think our bodies and our minds would all switch places at once.

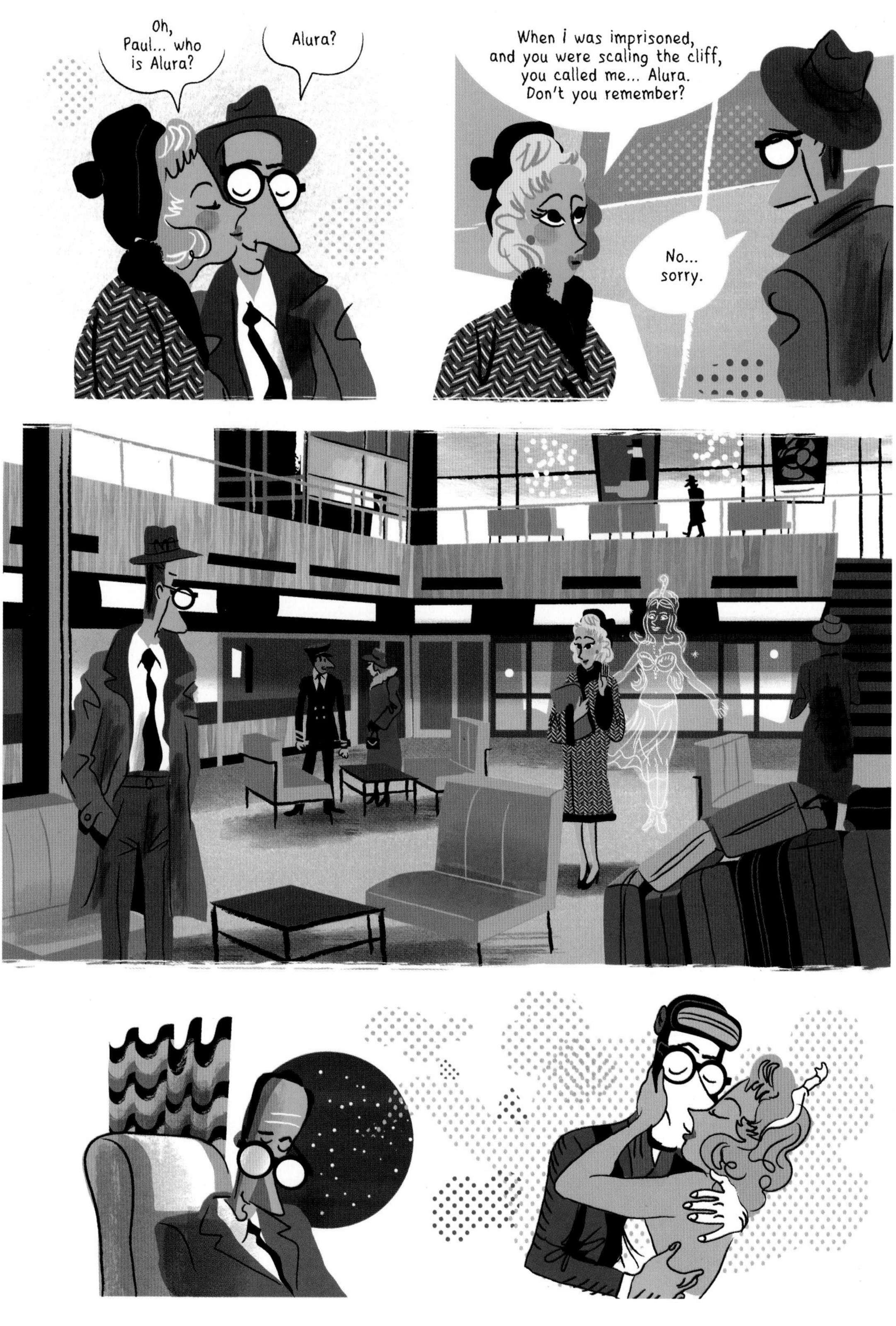
Oh, Paul... who is Alura?
Alura?
When I was imprisoned, and you were scaling the cliff, you called me... Alura. Don't you remember?
No... sorry.

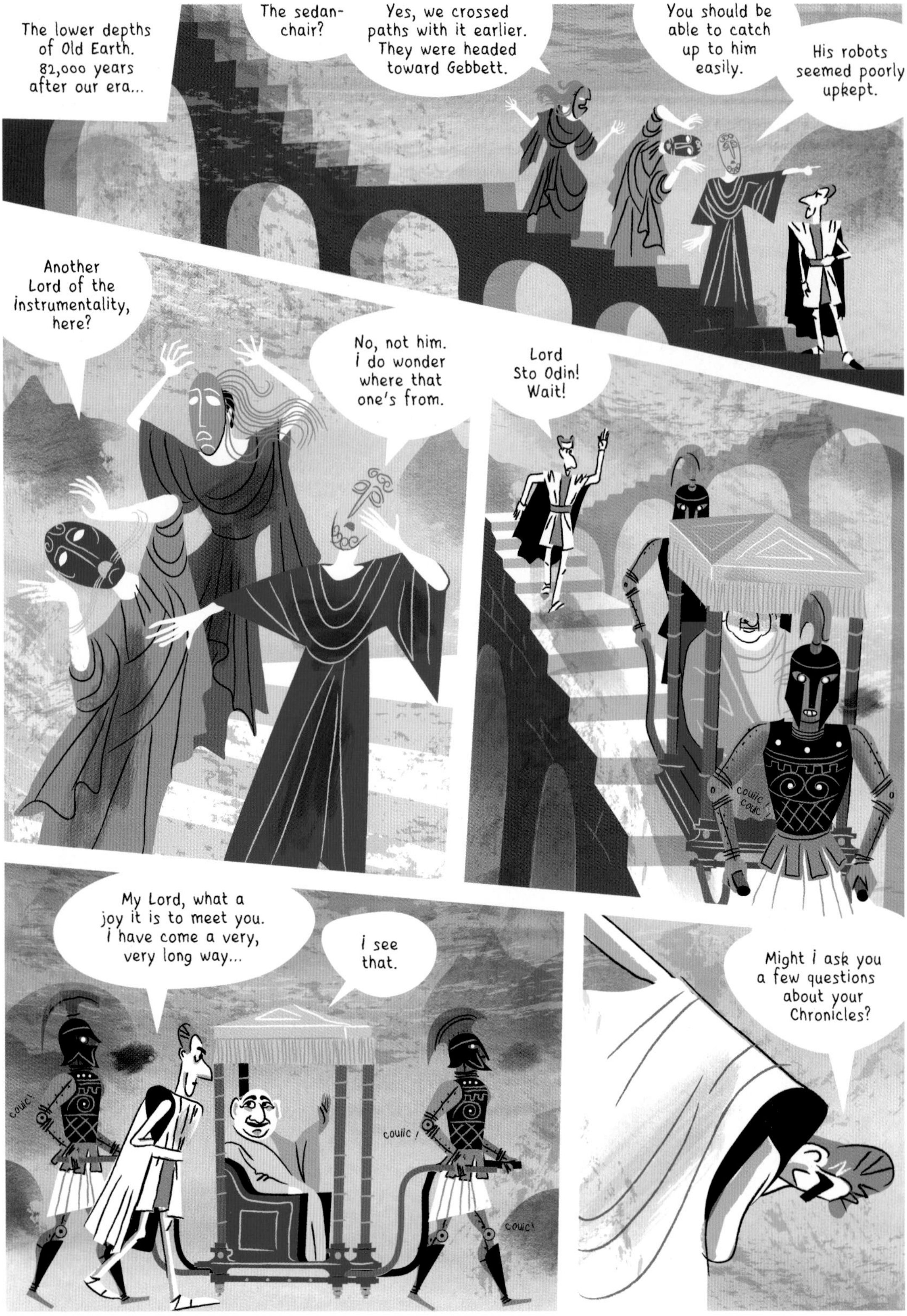

The lower depths of Old Earth. 82,000 years after our era...
The sedan-chair?
Yes, we crossed paths with it earlier. They were headed toward Gebbett.
You should be able to catch up to him easily.
His robots seemed poorly upkept.
Another Lord of the Instrumentality, here?
No, not him. I do wonder where that one's from.
Lord Sto Odin! Wait!
Couic ! Couic !
My Lord, what a joy it is to meet you. I have come a very, very long way...
I see that.
Couic !
Couic !
Couic !
Might I ask you a few questions about your Chronicles?

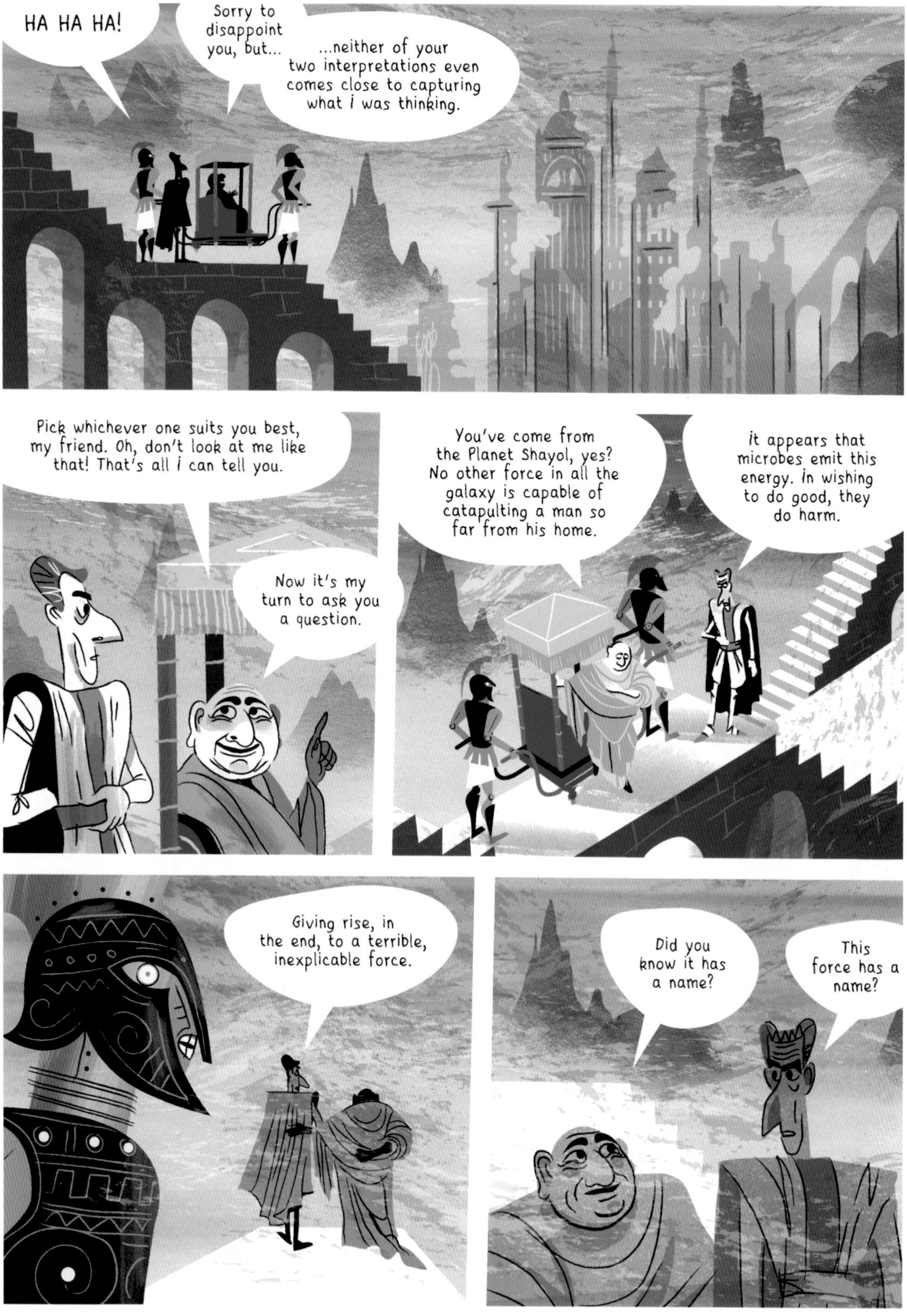
HA HA HA!
Sorry to disappoint you, but...
...neither of your two interpretations even comes close to capturing what I was thinking.
Pick whichever one suits you best, my friend. Oh, don't look at me like that! That's all I can tell you.
Now it's my turn to ask you a question.
You've come from the Planet Shayol, yes? No other force in all the galaxy is capable of catapulting a man so far from his home.
It appears that microbes emit this energy. In wishing to do good, they do harm.
Giving rise, in the end, to a terrible, inexplicable force.
Did you know it has a name?
This force has a name?

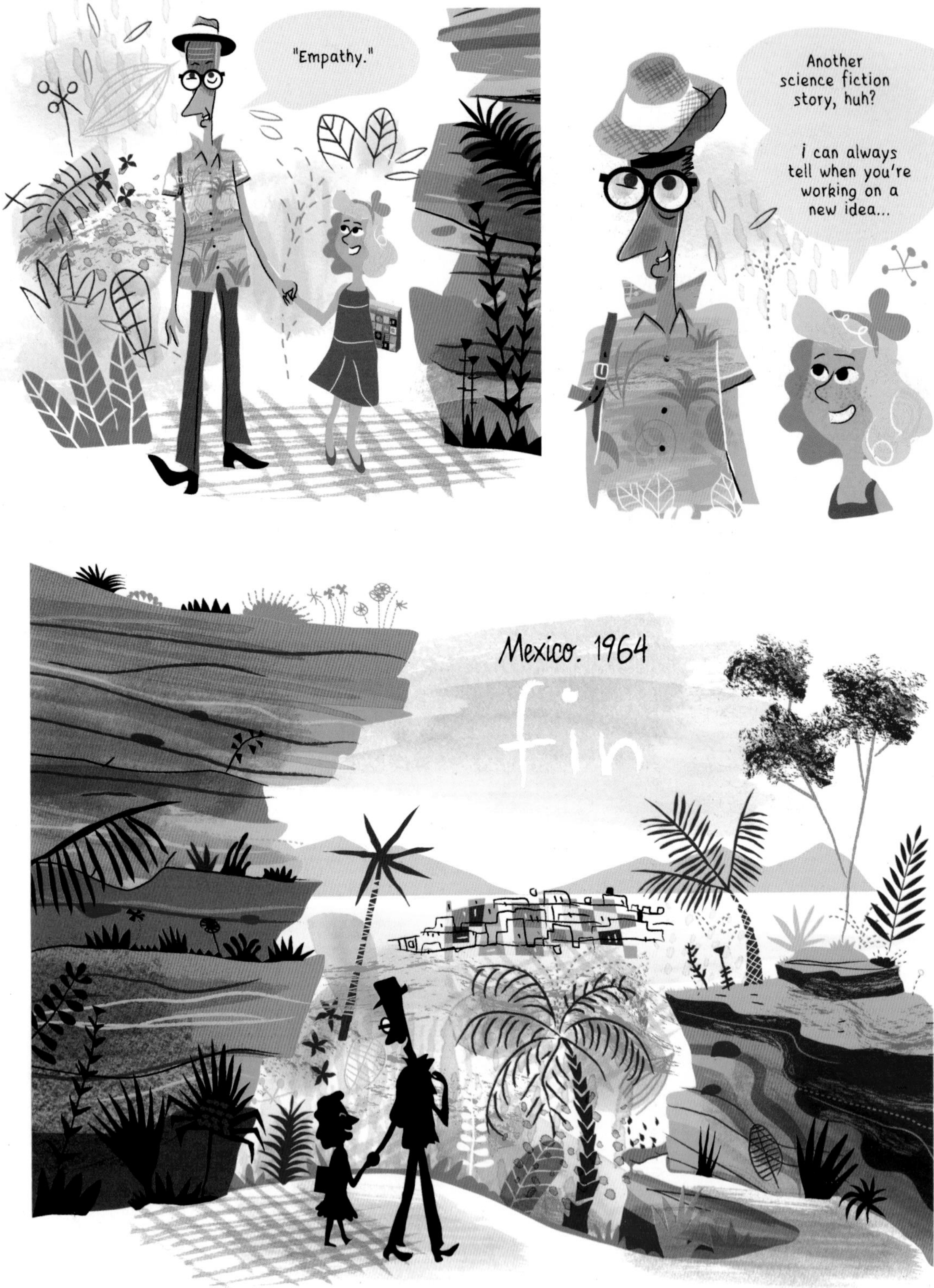
"Empathy."
Another science fiction story, huh?
i can always tell when you're working on a new idea...
Mexico. 1964
fin

Clérisse & Smolderen . 2012